You're About to Become a

Privileged Woman.

INTRODUCING
PAGES & PRIVILEGES™.

It's our way of thanking you for buying
our books at your favorite retail store.

GET ALL THIS FREE
WITH JUST ONE PROOF OF PURCHASE:

◆ Hotel Discounts up to 60% at home and abroad

◆ Travel Service - Guaranteed lowest published
airfares plus 5% cash back on tickets

◆ $25 Travel Voucher

◆ Sensuous Petite Parfumerie collection ($50 value)

◆ Insider Tips Letter with sneak previews of
upcoming books

◆ Mystery Gift (if you enroll before 6/15/95)

You'll get a FREE personal card, too.
It's your passport to all these benefits– and to
even more great gifts & benefits to come!
There's no club to join. No purchase commitment. No obligation.

As a *Privileged Woman*, you'll be entitled to all these *Free Benefits*. And *Free Gifts*, too.

To thank you for buying our books, we've designed an exclusive FREE program called *PAGES & PRIVILEGES™*. You can enroll with just one Proof of Purchase, and get the kind of luxuries that, until now, you could only read about.

*B*IG HOTEL DISCOUNTS

A privileged woman stays in the finest hotels. And so can you—at up to 60% off! Imagine standing in a hotel check-in line and watching as the guest in front of you pays $150 for the same room that's only costing you $60. Your *Pages & Privileges* discounts are good at Sheraton, Marriott, Best Western, Hyatt and thousands of other fine hotels all over the U.S., Canada and Europe.

*F*REE DISCOUNT TRAVEL SERVICE

A privileged woman is always jetting to romantic places. When <u>you</u> fly, just make one phone call for the lowest published airfare at time of booking—<u>or double the difference back</u>! PLUS—

you'll get a $25 voucher to use the first time you book a flight AND <u>5% cash back on every ticket you buy thereafter through the travel service</u>!

FREE GIFTS!

A privileged woman is always getting wonderful gifts.
Luxuriate in rich fragrances that will stir your senses (and his). This gift-boxed assortment of fine perfumes includes three popular scents, each in a beautiful designer bottle. <u>Truly Lace</u>...This luxurious fragrance unveils your sensuous side. L'Effleur...discover the romance of the Victorian era with this soft floral. <u>Muguet des bois</u>...a single note floral of singular beauty. This $50 value is yours—FREE when you enroll in *Pages & Privileges*! And it's just the beginning of the gifts and benefits that will be coming your way!

FREE INSIDER TIPS LETTER

A privileged woman is always informed. And you'll be, too, with our free letter full of fascinating information and sneak previews of upcoming books.

MORE GREAT GIFTS & BENEFITS TO COME

A privileged woman always has a lot to look forward to.
And so will you. You get all these wonderful FREE gifts and benefits now with only one purchase...and there are no additional purchases required. However, each additional retail purchase of Harlequin and Silhouette books brings you a step closer to even more great FREE benefits like half-price movie tickets...and even more FREE gifts like these beautiful fragrance gift baskets:

L'Effleur ...This basketful of romance lets you discover L'Effleur from head to toe, heart to home.

Truly Lace ...A basket spun with the sensuous luxuries of Truly Lace, including Dusting Powder in a reusable satin and lace covered box.

ENROLL NOW!
Complete the Enrollment Form on the back of this card and become a Privileged Woman today!

Enroll Today in *PAGES & PRIVILEGES*™, the program that gives you Great Gifts and Benefits with just one purchase!

Enrollment Form

□ *Yes!* I WANT TO BE A *Privileged Woman.*
    Enclosed is one *PAGES & PRIVILEGES*™ Proof of Purchase from any Harlequin or Silhouette book currently for sale in stores (Proofs of Purchase are found on the back pages of books) and the store cash register receipt. Please enroll me in *PAGES & PRIVILEGES*™. Send my Welcome Kit and FREE Gifts -- and activate my FREE benefits -- immediately.

NAME (please print)

ADDRESS   APT. NO

CITY   STATE   ZIP/POSTAL CODE

PROOF OF PURCHASE

Please allow 6-8 weeks for delivery. Quantities are limited. We reserve the right to substitute items. Enroll before October 31, 1995 and receive one full year of benefits.

NO CLUB!
NO COMMITMENT!
Just one purchase brings you great Free Gifts and Benefits!
(See inside for details.)

Name of store where this book was purchased_____

Date of purchase_____

Type of store:

      □ Bookstore   □ Supermarket   □ Drugstore

      □ Dept. or discount store (e.g. K-Mart or Walmart)

      □ Other (specify)_____

Which Harlequin or Silhouette series do you usually read?

Complete and mail with one Proof of Purchase and store receipt to:
  U.S.: *PAGES & PRIVILEGES*™, P.O. Box 1960, Danbury, CT 06813-1960
  Canada: *PAGES & PRIVILEGES*™, 49-6A The Donway West, P.O. 813,
           North York, ON M3C 2E8   **PRINTED IN U.S.A**

Cindy, Judy and Sherry—three women who grew up believing in fairy tales.

Thorne, John and Jeff—three men with no time for childish nonsense.

Watch them all meet their matches in

Legendary Lovers

Because sometimes, dreams really do come true....

Debbie Macomber

hails from the state of Washington. As a busy wife and mother of four, she strives to keep her family healthy and happy. As the prolific author of dozens of bestselling romance novels, she strives to keep her readers happy with each new book she writes.

Debbie Macomber

Legendary Lovers

Published by Silhouette Books
America's Publisher of Contemporary Romance

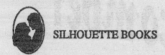

SILHOUETTE BOOKS

ISBN 0-373-20114-1

by Request

LEGENDARY LOVERS

Copyright © 1995 by Harlequin Enterprises B.V.

CINDY AND THE PRINCE
Copyright © 1988 by Debbie Macomber
SOME KIND OF WONDERFUL
Copyright © 1988 by Debbie Macomber
ALMOST PARADISE
Copyright © 1988 by Debbie Macomber

Printed in U.S.A.

CONTENTS

Dear Reader,

Once upon a time, in a land not so far away, there lived a girl, Debbie Macomber, who grew up dreaming of castles, white knights and princes on fiery steeds. Her family was an ordinary one with a mother and father and one wicked brother, who sold copies of her diary to all the boys in her junior high class.

One day, when Debbie was only nineteen, a handsome electrician drove by in a shiny black convertible. Now Debbie knew a prince when she saw one, and before long they lived in a two-bedroom cottage surrounded by a white picket fence.

As often happens when a damsel fair meets her prince charming, children followed, and soon the two-bedroom cottage became a four-bedroom castle. The kingdom flourished and prospered, and between soccer games and car pools, ballet classes and clarinet lessons, Debbie thought about love and enchantment and the magic of romance.

One day Debbie said, "What this country needs is a good fairy tale." She remembered how well her diary had sold and she dreamed again of castles, white knights and princes on fiery steeds. And so the stories of *Cinderella, Beauty and the Beast* and *Snow White* were reborn....

Debbie Macomber

CINDY AND THE PRINCE

Debbie Macomber

Chapter One

"Someday your prince will come," Vanessa Wilbur sang in a strained falsetto voice as she ran a feather duster along the top of the bookcase.

Studiously, Cindy Territo ignored her working partner and vigorously rubbed the thirty-story-view window, removing an imaginary smudge from the thick glass. The pair were janitorial workers for Oakes-Jenning Financial Services and for four nights a week they were responsible for cleaning the executive offices of the company's top officials. Tedious work, but it provided a supplement to Vanessa's family's income so she could pursue her dream of script writing, with high hopes of someday seeing her work performed on Broadway. And the job paid well enough to keep Cindy in computer school.

"You have to admit you spend more time cleaning

Mr. Prince's office than any of the others," Vanessa said, eyeing her friend suspiciously.

Unable to swallow her amusement, Cindy stuffed her cleaning rag into the hip pocket of her coveralls and laughed aloud. "Has anyone told you that you're a hopeless romantic?"

"Of course." Vanessa's eyes shone with unconcealed laughter. She held her feather duster upright, cocked her head to one side and released an exaggerated sigh. "Sometimes I think you, my friend, could be living a modern-day fairy tale."

"A what?" Cindy might be far more cynical than Vanessa, but one of them had to keep her head out of the clouds, she figured.

"A fairy tale."

Cindy did her best to ignore her friend and continued window washing—her least favorite task.

"Someday... some way... a handsome prince will come riding into your life on a white stallion and rescue you from all this."

Abruptly Cindy shook her head. "You've been spending too much time in dreamland again, my friend."

"No, I haven't," Vanessa objected and scooted onto the corner of a large mahogany desk, her short legs swinging. "In fact I believe it's fate. Think about it, girl. Your name is Cindy as in Cinderella and you clean the offices of a man named Prince, as in Prince Charming. Now doesn't that strike you as fate?"

"Thorndike Prince!" Cindy spewed out his name in a burst of laughter.

"And, as I mentioned, you do spend more time in his office than any of the others!"

"He's the first vice president. His office is largest, for heaven's sake."

"But..."

The idea was so ludicrous that Cindy was forced to choke back laughter. "Besides, he's got to be at least sixty...maybe even seventy."

"What makes you think so?"

"First, Oakes-Jenning Financial Services isn't going to make a thirty-three-year-old their first vice president, and second—"

"It's been done before," Vanessa interrupted. Folding her arms, she hopped down from the desk to glare stubbornly at her friend.

"And second of all," Cindy continued undaunted, "I clean his office; I know the man. He's staid, stuffy and sober-minded, and that's just the beginning."

"What do you mean?"

"He's so predictable. He eats the same sandwich— pastrami on rye—nearly every day for lunch and orders it from the same deli. He's so set in his ways that he's as probable as Santa Claus on Christmas Eve. The only thing he knows is business, business, business. Oh, I'm confident that he's dedicated and hardworking, but there's more to life than slaving away in some stuffy office and making oodles of money." A whole lot more—and Cindy sincerely doubted the first vice president knew anything about having fun.

"What do you think about the photograph of the gorgeous brunette that sits on his desk?"

A smile dimpled Cindy's cheeks. "Nothing. I'd venture a guess that Mr. Thorndike Prince has been sedately married to the same woman for fifty years."

"The photo," Vanessa reminded her.

"That's probably the old coot's granddaughter."

"Wrong!"

"Wrong?"

"Yup. How would you like to see a picture of your 'old coot'?"

From the twinkle in Vanessa's dark brown eyes, Cindy knew she was in for a shock. "And just where did you happen to find a picture of ol' Thorndike?"

"In the financial section of this afternoon's paper. Read it and weep, Cindy Territo." She reached inside her cleaning cart and whipped out the folded newspaper, shoving it under Cindy's nose.

One glance at the dark, handsome man in the photograph caused Cindy to suck in a surprised breath. She grabbed the newspaper and held it in both hands as she disbelievingly stared at the picture. "I don't believe it," she murmured in a voice so low it sounded gravelly. "He's, why, he's—"

"Gorgeous," Vanessa supplied with a smile a Cheshire cat would envy.

"Young." The word trembled out from Cindy's dry throat as she had trouble finding her voice. He was gorgeous, all right; she admitted that freely. Rarely had she seen a man more strikingly handsome. He was the type who would stand out in any crowd. Forceful. Persuasive. Vigorous. His face was square and serious, his chin proud and determined. His eyes stared back at her and even from the black-and-white image, Cindy could tell they were an intense gray. There wasn't a hint of amusement in those sharp, keen eyes, and Cindy guessed that the photographer had been lucky to obtain the picture. Perhaps most shocking of all was that Thorndike Prince couldn't be more than thirty-five... if that.

"Well?" Vanessa prodded.

"He isn't exactly the way I pictured him."

"You're right about that," Vanessa said with obvious pleasure. "Now all we need to do is to find a way for the two of you to meet."

"What?" Cindy tore her gaze from the newspaper, confident she'd misunderstood her friend.

"All we need is to come up with a way of getting the two of you together," Vanessa repeated. "You're perfect for each other."

Playfully, Cindy placed the back of her hand against her friend's forehead. "How long have you been running this raging fever?"

"I'm not sick!"

"Maybe not, but you're talking like a crazy woman."

"Come on, Cindy girl, dream a little."

"That's no dream—that's a nightmare." Her hand flew to the barely tamed blond curls sneaking out from beneath the red bandana tied at the back of her head. The blue pinstriped coveralls were reminiscent of a railroad worker's and did nothing to emphasize the feminine curves of her full hips and breasts.

"Naturally you wouldn't look like this."

"I certainly hope not."

"He'd like you, Cindy," Vanessa continued enthusiastically. "I know he would. You're bright and witty, and ol' Thorndike looks like he could use someone to fill his life with love and laughter. I think you may be right about him in that respect. I bet business is all he does think about. And you're so pretty with that naturally blond hair and those baby-blue eyes; the minute he sees you, it'll be like he's been knocked over the head."

Cindy released a wistful sigh. She didn't need to close her eyes to mentally picture her prince gazing down on her with such a look of tenderness that it stole her breath. Just the thought was enough to produce a warm, tingling sensation in the pit of her stomach.

A frown pinched Vanessa's prominent nose as her gaze grew serious. "We have one minor problem, though—that woman in the photograph on his desk. I doubt she's his sister. They could be serious."

"'Serious,'" Cindy repeated before she realized what she was saying. Brusquely she shook her head to shatter the mental image of Thorndike Prince leaning over to kiss her passionately. Within minutes Vanessa had nearly convinced her that at one look, the first vice president of Oakes-Jenning Financial Services would swoon at her feet. How easy it was to dream, but the reality of life faced her every day.

"Come on, Neil Simon, we've got work to do."

"Neil Simon?"

"You've apparently decided to turn your talent toward writing stage comedies."

"But, Cindy, I'm serious!"

"I'm not. Someone like Thorndike Prince isn't going to be interested in the cleaning woman who vacuums his office."

"You're underestimating the man."

"Enough! I've got work to do even if you don't."

Although Cindy returned to cleaning and scrubbing with a vigor that had been lacking earlier, her thoughts were far from the tasks at hand. Even when she left the Financial Center for the dark, windy streets of Manhattan, her thoughts centered on the tall, dark man in the photograph. It wasn't like her to be so affected by a man simply because he was good-looking. But Thorndike Prince was far more than handsome; something deep within her had instantly responded to him, had innocently, naively reached out to him. She saw in him the elusive qualities she'd been searching for in a man for the past twenty-two years. He was proud yet honest. Shrewd yet gentle. Demanding yet patient.

The December wind whistled down the canyon of tall office buildings and Cindy tucked the thick wool coat more snugly around her, burying her hands deep in her pockets. A quick glance at the clock in front of the jeweler's across the street told her Uncle Sal would be there any minute. No sooner had the thought formed when the sleek black limousine eased to a stop against the curb. The front door swung open as Cindy approached and she quickly climbed inside, savoring the warmth.

"You been waiting long?"

"Only a couple of minutes." Cindy gave her uncle a reassuring smile.

He removed the black driver's cap and unbuttoned the crisp chauffeur's uniform, letting out a deep breath. "Remind me to talk to your aunt. The cleaners must have shrunk this jacket."

"Right," Cindy said, swallowing a laugh. More than likely it was Aunt Theresa's cooking that was responsible for the tight jacket, but she wasn't about to tell her uncle that.

As the limousine wove through the New York traffic, Cindy stared out the window, more tired than she could remember.

"You're quiet tonight," her uncle commented thoughtfully.

"I'd think you'd count your blessings." Life in a large Italian family rarely left a moment's peace. Sal and Theresa's home was the hub of the Territo clan. Her aunt and uncle had raised Cindy as their own, loving her, nurturing her with all the warmth they gave their natural child. Cindy's own parents had divorced when she was too young to remember, and her mother had died when Cindy was five. She'd never heard from her father, and when she'd started grade school she'd taken the name Territo to avoid confusion.

Sal chuckled. "Maybe I should be grateful for the quiet. When I left the house this afternoon your aunt was blistering the sidewalk with her rantings."

"What happened now?"

"She found Tony and Maria necking on the fire escape again."

At fifteen, Cindy's cousin was already showing the potential for breaking many a young girl's heart. "That Tony's too hot-blooded."

Sal chuckled, sent a proud glance to his niece and playfully nudged her with his elbow. "He's too much like his old man, huh?"

"Right. He probably doesn't even feel the cold."

The car grew silent again, and once more Cindy felt her uncle's eyes on her. "You feeling okay?"

"I'm just tired."

"How many more weeks you got of school?"

"A couple." Two full weeks and then she could rest and concentrate on the fast-approaching Christmas holidays. Christmas was sneaking up on her this year. Although she had set aside the money from her last paycheck, she hadn't even started her shopping. There hadn't been time and wouldn't be until her computer classes were dismissed for the winter quarter.

Her uncle parked the limousine in front of the apartment building in a space reserved for him. Nothing was posted to claim this curb for Sal's limousine, but the neighborhood, out of love and respect, made sure there was room for him to park each night.

The apartment was quiet. Cindy and her uncle paused in the crowded entryway to remove their coats. Cindy hung hers on the brass coatrack while her uncle reverently placed his jacket inside the hall closet. His cap was tucked in place on the shelf above the rack.

"You hungry?" her uncle whispered.

"Not tonight." Aunt Theresa kept a large plate of food warming in the oven for them and her uncle and Cindy often sat in front of Johnny Carson and enjoyed their late-night dinner.

"You sure you're feeling okay?" Sal squinted his eyes as he studied her carefully.

"I'm fine. I think I'll take a hot bath and go to bed."

"You do that." Already her uncle was heading for the kitchen, eager for his meal.

Cindy's bedroom was tiny, as were all the bedrooms in the apartment. There was hardly room to walk between the double bed and the heavy mahogany dresser that had been her mother's as a child. The closet was little more than an indentation in the wall. A faded curtain hung in front of it, serving as the door. Cindy glanced around the room with fresh eyes. Thorndike Prince definitely wouldn't be interested in a woman who slept in a room such as this. Her thoughts drifted to the dark woman in the photograph on his desk. No doubt her bedroom was carpeted with lush Oriental rugs and decorated with a fancy brass bedroom set. Perhaps there was even a fireplace.... Cindy sighed and sat on the corner of her mattress feeling the hopelessness of it all. Vanessa had told her it was time to dream a little, and that was exactly what Cindy planned to do: she was going to save this special feeling she had for Thorndike Prince for her dreams.

After luxuriating in a tub filled with hot soapy water, Cindy fell into a deep, natural sleep.

The following day she even managed not to think about Vanessa's crazy schemes throughout her classes. Nor did she allow thoughts of her prince to invade her mind while she hurried home from school and changed into her work clothes. However, the minute she stepped into the Oakes-Jenning Financial Services building, Cindy was assaulted on all sides by dreams she had no right to entertain.

"Hi," Vanessa grumbled as she checked the supplies on her cleaning cart.

"What's wrong with you?" Of the pair, Vanessa was usually the one with the ready smile and quick conversation.

"Traffic was a nightmare."

"Hey, girl, this is New York. What do you expect?"

"A little sympathy would come in handy."

"Poor, Vanessa . . . poor, poor Vanessa." Soothingly, Cindy stroked her friend's arm. "Did that help?"

"A little," she grumbled and led the way to the service elevator. They rode it to the main floor, then transferred to the passenger one. Bob Knight, the security officer who guarded the front entrance, waved as they continued through the front foyer.

Cindy leaned her weight against the back of the elevator as the heavy door glided silently shut. Already she was concerned about cleaning Thorndike's office. The room would never be the same to her again. She couldn't just empty his garbage without wondering what was happening in his life and knowing she could never be a part of it.

"Hey, did you see that?" Vanessa cried excitedly, making a futile attempt to stop the elevator.

"See what?" Cindy was instantly alert.

The moment the elevator hit the thirtieth floor, Vanessa pushed the button that sent them backtracking in a rushing movement.

"Vanessa, what's going on?"

"Give me a minute and I'll tell you."

"Tell me what?" Cindy chuckled at the way her friend anxiously bit her bottom lip. "No doubt you've witnessed the living answer to life's difficulties? Perhaps you've discovered the secret to peace and goodwill for all mankind?"

The instant the doors glided open Vanessa grabbed Cindy's arm and jerked her out of the elevator. "Look at this," she cried, slapping her friend across the back as she shoved her in front of a large notice board.

"Look at what?" The only thing she could see was information about some type of party.

"Read it out loud," Vanessa instructed with tattered patience.

Shrugging her shoulders, Cindy complied. "The Oakes-Jenning Christmas Ball, 7:30 p.m., December 15. Hotel St. Moritz, Grand Ballroom. By invitation only."

"Well?" Vanessa's eyebrows arched with devilish humor.

"Well, what?" Gradually a dawning light seeped into Cindy's perplexed brain. "You're nuts! You couldn't possibly mean for me to..."

"It's the perfect way to get you two together."

"But..." So many excuses crowded Cindy's mind that she couldn't say them all. The first one to untwist itself from the tip of her tongue was the most obvious. "I don't have an invitation."

"Hey, there are ways—"

"Forget it!" Cindy hoped she'd said it in a way that would cancel all further arguments. She stepped back into the elevator and waited for Vanessa to join her.

"I'm not going to forget it and neither are you. It's fate...Kismet. I knew it the minute I saw Thorndike Prince's picture in the newspaper and so did you, so don't try to argue with me."

"I'm not arguing," Cindy replied calmly. "I simply refuse to discuss it."

"But why?"

Faking a yawn, Cindy cupped her hand over her mouth and idly glanced at her watch.

"All right, all right, I get the message," Vanessa grumbled under her breath. "But you aren't kidding me one bit. You're dying to attend that Christmas Ball."

Was she? Cindy asked herself as the night progressed. Dusting Mr. Prince's outer office granted her the solitude to think about the magic of a Christmas ball, and she quickly realized her friend was right once again. Cindy had never thought of herself as being so transparent, but she would gladly have sacrificed herself to the taunts of three ugly stepsisters for the opportunity to attend such a gala event. Only she didn't have any stepsisters and she wasn't Cinderella. But a ball... the Christmas Ball... Nowhere else would she have the opportunity to introduce herself to her prince and be accepted as his equal but in a place as enchanting as a Christmas ball. Perhaps Vanessa was fey....

Naw, Cindy discounted that thought. Her working partner simply possessed a wildly romantic heart. But then, so did charwoman Cindy.

Her feather duster ran across Thorndike Prince's secretary's desk and for the first time since she'd been hired by the janitorial department, Cindy wondered about the woman who spent so much of her day with Thorndike Prince. Mrs. Hillard rarely let anything go to waste. Even discarded pages of stationery were neatly trimmed into scratch pads, stapled together at the top corners. The woman's theme appeared to be Waste Not, Want Not.

Cindy spent only a bare minimum of time in Mr. Prince's office. Other than a dusting now and again and an occasional vacuuming, the room was surpris-

ingly neat, which was something she couldn't say
about the other executives' quarters. As she emptied
his garbage, a smile touched her deep blue eyes to note
the name The Deli Belly, the delicatessen from which
Thorndike ordered his lunch. He was apparently a
creature of habit, but then they all were, weren't they?

As Cindy moved from one office to the next she did
her utmost to contain her thoughts, but her mind
turned traitor, and the image of the crystal ball dangling from the center of the ballroom and the crowded
room full of dancing couples kept flitting into her
mind. In every image, Cindy and her prince were in
the center of the Grand Ballroom, arms entwined
around each other.

"Well?" Vanessa said, startling Cindy.

She recovered with astonishing dexterity. "Well,
what?"

"Have you been thinking about the ball, Cinderella?"

"It's not going to work." It was a measure of her
fascination with Thorndike Prince to admit she'd
given the matter a second thought. It was an impossible scheme from beginning to end.

"It'll work," Vanessa said with blind optimism.

"Then where's my fairy godmother?"

With a saucy grin, Vanessa polished her nails
against the yoke of her cotton shirt. "Hey, sweetie,
you're looking at her."

"And my coach led by two perfectly matched white
stallions. And how about turning mice into footmen?
Is that trick up your sleeve as well?"

For a moment Vanessa looked concerned, then she smiled and flexed her fingers. "I'm working on those. There's no need to worry."

"Are you working on a floor-length chiffon gown at the same time?"

"Sure..."

"If I were a fairy godmother, I'd tackle the invitation business right away."

"Right." For the first time Vanessa looked daunted. "I didn't realize this was going to be such a headache."

"And that's only the beginning."

"I don't think I want to hear it all."

Cindy turned back to her cart, pushing it down the wide hallway, humming as she went. It was nice to dream, but that was all it could ever be for her and the prince: a fanciful dream.

Almost by rote, Cindy picked up the green metal garbage can of the secretary to the third vice president and dumped its contents into the large plastic bag on the end of her cart. As she did so a flash of gold caught her eye. Out of curiosity, she reached for it, and when she read the gilt printing, her heart rushed to her throat, nearly choking off her breath.

Holding the paper in both hands, she walked out of the room in a daze. "Vanessa!" she cried. "Vanessa, hurry. I don't believe it.... I think I'm living through an episode of *Twilight Zone*."

Her partner met her in the hallway. "What is it?"

"Look." Reverently, she handed the folded piece of paper to her friend.

"It's an invitation to the ball," Vanessa whispered, raising her round, shocked eyes to meet Cindy's. "I don't believe it!'' Then her dark eyes brightened as she waved an imaginary wand over Cindy's head. "Did you feel the fairy dust?"

"It's coming down like rain, my friend," Cindy cried shaking her head with awe and wonder.

"Where did you find it?"

"In the garbage."

"You've got to be kidding!"

Cindy shook her head. "They must have been mailed out last week sometime."

"And apparently Miss Reynolds has decided not to attend, in which case you will humbly accept on her behalf."

"But—"

"It's fate! Surely you're not going to argue with me now!"

"No." Cindy was more than willing to accept this unexpected gift. She'd attend this ball and satisfy her inquisitiveness regarding Thorndike Prince. She'd indulge herself this one time and only this once.

On the evening of December 15, Cindy's stomach was a mass of nerves. A beehive would have held less rumbling activity. Her cousin, Tony, knocked on her bedroom door and called, "Vanessa's here."

"Okay, tell her I'll be right out." Squaring her shoulders, Cindy forced herself to smile and walked into the living room, where her family and Vanessa were impatiently waiting.

Her friend stood as Cindy entered the room. "Oh, Cindy, you're . . . beautiful."

Cindy's aunt dabbed the corner of one eye and murmured something in Italian. "She looks just like her mother."

Vanessa didn't seem to hear her. "Where did you ever find such an elegant gown?" The sweetheart neckline was trimmed with the finest lace and was worn off the shoulders. The bodice fit snugly against her torso and the waistline was slightly raised. The skirt was made up of layer upon layer of pale blue chiffon that formed wide-tiered ruffles.

"Do you like it?" Slowly she whirled around, letting Vanessa view the full effect.

"I'm speechless."

For Vanessa, that was saying something. Cindy's gaze rested lovingly on her aunt.

Aunt Theresa lifted her hand in mock salute. "It was nothing . . . an early Christmas gift."

"She made it?" Vanessa gasped.

"A dress is not made," Theresa chided mockingly. "It is sewn with loving fingers."

"Where'd you get the purse?"

Cindy lifted the small pearl-beaded clutch. "My Aunt Sofia."

"And the combs?"

Cindy's hands flew to her hair, swirled upon her head and held in place by pearl combs. "Those were my mother's."

"You look more like a princess than anyone I've ever seen. I don't know what to say."

"For once," Cindy laughed.

Vanessa walked circles around her a couple of times, shaking her head in wonder.

"How are you getting there?"

"My uncle's dropping me off and picking me up later."

"Excellent plan."

"Listen." Suddenly Cindy's nerve abandoned her. She was living her dream just as she'd always wanted, but something deep inside her was screaming that she was playing the part of a fool—a romantic fool, but a fool nonetheless. "I'm not sure I'm doing the right thing. Sheila will probably be there." On close examination of the brunette in the photograph on Thorndike's desk, Cindy and Vanessa had seen the other woman's bold signature across the bottom of the picture.

"She might," Vanessa agreed. "But you'll do fine." For good measure she added another imaginary sparkling of fairy dust. "The enchantment is set, so don't worry."

"What? Me worry?" Cindy said, crossing her eyes and twisting her face like her favorite madcap character.

Everyone laughed, nearly drowning out the sound of the honk from the limousine in the street below.

"You ready?" Aunt Theresa asked, draping a warm shawl around Cindy's shoulders.

"As ready as I'll ever be," she said, expelling a deep breath.

Her Uncle Sal was standing outside the limousine, holding open the back door for her. "You ready, Miss?" he asked in a dignified voice that nearly dissolved Cindy into giggles.

She climbed into the back and realized that of all the nights she'd ridden with her uncle, this was the first time she'd ever been seated in back. "Hey, this is nice," she called forward, running her hands along the smooth velvet cushion, astonished at all the space.

"We have one problem," her uncle informed her, meeting her gaze in the rearview mirror.

"What's that?"

"I'm sorry, kiddo, but I've got to have the limo to pick up the Buckhardt party before one."

"That won't be any problem," Cindy returned cheerfully. "Cinderella is supposed to leave the ball before midnight anyway."

Chapter Two

Bored, Thorne Prince stood in the farthest corner of the ballroom, with a look of studied indifference on his face. He idly held a glass of champagne. He hated these sort of functions; they were a waste of his valuable time. He'd been obligated to attend this silly Christmas party, but he held out little hope of enjoying it. To complicate matters, Sheila couldn't attend with him. She, at least, would have made the evening tolerable. Hoping he wasn't being obvious, Thorne glanced at his gold wristwatch and wondered if anyone would notice if he silently slipped away.

"Prince, old boy, good to see you." Rutherford Hayden stepped to his side and slapped him hard across the back.

Thorne's response was a grim smile. He had no use for the man who was looking to further himself in the company by ingratiating himself with Thorne by means other than job skills and performance.

"Fine party."

"Yes." If the man hoped to engage Thorne in long-winded conversation, he was going to be disappointed.

A moment of awkward silence passed during which Thorne did nothing to ease the tension. Rutherford paused and cleared his throat. "I've been giving some thought to your suggestion regarding the Hughes account, and I—"

"It was an order, not a suggestion." The hard line of Thorne's mouth remained inflexible. Damn! Hayden was going to trap him into talking business, and he'd be stuck with this inept bore half the night. To refuse would only heighten the already growing dislike between them. In spite of his incompetence, Hayden had the ear of Paul Jenning, the company president. Apparently the two had been high-school chums and on occasion played golf together.

"I'm back," Cindy said, feigning breathlessness as she sauntered up to Thorne's side. She gazed at him with wide, adoring eyes. "Thank you for holding my champagne." She took the glass from his lifeless hand and turned her attention to Hayden. "It's good to see you again, Ruffie." Deliberately she used the nickname she knew he disliked. A woman didn't empty a man's wastepaper basket for a year without learning something about him. Cindy was a silent witness to the habits, likes and dislikes of all the occupants of the executive offices.

Rutherford Hayden glanced from Cindy to Thorne, then back to her again. "I'm afraid I don't recall the pleasure."

"Cindy," she informed him and offered him her hand. He politely shook it, and Cindy fluttered her lashes for the full, dazzling effect.

"'Ruffie'?" Thorne asked, cocking one eyebrow, mocking amusement evident in his voice.

"Yes, well . . ." Rutherford looked into the dancing couples that occupied the extensive ballroom floor. "I won't keep you any longer. We can discuss this Hughes matter another time."

"Good idea." Thorne knew from the way Hayden's eyes were scanning the crowd that he would move on to easier prey.

"Nice seeing you again, Tami."

"Cindy," she corrected, taking a sip of the champagne. The bubbly liquid slid down the back of her throat, and she smiled beguilingly up at the irritating man.

As soon as Hayden was out of earshot, Cindy turned and handed the glass back to Thorne.

"Now," she said, her eyes twinkling. "I won't disturb you any longer," she murmured sweetly. "You can get back to your pouting. But you really shouldn't brood, you know—age lines."

Thorne's mouth sagged open with complete astonishment. "'Pout—ing'?"

"It's true," she said without so much as blinking. "You're a sad disappointment to me, Thorndike Prince."

Thorne hadn't the foggiest notion who this chit was, but he gave her points for originality. "I'm devastated to hear it."

"I don't doubt it." If he didn't possess the common sense to recognize her as his Cinderella, then there was little she could do about it.

"Just who are you?"

"If you don't know yet, then we're in worse shape than I thought."

"Cindy who?" He studied her closely and couldn't recall ever meeting her.

"If you had a lick of sense, you'd recognize me."

"We've met?"

"Sort of..." Cindy hedged, her nerve flagging. "All right, since you're obviously not the prince I thought, I guess it won't do any harm to tell you. I'm Cinderella, but unfortunately, you're not my prince—you're much too cynical."

"Cinderella?" Thorne felt laughter expand his chest and would have let it escape if she'd shown the least bit of amusement, but she was dead serious.

"You needn't worry," Cindy said. "I won't trouble you any longer. You can go back to your brooding." With that, she sashayed away, leaving him without so much as glancing over her shoulder.

Pouting! Brooding! Of all the nerve! No one spoke to him like that! A Prince neither pouted nor brooded!

Gradually the anger wore away and a hint of a smile wooed the edges of his mouth. Before he knew what was happening, Thorne grinned. The amusement swelled within him and he forced back the desire to laugh outright. He didn't recall that the Cinderella of old had this much grit. This one did—rare grit—and almost against his will he sought her out in the crowded room. He found her standing against the wall opposite his own. Willingly her eyes met his, and she raised her champagne glass in a silent toast. Her eyes were a brilliant, bottomless shade of vibrant blue, and even from this distance he could see them sparkling at him. *Alluring.* That was the word that flashed into Thorne's mind. She was the most utterly appealing woman he'd seen in ages.

From the way her eyes held his, he saw she was interested and interesting. It wasn't unusual for a woman to approach him; he was intelligent enough to know he was considered a "good catch," and many a debutante would like to sink her eyeteeth into him. He knew that in time this woman, too, would return to his side to strike up another conversation. He'd play this one cool, but given the right incentive he'd forgive her for insulting his pride. Although—damn it all—she was right; he had been pouting. But brooding—now that was going too far.

For her part, Cindy was acutely disappointed in Thorndike Prince. He was everything she'd expected and nothing like she'd hoped. A contradiction in terms, she realized, but she could find no other way to describe her feelings. He was so cynical—as though the beauty of this lovely evening and the Christmas season left him untouched. For hours she'd been studying him. At first she'd been captivated, enticed. Only later did her fascination begin to dim. Whimsically, she'd built him up in her mind, and he'd fallen far short of her expectations. He was her knight in shining armor. Her hero. The man of her dreams.

She'd imagined him gallant and exciting and had found him bored and cynical. Twice he'd glanced at his watch and once . . . once, he'd even had the audacity to *yawn*. Life appeared to be so predictable and mundane to Thorndike Prince that the beauty that surrounded him did little to faze him.

Cindy was disappointed, but she refused to waste this precious evening. She'd made her pitch and announced who she was. Mission accomplished. She was convinced she'd best forget about her prince, but there wasn't any reason to waste this night. Cindy intended to have a marvelous time and not surprisingly she did just that as she mingled with the guests, placing names with faces. Feeling a bit smug because she knew their secrets and they knew nothing of her, she danced, nibbled on the hors d'oeuvres and tapped the toe of her high-heeled shoe to the lighthearted beat of the orchestra music.

An hour. Thorne had been waiting an hour for the mysterious Cinderella to return and she'd ostentatiously remained on the other side of the ballroom. Except for the silent toast she'd given him earlier, she'd granted him little more than a disinterested glance now and again. Once, she'd danced with Barney, a young executive, and Thorne had been hardpressed not to cross the room and inform her that James Barney was no prince! But the thought of taking such an action was so utterly irrational that Thorne had been stunned ever to have entertained it.

Another time, the sound of her laughter had drifted over to him, and Thorne thought he couldn't remember ever hearing anything more musical. She intrigued him. He discovered he couldn't stop watching her. An unreasonable anger began to build inside him when she danced with two other men.

Finally when he could tolerate it no longer, Thorne reached for another glass of champagne and marched across the room.

"I think you'd best explain yourself," he said without preamble.

At first Cindy was too stunned to speak. "I beg your pardon."

"I'll have you know, I never brood." Her blue eyes fairly gleamed like liquid sapphire as a smile brought her mouth into the most sensuous movement he'd ever witnessed. "And this business about being Cinderella—now that's going a bit overboard, don't you think?"

"No, but please call me Cindy. Cinderella is such an outdated name."

She laughed then, that sweet, musical laugh that had fascinated him earlier. He stared at her, unable to look away. She reminded him of snowflakes and kittens, innocence and youth. It took all his restraint not to reach out and pull her into his arms. Good Lord, he hadn't drunk that much champagne. "Would you care to dance?" he found himself asking.

She nodded eagerly, and Thorne escorted her onto the floor, his hand guiding her at the small of her back. When they reached the outer fringes of the dance floor, Thorne turned her into his embrace. In the beginning he held her at arm's length, almost afraid of what would happen to him if he brought her soft feminine body against his own. Maybe she'd disappear, vanish into thin air. He half expected to wake up from this trance and find the entire company staring at him while he swirled around the room all alone.

Although Thorne held up the pretense of dancing, all of his concentration was focused on merely looking at his intriguing partner. On closer inspection he found her to be truly lovely; she was more than pretty, she was breathtakingly beautiful. Innocent yet enticing. Docile yet challenging. Her skin looked as soft as satin and felt as warm as a spring day. He didn't dare think about what that marvelous little mouth would taste like. He resisted the instinct to bring her into the circle of his arms, although their movements were awkward and strangely out of sync.

Finally Cindy shook her head, stopped dancing and dropped her arms. Her gaze found his, her disappointment keen. In the space of a few hours, her prince had managed to shatter every illusion she dared to form about him. "Not only are you a terrible disappointment to me, but you can't dance worth a darn, either." Disgusted, she stared at him, defying him to disagree with her.

Thorne didn't—she was right. Without saying a word, he brought her back into his arms, only this time he held her the way he'd wanted to from the first, pressing her body intimately to his. Her full breasts brushed against his torso. Thigh aligned to thigh. No more games, no more secrets.

Cindy slipped her arms around his neck and lay her head along the chiseled line of his jaw. The music was a favorite Christmas melody, and her eyes drifted shut as she wrapped herself in the enchantment of the song.

They moved as one, as though they had spent a lifetime practicing together for this one night. A woman had never felt more right in Thorne's arms. A man had never seemed more in command as he led Cindy from one end of the dance floor to the other without missing a step, guiding, leading, dictating every action.

"Do you always hum along with the music?" Thorne asked unexpectedly.

Cindy's eyes flew open and she nearly stumbled over his feet as her step faltered. "I'm sorry...I didn't realize."

"No problem," Thorne murmured, chuckling; he cradled the back of her head and guided her temple to its former position against his jaw. After she'd called him a cynic, a brooding one to boot, he felt he owed her a bit of honesty as well. "You were only slightly off-key."

Cindy could feel him smile and she relaxed, not wanting to do anything to disturb the wonder of the moment.

Maybe she'd been wrong. Maybe, just maybe, he could be her prince after all. Thorne was holding her just as she'd dreamed and from the way his arms tightened around her at the end of the song, it felt as though he never intended to let her go.

"Would it be selfish to request another dance?"

"Cinderella's prince did," Cindy whispered, her heart tripping with a glorious melody that had nothing to do with the orchestra's music.

"Then I should, don't you think?"

It was all Cindy could do to nod. They danced again and again and again, neither speaking, each savoring the simple pleasure of being held. The only thought in Thorne's mind was the woman in his arms.

The only thought in Cindy's mind was that fairy tales can come true; she was living one.

"You say I'm a disappointment to you?" he ventured at the end of the dance. He couldn't hold her any longer without trying to discover everything he could about her.

Cindy lifted her head and gazed at him. "Not anymore."

Thorne felt the full dazzling impact of her blue eyes on him. "Not anymore?" he repeated, smiling despite his effort not to. "Have we met before?" He was sure they hadn't; he wouldn't have forgotten her or those incredible blue eyes, but one look and she'd seen straight through him.

"Never," she confirmed.

"But you know me?"

Cindy dropped her gaze. "Yes and no."

"You *are* an employee of Oakes-Jenning?"

"Yes." Amusement slashed her soft mouth until the corners quivered with the effort to hold back a smile. "Did you think I'd crashed your precious party?" That was so close to the truth that she quickly averted her gaze.

Thorne ignored her obvious enjoyment of this one-sided conversation. "How did you know Rutherford Hayden's nickname is Ruffie?"

"The same way I know you hate tuna salad." Cindy's gaze fell upon the rows and rows of tables loaded with a spectacular menu of salads, meats and cheeses. "Now, if you'll excuse me, I'd like to get something to eat."

He took a step forward in an effort to stop her. "No."

"No?"

Thorne realized he must sound like an idiot, but he didn't want to let her go. "Would you mind if I joined you?"

"Not at all," she said, her heart leaping for joy once again.

"My mother sent you, didn't she?" Thorne breathed a sigh of relief; he had it all figured out. His mother had been after him for years to give her grandchildren. She must have hunted for months to find someone as perfect as Cindy.

"Your mother? No."

The honesty in her eyes couldn't be doubted. But even if his mother had put Cindy up to this, it didn't explain the instant, overwhelming attraction he felt for her.

Bemused, Thorne followed her through the long line that had formed at the buffet tables, heaping his plate with a wide variety of the offerings.

"What? No pastrami?" Cindy teased after they'd found a table in the crowded room.

Thorne paused, his napkin only half unfolded. His eyes cut through her. "I had a pastrami sandwich for lunch. You couldn't have known that, could you?"

"No. It was an educated guess." Cindy focused her attention on buttering her dinner roll.

"An educated guess? Like my not liking tuna?"

"No." Deliberately she took a bite of her seafood salad, tasting shrimp, crab and another delicacy she couldn't name.

Patiently Thorne waited until she had finished chewing. "But you know me?"

"A little." Not nearly as well as she wanted to.

"How?"

"I *do* work for Oakes-Jenning," she said and glanced at the huge green olives he'd removed from the top of the dainty sandwiches. "Are you going to eat those?"

Thorne's gaze followed her own to his plate. "The green olives—good grief, no."

"Can I have them?"

Without ceremony, Thorne delivered three to her plate, then fastidiously wiped his hands clean on the linen napkin.

Eagerly Cindy picked up an olive and placed it between her lips, luxuriously sucking out the pimento, then popping the entire thing in her mouth. When she'd finished, she paused to lick the tips of her fingers free of juice. Thorne's scowl stopped her when she reached for another. The lines at the side of his mouth had deepened, and she noted the vein pulsing in his temple. Alarm filled her. Her worst fear had been realized: unwittingly, she'd committed some terrible faux pas.

"What did I do wrong?" she asked in a fear-laced whisper. She dropped her hands to her lap and clenched the napkin, watching him expectantly.

For a long moment, their eyes locked and held. Thorne had been mesmerized, watching her eat the olive. Such a simple pleasure, and she'd made it appear highly sensuous. He couldn't seem to take his eyes off her—or off the tempting shape of her mouth. Again he felt the overwhelming urge to kiss her and experience for himself the sweetness of her lips. Her eyes, her mouth, the curve of her cheek. Everything about her completely and utterly captivated him. For years women had used their bodies and their wits in a effort to entice him. But no woman had ever had the effect on him that this one did with the simple act of eating an olive.

"What did you do wrong?" Thorne repeated, shaking his head to clear his befuddled thoughts. "What makes you think you did anything wrong?"

"You were looking at me...funny."

He smiled then, forcing the edges of his mouth to curve upward. "Then I apologize."

Cindy relaxed and reached for the second olive. Thorne's gaze widened and he groaned inwardly, setting his fork beside his plate.

The music started up again long before they'd finished their meal and unconsciously Cindy tapped her toe to the beat. Christmas was her favorite time of year, and the orchestra seemed to know all the carols she loved best.

"Would you like to dance again?" Thorne asked.

Cindy nodded. She wouldn't refuse the opportunity to be in her prince's arms. This was her night, a night for enchantment, and she wanted to remember and relive every moment of it for the rest of her life. Tomorrow she would go back to being plain, simple Cindy, the girl who cleaned his office. But tonight...tonight she was the alluring woman he longed to hold in his arms.

By unspoken agreement they stood together and walked to the center of the dance floor. Thorne turned Cindy into his arms, holding her close, savoring the feel of her, that special scent that was only hers, and the warmth of her nearness. He felt as if he were a hundred years old in ways she knew nothing about and, conversely, that he'd just turned twenty-one all over again. She did this to him and he hadn't an inkling why.

Thorne's arms tightened around her, anchoring her against him. Both his hands were around her waist and he laid his cheek along hers and closed his eyes. To think that only a few hours earlier he'd been contemplating sneaking away from this party, having found it a deadly bore. Now he dreaded the time it would end, praying that each minute would stretch out so that nothing would destroy this night and his time with this woman.

Cindy pressed her cheek to his and prayed she'd always remember every minute of this night. She planned to store each detail in her heart. She couldn't possibly hope to explain it to anyone; mere words were inadequate to describe the warm feeling she shared with Thorne. This magical, mystical night was hers and hers alone. She would have a lifetime to treasure these precious hours and relive each minute over and over in her mind.

Even when the music became lively, Thorne held her as though it were the slowest dance of the night. He wanted to kiss her so badly that he was forced to inhale sharp, even breaths several times to restrain his desire. Thorndike Prince did not make a spectacle of himself on the dance floor for any reason. However he soon discovered that the temptation was too strong. Her nearness was more than any sane man could resist and he turned his head ever so slightly and ran his mouth over her ear.

Cindy released a sigh of pleasure and moved her hands to the back of Thorne's neck, running her finger through the thick dark hair. When his lips sought the hollow of her throat, she groaned his name in a low, aching sigh.

Unexpectedly Thorne dropped his arms and reached for her hand. "Let's get out of here," he said in a voice that sounded strangely unlike his own.

He led her off the ballroom floor as though he couldn't leave fast enough. "Did you bring a coat?"

"A shawl."

Irritably he held out his hand, palm upward. "Give me your ticket."

Her fingers shook as she opened the beaded clutch and retrieved the small tab. "Where . . . where are you going?"

He sounded almost angry, certainly impatient. "Anywhere but here," he mumbled.

He left her then and Cindy stood alone, pondering the strangeness of his actions. She wanted to ask him more, longed to know why he looked as though he wanted to rip her limb from limb. But when he returned she said nothing, silently following him as he led her out of the ballroom and into the hallway to the elevator.

A male voice called out to them. "Thorne, you're not leaving, are you?"

Cindy twisted her head around at the unexpected sound of the voice, but Thorne applied pressure to her back, directing her forward.

"That man was talking to you."

"I have no desire to talk to anyone," he said stiffly, escorting her into the crowded elevator. They stepped off at the ground floor and Thorne led her to the entrance of the hotel.

The doorman stepped forward and asked. "Taxi, sir?"

Thorne looked at the man as though he hadn't heard him. He decided quickly, glancing at Cindy. "No." He grabbed her hand then, and guided her across the busy street to the paved pathway that led to the interior of Central Park.

"Thorne," Cindy whispered, uncertain. "Why are you so angry?"

"Angry?" He paused in front of the large fish pond.

The moon beamed golden rays all around them, and Cindy could see that his face was intent, his mouth bracketed with harsh lines. His gray eyes were narrowed and hard, yet when they rested on her she saw them soften.

"I'm not angry," he said at last, his breathing labored. "I'm..." He paused and rammed his hands into his pants pockets. "I don't know what I am. You're right, I am angry, but not at you."

"Then who?"

He shook his head and his eyes grew warm and lambent as he studied her upturned face. Almost as though he didn't know what he was doing, Thorne pulled his hands from his pockets and cupped her face, staring at her with a thoroughness that brought a heated rush of color to her cheeks. "You're so beautiful," he whispered with a reverence that shook his voice.

Cindy dropped her eyes.

His grip tightened almost imperceptibly. "It's true," he continued. "I've never known anyone as lovely."

"Why did you bring me here?"

Thorne expelled his breath in a low rush, and his words were an odd mixture of anger and wonder. "For the most selfish of reasons. I wanted to kiss you."

Cindy's questioning gaze sought his. "Then why haven't you? Cinderella's waiting."

He smiled then. "You're taking this prince stuff seriously, aren't you?"

"Very."

He ran his thumb across her bottom lip and his eyes grew serious. "I've never experienced anything like this."

"Me either." It was important that he know this phenomenon was as much a shock to her. She hadn't expected anything like this to happen, hadn't believed it ever would. When she'd first seen him, her disappointment had been acute and profound. But all that had changed the moment he'd come to her and asked her to dance. From that time forward he had magically been transformed into the prince who'd dominated her dreams for weeks. He was everything she'd imagined and a thousand things more.

"I haven't any right," he said, but his mouth inched closer to hers as though he wanted her to stop him.

She couldn't—not when she longed for his kiss the way she did; not when every cell of her being was crying out for the taste of his mouth over hers.

The ragged beat of his heart echoed her own as Cindy flattened her hands against his chest and slowly, deliberately, tilted her face to receive his kiss. They were so close their breath mingled. Cindy parted her lips, eager now. She stood on tiptoe as Thorne gently lowered his lips onto hers. His mouth was firm and so unbelievably tender that Cindy felt a tear form at the corner of her eye. Their mouths clung, and Cindy's hands crept upward to meet behind his neck.

"Oh, Lord—so sweet, so very sweet," Thorne groaned and buried his face in the milky-smooth slope of her neck. "I knew it would be like this. I knew it would be this sweet." His breathing was ragged, uneven.

Cindy felt as though she'd been shocked, stunned into speechlessness. Her whole body went numb, tingling with wonder. As difficult as it was, she resisted the urge to place her fingers to her lips to test the sensation. Thorne looked equally shaken. They broke apart and Cindy teetered for a moment until she found her balance.

Their eyes met and held for a timeless second. When Thorne reached for her, Cindy walked willingly into his arms, as though it were the only place in all creation where she truly belonged. His mouth was eager, hungry upon hers, twisting, turning, tasting, testing as though he had to reexperience these sensations and hadn't believed this wonderful feeling could be real.

When he released her, Cindy was weak and trembling. She looked up at Thorne and noted he was unnaturally pale.

Without questioning her, Thorne took a step back and removed his heavy overcoat. Gently, he placed it over her shoulders. "You're cold," he whispered. His hands lingered on her shoulders, and it looked as though he had to restrain himself from kissing her again.

"No," she murmured, shaking her head. "It's not the cold. It's you—you make me tremble."

"Look what you do to me." He captured her hand and placed it over his pounding heart. A frown drove his dark brows together. "I'm no schoolboy. What's happening to us?"

Cindy smiled and pressed a gentle kiss to the corner of his mouth. "Magic, I think."

"Black magic?" He regarded her suspiciously, but his eyes were smiling.

"No, this is the very best kind."

He agreed. Nothing that felt this good, this wonderful, could ever be wrong. He placed his arm around her shoulder and led her to one of the many benches that faced the huge fish pond.

Silently they sat together, neither speaking, neither needing words. Thorne continued to hold her simply because releasing her was unthinkable. His mind whirled with a hundred questions. He prayed she was a secretary so he could make her his own. He didn't care what strings he had to pull; he wanted her working with him. Mrs. Hillard was looking to retire, and the thought of greeting each day with Cindy was enough to... The thought crystallized in his mind. He *was* going crazy. The cardinal rule of any office was never to become romantically involved with an employee.

He must have given her a shocked look because Cindy's gaze met his and her eyes softened with such compassion that Throne could barely breathe.

"It's all right," she whispered.

"But..."

"No," she said and pressed her fingers to his lips, silencing him.

He gave her a funny look. Could she read his thoughts as well? Was she clairvoyant? She couldn't possibly have known what he'd been thinking, yet she showed him in a glance that she understood his very soul.

"You don't need to tell me," Cindy spoke after a long moment. "I already know about Sheila."

Chapter Three

"Sheila." The name seared through Thorne's mind. Good Lord, he was practically engaged to the other woman and here he was sitting beside Cindy and madly plotting to keep her in his life. He thrust his face toward her, his mouth gaping open as one thought quickly stumbled over another. He had to explain. He had to let Cindy know—only he wasn't sure how he was going to unscramble his own mind, let alone reassure her. It was as though Sheila meant nothing to him. Nothing. Yet a few days before, he'd contemplated giving her an engagement ring for Christmas. He'd actually been entertaining the idea of marriage and starting a family.

The twisting, churning trail of his thoughts must have been visible in his eyes, because Cindy's gaze softened and she smiled with such sweet understanding that the panic that gripped him was instantly quelled.

He looked so astonished, so shocked, that Cindy placed her index finger across his lips. "Shh. You don't need to tell me anything; I understand."

If she did he wished to hell she'd explain things to him. Thorne felt like a scheming hypocrite. He was nearly engaged to one woman and so attracted to another he could barely take his eyes off her. Even now when she'd brought Sheila's name between them, he couldn't force himself to leave Cindy. By all that was right, he should stand up and walk away. He should escape before whatever was happening this enchanted evening could mark him. His gut reaction was that Cindy's imprint on him could well be indelible. It was crazy, the things he was thinking. Insane to want her working with him. Absurd to seriously consider dating an employee. His mother would be stunned, his father amused. They'd been after him for years to settle down, but they'd made it abundantly clear that they expected him to marry the right type of woman.

"You're angry now," Cindy said, studying the dark emotion as it wove its way across his face, pinching his eyes and mouth, drawing his brow together in a deep frown.

"Not angry," he countered. "Confused."

"Don't be."

He took her hand in his, weaving their fingers together. She had beautiful hands. Each finger was narrow and tapered, and intuitively Thorne felt the gentle comfort she would be capable of granting with a mere touch. The nails were clipped to a respectable length,

neither too long nor too short. He supposed she had
to keep them short in order to type properly.

"Who are you?" he asked, astonished that even her
fingers could entice him.

Cindy felt the magic slowly dissipating. "I . . . I already told you."

"Cinderella?"

"Yes."

"And I'm your prince?"

"Yes." She nodded vigorously. "I've dreamed of
you so often, and then I met you, and I knew you were
everything my fantasies had promised."

He forced her gaze to meet his by placing his index
finger beneath her chin. Studying her intense blue eyes
was like looking into the crystal-clear water that ran
off the mountains during spring thaw. She was incapable of deception. Unbelievably sweet. Completely
innocent. She was everything he'd dared hope he'd
find in a woman—yet had never believed he'd find.
She was unexpected sunshine and warmth on a winter
day. Laughter and excitement in the middle of a deep,
dark void. Love when he least anticipated it and was
least prepared to deal with it. "You claimed I disappointed you."

"That was before. Now I know who you really are,
and I can hardly believe it's true."

"Oh, Cindy." He couldn't stop himself. He lowered his mouth to hers and kissed her again, wrapping his arms around her, holding her against him,
savoring the feminine feel of her as she pressed her
softness to his hard chest. She tasted like heaven, and
her lips promised him paradise. "Cindy," he whispered against her mouth. Never had a name been more

lovely. He kissed her again and drew her bottom lip gently between his teeth.

Cindy leaned into him and parted her mouth to the pressure of his tongue. She could barely breathe past the pagan beat of her heart. She feared she'd wake up any minute and discover this had all been a dream.

Thorne heaved a sigh that came all the way from the marrow of his bones and held her so close that his arms ached.

"Thorne..."

"I'm hurting you?" He relaxed the pressure instantly and ran his hands down the length of her back and up again to rest on the curve of her shoulders. His thumb stroked the pulse that was rapidly pounding near the hollow of her throat. Reluctantly he eased her away from him. "Tell me about yourself. I want to know everything."

Cindy dropped her gaze and laughed lightly to hide her uneasiness. She couldn't tell him anything. "There isn't much to tell."

She placed her hands on the side of his face and slowly rubbed his jaw. "I see such pride in you. Stubborn pride," she amended with a gentle smile. "And mind-bending determination. Were you always like this?"

Thorne could deny neither; she read him as easily as she would a billboard. He could disguise his thoughts and reactions from others, but not from Cindy. "Always, I think. My mother claims that when I was fourteen months old, I tossed my bottle against the wall and refused to drink out of anything but a cup from then on. That was only the beginning. When other children were riding tricycles, I wanted a two-wheeler. I was reading by age five and not because I was gifted. My older sisters read and I was hell-bent to do anything they could.''

"I refused to give up my blanky until I was six,'' Cindy admitted sheepishly. It had been her only comfort after her mother had died, and she'd clung to it feverishly, initially refusing to accept the love her aunt and her uncle had offered.

"You must have been a beautiful baby.''

"I had buckteeth and freckles.''

"I wore braces and corrective shoes.''

Cindy laughed. "You were always the sportsman, though, weren't you?''

Thorne's eyes momentarily clouded. "Yes.''

"Something happened.'' Cindy could see it: a flash of some memory that came so briefly that another person might have missed it.

His heart hammered relentlessly, squeezing with rare emotion. He'd hadn't thought about the accident in years. He'd only been a child. Ten years old.

Cindy saw the pain in his eyes and although she didn't understand it, she knew she had to comfort him. She lifted her hand and gently touched his face. "Tell me,'' she whispered in a low, coaxing tone. "Tell me. Tell me everything.''

Sensation raced through Thorne like wildfire. He caught her hand, raised it to his mouth and kissed her palm. "I fell from my horse. I thought I was dead, then I realized that death wouldn't hurt that much. I was barely conscious; every breath I drew was like inhaling fire.''

Cindy bit her bottom lip. The thought of Thorne in pain, even discomfort that he'd suffered years before, was more than she could bear. "Broken ribs?"

"Six, and a bruised kidney."

Her fingers tightened over his. There was more than the physical pain he was remembering; something far deeper, far more intense, punctured his memory. "What happened?"

He gave her a long, hard look. "I already told you. I fell off the horse."

"No. Afterward."

"Afterward," he repeated in a tight murmur. He remembered lying in bed in his darkened room hours later. The pain hadn't gone away. If anything, it had grown so much worse he wished he had died just so he wouldn't have to bear the agony any longer. One eye had been so severely bruised it had swollen shut. The side of his face was badly scraped, and the incredible ache in his jaw wouldn't go away. Two days later, the doctor discovered that it, too, had been broken in the fall.

His father was away much of the time, traveling for business, when Thorne was a boy, but he'd come the afternoon of the accident to see his son. Thorne had looked up at his father, grateful he was there. Tears had welled in Thorne's eyes, but instead of offering comfort, the elder Prince had spoken of what it meant to be a man and how a true man never revealed his emotions and certainly never cried.

"Thorne," Cindy prompted.

"My father forced me out of bed and into the saddle." He'd never told anyone about that incident. It made his father sound heartless and cruel. Thorndike, Sr. was neither—only proud and stubborn like his son. Thorne paused and his eyes narrowed. "Why am I telling you this?"

"You needed to," she answered simply.

Thorne looked startled. She was right. He had needed to tell someone about the accident, only he hadn't recognized the necessity of it himself. Until tonight with Cindy. Unexpectedly, he felt like laughing.

"Let's walk," he said, coming to his feet.

Cindy joined him and he tucked her hand into the crook of his elbow, folding his hand over her fingers. "This really is an enchanted evening, isn't it?"

"Magical," she returned, her eyes smiling softly into his.

They strolled along the walkway that led around the pond. Thorne felt like singing, which of course was ridiculous. He didn't sing. Not even in the shower. "Is there some deep, dark secret about yourself you should tell me?"

"Plenty," she answered, swallowing a laugh.

"Tell me just one so I won't feel like such a fool."

"Okay." She experienced an overwhelming urge to throw back her head and laugh. "No one knows this."

"Good." Thorne was pleased to hear it.

She hesitated. "You'll probably find this amusing, but I promise you, it isn't."

"I won't laugh," he promised and crossed his heart, vowing his silence.

She regarded him steadily, uncertain she could trust him with something this silly. "I still have my blanky."

"Do you sleep with it?"

"Of course not." She was offended until she realized he was silently amused by her admission. She bit back an angry response. He'd shared something profound with her. Her threadbare blanky was a little thing. "It's tucked away in a bottom drawer."

His eyes fairly sparkled.

"Thorndike Prince, you're laughing at me!"

"I swear I'm not." He gave her a look of childlike innocence. "Tell me something more."

"Never," she vowed, a chuckle punctuating her words.

Thorne paused and draped his arm over her shoulder. He lifted his gaze to the clear night sky. Stars filled the heavens, glimmering, glinting, glistening across the tops of the skyscrapers. "It's a beautiful night."

Cindy's gaze followed his. "Shall we make a wish?"

He turned his gaze to her. "A wish?"

"Upon a star." She twisted so she stood directly in front of him. "You haven't done this in a long time, have you?"

"No." There had seldom been time for childish games. In some ways, Thorne had never been allowed to be a boy. Responsibilities had greeted him at the bassinet. He was the only son, and as he was born after two daughters, great things had been expected of him.

"Then do it now," she urged gently, tossing back her head to gaze into the heavens. She picked out the brightest star, lowered her lashes and wished with all her heart that this night would never end. "Okay," she whispered when she'd finished, "it's your turn."

He stared at her blankly. "You're sure you want me to do this?"

"Yes," she answered simply.

Like Cindy, he raised his head and studied the heavens. "You don't honestly believe in this, do you?"

"You're asking Cinderella something like that? Of course, I believe. It's required of all princesses in fairy tales."

"What should I ask for?"

It took Cindy a moment to realize that whatever Thorne wanted in life he purchased without a second thought. He probably had every material possession he could possibly want.

"Ask for something you never expected to receive," she instructed softly.

Thorne dropped his gaze to Cindy. He'd never thought to meet anyone like her. Someone so pure and good. Someone so honest and forthright. A woman who stirred his mind as well as his heart. A woman of insight and laughter. He felt like a teenager next to her, yearning to find a way to please her—to thank her for giving him this priceless gift of joy.

His eyes melted her soul. He was looking at her as she'd always imagined great heroes viewed the loves of their lives. The way Heathcliff regarded Catherine or Mr. Rochester saw Jane Eyre. The bored, cynical look that tightened his features when she'd first arrived at the party had been replaced with one of tender gentleness.

"Close your eyes," she told him when she found her voice. "You have to close your eyes to make your wish come true."

Reluctantly Thorne did as she requested, but he didn't need any stars or any wishes to be granted his lone request. Without his even asking, it had already come true: everything he'd ever wanted was standing no more than a few inches from him. And if he doubted, all he had to do was reach out and touch her. Cindy was his, and he'd found her in the nick of time. To think that only a few hours before, he'd dreaded attending this party. The thought astonished him. Now he'd thank God every day of his life that he had been there to meet Cindy.

"Have you finished?" she whispered, surprised at the inordinate amount of time he took to make his request of the heavens.

Slowly Thorne opened his eyes. "Are you going to tell me your wish?" he asked, bringing her against his side once more. He had to keep touching her to believe she was real and he wasn't in the middle of some fever-induced hallucination.

"I might as well," she said softly. "There's no possibility it will ever come true."

"Don't be so certain. I thought we'd already agreed this night is filled with magic."

"It couldn't come true." Her footsteps matched his own as they continued strolling. As much as she wished it to be, her request was an impossibility, and she'd best accept it as such. "I asked that this night would never end."

"Ah." Thorne understood her reasoning. "But in some ways it never will."

"How's that?" Cindy turned her head to better study his expression. When she'd first conceived this plan, she'd counted on the magic to work for her. Now that she saw how greatly Thorne had been affected by her schemes, she marveled at the potency of the stars to grant her wishes.

"This night will last forever," Thorne said thoughtfully.

"But how?" Cindy didn't understand because midnight loomed and she knew she must leave him. There was no turning back for Cinderella.

"It will live in our hearts."

The tear that sprang to the corner of Cindy's eye was so unexpected and so profoundly felt that she hurriedly turned her head away in an effort to hide it from Thorne. She hadn't expected . . . hadn't dared to hope he would be so romantic.

"That's beautiful," she said in a choked whisper. "Prince Charming himself couldn't have said it any better."

"Only Cinderella would know that."

Cindy smiled, letting the wonder of this night dispel all doubts.

"So you're still claiming to be Cinderella?"

"Oh, yes, it's quite true."

His steps slowed. "Do you have two ugly stepsisters?"

"No," she answered, grateful he'd steered the conversation to lighter subjects.

"What about a fairy godmother?"

"A wonderful but ordinary godmother," she answered, convinced her aunt would appreciate the compliment. "But that doesn't mean she lacks magical powers."

"Did she turn the mice into horses for your carriage?"

Cindy frowned. "I don't exactly have a carriage."

"Yes, you do," Thorne said, leading her onto the sidewalk along Central Park Avenue South. Horse-drawn carriages lined the streets, seeming to wait for her command. "Your carriage awaits you, my lady," Thorne told her formally, bowing low as a knight of old would have done for his princess.

As if reading Thorne's thoughts, the middle-aged driver, who wore a black top hat, stepped forward and opened the carriage door. Cindy accepted his hand and climbed inside. The black leather cushion creaked when she sat, and Cindy tucked her dress around her. She continued to wear Thorne's overcoat and wondered guiltily if he was chilled. The warmth of the look he gave her when he climbed in after her chased away any doubt.

Sitting beside Cindy, Thorne placed his arm around her shoulders. "I've lived in Manhattan for the past six years and I've never done this."

"Me either," Cindy admitted, feeling as excited as a child.

"I may have confused the driver, however," Thorne claimed, his eyes twinkling with merriment. "I told him we wanted to survey our kingdom."

Cindy laughed. "Oh, dear, the poor man. He must think we're both crazy."

"We are, but I don't mind. Do you?" His eyes grew sober. When Cindy was with him it didn't matter if the world found his behavior amusing.

"Not in the least."

The driver jumped into the carriage box and gently urged the horse onto the street. The giant wheels at Cindy's side drowned out the sound of the horse's shoes as they clapped noisily against the pavement.

"I've always wanted to do this," Cindy admitted. "Thank you, Thorne." She laid her head upon his shoulder and drew in a deep breath. She yearned to hold on to this moment for as long as possible before having to relinquish it.

Thorne intertwined his fingers with hers and raised her hand to his mouth to brush a kiss across her knuckles. "I know so little about you."

"You know everything that's important."

"I feel like I do," he said after a moment. "I know this sounds loony, but it's as if I've known you all my life."

Cindy understood. "In some ways, I think that I might have been born for this night."

"I feel like I've been born for you."

Cindy went stock-still. It became difficult to swallow. They had only tonight. Only these few hours, and when it was midnight, she would be forced to go back to being the girl who cleaned his office. A nobody. Certainly no one who would ever interest Thorndike Prince, first vice president. Her mind spun with countless possibilities, but they all ended with the same shattering reality. She couldn't change who she was, and he couldn't alter the man he had become. There could be no middle ground for them.

"You're terribly quiet all of a sudden," Thorne observed. He liked having her close to him. He loved touching her and kissing her. But the fascination he felt for her wasn't physical. The only word he could think of that might describe his feelings was *spiritual*. Something buried deep within him had reached out and met a significant inner part of the woman at his side. His inner personality had connected with hers. With her, he experienced a wholeness, a rightness that had been missing from his life.

"Let's not think beyond anything but this night," Cindy said softly. Her mind was conjuring up ways in which she could meet him again, but she quickly realized the impossibility of it all. As it was, she had stolen this one night. There could be no others. Ever. A sadness surrounded her heart, pressing against her with such heaviness that she nearly gave up breathing, the effort was so great.

"We'll share forever," Thorne returned quickly. "And all the nights for the rest of our lives." He knew he was rushing her. Good God, they'd only met a few hours before, and he was practically asking her what names she planned to give their children. The thought stunned him. He, Thorndike Prince, who had always been described as an unemotional, hard-hearted cynic, was talking like a lovesick teenager. And loving it. He'd been ignorant before meeting Cindy. Stupid. Now that he'd met her, he understood what drove men to impossible feats in the name of love. He'd walk over hot coals to get to Cindy. Hell, he'd walk across water just to be at her side. Nothing would stop him now that he'd discovered her.

"I want you to meet my family." He shocked himself by making the suggestion.

"Your family?" Cindy repeated, stunned.

"Yes." He'd talk to both his mother and his father first. They'd be surprised, of course, since they'd been expecting him to announce he was marrying Sheila. Sheila. He nearly laughed aloud. He couldn't even remember what the other woman looked like.

His parents could be his and Cindy's biggest hurdle. But once they met her they wouldn't question his actions. After the initial shock his mother would love her, Thorne was certain of that. His father was another matter, but given time, he would respect Thorne's decision. Things could get a bit sticky with Sheila, but she was a reasonable woman. She wanted what was best for Thorne, and as soon as he explained, Thorne was convinced the other woman would understand.

Within a matter of hours a secretary with a saucy grin had turned his life upside down. And Thorne loved it.

"I...can't meet your family." Cindy's mind was in turmoil.

"Of course you can. They're going to love you."

"Thorne—"

"Stop." He pressed his finger across her lips just as she'd done to him earlier. "Here," he said, and placed her hand over his heart. "Feel how excited and happy I am. I feel alive for the first time in years. You've done that for me. I want to laugh and sing and dance, and I never do any of those things."

"But, I can't—"

"I know I'm probably going a thousand times too fast for you. I realize it all sounds crazy, but I've been waiting years for you. Years." He framed her face with his hands as his gaze studied hers. His thumbs ran over his lips before he kissed her with infinite gentleness. His mouth lingered over hers as if he couldn't get his fill of her and never would. "What took you so long, Cindy, love? What took you so very long?"

Cindy swallowed a sob at the tenderness she saw in his eyes. "Thorne, please...don't..."

His mouth stopped her, kissing her again until her senses spun at breakneck speed, careening down a slope of reality. There was no question of refusing herself the luxury of his touch. Nor was there a question of disillusioning him. Soon enough he would discover the truth. Soon enough he would know she wasn't who she pretended to be. She was no princess. No royal blue blood flowed through her veins. Her family name wasn't going to cause any banker's heart to react with excitement.

"I'd be honored to meet your family," she said softly.

"Tomorrow, then."

"Whenever you wish." She couldn't meet his eye, knowing there were no tomorrows for them.

They had so little time together. So little time. She couldn't ruin everything now. Maybe it was wrong not to tell him she was the janitorial worker who cleaned his office and that she had no intention of embarrassing him in front of his family. But it couldn't be any more wrong than crashing the party and seeking out Thorndike Prince in the first place.

The carriage driver paused to clear his throat. Irritated, Thorne broke away from Cindy and noted they'd completed the circle and were back.

"Shall we go around again?" On the first trip, he had gotten her to agree to meet his family. He'd seen the reluctance in her eyes and realized how much the thought had intimidated her. Yet she'd agreed. He yearned to hold her and assure her he would never leave her, that with a little time and patience his family would be as impressed with her as he was.

Somewhere in the distance a clock began to chime. Cindy paused, counting the night-piercing tones that seemed to peal on endlessly. "Midnight," she cried,

her heart beating frantically. "It's midnight. I've...
I've got to leave. I'm sorry...so sorry."

"Cindy." Thorne reached out for her, but already
she was rushing away. He ran a few steps, his pace
matching hers. "I'll take you home. Don't worry
about missing your ride—I'll see you safely home."

Tears filled her eyes as she handed him his coat and
paused to wrap her arms around him, hugging him
with all the emotion stored in her heart. "You don't
understand."

She was right about that, Thorne mused. She
looked stricken—frightened and so unbelievably unhappy that he longed to ease whatever pain she was
suffering.

"It was the most wonderful night of my life.
I'll...remember it, and I'll always...always remember you."

"You won't get a chance to forget me." He tried to
keep her with him, but she whirled around and picked
up her skirts, racing away as though the very demons
of hell were in wild pursuit.

Stunned into immobility, Thorne watched her race
into traffic. She'd crossed the busy street and was
halfway down the sidewalk, when she turned around
abruptly. "Thank you," she yelled, raising her hand
to wave. "Thank you for making all my dreams come
true." She covered her mouth with her hand and even
from the distance Thorne could see she was weeping.
She ran then in earnest, sprinting to the corner. The
instant she reached it a long black limousine pulled up.
As if by magic, the door opened and Cindy slid inside. The limo was gone before Thorne had a chance
to react.

"Sir."

For a moment Thorne didn't respond to the voice beckoning him.

"She dropped these." The carriage driver handed Thorne two pearl combs.

The older man with the black top hat stared at Thorne. "Had to be home by midnight, did she?"

"Yes," Thorne responded without looking at the other man.

"Sounds like Cinderella."

"That's who she said she was."

The other man chuckled. "Then you must be Prince Charming."

Still, Thorne didn't move. "I am."

The carriage driver found that all the more amusing. "Sure, fella. And I'm Mr. Rockefeller himself."

Chapter Four

The first thing Thorne thought about when he woke early the following morning was Cindy. He'd drifted into a deep, restful sleep, picturing her sweet face, and he woke cursing himself for not getting her phone number. Being forced into waiting an entire day to see her again was nearly intolerable, but she'd left in such a maddening rush that he hadn't thought to ask her for it. Now he was paying the price for his own lack of forethought.

After he'd showered, he stood in a thick robe in front of his fourteenth-floor window. Manhattan stretched out before him like a concrete jungle, bold and brash. The crazy thing was how much he felt like singing. He'd been shocked to find himself humming in the shower. He gripped with both hands the towel that was draped around his neck and expelled a long, thoughtful sigh. It was almost as if he'd been reborn.

The world below buzzed with activity. Cars crowded the streets. A Circle Line tourist boat cruised around the island. Funny, he hadn't paid much attention to the Hudson River or seaport or any of the other sights in a long while. Now they sparkled like a thousand facets in a flawless diamond. It was ridiculous to believe he might be in love, but he felt breathless with excitement just thinking about Cindy.

The phone rang and Thorne reached for it expectantly. It was unrealistic to hope it was Cindy calling, and yet he nearly sighed with disappointment when his mother's voice greeted him.

"Thorne, it's your mother."

"Good morning, Mother."

"You certainly sound in a cheerful mood. How was the Christmas Ball?"

"Fabulous."

"Did Sheila attend with you?"

"No, she couldn't get away." His mother liked to keep close tabs on her children. Thorne tolerated her frequent calls because she was his mother, and her motivation was innocent enough, although he'd made it clear that his personal life was his own. She wanted him settled, sedately married and producing enough grandchildren to keep her occupied. His sisters had done their share and now it was his turn.

He spoke again, remembering that he'd asked Cindy to meet his family. "Mother, listen, I'm pleased you phoned. There's someone I'd like to bring to the house. Would it be possible to have her to dinner soon?"

"Her?"

"Yes, if it's not inconvenient, perhaps we could set it up for Christmas week."

"Do you have some exciting news for us, darling?"

Thorne weighed his words. "I suppose you could say so." He'd met the woman he planned to share his life with. It didn't get much more exciting than that, but he wasn't about to announce that to his family. After all, he'd just met Cindy. They'd scoff at him, and even Thorne had to admit he was behaving like a romantic fool.

"I believe your father and I may have already guessed your news." His mother's voice was soft and lilting with excitement.

"It's not what you think, Mother." Thorne paused and chuckled. "Or *who* you think, for that matter. I met someone wonderful last night...someone very special. I suppose it was a bit presumptuous of me, but I invited her over to meet you and Dad." The invitation alone must have been a shock to his mother, Thorne realized. He rarely introduced his lady friends to his family.

The short silence that followed was heavy. "This someone you met...she isn't by chance...Sheila?"

"Her name is Cindy, and we met at the Christmas Ball." Even his own mother would assume he'd lost his mind if he were to tell her that the minute he'd held Cindy, he'd known she was going to be special in his life.

"Cindy." His mother repeated it slowly, as though testing it on her tongue. "What's her last name?"

Thorne realized his mother was really inquiring about her family. He hated to admit it, but his own mother was a terrible snob.

"Surely she has a surname?" his mother taunted, obviously displeased about this unexpected turn of events.

Thorne hesitated. Now that he stopped and thought about it, he realized he didn't know Cindy's surname. "I don't believe she told me."

"You don't know her last name?"

"I just told you that, Mother. But it isn't any problem. I'll see her again Monday morning." Even as he said it, it sounded like an eternity, and Thorne wasn't entirely convinced he could wait. "She's an employee of Oakes-Jenning."

Another lengthy pause followed. "You haven't said anything to Sheila?"

"Of course not, I only met Cindy last night. Listen, Mother, I probably am making a mistake even mentioning her to you like this, but—"

"It's just a shock, that's all," his mother responded calmly, having regained her composure. "Do me a favor, son, and don't say anything to Sheila yet."

"But, Mother—"

"I wouldn't want you to mislead the poor girl, but you might save yourself a considerable amount of heartache until you and... What was her name again?"

"Cindy."

"Ah, yes, Cindy. It would be better if you sorted out your feelings regarding Cindy before you say something to Sheila that you'll regret later."

"Cindy knows all about Sheila."

"Yes, but Sheila doesn't know about Cindy, and my guess is that it would be best to let this new...relationship simmer for a time until you're sure of your feelings."

Thorne's jaw tightened. He'd been foolish to mention Cindy to his mother. It was too soon. Later, when they saw how much he'd changed, they'd want to know the reason; he could explain Cindy then.

"Thorne?" His mother prompted. "Do you agree?"

For a moment he had to stop and think what she was asking him to agree to. "I won't say anything to Sheila," he promised.

"Good." Her relief came in the form of an exaggerated sigh.

"You must have phoned for some reason, Mother."

"Oh, yes," she said and laughed nervously. "It was about Christmas Day...I was wondering if you minded...if I invited Sheila."

"Perhaps it would be best if you didn't." Although Christmas was only a little more than a week away, Thorne had hoped to share this special day with Cindy. Christmas and every day in between.

The pause that followed told Thorne his objection came too late.

"I'm afraid...I happened to run into her yesterday when I was shopping...and, oh, dear, this is going to be a bit messy."

"Sheila's already been invited," Thorne finished for his mother. He closed his eyes to the cloudburst of anger that rained over him and quickly forgave her interfering ways. She hadn't meant to cause a problem. It must have seemed only natural to extend the invitation when he'd recently indicated he was considering marrying the other woman.

"Will that be so very uncomfortable, darling?"

"Don't worry about it, Mother. I'm sure everything will work out fine." Cindy would understand,
Thorne realized. She was an incredible person who
revealed no tendencies toward unreasonable jealousy.

"I do apologize, but your father and I both thought
Sheila would be joining our family . . . permanently."

"I know, Mother, this change of heart is rather unexpected."

The remainder of the conversation with his mother
was brief and Thorne hung up the phone, more confident than ever about his powerful feelings for Cindy.
Just remembering the way she'd strolled up to him at
the ball and announced that she was Cinderella
brought a quivering smile to the corners of his mouth.
And then she'd told him what a sorry disappointment
he was to her. Thorne laughed out loud. Monday
morning couldn't come soon enough to suit him. Not
nearly soon enough.

Cindy woke to a pounding headache. Her head
throbbed with pain and she placed her hand over her
eyes to block out the light. She didn't suffer from these
often, but when she did they were debilitating. Her
mouth felt dry and her tongue swollen. Carefully she
rolled onto her back and stared at the ceiling, waiting
for the discomfort to pass.

The evening with Thorne had been so much more
than she'd dared to dream. She hadn't been able to
sleep for hours after her Uncle Sal had dropped her off
in Little Italy. She lay in bed and continued to relive
every part of the evening. The night had been perfect—from their awkward beginning when she'd in-

troduced herself, to the tenderness she'd seen in his gaze when he looked down on her in the carriage. An aching sob built up in her chest until she was forced to bite down on her bottom lip to hold it inside.

She'd been wrong to play the role of Cinderella. It would have been so much easier never to have met Thorne. Now she was forever doomed to hold this ache within her breast for having so flippantly tempted fate.

When she'd arrived home, even before she'd undressed, Cindy had sat on the end of her bed and tried to picture Thorne in her home. The mental image was so discordant that she'd been forced to cast the thought from her mind. If Thorne were to see this apartment and the earthy family she loved, he would be embarrassed. Thorne Prince didn't know what it meant to live from paycheck to paycheck or to "make do" when money was tight. He might as well live on another planet in a neighboring solar system, he was so far removed from her way of life.

"Cindy." Her aunt knocked gently at the bedroom door. "Are you awake?"

Cindy sat up awkwardly and leaned against her headboard. "I'm up...come on in."

Slowly, her aunt opened the door. Her eyes met Cindy's. "It's nearly noon. Are you feeling ill?"

It was unusual for Cindy to stay in bed for any reason. "A headache."

Aunt Theresa sat on the edge of the bed and brushed the hair away from Cindy's brow. "Did you have a good time last night?" she asked softly, studying her niece.

Cindy's gaze dropped to the patchwork quilt that served as her bedspread. "I had a wonderful time."

"Did Cinderella meet her prince?"

Cindy's eyes glistened at the memory. "I spent most of the evening with him."

"And was he everything she expected?"

Cindy nodded because speaking was impossible. She leaned forward enough to rest her head on her aunt's shoulder.

"And now?" The older woman probed.

"And now Cinderella realizes what a terrible fool she was because at midnight she turned back into plain, simple Cindy Territo." A tear scorched her cheek and her arms circled her aunt's neck. As she had as a child, Cindy needed the warmth and security of her aunt's love.

"My darling girl, you are neither plain nor simple."

Cindy sniffled and sadly shook her head. "Compared to other women he knows, I am."

"But he liked you."

"He thought I was a secretary."

"Nevertheless he must have been impressed to have spent the evening in your company. Does it matter so much if you're a secretary or a charwoman?"

"Unfortunately, it does."

"It seems to me you're selling your prince short," her aunt said soothingly, stroking the back of Cindy's head. "If he's everything you've said, it wouldn't matter in the least."

Cindy said nothing. She couldn't answer her aunt's questions. Her own doubts were overwhelming.

"Do you plan to see him again?" Theresa asked, after a thoughtful moment.

Cindy closed her eyes to the searing disappointment and emotional pain. "Never," she whispered.

Monday morning Thorne walked crisply into his office fifteen minutes ahead of his usual routine. Mrs. Hillard, his secretary, looked up from the work on her desk, revealing mild surprise that her employer was early.

"Good morning, Mrs. Hillard. It's a beautiful day, isn't it?"

His secretary's mouth dropped open. "It's barely above freezing and the weathermen are forecasting a snowstorm by midafternoon."

"I love snow," Thorne continued, undaunted.

Mrs. Hillard rolled out her chair and stood. "Are you feeling all right, sir?"

"I'm feeling absolutely wonderful."

"Can I get you some coffee?"

"Please." Thorne strolled toward his desk. "And contact Wells in personnel, would you?"

"Right away." A minute later she delivered his coffee. The red light on his phone was lit, and Thorne sat in his chair and reached for the receiver.

"This is Thorndike Prince," he began in clipped tones. "Would you kindly check your files for the name Cindy. She works on the executive floor. I'd like her full name and the office number."

"Cindy?" The tinny voice of the personnel director came back over the phone.

"Unfortunately, I don't have her surname."

"This may take some time, Mr. Prince; I'll have to phone you back."

Thorne thumped his fingers against the top of his desk in an effort to disguise his impatience. "No problem. I'll wait to hear from you." He replaced the receiver and leaned back in his chair, holding the coffee in both hands. He gazed out the window and noted for the first time the thick, angry clouds that threatened the sky. A snowstorm, Mrs. Hillard had said. Terrific! He'd take Cindy for a walk in the falling snow and warm her with kisses. They'd go back to the park and feed the pigeons and then to his apartment and drink mulled wine. He'd spent one restless day without her and he wasn't about to waste another. His head was bursting with things he wanted to tell her, things he found vitally important to share. Today he'd learn everything he could about her. Once he knew everything, he'd take her in his arms and tell her the magic hadn't quit working. The spell she'd cast on him hadn't faded and couldn't. If anything, it had grown stronger with every passing minute.

The phone pealed and he jerked the receiver off its cradle. "Prince here."

"This is Mr. Wells from personnel."

"Yes."

"Sir—" he paused and cleared his throat "—I've checked all our records and I don't find anyone with the name Cindy or Cynthia employed on the executive floor."

"Then look again," Thorne said stiffly. The incompetence he was forced to deal with on a day-to-day basis was enough to try the patience of any man.

"Sir, I've checked the files three times."

"Then I suggest you do so again." Thorne slammed down the phone. The only way he was going to get Cindy's name was to go down there himself and locate it. Nothing irritated him more than this kind of flaming stupidity.

A half hour later, Thorne was forced to agree with Wells. There wasn't a secretary in the entire company with the name Cindy. Thorne slammed the filing-cabinet drawer shut with unnecessary force.

"Who was in charge of the Christmas Ball?" he demanded.

Mr. Wells, a diminutive man who wore a bow tie and glasses, cleared his throat. "I was, Mr. Prince."

"The ball was by invitation only; is that correct?"

"Yes, sir, I received my instructions from—"

"I want the list."

"The list?" He pulled out a file and handed Thorne several sheets of paper. "The name of every employee who received an invitation is here, except one and—"

"Who?" Angrily Thorne whirled around to face the other man, prepared to do whatever was necessary to learn the name.

"Myself," Wells admitted in a choked, startled voice.

Thorne's gaze scanned the list, then again much more slowly, carefully examining each name. No one named Cindy was there.

"How many extra invitations were printed?"

"A dozen...I have a list here." Wells pulled a sheet of paper from the file and Thorne took it and counted the names typed on it. Exactly twelve.

"Sir... perhaps this Cindy crashed the party.... There are ways," he stammered. "The hotel staff does all it can to assure that only those with an invitation are granted admission, but... it's been known to happen."

"Crashed the ball..." Thorne repeated, stunned. He paused and rubbed a hand over his face. That was exactly what had happened. The instant he heard Wells say it, he recognized the truth. "Thank you for your trouble."

"It was no problem, Mr. Prince. Perhaps if you could describe the girl, I could go through our files and locate several pictures. It could be that she is employed by Oakes-Jenning, but is assuming another name."

Thorne barely heard the other man. "That won't be necessary." He turned and left the office, reaching his own without remembering having stepped into the elevator.

Mrs. Hillard stood when he entered the room, her hands filled with the mail. Thorne gave her a look that told her he'd deal with his correspondence later, and she sat back down again.

For two days he'd been living in a dreamworld, Thorne realized. He'd been acting the part of an idiotic, romantic fool. The joyful expectation drained out of him and was replaced with a grim determination not to allow such folly to overtake him a second time. He'd put Cindy out of his mind and his heart as easily as he'd instilled her there. She was a fraud who had taken delight in duping him. Well, her plans had worked beyond her greatest expectation. He slumped into his chair and turned to look at the sky. Mrs. Hillard was right. The weather was terrible, but then so was the day.

Chapter Five

Thorne's violent sneeze tore the tissue in half. He reached for another in the nick of time. His eyes were running, he was so congested he could barely breathe and he had a fever. He felt thoroughly miserable, and it wasn't all due to this wretched cold. He'd gotten it the night he'd given Cindy his coat. Cindy. She haunted his dreams and filled his every waking thought. He wanted to hate her, shout at her and...and take her in his arms and hold her to him for all time. There were moments when he despised her, and then there were other times, usually at night, when he'd lie back and close his eyes. She came to him then, in those quiet moments, and tortured him, playing back every minute of their enchanted evening together. He'd be on the ballroom floor with her in his arms; a second later he'd recall with vivid clarity the agony in her eyes as she tearfully told him goodbye.

When she repeated over and over how sorry she was, the words seemed to echo around the canyons of his mind like piercing rifle shots in the night.

Thorne picked up the pearl comb and fingered it for the thousandth time in the past five days. He'd kept it with him constantly, seeking some clue from it, some solace. He found neither. He'd taken it to a jeweler and learned it was a moderately inexpensive comb that was perhaps twenty-five years old—certainly of little value beyond sentimental. It wasn't as if he could take it around the executive floor and try it on women's heads to see if it would fit. Cinderella had left him a useless white elephant. He couldn't trace her with a common pearl hair clip.

Other than the comb, Thorne had nothing with which to find Cindy. The crazy part was that he wasn't completely convinced he wanted to see her again. She'd lied to him, played him for a fool and mercilessly shattered his dreams—serious crimes for a woman he'd known for less than ten hours... and yet he couldn't stop thinking about her. Every minute. Every day. God knew, he wanted to cast her from his mind—to condemn her to the deepest, darkest reaches of hell . Then and only then could she fully appreciate what she'd done to him.

Thorne's thoughts were followed by another thunderous sneeze. He pressed the intercom button and summoned his secretary. "Did you get that orange juice?" he demanded.

"It's on its way," she informed him in a crisp, businesslike tone.

"Good." Thorne pulled open the top desk drawer and reached for the aspirin bottle. Lord, he was miserable, in both body and spirit.

Cindy inhaled a deep breath and forced herself into Thorne's office. It was torture to be inside the room where he spent so much of his time. She could feel his presence so strongly that she kept looking over her shoulder, convinced he was there, standing behind her. She wondered what he would say to her—if he hated her or if he even thought about her—then decided she'd rather not know. Her heart felt weighed down with a multitude of regrets.

Pushing Thorne out of her thoughts, she ran the feather duster over the top of his desk. Something small and white fell from the desktop and rolled onto the carpet. Cindy bent over and picked it up. A pearl. She held it in the palm of her hand and stared at it with open fascination. Thorne had her mother's combs! Cindy had thought they were lost to her forever. Not until she was home did she realize they'd fallen from her hair, and she'd been devastated over their loss. She had so few of her mother's personal possessions that losing even one was monumental.

"What's that?" Vanessa asked, standing in the open doorway, her feather duster stored in her hip pocket.

Cindy's hand closed over the pearl. Knowing that Thorne had the combs gave her a secure feeling. "A pearl," she said, tucking it inside the pocket of her coveralls.

Vanessa studied her closely. "Do you think it might be from your mother's combs?"

"I'm sure it is." If she were to leave part of herself with him, then something that was of such high value to her was fitting.

"Then your prince must have them."

Cindy nodded, comforted immeasurably by the information. "One, at least."

"How do you plan to get it back?"

"I don't," Cindy said and continued dusting, praying Vanessa would return to her own tasks so Cindy could keep her thoughts to herself.

"You aren't going to get them from him? That's crazy. You were sick about losing those combs."

"I know."

"Well, good grief, Cindy girl, here's the perfect opportunity for you to see your handsome prince a second time. Grab it, for heaven's sake!"

Cindy's mouth quivered. "I don't want to see him again."

"You might be able to fool your family, but you won't have such an easy time with me," Vanessa pressed, her mouth grim and her eyes revealing her disapproval. "You told me the ball was the happiest, most exciting night of your life."

Cindy's back stiffened. The warm, fairy-tale sensations the ball had aroused were supposed to last a lifetime, and instead the evening had left Cindy yearning for many, many more. "The night was everything I dreamed, but don't you see? I was playing a role... I was glamorous and sophisticated and someone totally different from the Cindy Territo you see now. The show closed, the part is cancelled and I've gone back to being just plain me: Cindy Territo, janitorial worker, part-time student."

"Cindy—the woman in love."

"Stop it, Vanessa!" she cried and whirled around to face her friend. "Adults don't fall in love after one night. Not true love—it just doesn't happen!"

Suavely Vanessa crossed her arms and leaned her hip against the side of Thorne's rosewood desk. "That's not what I hear."

Cindy snorted softly. "That's not love...that's hormones. It wasn't like that with Thorne and me; I don't think I can explain it...I've never felt anything like this with any man." She couldn't find the words to explain to her friend that what she shared with Thorne wasn't physical, but spiritual.

"And you're convinced it can't be love?" Vanessa taunted.

"It's impossible...I don't want to talk about him or that night again. I...we have to put it out of our minds." She reached for Thorne's wastepaper basket and unceremoniously dumped it inside her cart. When she saw the contents her eyes widened with self-recriminations. "Vanessa, look." She picked up a discarded aspirin box and another for a multisymptom-cold remedy. "Thorne's sick."

"He must have gone through a whole box of tissues from the looks of it."

"Oh, no." Cindy sagged into his chair, lovingly stroking the arm as though it were his fevered brow. She longed to be with him. "The night of the ball," she began, her voice strained with regret, "when we went into the park, he gave me his coat so I wouldn't catch cold."

"At a price, it seems."

Cindy's face went pale, and she looked distractedly at her friend before turning her head away and closing her eyes. "It's all my fault. Christmas is only a few days away.... Oh, dear, I did this to him."

"What do you plan to do about it?"

"What can I do?" If Cindy was miserable before, it was nothing compared to the guilt she suffered now, knowing her prince was ill because of something she'd done.

"Make him some chicken soup and take it to him," Vanessa suggested thoughtfully.

Cindy's eyes widened. "I couldn't."

"This is the same woman who sauntered up to Thorndike Prince and announced he was a sad disappointment to her?"

"One and the same," Cindy returned miserably.

Vanessa shook her head and frowned. "You could have fooled me."

If anybody was a fool, Cindy determined the following afternoon, it was she. She'd spent the morning chopping vegetables into precisely even pieces and adding them to a steaming pot of stewing chicken while her aunt made up a batch of thick, homemade noodles.

"Maybe I should have Tony deliver it to him for me," Cindy suggested, eyeing her aunt speculatively.

"Tony and Maria are going to a movie, and you can bet that your prince isn't going to hand over those combs to my son without getting whatever information he could out of him." The way she was regarding Cindy suggested that Thorne would use fair means or foul to find out what he could.

"Thorne wouldn't hurt anyone," Cindy defended him righteously, and from the quick smile that lit up the older woman's features, Cindy realized she'd fallen neatly into her aunt's trap.

"Then you shouldn't have any qualms about visiting him. It's not Tony or anyone else he wants to see—it's you."

Cindy raised questioning eyes to the woman who had so lovingly raised her. "I'm not entirely convinced he does want to see me."

"He kept the combs, didn't he?"

"Yes, but that doesn't mean anything."

"No man is going to carry around a pair of women's hair combs without a reason."

"Oh, Aunt Theresa, I feel like such an idiot. What if he hates me? What if—"

"Will you stop with the what ifs! The soup is finished. Take it to him and go from there."

"But..." She strove to keep the telltale emotion from her voice. But it wouldn't take a fortune-teller to see that she was as nervous as a cat in a roomful of rocking chairs. Today...if she saw Thorne, there would be no fancy gown with dimmed lights to create an illusion of beauty and worldliness. No moonlight and magic to entice him. Her plaid wool skirt, shell-knit sweater and leather pumps would tell him everything.

Theresa caught her by the shoulders. "Stop being so nervous, it's not like you!"

Cindy forced a smile and nodded. She'd go to him because she must. Her actions were already mapped out in her mind. She'd arrive at his apartment, give him the soup and tell him how sorry she was that he'd gotten a cold. Then, depending on how he responded to her, she'd ask for her mother's combs. But only if he showed signs of being pleased to see her. Somehow she doubted he would.

The television droned in the background, but Thorne couldn't force any interest in the silly game shows that ran one after another. They, however, were only slightly less boring than the soap operas that aired on the other channels. He felt hot, then chilled. Sick and uncomfortable. Sleepy from medication and wide-awake. It was only three days until Christmas and he had all the love and goodwill of an ill-tempered, cantankerous grinch!

The small tree that decorated the corner of the living room was testimony to his own folly. He'd enthusiastically put it up the day after meeting Cindy, and now it sat there taunting him, reminding him what a fool he was to believe in romantic dreams. In three days' time he would be obligated to arrive at his parents' home and face them and Sheila. The thought was not pleasant. All he wanted to do was bury his head in the sand and insist the world leave him alone!

He sighed and reached for a glass of grapefruit juice and another cold tablet. Discarded cold remedies crowded the surface of his glass coffee table. He'd taken one pillow from his bed and stripped away the bedspread in an effort to get comfortable in the living room.

The doorbell chimed and he twisted around and glared at it with open hostility.

Seemingly undaunted, the bell rang a second time. "Go away," he shouted. The last thing he wanted was company.

This time the ring was followed by loud knocking.

Furious, he shoved the covers aside and stormed to the front door. With equal force he jerked it open and glared angrily at the young woman who stood before him. "I said go away!" he shouted, in no mood to be civil. "I don't want to..." His voice faded to a mere croak. "Cindy?" He was too shocked, too stunned to do anything, even breathe. The first thing that came to his mind was to haul her into his arms and not let her leave until she told him who she was. But the impulse was followed immediately by an all-consuming anger. His face went hard as he glared at her with contempt.

Cindy stood frozen in front of him, unable to force a coherent word from her vocal cords. A rush of color heated her face. This was a hundred times worse than she'd imagined. Thorne hated her. Dismayed and disheartened, she handed him the large paper sack. "I...learned you were sick."

"What's this?" Knowing her, he could well suspect arsenic.

"Chicken soup."

Thorne's eyes lit up with sardonic amusement. She resembled a frightened rabbit standing in front of a hungry wolf. He wanted her to fret and wondered how anyone could look so innocent and so completely guileless when he knew her to be a liar and a cheat. "You might as well come in," he said gruffly, stepping aside to allow her entrance.

"I can only stay a minute," she said shakily.

"I wouldn't dream of inviting you to stay longer," he answered, in an effort to be cruel. He was rewarded when he watched the color drain from her soft features. Good. He wanted to hurt her. He wanted her to experience just a taste of the hell she'd put him through.

She caught her breath and nodded, saying without words that she understood.

He set the soup on the coffee table and slumped onto the white leather sofa. "I won't apologize for the mess, but as you evidently heard, I haven't been feeling well." He motioned toward the matching chair across from him. "I know what you want."

Surprise rounded her deep blue eyes. "You do?"

"It's the combs, isn't it?"

Cindy nodded and sat on the edge of the cushion, folding her hands primly in her lap. She clasped her fingers together so tightly that she was certain she'd cut off her circulation. "They were my mother's... You have them?"

"Both."

She sighed with relief. "I thought I'd lost them."

"You knew damn good and well I had them."

Cindy opened her mouth to argue with him but quickly closed it. He couldn't believe anything but ill of her, and she couldn't blame him.

"What? No heated defense?"

"None. You have the right to hate me. I lied to you, but not in the way you think."

"You're sure as hell no secretary."

"No, but if you remember, I never said I was."

"But you didn't stop me from thinking that."

Cindy dropped her eyes to her clenched hands. "As I said before, you have every right to be angry, but if it's any consolation to you—I am deeply and truly sorry."

His gaze narrowed, condemning her. "Such innocent eyes. Who would have guessed that such deception, such cleverness lay just below the surface? You, my dear, should be employed by the War Department. Your country would be well served by your deceitfulness."

Cindy clamped her teeth together with such force that her jaw ached. Every word was a slap in her face and it hurt, it hurt so terribly. His eyes were so cold and filled with such contempt. "If I could have the combs...I'll be on my way."

"Not quite yet." He stood and joined her, pulling her to her feet. "You owe me something for all the lies you told...for deceiving me into thinking you were kind and good." For filling his head with dreams and shattering the unspoken promises she'd given him so freely.

Frightened, Cindy drew back sharply.

His eyes narrowed fiercely on her flushed face and his hands tightened around her upper arm. He pulled her against him and slanted his mouth over hers, mercilessly moving his lips against hers.

Cindy went still with shock, giving up the struggle, letting him do as he would. Fighting would only aggravate him.

Thorne felt her submission and the distress that coursed through her veins as her heart pounded against his own. He loosened his grip and drew back slowly. She'd gone deathly pale, and he was instantly filled with overwhelming regret. He dropped his hands and watched as she took a stumbling step away from him.

"I apologize for that," he said hoarsely, condemning himself. He was wrong about her. She wasn't cold and calculating, but warm and generous. It was all there for him to read in her clear, blue eyes. Her chin shook slightly and those magical eyes stared up at him, glimmering with deep hurt. He longed to soothe away the hurt he had inflicted. Utterly defeated, he turned and walked away. "I'll get the combs."

Thorne hesitated halfway down the hall that led to his bedroom. The floor seemed to pitch and heave under him, and he sagged against the wall in an effort to keep from falling. He knew it was the medication—the doctor had warned him about the dizzying effect.

"Thorne..." Cindy was at his side, wrapping an arm around his waist, trying to support him.

"I'll be fine in a minute."

Her hold tightened. "You're sick."

His breathless chuckle revealed his amusement. "Are you always so perceptive?"

"No." She tried to help him. "Let me get you into bed."

"Those are misleading words, Cinderella. I'm sure your fairy godmother would be shocked."

"Quit joking, I'm serious."

He turned his head and his gaze pinned hers. "So am I."

"You're to sick to make love."

"Wanna bet?"

"Thorne!" Her face filled with hot color. As best she could, Cindy directed him into the bedroom. The huge king-size bed dominated the middle of the room and was a mess of tangled sheets and blankets. She left him long enough to pull back the covers and fluff up the pillow.

Because he felt so incredibly weak, Thorne sat on the edge of the mattress and ran a weary hand over his face. Under normal circumstances he would have been humiliated to have a woman fuss over him like this, but nothing about his relationship with Cindy was the least bit conventional.

"Here, let me help you," she insisted, urging him to lie down.

"No." He brushed her hand away.

"You need to rest."

"No," he repeated, louder this time.

"Thorne, please, you're running a fever."

"If I do fall asleep," he said, holding her gaze, "you'll be gone when I wake." His mouth curved into a sad smile. "Will you promise to stay?"

Cindy hesitated.

"It's your fault I'm sick." A little guilt went a long way when used properly.

"I'll stay until you wake."

"Do you promise?"

She nodded.

"Say it, Cindy."

"I'll be here," she cried, angry that he couldn't trust her. "I wouldn't dream of leaving you like this."

He fell against the pillow and released a long sigh. "Good," he said and closed his eyes. For the first time in days he felt right. From the moment Cindy had left him standing in the park, it was as though a part of himself had been missing. Now she was here, so close that all he had to do was reach out and touch her to be whole again.

Standing at his side, Cindy drew the covers over his shoulders and lingered beside the bed. She wouldn't leave the room until she was sure he was asleep. He looked almost childlike, lying on his side, his brow relaxed and smooth. The harsh lines around his mouth were gone, as were the ones that fanned out about his eyes.

A minute later, his lashes flittered open and he looked around, startled.

"I'm here," she whispered and ran her hand across his brow to reassure him.

"Lie down with me," he pleaded and shifted to the far side of the bed, leaving more than ample room for her slim body.

"Thorne, I can't."

"Please." His voice was barely discernible, hardly more than a whisper.

No one word could ever be more seductive. "I shouldn't."

He answered her by gently patting the mattress at his side; his eyes were still closed. "I need you," he said softly.

"Oh, Thorne." She pressed her lips tightly together and slowly slipped off her shoes. He was blackmailing her and she didn't like it one bit. As soon as he was well she'd let him know in no uncertain terms what she thought of his underhanded methods.

Keeping as close to edge of the bed as possible without falling off, Cindy eased herself onto the mattress, lying stiff and tense at his side. Thorne was under the covers while she remained on top, but that did little to diminish her misgivings.

Gradually, so that she was hardly aware of what he was doing, Thorne eased himself closer to her so he could feel the warmth of her body against his. Sleep was so wonderfully inviting. He slipped his arm over her ribs and brought her close, cuddling her. He felt the tension leave her limbs, and for the first time since the Monday following the Christmas Ball, Thorne Prince smiled.

Cindy woke two hours later, stunned that she'd slept. The room was dark and she lay watching the shadows dance on the bedroom walls, thinking. Her mind was crowded with conflicting thoughts. She should leave him while she could, with her heart intact; but she'd promised him she wouldn't. No matter what the consequences, she wouldn't lie to him again. She couldn't live with herself if she did.

As gently as possible, Cindy slipped from his arms and tiptoed across the plush carpet. Clothes littered the floor and she automatically picked them up as she made her way out of the room. She found towels in the bathroom and added those to the load of shirts in the washing machine.

Dirty dishes filled the kitchen sink, and, humming as she worked, Cindy placed those in the dishwasher and turned it on as well. The pots and pans, she scrubbed by hand. She had finished those when she turned around and discovered Thorne, standing in the middle of the kitchen, watching her.

"I'd thought you'd left," he murmured, and rubbed a hand over his eyes. He'd woken to find her gone and momentary terror had gripped his heart. It wasn't until he'd realized she was in the other room that he'd been able to breathe again.

"No, I'm here," she said foolishly.

"I certainly don't need you cleaning for me. I've got a woman who comes in for that."

"What's her name?"

He stared at her blankly, astonished at the inane conversation they were having. "Hell, I don't know, she's not important; I wouldn't know her if I met her on the street."

Cindy turned around to face the sink and bit her bottom lip at the pain. With slow, deliberate movements, she rinsed out the dishrag and wrung it dry. Patiently, she folded it over the faucet and dried her hands on the kitchen towel.

"Cindy." He touched her shoulder, but she ignored him.

"I promised you I wouldn't leave while you were sleeping," she said, her eyes avoiding his. "But I have to go now. Could I please have the combs?"

"No."

"No?"

"They belonged to your mother, didn't they?"

Cindy nodded.

"Then obviously they mean a great deal to you?"

"Yes...of course." She didn't understand where he was directing the conversation.

"Then I'll keep them until I find out why it's necessary for you to disappear from my life."

Cindy was too shocked to think straight. "That's blackmail."

"I know." He looked pleased with himself. He had her now. "I'll feel a whole lot better once I shower and shave." He ran his hand over the side of his face. "Once I'm finished, we'll talk."

Cindy's fingers gripped the counter behind her. "Okay," she murmured. She hated lying to him, hated misleading him, but she had no intention of staying. None. She couldn't. She'd kept her promise—she hadn't left while he slept. Now he was awake and so was she. Wide-awake.

The minute she heard the shower running, Cindy sneaked to the bedroom and retrieved her shoes. She was all the way to the front door before she hesitated. A note. He deserved that much.

She found paper and a pen in the kitchen and wrote as fast as her fingers could move. She told him he was right in assuming the combs meant a great deal to her. So much so that she wanted him to keep them in memory of the night they met. She told him she'd always remember him, her own dashing Prince Charming, and that their time together was the most special of her life. Tears filled her eyes and her lips trembled as she signed her name.

She left the paper on top of the television where he was sure to find it. Soundlessly she made her way to the front door. She paused, blinded by tears. Her fingers curled around the knob and she inhaled a wobbly sniffle. Everything within her told her to walk out the door and not look back. Everything that is, except her heart. Cindy felt as if it were dissolving with every breath she drew. She pressed her forehead against the polished mahogany door and cupped her mouth with her hand in an effort to strengthen her resolve.

"I didn't think I could trust you." Thorne said bitterly from behind her.

Chapter Six

Thorne's harsh words cut savagely into Cindy's heart. With tears streaming down her cheeks, she turned to face him, all the pent-up emotion in her eyes there for him to read. He had to see that it was killing her to walk away from him. She was dying by inches.

One look at the pain etched so plainly in her tormented features and Thorne's anger evaporated like dew in the midmorning sun. He moved across the room. "Oh, Cindy," he groaned and reached for her, wrapping her in his arms. At first she resisted his comfort, standing stiff and unyielding against him, but he held her nonetheless because he couldn't bear to let her go. His hands cupped her face and he directed her mouth to his, kissing her again and again until she relaxed and wound her arms around his neck. Thorne could feel her breath quicken and he knew he'd reached her.

Cindy's heart stopped and then surged with quick, liquid fire. Having Thorne hold and kiss her only made leaving him all the more difficult. Yet she couldn't resist him. She could barely breathe past the wild pounding of her heart. She shouldn't have come to him, shouldn't have asked for the return of her mother's combs. But she had—seeking some common ground, praying to forge a trail that would bridge the gap between their lives. Only there was no path, there was no structure to span the Grand Canyon between his wealth and her indomitable pride. His words about his cleaning woman had proven how unfeasible any relationship between them would be.

"No." She eased herself away from him. "Please, don't try to stop me.... I must go."

"But why?"

She pinched her lips together and refused to answer him.

Thorne ran his hand down her thick blond hair to her shoulder. He drew in a calming breath and released it again, repeating the action several times until he could think clearly.

"You're married, aren't you?"

"No." Her denial came hot and fast.

"Then why do you insist upon playing this childish game of hide-and-seek?"

She dropped her head and closed her eyes, unable to look at him any longer. "Trust me, it's for the best that we never see each other again."

"That's ridiculous. We're perfect together." He was nearly shouting at her. He paused and dropped his voice, wanting to reason with her calmly. "I *need* to be with you. That one night was the most wonderful of my life. It was like I'd suddenly woken up from a deep coma. The whole world came alive for me the minute you arrived. At least give us a chance. That isn't so much to ask, is it?"

A tear slipped from the corner of her eye, scorching her face as it rolled down her cheek.

"Cindy, don't you realize I'm crazy about you?"

"You don't know me," she cried.

"I know enough."

"It was one night, don't you see? One magical night. Another could never be the same. It's better to leave things as they are than disillusion ourselves by trying to live a fantasy."

"Cindy." He stopped her, pressing his lips hungrily over hers, kissing her until she was weak and clinging to him. "The magic is stronger than ever. I feel it and so do you. Don't try to deny it."

She leaned her forehead against his chest, battling the resistance her heart was giving her. But she couldn't deny the truth any more than she could stop her heart from racing at his slightest touch.

"One more night," Thorne said softly, enticingly, "to test our feelings. Then we'll know."

Cindy nodded, unable to refuse him anything when he was holding her as if she were an enchanted princess and he were her promised love. Her heart lodged in her throat and when she did speak, her voice was hardly above a whisper. "One more night," she said. "But only one." Any more and it would be impossible to do what she must.

Thorne felt the tightening in his chest subside and the tension seep out of him. He wanted to argue with her; he wanted a lot more than one night—but she looked so confused and uncertain that he didn't dare press her. For now he would be satisfied with the time she could freely give him. Afterward he'd fret, but not now, when she was in his arms.

He grinned. "Where would you like to go? A play? Bobby Short is playing at the Carlyle, and if you haven't heard him, you should. He's fabulous."

"Thorne." Her hand on his arm stopped him. "You're ill."

"I feel a thousand times better." And he did!

"We'll stay right here," she countered, and breaking out of his arms, she strolled into the kitchen. She held Thorne by the hand and dragged him with her. With all the authority of a boot-camp sergeant, she sat him down and proceeded to inspect his freezer and cupboards.

Thorne watched, amazed, as she organized their meal. Before he knew what was happening, Cindy had him at the counter, ripping apart lettuce leaves for a salad. It was as though she'd worked in his kitchen all her life. She located frozen chicken breasts, thawed them in the microwave and placed them in the oven with potatoes wrapped in aluminium foil. Then she searched his cupboards for the ingredients for a mushroom sauce.

Thorne paused long enough in his task to choose a compact disc. Soon music surrounded them as they sat in the living room. Thorne's arm was around her shoulders and she bent her arm to connect her fingers with his. Her head was on his shoulder. Thorne stretched his legs out in front of him and crossed them at the ankles. The moment was serene, peaceful. Thorne had never known a time like this with a woman. Others wanted parties and good times, attention and approval. He hadn't married, hadn't even thought of it until recently. He'd given up looking for that special someone who would fill his days with happiness and love. With Sheila, he'd been willing to accept "close enough," confident he'd never experience what Cindy made so simple. Yet here she was in his arms, and he was willing to do everything humanly possible to keep her there.

Cindy let her head rest on Thorne's shoulder. These few moments together were as close to paradise as she ever hoped to come in this lifetime. She found it astonishing that they didn't need to speak. The communication between them was so strong it didn't require words, and when they did talk, they discovered their tastes were surprisingly similar. Cindy loved to ski, so did Thorne. They'd both read everything Mary Stewart had ever written and devotedly watched reruns of *I Love Lucy*. Both Cindy and Thorne were so familiar with the old black-and-white television comedy that they bounced dialogue off each other, taking on the roles of Lucy and Ricky Ricardo. Excited and happy, they laughed and hugged each other.

Cindy couldn't believe this was happening and held him to her, breathless with an inexplicable joy. Somehow she'd known they'd discover the night of the Christmas Ball hadn't been a fluke.

Thorne couldn't believe how right they were together. Perfect. They loved the same things, shared the same interests. He'd never hoped to find a woman who could make him laugh the way Cindy did.

When dinner was ready, Thorne lit candles, placed them in the center of the dining-room table and dimmed the overhead lighting. The mood was wildly romantic.

"The fairy dust is so thick in here I can barely see," Cindy teased as she delivered their plates to the table.

"That's not fairy dust."

"No?"

"No," he said, and his eyes smiled into hers. "This is undiluted romance." He pulled out her chair for her and playfully nuzzled her neck once she was seated.

"I should have recognized what this is; you'll have to pardon me, but I've been so busy with school that I haven't dated much in the past—" She stopped abruptly, once she realized what she'd said.

Thorne sat down across from her and unfolded the linen napkin. "You attend school?" He'd been so careful not to question her, fearing she'd freeze up on him if he were to bombard her with his need to find answers. From the moment she'd arrived, he'd longed to discover how she'd known he was ill. Cindy was like a complex puzzle. Every tidbit of information he'd learned about her was a tiny interlocking piece that would help him reveal the complete picture of who and what she was—and why she found it so necessary to hide from him.

"I attend classes," she admitted, feeling awkward. Without being obvious, she tried to study his reaction to the information, but his face was an unreadable mask. He'd been in business too long to show his feelings.

"What are you studying?"

"Books." Her stomach tightened and fluttered and she gave him a reproving glance before returning her attention to her meal.

Thorne's grip on his fork tightened as he watched Cindy visibly withdraw from him. Her eyes avoided his, she sat stiff and uneasy in the chair; her mouth was pinched as though she were attempting to disguise her pain. Intuitively he knew that if he continued to press her for answers, he'd lose her completely. "I won't ask you anything more," he promised.

She smiled then and his heart squeezed with an unknown emotion. The ache caught him by surprise. He didn't care who Cindy was. She could be an escaped convict and it wouldn't matter. He wanted to tell her that no matter what it was that troubled her, he could fix it. He'd stand between her and the world if that was what it took. Forging rivers, climbing mountains, anything—he'd do it for her gladly.

After they'd finished eating, Cindy cleared the table. Thorne moved across the living room to change the music.

With tears blinding her, Cindy reached for her coat and purse.

"Do you like easy listening?" Thorne asked without turning. "How about country and western?"

"Anything is fine." Cindy prayed he didn't hear the catch in her voice. She shot him one last look, thanking him with her eyes for the second most magnificent night of her life. Then silently, she slipped out the front door and out of her dreams into the cold harsh world of reality.

"I've got the music to several Broadway shows if you'd prefer that."

His statement was met with silence.

"Cindy?"

He walked into the kitchen. She was gone.

"Cindy?" His voice was hardly audible. He didn't need to look any further. He knew. She'd slipped away when he'd least expected it. Vanished into thin air. He found the note propped on top of the television. She asked him to forgive her. He stared at the words coldly, hating them almost as much as he hated her at that moment.

Thorne folded the paper in half and viciously ripped it, folded it a second time, tore it and folded it again and again until the pieces were impossibly thick. His face went rigid and a muscle worked convulsively in his jaw as he threw her note in the garbage. He stood, furious with her, furious with himself for being caught in this trap a second time.

"Damn you, Cindy," he muttered, and slapped his fist against the counter. "Damn you." He snapped his eyes closed in an effort to control his overpowering anger. Fine, he told himself. If this was the way she wanted it, he'd stay out of her life. Thorndike Prince didn't crawl for any woman—they came to him. His face hardened grimly and his eyes narrowed. He didn't need her. He'd get along perfectly without her and the silly games she wanted to play. He was more determined than ever to put her out of his mind forever. This time he meant it.

Christmas Day was a nightmare for Cindy. She smiled and responded appropriately to what was going on around her, but she was miserable. She couldn't stop thinking about Thorne. She wondered who he was with and what he thought of her . . . or *if* he did. After the sneaky way she'd left him, Cindy believed he probably hated her. She certainly couldn't blame him.

"Cindy, Cindy..." Her four-year-old cousin crawled into her lap. "Will you read to me?"

Carla had always been special to Cindy. The little girl had been born to Cindy's Aunt Sofia when she was in her early forties. Sofia's three other children were all in their teens and Sofia had been shocked and unhappy about this unexpected pregnancy so late in life. Then Carla had arrived and the child was the delight of the Territo family.

"Mama's busy and all Tony wants to do is talk to Maria."

"Of course, I'll read to you." She gave Carla a squeeze around the middle.

"You're my favorite cousin," Carla whispered close to Cindy's ear.

"I'm glad, because you're my favorite cousin, too," Cindy whispered back. "Now, do you have a book or do you want me to choose one?"

"Santa brought me one."

"Well, good for Santa." Her eye caught her Aunt Sofia's and they exchanged knowing glances. Carla might be only four, but the little girl was well aware that Santa looked amazingly like Uncle Carl, after whom Carla had been named.

"I'll get it," Carla crawled off Cindy's lap, raced across the room and returned a minute later with a wide grin. "Here," she said and handed the large picture book to Cindy. "Read me this one. Read me 'Cinderella.'"

Cindy's breath jammed in her lungs and the brimming tears stung her eyes. "'Cinderella'?" she repeated as the numbing sensation worked its way over her body. She prayed it would anesthetize her from the trauma that gripped her heart.

"Cindy?" Carla's chubby little hands shook Cindy's knee. "Aren't you going to read to me?"

"Of course, sweetheart." Somehow she managed to pick up the book and flip open the front cover. Carla positioned herself comfortably in her cousin's lap, leaned back and promptly inserted her thumb in her mouth.

It demanded all Cindy's energy to open her lips and start reading. Her throat felt incredibly dry. "'Once upon a time...'"

"...in a land far away," Mary Susan Clark told her five-year-old son, who sat on the brocade cushion at her feet.

Thorne's gaze rested on his sister, who was reciting the fairy tale to her son, and his heart rate slowed with anger and resentment. "Do you think it's such a good idea to be filling a young boy's head with that kind of garbage?" Thorne demanded gruffly.

Mary Susan's gray eyes widened with surprise. "But it's only a fairy tale."

"Thorne." His mother's puzzled gaze studied his. "It's not like you to snap."

"I apologize," he said with a weak smile. "I guess I have been a bit short-tempered lately."

"You've been ill." Sheila, with her dark brown eyes and pixie face, automatically defended him. She placed her hand in his and gave his fingers a gentle squeeze.

Sheila was a nice girl, Thorne mused: pleasant and loyal. Someday she'd make a man an excellent wife.

Maybe even him. Thorne was through playing Cindy's games. Through believing in fairy tales. He couldn't live like this. Cindy didn't want to have anything to do with him, and he had no choice but to accept her wishes. Sheila loved him—at least she claimed she did. Thorne didn't know what love felt like anymore. At one time he'd thought he was in love with Sheila. Maybe not completely, but he'd expected that emotion to come in time. Then he'd met Cindy, and he was head over heels in love for the first time in his thirty-three years. Overnight, he'd been hooked. Crazy in love. And with a woman who'd turned her back on him and walked away without a second thought. It didn't make sense. Nothing did anymore. Nothing at all. Not business. Not life. Not women.

Thorne and Sheila had been seeing each other for nearly six months and Thorne knew she'd hardly been able to conceal her disappointment when an engagement ring hadn't been secretly tucked under the Christmas tree. But she hadn't questioned him. He wished she wasn't so damned understanding; he'd have liked her better if she'd gotten angry and demanded an explanation.

Thorne noticed his mother studying him and he made an effort to disguise his discontent. Smiling required a monumental effort. He managed it, but he sincerely doubted that he'd fooled his mother.

"Thorne, could you help me in the kitchen?"

The whole family turned their attention to him. The old ploy for talking privately wasn't the least bit original.

"Of course, Mother," he said with the faintest sardonic inflection. He disentangled his fingers from

Sheila's and stood, obediently following Gwendolyn Prince out of the room.

"What in heaven's name is the matter with you?" she demanded, the minute they were out of earshot. "It isn't that... that girl you mentioned, is it?"

"What girl?" Feigning ignorance seemed the best possible response.

"You haven't been yourself..."

"Since the night of that Christmas Ball," Cindy's Aunt Theresa said softly.

The silence that followed grated on Cindy's frayed nerves. "I know," she whispered. "You see, there's something I didn't know... fairy tales don't always come true."

"But, Cindy, you're eating your heart out over him."

"We said goodbye," she answered, her eyes pleading with her aunt to drop this disturbing subject. Accepting that she would live her life without Thorne was difficult enough; rehashing it with her aunt was like tearing open a half-healed wound.

"But you haven't stopped thinking about him."

"No, but I will in time."

"Will you, Cindy?" Theresa's deep brown eyes revealed her doubt.

Her gaze pleaded with the older woman's. "Yes," she said and the words were a vow to herself. She had no choice now. When she'd left Thorne's apartment it had been forever. Although the pain had been nearly unbearable, it was better to sever the ties quickly and sharply than to bleed to death slowly.

* * *

"Mother and I are planning a shopping expedition to Paris in March," Sheila spoke enthusiastically, sitting across the green table from Thorne.

They were at one of Thorne's favorite lunch spots. Sheila had made it a habit to drop by unexpectedly at the office at least once a week so they could have lunch. In the past, Thorne had looked forward to their get-togethers. Not today. He wasn't in the mood. But before he'd been able to say anything to Mrs. Hillard, she'd sent Sheila into his office, and now he was stuck.

"Paris sounds interesting."

"So does the chicken," Sheila commented, glancing over the menu. "I hear the mushroom sauce here is fabulous."

Thorne's stomach clenched violently. "Baked chicken breast served with mushroom sauce," he repeated, remembering all too well his last evening with Cindy and the meal she'd prepared for him.

"I hope you'll try it with me," Sheila urged, gazing adoringly at him.

Thorne's mouth thinned. "I hate mushrooms."

Sheila's gaze dropped again to the menu and she pressed her lips tightly together. "I didn't know that," she said after a long minute.

"You do now," Thorne snapped, detesting himself for treating her this way. Sheila deserved better.

The waiter stepped to the table, his hands clenched behind his back, and he smiled down on them cordially. "Are you ready to order?"

"I believe so," Thorne said, closing his menu and handing it to the other man. "The lady will have the chicken special and I'll have a mushroom omelet."

Sheila gave him an odd look, but said nothing.

During lunch Thorne made a sincere effort to be pleasant. He honestly tried to appear interested when Sheila told him about the latest trends in fashion she hoped to wear once she returned from France. He even managed to stifle a yawn when she hinted at the possibility of buying several yards of exclusive French lace. It wasn't until they'd left the restaurant and were walking toward his office that Thorne caught the implication. French lace—wedding gown.

"And I was thinking . . ."

Sheila's voice faded and Thorne quickened his pace. There. The blonde, half a block ahead of him. Cindy. Dear God, it was Cindy.

"Thorne," Sheila announced breathlessly. "You're walking so fast, I can't keep up with you."

Without thought, he brushed her arm from his. "Excuse me a minute." He didn't remove his gaze from Cindy, fearing he'd lose her in the heavy holiday crowds.

"Thorne?"

He ignored Sheila and took off running, weaving in and around the moving bodies that filled the sidewalk on the Avenue of the Americas.

"Cindy!" He yelled her name, but either she didn't hear or else she was trying to escape him. Again. He wouldn't let her. He'd found her now. Relief flowed through him and he savored the sweet taste of it. He had dreamed something like this would happen. Somehow, some way he'd miraculously stumble upon her. Every time he stepped out of his apartment, he found himself studying faces, looking. Seeking. Searching for her in a silent quest that dominated his every waking thought. And now she was only a few feet from him, her brisk pace no match for his easy sprint. Her blond hair swished back and forth, hitting the top of her shoulders. Her dark navy wool coat was wrapped securely around her.

Sharply Thorne raced around two couples, cutting abruptly in front of them. He didn't know what he'd do first: kiss her or shake her until she begged him to stop. Kiss her, he decided.

"Cindy." He caught up with her finally and placed his hand on her shoulder.

"I beg your pardon." The woman, over fifty, shouted and slapped his hand away. She didn't even resemble Cindy. She was older, plain, and embarrassed by his attention.

Thorne blinked back the disbelief. "I thought you were someone else."

"Obviously. Mind your manners, young man, or I'll report you to the police."

"I apologize." He couldn't move. His feet felt rooted to the sidewalk and his arms hung lifelessly at his sides. Cindy was driving him mad; he was slowly but surely losing his mind a minute at a time.

"Decent women aren't safe in this city anymore," the woman grumbled and quickly stepped away.

"Thorne! Thorne!" Sheila joined him, her hands gripping his arm. "Who was she?"

"No one." He couldn't stop looking at the blonde as she made her way down the street. He would have sworn it was Cindy. He would have wagered a year's salary that the woman who couldn't escape him fast enough had been Cindy. His Cindy. His love.

"Thorne," Sheila droned, patting his hand. "You've been working too hard. I'm worried about you."

"I'm fine," he snapped. "Just fine."

The pinched look returned to Sheila's face, but she didn't argue. "March gives you plenty of time to arrange a vacation. We'll have a marvelous time in Paris. I'll take you shopping with me and let you pick out my trousseau."

"I'm not going to Paris," he barked.

Sheila continued to pat his hand. "I do wish you'd consider it, Thorne. You haven't been yourself lately. Not at all."

He couldn't agree more.

Two hours later Thorne sat at his desk reading over the financial statements the accounting department had sent up for him to approve.

"Mr. Williams is here," his secretary informed him.

Instantly Thorne closed the folder. "Send him in."

"Right away," Mrs. Hillard returned crisply.

Thorne stood to greet the balding man with a wide space between his two front teeth. He wore a suit that looked as if it hadn't been dry-cleaned since it came off the rack at Sears ten years before. His potbelly gave credence to the claim that Mike Williams was the best private detective in the business: from the looks of it, he ate well enough.

"Mr. Williams," Thorne said, extending his hand to the other man.

They exchanged brisk handshakes. The man's grip was solid. Thorne approved.

"What can I do for you?"

Thorne motioned toward the chair and Mike sat.

"I want you to find someone for me," Thorne said, without preamble.

Mike nodded. "It's what I do best. What's the name?"

Thorne reclaimed his chair and his hands gripped the armrest as he leaned back, giving an impression of indifference. This wasn't going to be easy, but he hadn't expected it would be. "Cindy."

"Anything else?" The detective reached for his pencil and pad.

"I'm not completely sure that's her name. It could have been contrived." Thorne was braced to accept anything where Cindy was concerned. Everything and anything.

"Where did you meet her?"

"At a party. The one put on by this company—she doesn't work here, I've already checked."

Williams nodded.

"She did leave these behind." Thorne leaned forward to hand the detective one pearl comb. "But I've had it appraised and the comb isn't uncommon. She claimed they belonged to her mother. There are no markings that would distinguish them from ten thousand identical combs."

Again Williams nodded, but he carefully examined the comb. "Can I take this?" he asked and stuck it in his pocket.

Thorne agreed with a swift nod of his head. "I'll want it back."

"Of course."

They spoke for an additional fifteen minutes and Thorne recalled with as much clarity as possible every meeting with Cindy.

Williams stopped him only once. "A limo, you said."

"Yes." Thorne scooted forward in his chair. He'd forgotten that. Cindy had gotten into a limousine that first night when she'd escaped from him. She'd handed him his coat, run across the street and immediately been met by a long black limousine.

"You wouldn't happen to remember the license plate, would you?"

"No." Disgustedly, Thorne shook his head. "I'm afraid I can't."

"Don't worry about it. I have enough." Williams briefly scanned the details he'd listed and flipped the pad closed. Slowly, he came to his feet.

"Can you find her?" Thorne stood as well.

"I'll give it my best shot."

"Good." Thorne hoped the man couldn't see how desperate he'd become.

A cold northern wind bit into Cindy's arms as she waited on the sidewalk outside the Oakes-Jenning building well past midnight. She was exhausted—both physically and mentally. She hadn't been sleeping well and the paper she should be writing during the holiday break just wouldn't come, although she'd done all the required research. It was Thorne. No matter what she did, she couldn't stop thinking about him.

Her Uncle Sal pulled to a stop at the curb. Cindy stepped away from the building and scooted inside to the front seat beside him.

"Hi," she greeted, forcing a smile. Her family was worried about her and Cindy did her best to ease their fears; she'd be fine, given time.

"A private detective was poking around the house today," her uncle announced, starting into the traffic.

Cindy felt her heart go cold. "What did he want?"

"He was asking about you."

Chapter Seven

"Asking about me... What did you tell him?"

"Not a damn thing."

"But..."

"He wanted to look at my appointment schedule for December 15, but I wouldn't let him."

The chilly sensation that had settled over Cindy dropped below freezing. Her uncle's refusal would only create suspicions. The detective would be back, and there would be more questions Sal would refuse to answer. The detective wouldn't accept that, and he'd return again and again until he had the information he wanted. This stranger would make trouble for her family. Cindy could see it as clearly as if it were printed across the sky in huge, bold strokes. In a hundred years, she would never have guessed that Thorne would go to such lengths to locate her. She had to find a way to stop him ... a way to make him understand and leave things as they were.

Cindy went to bed thinking about the situation and arose more tired and troubled than she was before she'd slept. Repeatedly she examined her own role in this rash venture. Playing the part of Cinderella for one night had seemed so innocent, so adventurous, so exciting. She'd slipped into the fantasy with uncanny ease, but the night had ended with the stroke of midnight and she could never go back to being a fairy-tale figure again. She'd let go of the illusion and yes, it had been painful, but she'd been given no choice. The consequences of that one foolhardy night would follow her all the days of her life.

She had never dreamed it would be possible to feel as strongly about a man in so short a time as she did about Thorne. But the emotion wasn't based on any of the usual prerequisites for love. It couldn't be. They had only seen each other twice.

Thorne might believe he felt as strongly about her, Cindy realized as her thoughts rambled on, but that wasn't real either. She was a challenge: the mystery woman who had briefly touched his life. Once he learned the truth and realized she'd made a fool of him, it would be over. Given no other option, Cindy realized she'd have to tell Thorne who she really was.

"He could fire me," she said aloud several soul-searching hours later. Her hands clenched her purse protectively under her arm as she stood outside the Oakes-Jenning Financial Services building. Employees streamed out in a steady flow. Cindy stood against the side of the building, back just far enough to examine their faces as they made their way out the heavy glass doors. They all looked so serious, somber and grave. Cindy didn't know much about the business world, but it certainly seemed to employ dour souls. Thorne included.

For most of the afternoon, Cindy had weighed the possible consequences of telling Thorne the truth. Losing her job was only one of several unpleasant options that had crossed her mind. And ultimately he could hate her, which would be so much worse than anything else he could do to her. She wanted to scream at him for being so obstinate, so willful, so determined to force himself into her life. He had to know that she didn't want to be found, and yet he'd ignored her wishes and driven her to this. He'd forced her into doing the one thing she dreaded most: telling him the truth.

Her tenacity hardened as she watched Thorne step outside the building, his face as staid as the others. He carried a briefcase in his hand and walked briskly past her. Unseeing. Uncaring. As oblivious to her then as he was every morning when he walked into his clean office.

"Thorne." She didn't shout, her voice was little more than a whisper.

Abruptly he stopped, almost in midstride, and turned around. "Cindy?" His gaze scanned the sea of faces that swam before him. "Cindy?" he repeated, louder this time, uncertain if this was real. He'd been half out of his mind for days on end. Nothing shocked him anymore. He'd recognized her voice instantly, but that too could be part of his deep yearning to find her. She was here and she'd called to him, and he'd uproot this sidewalk before he'd let her escape him again.

"Here." She took a step closer, her hands clenched into hard fists at her side. "Call off the detective. I'll tell you—" She wasn't allowed to finish.

Thorne dropped the briefcase onto the cement, gripped her shoulders and roughly hauled her into his arms. His mouth came down on hers with such force that he drove the breath from her lungs. His hand dug into her hair as he tangled the thick blond tresses with his fingers, as though binding her to him for all time. His mouth slanted over hers and left her in little doubt regarding the strength of his emotions.

Cindy's first reaction was stunned surprise. Her hands hung uselessly at her sides. She'd expected him to be furious, to shout at her and demand an explanation. But not this. Never this.

Once the initial shock of his kiss faded, she surrendered to the sheer pleasure of simply being in his arms. She held on to him, wrapping her arms around him, relishing the rush of sensations that came springing up from within her like the profusion of flowers that follows a spring rain. She couldn't have pushed him away had her life depended on it. The rock-hard resolution to ruthlessly end their nonrelationship had melted the minute he'd reached for her.

"This had better not be a dream," Thorne said, moving his lips against her temple. "You taste so unbelievably real."

Cindy flattened her palms against his chest in an effort to break away, but he held her steadfast. "Thorne, please, people are looking."

"Let them." He kissed her again, with such hunger and greed that she was left breathless and utterly boggled. Disoriented, she made a weak effort to break loose of his grip, but Thorne had backed her against the side of the building and there was nowhere to move. And even if there had been, she was convinced he wouldn't have released her.

"Thorne," she pleaded. Every second he continued to hold her ate up her determination to explain everything. He felt so warm and vital...so wonderful. "Please...don't," she begged as he covered her face with kisses. Even as she was speaking, pleading with him to stop, she was turning her head one way and then another to grant him freedom to do as he wished.

"I'm starving for you," he said before feasting on her mouth one more time.

"Please." The sob worked its way up her windpipe. She was so weak-willed with Thorne. She could start out with the firmest of resolves but ten seconds after being with him, she had all the fortitude of a roasted marshmallow.

"Cindy, dear God—" his arms tightened "—I've been crazy these past few days without you."

The time hadn't been any less traumatic for Cindy. "You hired a detective?"

"He found you?"

"No...I heard you were looking." Lovingly her hands framed his face. "Thorne, please call him off." She viewed the private detective as a dog nipping at her heels. An irritant who had the power to turn her life upside down and intimidate those she loved most. "I'll tell you everything you want to know...only, please, please, don't hate me."

"Hate you?" His look was incredulous. "It isn't in me to feel any different than I did the night we met."

For the first time he seemed to notice the stares they were generating. "Let's get out of here." He reached for her hand and marched her purposefully away.

"Thorne," she cried, tossing a surprised glance over her shoulder. "Your briefcase."

He looked so utterly astonished that he could have forgotten it, Cindy laughed outright.

Without hesitating, he turned and went back to retrieve it, dragging her with him. "Do you see what you do to me?" His words were clipped, almost angry.

"Do you know what you do to me?" she returned with equal consternation.

"I must have one hell of an effect on you, all right. You can't seem to get away from me fast enough. You sneak away like a thief in the night and turn up when I least expect it. I don't sleep well, my appetite is gone and I'm convinced you're playing me for a fool."

"Oh, Thorne, you don't honestly believe that, do you?" She came to an abrupt stop. People walked a large circle around them, but Cindy wasn't concerned. She couldn't bear it if Thorne believed anything less than what she truly felt for him. "I think I'd rather die than let you assume for one minute that I didn't care for you."

"You have one hell of a way of showing it."

"But, Thorne, if you'd stop and give me time to—"

Undaunted by the traffic, Thorne paraded them halfway into the street, his arm raised. "Taxi!"

"Where are we going?"

A yellow cab pulled up in front of them. Thorne ignored her question as his hand bit unmercifully into her elbow. He opened the car door for her and climbed in beside her a second later.

Before Cindy had an opportunity to speak, Thorne draped his elbow over the front seat and spoke to the driver. When he'd finished he leaned back and stared at her as though he still weren't completely convinced she wasn't a ghostly illusion.

Cindy didn't know what she'd expected. She hadn't thought about where she'd talk to Thorne, only that she would. Over and over she'd rehearsed what she wanted to say. But she hadn't counted on him hauling her halfway across Manhattan to some unknown destination. From the looks he was giving her now, he didn't appear any too pleased with finding her.

Thorne relaxed against the cushion and expelled a long sigh. "Do you realize we've been to bed together and I don't even know your name?"

Cindy felt more than saw the driver's interest perk up. Color exploded into her cheeks as she glared hotly at Thorne. "Would you kindly stop?" she hissed. He was doing this on purpose, to punish her.

"I don't think I can." He regarded her levelly. "Look at me! I'm shaking like a leaf. You've got me so twisted up inside, I don't know what's real and what's not anymore. My parents think I need to see a shrink and I'm beginning to agree with them!"

Cindy covered his hand with her own. "I'm certainly not anything like the Cinderella you met that night." Her voice was a raw whisper, filled with pain. "I thought I could pretend to be something I'm not for one glamorous night, but it's all backfired. I've hated deceiving you—you deserve better than me."

"Is your name really Cindy?"

She nodded. "That's what started it all. Now I wish I'd been named something like Hermione or Frieda—anything but Cindy. If I had, then maybe, just maybe I wouldn't have believed in that night and decided to do something so stupid."

"No matter who you are and what you've done," Thorne told her solemnly, "I'll never regret the Christmas Ball."

"That's the problem—I can't either. I'll treasure it always. But Thorne, don't you see? I'm not Cinderella; I'm only me."

"In case you haven't noticed, I'm not exactly Prince Charming."

"But you are," Cindy argued.

"No. And that's been our problem all along; we each seemed to think the other wanted to continue the fantasy." He placed his arm around her and drew her close to his side. "That one evening was marvelous, but it was one night in a million. If we're to develop a relationship, it has to be between the people we are now."

Cindy leaned against him, sighed inwardly and closed her eyes as he rubbed his chin across the top of her head.

"I want to continue being with Cindy," he said tenderly, "not the imaginary Cinderella."

"But Cindy will disappoint you."

"If you're looking for Prince Charming in me, then I fear you're in for a sad awakening as well."

"You don't even know who I am."

"It doesn't matter." Her sweet face commanded all his attention. He read her lovely blue eyes as easily as a child's reader. Something deep inside her was insecure and frightened. She'd bolted and run away from him twice, her doubts overtaking her. No more. Whatever Williams had dug up about her had worked. She was here because he'd gotten close to her, close enough to bring her back to him.

She really was a lovely creature. Gentle and good. Beautiful in ways that stirred his heart. Her eyes were wide and inquiring, her lips moist from his recent kisses. He'd found his Cindy and could on go with his life again. The restless feeling that had eaten at him these past few days was dissipating every moment he spent with her. He was a man who liked his privacy, and overnight he'd discovered he was lonely and couldn't adjust to the solitude. Not when he'd found the one woman he meant to share his world with. All he had to do was convince her of that. Only this time, he'd be more cautious. He wouldn't make demands of her. She could tell him whatever was troubling her when she was ready. Every time he started questioning her, it ended in disaster.

Cindy sat upright, holding her back stiff as she turned her head and glanced out the side window. He was right. They couldn't go back to the night of the Christmas Ball. But she wasn't completely convinced they could form a compatible relationship as Thorne and Cindy.

"You say it doesn't matter now," she said thoughtfully, "but when I tell you that I'm the girl who—"

"Stop." His hand reached for hers, squeezing her fingers tightly. "Are you married, engaged or currently involved with another man?"

She twisted around and glared at him for even suggesting such a thing. "No, of course not."

"Involved in any illegal activity?"

She scooted several inches away from him and sat starchly erect, shocked that his questions could pain her heart so. Her brow knitted with consternation. "Is that what you think?"

"Just answer the question."

"No." The lone word had difficulty making it up her throat. She looped a thick strand of honey-colored hair around her ear in nervous agitation. "I don't cheat, rarely lie and am disgustingly law-abiding—I don't even jaywalk, and in New York that's something!"

Thorne's warm smile chased the chill from her bones. "Then who and what you are is of no importance. You're the one who seems to be filled with objections. What I feel for you appears to be of little consequence."

"That's not true, I'm only trying to save you from embarrassment."

"Embarrassment?"

"My family name isn't linked with three generations of banking."

"I wouldn't care if it was linked with garbage collecting."

"You think that now," she snapped. He didn't realize how close he was to the truth!

"I mean that. I'm falling in love with a girl named Cindy, not a fairy-tale figure who magically appeared in my life. She's wonderfully bright and funny and loving."

Falling in love with her! Cindy's heart felt like it was going to burst with happiness just hearing him suggest such a marvelous thing. Then she realized the impossibility of a lasting relationship between them. Dejectedly she lowered her gaze. "Please don't say that."

"What? That I'm falling in love with you?"

"Yes."

"It's true. All I know is that you've been driving me insane the past few weeks. How can I know what I really feel if you keep jumping in and out of my life?"

"But you hardly know me," she cried. Yet it hadn't deterred her from falling head over heels for him.

The taxi came to a stop in the heavy traffic. The driver placed his hand along the back of the seat and twisted around. "Central Park is on your left."

"Central Park?" Cindy echoed, pleased at his choice of locations to do their talking.

"I thought we should return here and start over again." He diverted his attention for the moment while handing the driver several crisp dollar bills. A moment later, he joined Cindy on the sidewalk. He tucked her hand in the crook of his arm and smiled seductively down on her.

Her returning smile was feeble at best.

"Hello, there," he said softly. "I'm Thorne, which is short for Thorndike, which was my father's name and his father's before him."

"I'm a first-generation Cindy."

"Well, Cindy, now that we've been properly introduced, will you have dinner with me tonight?"

"I . . . can't." She hated to refuse him, but she couldn't spend time with him when she was paid to clean his office. As it was, she was due there within the half hour.

His face tightened briefly. "Can't or won't?"

"Can't." Regret weighted the lone word.

"Tomorrow, then."

"But it's New Year's Eve." Surely he had other places to go, and far more important people to spend the evening with than she. Arguments filled her head and were dispelled with one enticing look from Thorne.

"New Year's Eve or not, I'll pick you up and we'll paint the town." He felt Cindy tense and understood why. Quickly he amended his offer. "All right, I'll meet you somewhere. Anyplace you say."

"In front of Oakes-Jenning." Although it was a holiday, she would be working; she couldn't afford to turn down time and a half. "I . . . won't be available until after eleven-thirty."

"Fine, I'll be there."

"You're late," Vanessa informed Cindy unnecessarily, when she ran breathlessly into the basement supply room.

"I know."

"Where were you?"

"Central Park." Her hands made busy work filling her cart with the needed supplies. She'd left after promising Thorne she would meet him the following night. His gaze had pleaded with her to give him something to hold on to—a phone number, a name, anything. But Cindy had given him something of far more value: her word. Letting her go had been a measure of his trust. She could see that he wasn't pleased, but he hadn't drilled her with questions or made any other demands on her.

What he'd said made sense. Neither one of them could continue playing the role of someone they weren't. Cinderella was now Cindy and Prince Charming had gone back to being Thorne. They'd been a bit awkward with each other at first, but gradually that uneasiness had evaporated and they'd quickly become friends.

Cindy was beginning to believe that although there were plenty of obstacles blocking their paths, together they could possibly overcome them. There hadn't been much time to say the things she must because Cindy had been forced to rush to work. She hadn't explained that to Thorne, and watched as a jealous anger marred his face.

"What are you thinking?" Vanessa asked her, studying her friend.

"Nothing."

"Nothing," her friend complained. "Oh, good grief, are we back to that?"

Cindy relented. "I'm seeing Thorne tomorrow night."

"You are?" Even Vanessa sounded shocked. "But it's New Year's Eve...oh, heavens, girl, did you forget we have to work?"

"No...I told him I wouldn't be ready until after eleven-thirty."

"And he didn't ask for any explanation?"

"Not really." The questions had been there, his eyes had been filled with them, but he hadn't voiced a single one. Cindy felt her friend regarding her thoughtfully and made busywork around the cart, taking the items she needed before heading for the upper floor.

Oh, Lord, she only hoped she was doing the right thing. Thorne kept insisting that who she was didn't matter to him. She was going to test that and in the process wager her heart and her happiness.

"Thorne, it's your mother."

Thorne frowned into the telephone receiver. He could tell by the slight edge to her voice that she was going to bring up an unpleasant subject: Sheila. The other woman was quickly becoming a thorn in his side.

"Yes, Mother," he returned obediently.

"Your father and I are having a New Year's Eve party tomorrow night and we'd like you to attend."

Parties had never been his forte, which was one of the reasons his mother had been so keen on Sheila, who loved to socialize. Sheila would be good for his career, his father had once told him. At the time, Thorne had considered that an important factor in choosing a wife. Not anymore.

"I apologize, Mother, but I'll have to decline, I've already made plans."

"But, Sheila said—"

"I won't be with Sheila," he responded shortly.

"Oh, dear, is it that Cheryl woman again? I'd thought that was over."

"Cindy," he corrected, swallowing a laugh. He knew his mother too well. She remembered Cindy's name as well as she did her own.

"I see." His mother returned, her voice sharpening with disapproval. "Then you haven't said anything to Sheila."

"As I recall, you advised me against it," he reminded her.

"But, Thorne, the dear girl is beside herself with worry. And what's this about you chasing a strange woman down some sidewalk? Really, Thorne, what has gotten into you?"

"I'm in love."

The shocked silence that followed his announcement nearly made him laugh right into the phone. His parents had been waiting years for him to announce that he'd chosen a wife, and now that he was in love, one would think he'd committed a terrible crime. However, Thorne was convinced that once his parents met Cindy, they'd understand, and love her, too.

"Are you claiming to love a woman you hardly know?"

"That's right, Mother."

"What about her family?"

"What about them?"

"Thorne!"

His mother sounded aghast, which only increased Thorne's amusement. "You'd feel better if you could meet her?"

"I'm not sure...I suppose it would help."

"Dinner, then, the first part of next week. I'll clear it with Cindy and get back to you."

"Fine." But she didn't sound enthusiastic. "In the meantime, would you talk to Sheila? She hasn't heard from you all week."

"What do you suggest I say to her?"

"Tell her...tell her you need a few days to think things through. That should appease her for now.

Once I've had a chance to... meet your Cheryl, I'll have a better feel for the situation.''

"Yes, Mother," he said obediently and replaced the receiver. Family had always been important to Thorne, but he wouldn't allow his mother or any other family member to rule his life.

Leaning back, Thorne folded his arms behind his head. He felt good, wonderful. He'd never looked forward more to a night in his life. New Year's Eve with Cindy. And with it the promise of spending every year with her for the rest of his life.

The following day, Thorne only worked until noon. He did some errands, ate a light dinner around six, showered and dressed casually. The television killed time, but he discovered he couldn't keep his eyes off the wall clock. He'd leave around eleven, he'd figured. That would give him plenty of time to get to Oakes-Jenning, and from there he'd take Cindy to Times Square. It was something he'd always wanted to do, but had never had the chance. They could lose themselves in the crowd and he'd have every excuse to keep her close.

The doorbell chimed around eight, and Thorne hurried for the front door, convinced it was Cindy. Somehow, some way, she'd come to him early. His excitement died an untimely death when he found Sheila standing in the outside hallway.

"Sheila."

"Hello, Thorne." She glanced up at him through seductively thick lashes. "May I come in?"

He stepped aside. "Sure."

"You're looking delightfully casual." She entered the apartment, removed her coat, sat on the sofa and crossed her legs.

"This is a surprise." He stood awkwardly in the center of the room and buried his hands in his pockets.

"I haven't heard from you since our luncheon date and thought I'd stop in unannounced. I hope you don't mind?"

Thorne would have preferred to choose another day, but since she'd come, there was probably no better time than the present to tell her about Cindy. "I'm glad you did." At the light of happiness that flashed in her eyes, Thorne regretted his poor choice of words.

She folded her hands in her lap and regarded him with such adoration that Thorne felt his stomach knot.

"Sometimes I do such a terrible job of explaining my feelings," she said softly and lowered her gaze to her hands. She smoothed out a wrinkle on the thigh of her purple satin jumpsuit and released a soft, feminine sigh. "I want you to know how very much you mean to me."

The knot in Thorne's stomach worked its way to his chest, painfully tightening it. "I treasure your friendship as well."

She arched her pencil-thin brows. "I thought we were so much more than simply friends."

Thorne claimed the ottoman and scooted it so that he sat directly in front of her. "This isn't easy, Sheila."

"Don't." She stopped him. "I already know what you're going to say.... You've met someone else."

"I don't want to hurt you." They had been seeing each other steadily for months, and although he realized how mismatched they were, Sheila hadn't seen it yet, and he honestly wished to spare her any emotional pain.

"But you see, darling you don't need to. I understand about these things."

"You do?" Thorne hadn't the foggiest notion what there was for her to understand.

"A woman must accept this sort of thing from her husband. I know Daddy's had his women on the side. Mother knows and approves."

Thorne surged to his feet. "You're saying you expect me to have an affair?"

"Just to get her out of your system. I want you to know that I understand."

Years of discipline tempered Thorne's response. He was so furious that it took all his restraint to continue being civil, following Sheila's generous announcement. He marched to the plate-glass window and looked out, afraid to speak for fear of what he'd say. Instead he analyzed his anger.

"Thorne, you look upset."

"I am." He realized he was so outraged because Sheila's seeming generosity had subtly insulted Cindy by suggesting she belonged on some back street.

"But, why?"

"Cindy isn't that kind of woman," he said, and turned around. "And neither are you."

A gust of feminine tears followed. Embarrassed, Thorne retrieved a box of tissues and held Sheila gently in his arms until she'd finished weeping.

Dabbing her eyes, Sheila announced that she needed something to drink and nodded approvingly when Thorne brought out a bottle of expensive French wine he knew she enjoyed. He had plenty of time to soothe her wounded ego. Cindy wouldn't be available until almost midnight.

Once Sheila had dried her eyes, she was good company, chatting about the fun times they'd shared over the months they'd been seeing each other and getting slightly tipsy in the process.

Slowly, Thorne felt his anger evaporate. Sheila did most of the talking, and when she suggested they have a cocktail at the Carlyle, Thorne agreed. It was hours before he could meet Cindy.

The Carlyle was crowded, as were two of Sheila's other favorite hangouts where they stopped for drinks.

"Let's drop by at your parents'," she suggested casually, swirling the ice in her empty glass.

"I can't, I'm meeting Cindy in a couple of hours." He raised his arm to look at his watch and the air left his lungs in one disbelieving gasp. "I'm late."

"But, Thorne..."

It was already eleven forty-five and he was at least another fifteen minutes from Oakes-Jenning. The regret seared through him like a hot coal.

"You can't just leave me here!" Sheila cried, trotting after him.

He handed the stub to the hatcheck girl and paced restlessly until she returned. When she did, Thorne thrust the girl a generous tip for being prompt.

"Thorne." Sheila gave him a forlorn look, her eyes damp with tears. "Don't leave me."

Chapter Eight

All New York seemed alive with activity to Cindy. New Year's Eve and it could have been noon for all the people milling in the streets. Times Square would already be a madhouse, filled with anxious spectators waiting for the magical hour when the Big Apple would descend, marking the beginning of another New Year.

Cindy felt wonderful. Free. Thorne might have claimed not to be Prince Charming, but he'd demonstrated several princely qualities. From the way he'd searched for her, he seemed to hold a deep, genuine affection for her. Surely he wouldn't have hired a private detective to find her if he didn't care. Nor would he have been satisfied with the cloak of secrecy she wore like a heavy shroud. He wasn't pleased with the way she kept magically popping in and out of his life, but he accepted it. He claimed it didn't matter who or what she was, and to prove his point he'd refused to listen when she'd yearned to explain everything. He didn't demand answers when the questions were clearly etched in his eyes, nor did he make any unreasonable demands of her. She'd told him she couldn't meet him until eleven-thirty, and without voicing any qualms he'd accepted that.

A police car, with its siren screaming, raced down the street and Cindy watched its progress. A glance at her watch told her Thorne was fifteen minutes late. After months of cleaning up after Thorne, Cindy would confidently say that he was rarely tardy for anything. He was too much the business tycoon to be unaware of the clock.

Remembering the police car, Cindy stepped to the curb and looked up and down the street. Unexpectedly, alarm filled her. Perhaps something had happened to Thorne. Perhaps he was hurt and bleeding—maybe he'd suffered a relapse and was ill again.

Cindy couldn't bear to think of him in pain. She'd rather endure it herself than have him suffer. It took her another five minutes to reason things out. Thorne was perfectly capable of taking care of himself, and she was worrying needlessly. He'd gotten hung up in traffic and would arrive any minute. If he was hurt, she'd know. Somehow, some way, her heart would know. By fair means or foul, Thorne would come to her, no matter what the circumstances. All she had to do was be patient and wait. He couldn't look at her the way he did and ask her to spend this night with him and then leave her standing in the cold. She'd stake her life on it.

Thirty minutes later, Cindy's confidence was dying a slow, painful death. She was cold. Her face felt frozen and her toes were numb. She'd been silly enough to wear open-toed pumps and was paying the price of her own folly. She hunched her shoulders against the cutting cold as the wind whipped her hair back and forth across her face. Resentfully she thought of how hard she'd worked, rushing from one office to another to finish in record time, and how quickly she'd showered and changed clothes all so she could spend extra time with her hair and makeup. She'd wanted this night to be perfect for Thorne. After forty-five minutes of standing in the wind, her hair was a lost cause and her makeup couldn't have fared any better.

Another fifteen minutes, Cindy decided. That was all the time she'd give him.

And then fifteen intolerable, interminable minutes passed.

Five more, she vowed, and that was it. She'd walk away and not look back. Thorne would have a logical explanation, she was convinced of that, but she couldn't stand in the cold all night or she'd freeze to death.

Dejected, discouraged and defeated, Cindy waited out the allotted five minutes and decided there was nothing more she could do but leave. Tucking her coat more securely around her, she walked to the corner and paused. Not yet. She couldn't leave yet. What if Thorne arrived and they just missed each other? She couldn't bear for him to find her gone. He'd be frantic.

She pulled her hand from her pocket and examined her watch one last time. Maybe she should wait another minute or two—it wouldn't hurt anything. Her toes were beyond feeling and a couple more minutes wouldn't matter.

A niggling voice in the back of her mind tried to convince her that Thorne had left her waiting in the cold as just punishment for brusquely disrupting his staid, regimented life.

Forcefully, Cindy shook her head. She refused to believe it. The voice returned a moment later and suggested that Thorne was with another woman. Sheila. This possibility seemed far more feasible. The photograph of the other woman remained on prominent display in his office. A hundred doubts crowded each other as they battled for space in her troubled thoughts. Sheila. He was with Sheila!

Determined now to leave, Cindy buried her hands deeper in the satin-lined pockets of her heavy wool coat. It was too late to ring in the New Year with Thorne. Too late to believe that a relationship between them could work. Too late to demand her heart back!

Hunched against the piercing wind, her collar as close to her face as she could arrange it, Cindy turned and walked away. The tightness in her chest was nearly debilitating.

The sound of tires screeching to a halt and a car door slamming startled her.

"Cindy!"

She turned around sharply to discover Thorne frantically racing toward her.

Breathless, he caught her in his arms and held her to him. Roughly he pushed the hair from her face as though he needed to read her face and see for himself that she was safe and secure in his arms. "Oh, dear God, Cindy, I'm sorry, so sorry."

Every wild suspicion died the minute Thorne reached for her. He was so unbelievably warm and he held her as though he planned to do it a good long while. "You came," she murmured, laughing with pure relief. "You came." She wound her arms around his middle and tucked her head beneath his chin, savoring the warm, masculine feel of him. She noted there was something different about his usually distinctive masculine scent, as if it were mingled with some other fragrance.... But she was too deliriously happy at being in his arms to puzzle it out right now.

"You must be half-frozen," Thorne moaned, nuzzling her hair.

"Three-quarters," she jested. "But it was worth every second just to be with you now."

He kissed her then, his mouth cherishing hers, hungry yet gentle, demanding yet tender. Cindy absorbed his warmth, focusing on him like a tropical orchid turning toward the sun, seeking its nourishing rays as the source of all life.

Thorne lifted his head, cupped her chilled face with both hands and released a sigh that came from deep within him. He'd been overwrought, checking his watch every ten seconds, half crazy with fear that she'd walk out of his life and he'd never find her again. The traffic had been a nightmare, with the streets crammed with cars and people. His progress had been severely impeded until he'd decided he could arrive faster if he'd walked. He hadn't dreamed she'd still be there waiting, although he prayed she was. An hour she'd stood and waited in the freezing cold. He cursed Sheila and then himself.

"Let's get out of here," he said breathlessly. Looping his arm around her waist, he led her back to the taxi and helped her inside. He paused long enough to give the driver instructions to a drive to a nearby restaurant.

Once inside the cab, Cindy removed her shoes and started to rub some feeling back into her numb toes.

"Let me do that," Thorne insisted, placing her nylon-covered feet between his large hands and rubbing vigorously.

Cindy sighed, relaxed and leaned against the back of the cushioned seat.

"Any better?"

She nodded, content just to be with Thorne. "Where are we going?"

"Someplace where I can get some Irish coffee down you."

"I'm Italian," she said with a generous smile.

"Italian?" He eyed her curiously, surprised at her unexpected announcement. "But you're blond."

"There are plenty of us, trust me."

They arrived at the restaurant, but it wasn't one that Cindy recognized. Thorne gave her his hand to help her climb out of the taxi. He paid the driver and escorted her inside the lounge. They were given a table immediately, although the place was crowded. Cindy was convinced the large bill Thorne passed the maître d' had something to do with the waiting table.

Once they were seated, Thorne leaned against the back of the oak chair and ran a hand over his face. "I feel like I've been running a marathon," he said, expelling his breath.

"What happened?"

The waitress arrived and Thorne placed their order for drinks, glad for the interruption. He was going to mislead Cindy. It was only a lie of omission, but it still didn't sit right with him. He expected her to be honest with him, and it felt wrong to be less so with her. "I miscalculated the time and got caught in traffic. I didn't dare to hope you'd still be there; I don't know what I would have done if you'd left."

"I'd already decided to contact you in the morning."

He momentarily closed his eyes. "Thank God for that."

"You wanted to give us—the unprincely Thorne and the unadorned Cinderella—a chance, and I agreed, didn't I?"

"Yes."

His smile was capable of delaying an ice age, Cindy determined. He looked at her the way a starving man would survey a Thanksgiving feast. His gaze was tender and loving, warm and enticing. "We didn't ring in the New Year." His words revealed his regret.

"I know." She dropped her gaze because looking at him was much too intense, like staring into the sun for too long. She was becoming blind to the facts that surrounded their unusual relationship, ignoring the overwhelming potential for injury.

The waitress arrived with their drinks and Cindy sipped the liquor-laced coffee. It was hot, sweet and potent, burning a path down her throat and instantly spreading its warmth to her farthest extremities. The tingling sensation left her toes and fingers almost immediately.

"Next year we'll make it to Times Square?" Thorne suggested, his voice lifting slightly on the end of the statement, turning it into a question.

"Next year," she agreed, desperately wanting to believe they would be together twelve months from now. It was preferable not to look ahead with Thorne, to live for the moment, but she couldn't help herself.

"Are you hungry?" he asked next.

"Famished." She hadn't eaten anything since early afternoon, not wanting to spoil her appetite.

"Good. Do you want to order dinner now or would you rather have another cocktail?"

"Dinner," Cindy returned confidently. "But if you want another drink, don't let me stop you."

He picked up the menu and shook his head. "I've had a bottle of wine and a couple of cocktails before I caught up with you."

Cindy lifted the menu and mulled over the information he'd let slip. He'd lost track of the time, he'd claimed. That's easy enough to do when having a good time in the company of a beautiful woman. Her earlier suspicions resurrected themselves, bubbling to the surface of her mind like fizz in club soda—popping and hissing with doubts. Thorne had been with Sheila. He'd brought in the New Year with the other woman when he had asked to share the moment with her. He hadn't been with Cindy, but with Sheila, the woman whose picture sat prominently on his desk. Cindy was as convinced he'd been with the other woman as she was that the faint scent she'd noted on Thorne's jacket earlier was perfume. Sheila's perfume.

All the special excitement she experienced every time she was with Thorne whooshed out of her like air from a punctured balloon. She felt wounded. The commotion and noise from the restaurant that surrounded her seemed to fade into nothingness.

"Have you decided?" Thorne asked.

She stared at him blankly, not understanding what he was asking until she realized he was inquiring about her dinner selection. "No. What do you suggest?" It amazed her that she could speak coherently. There would be no next year for them—probably not even a next week. She'd be astonished if they made it through dinner.

You're overreacting, she told herself. *He had a drink with another woman. Big deal.* Thorne wasn't her exclusive property. But he'd obviously held Sheila, wrapped his arms around her...even kissed her. He must have, or the cloying scent of expensive perfume wouldn't be wafting from him.

Deliberately she set the menu aside and glared at him, not knowing what to do.

"Cindy?"

"Hum?" She made a conscious effort to look attentive.

"What's wrong? You don't look right."

"I'm fine," she lied. How could she be anything close to normal when the fragile walls of hope and expectation were crumbling at her feet? Her dreams had become ashes, burning hotly. Again she told herself that she was making too much of it. She had little to go on but conjecture, yet in her heart she knew. Thorne had left her standing in the miserable cold, alone, while he toasted the New Year with Sheila.

"If you'll excuse me a minute, I think I'd like to freshen up." Somehow she managed to keep her voice level, revealing none of the emotion that rocked her heart and her head.

"Of course." He stood when she did, but as she moved to turn away, his hand reached for her, stopping her. A frown marred his face. "There are tears in your eyes."

She hadn't realized she was crying. She rubbed the moisture from her face. "What would I have to cry about?" The words came out as if she were riding on a roller coaster, heaving in pitch, squeezing between the tightness that gripped her throat.

"You tell me."

Cindy reached for her coat and purse, the tears flowing in earnest now. The one drink had gone to her head on an empty stomach and she swayed slightly. "I suddenly figured everything out. I lost the feeling in my toes waiting for you."

Thorne blinked. She wasn't making the least bit of sense. "What do your toes have to do with the fact that you're crying?"

She jabbed a finger in his direction. "You... were... with... Sheila, weren't you?"

His chin jutted out with determination and fiery anger. He forced her to sit down and took the chair directly across from her. He wouldn't back down from the fierce anger in her gaze. She accused him of a multitude of crimes with one searing glare, and Thorne realized his mistake: he should have leveled with her earlier—he would have if he hadn't feared exactly this reaction. "Yes, I was with Sheila."

She leaned halfway across the small table, her eyes spitting fire. "For more than an hour I waited in the cold and wind, never once doubting you'd come. You're right, Thorne, you're no Prince Charming."

"At the moment there isn't the faintest resemblance between you and Cinderella, either."

She ignored that. "If I had the least bit of magic left in me, I'd turn you into a frog."

"I'd make you kiss me." Lord, he loved her. They were actually arguing, laying their feelings on the table the way a world-class poker player would turn over his cards.

"I don't think it would do any good," Cindy said hotly. "Me kissing you, that is. You'd still be a frog."

"That could be, but I sincerely doubt it."

Cindy bit into her bottom lip. Thorne seemed to think this witty exchange was fun while she was devastated. He was so casual about it, and that hurt.

Thorne immediately sensed the change in Cindy. "I didn't want to be with Sheila," he said, his eyes dark and serious. "I begrudged every minute that I wasn't with you."

Cindy didn't know what to believe anymore.

"Then why..."

"I was trapped," he said, and although his voice revealed his pride, his eyes pleaded with her for understanding. "I would have given anything to welcome in the New Year with you. God willing, I will next year."

Hours later, when she crawled into bed, she wasn't any more confident than she had been in the restaurant. They'd both ordered lobster and talked for hours, their earlier dispute quickly shelved because their time together was too precious to waste arguing. It astonished Cindy the way they could talk. They liked the same things, shared the same interests, bounced ideas off each other and lingered so long over coffee that the waitress grew restless. Only then did Cindy and Thorne notice that they were the only couple left in the restaurant.

"When can I see you again?" he asked.

"Soon," she promised, buttoning her coat. "I'll contact you."

He hadn't liked that, Cindy could tell by the hard set of his mouth. Before they parted, he made her promise that she'd get in touch with him. She would.

Now, as early-morning shadows danced across the walls, Cindy lay in her bed undecided. Because she'd given Thorne her word, she would meet him, but this had to be the end of it. Oh, heavens, how often had she said that? Too often. And each time, walking away from him had grown more difficult. He was like an addictive drug, trapping her more with each contact, filling her with longing for him. He was so wonderfully good for her and so disastrously bad for her. She didn't know what she was going to do anymore. Thorne was in her blood.

Thorne stood on the dock as large sea gulls circled overhead. The Staten Island ferry, filled with crowds of tourists who'd taken the twenty-five-cent ride for a closer view of the Statue of Liberty, was slowly advancing toward the long pier.

Cindy had said she'd meet him here. She hadn't shown up yet, but it was still too early to be concerned. It had been a week since he'd last seen her. His fault, not hers. He'd been out of town on business and had returned home to find a note taped to his apartment door. She'd set the time and the place for this meeting. How she'd known he would be free this afternoon was beyond him. Where and how she got her information no longer concerned him. Seeing and being with her were of primary importance. Nothing else mattered.

He had to find a way to assure her that she was the most important person in his life. The incident with Sheila had been left unsettled between them. Thorne could see from Cindy's taut features that she wanted to believe that whatever he shared with Sheila was over. But she had her doubts, and he couldn't blame her.

Briefly he thought about the large diamond he kept in the safe at the office. He wanted it on her finger and her promise to be his wife, but he knew better than to ask her, although the question burned in him like a smoldering fire. The timing had to be right. It wasn't yet. When she completely trusted him, when she opened up to him and told him everything, then he could offer her his life.

For now, all he could do was love her, dispel the doubts one at a time. Today he'd come up with a way of doing that.

"Hi." Cindy joined him on the dock. Her hands were buried deep inside her pockets as she stood, looking into the wind.

Slow, grateful relief poured over Thorne like thick honey. She'd come; he could relax and smile again.

"Hi, yourself," he responded with a smile, resisting the urge to take her in his arms.

"How was Kansas City?"

He smiled, because she'd amazed him again. She'd known where he'd been and for how long. "Dull. I was in a rush to get back to you. Did you miss me?"

Cindy nodded, although she'd rather not admit as much. The week they'd spent apart had seemed a lifetime. For seven days she'd told herself she'd better get used to living without him being the focal point of her existence. "School started up again, I've been busy."

"But you still thought about me?"

Every minute of every day. "Yes," she answered starkly.

The ferry docked and they stood and watched silently as the passengers disembarked.

"I haven't been to the Statue of Liberty since it's been refurbished, have you?" Thorne asked, watching her. It was obvious something was troubling her. Cindy wasn't this quiet this long, without something weighing on her mind.

"No." The wind swirled her hair around her face and she lifted a strand of hair from her cheek.

Thorne studied her. She looked so troubled, so uncertain that he gently pulled her into his embrace, holding her close.

She sighed and leaned against him, relishing his touch after seven tedious days of being without him. She'd never be the same after Thorne. She would go on with her life because there was no option to do anything else. But she'd never be the same.

"Are you ready to talk?" he asked softly, raising her chin so she would meet his gaze.

At one time she had been, but not anymore. It seemed they took one step forward, then quickly re-

treated two. Just when she was beginning to feel secure and right about loving him he'd left her waiting
while he was with Sheila. Although he'd repeatedly
claimed the other woman meant nothing to him, he
continued to keep her picture on prominent display on
his desk. And recently, quite by accident, she discovered the receipt from Tiffany's for a diamond ring. If
she'd been insecure about her position in Thorne's life
before, now she was paranoid.

"Cindy?" he prompted.

Sadly she shook her head, then brightened. "Shall
we walk along the water to get in line for the Statue of
Liberty ferry?"

"No."

"You don't want to go?"

"I have a surprise for you."

"A surprise?" Her heart rocketed to her throat.

He reached for her hand. "We're going someplace
special today."

"Where?"

"That's the surprise." He smiled down on her and
reached for her hand.

Again Cindy was convinced dinosaurs would still be
roaming the world if Thorne's smile had been around
to halt the flowing ice.

"My car's parked down the street."

"Your car?"

"We can't reach . . . this place by subway."

Despite her reservations, Cindy laughed. "I'm not
sure I like surprises."

"This one you will." His fingers tightened around
hers. "I promise." Cindy would know for certain her
position in his life after today.

"Are you sure this is . . . someplace I want to go?"

"Now that may be in question, but you've already agreed."

"I did? When?"

Thorne kissed the top of her nose. "The night we met."

Cindy shuffled through her memories and came back blank. "I don't recall agreeing to anything."

Thorne pretended shock, then shook his head in mock despair. "How quickly they forget."

"Thorne!" He led her up the street.

"This isn't anyplace fancy is it?" She wore crisp blue jeans, a pink turtleneck sweater and loafers with hot pink socks.

"You're perfect no matter what you wear."

"I suppose this is some fancy restaurant where everyone will be in a tux."

"No restaurant."

"But we are eating?" She certainly hoped they would be. As usual, she was starving. Why, oh, why did it always happen this way? She'd be so uneasy, so certain nothing would ever work between them, and ten minutes after being with Thorne, she would gladly hand over her soul. The thought of being separated from him was unthinkable. She was crazy in love with this man.

"Are you worried about your stomach again?"

"Don't worry, it's something lobster will cure," she joked and was rewarded with a smile.

Cindy would have bet anything Thorne drove a Mercedes in a subdued shade of gray or steely blue. She was wrong—his car was a Corvette, bright red and so unlike him that she stood with her hands on her hips and shook her head.

"I bought it on impulse," he said a bit sheepishly, holding open the passenger door for her.

She climbed inside, amazed at how close to the ground they were. When she had trouble with the seat belt, Thorne leaned over and snapped it into place, teasing her unmercifully about her lack of mechanical ability, then kissing her soundly when she blushed.

Once they were on the Jersey turnpike, Cindy grew all the more curious. "Just how many days will we be traveling?"

"Forty-five minutes," he answered.

"That long, huh? Aren't you going to give me any clues?"

Thorne resolutely shook his head. "Not anything more than I've already told you."

He was in such a good mood that it was impossible to be serious. Soon they were both laughing, and Cindy didn't notice when he exited from the freeway. He drove confidently through a neighborhood of luxurious homes.

"This must be quite some place."

"Oh, it is," he promised.

When he turned into a long circular driveway that curved around a huge water fountain, Cindy's curiosity was all the more sharp. She'd never seen a more opulent home. Two floors with huge white pillars dominated the front. It looked like something out of *Architectural Digest*.

"Wow." She couldn't find any other word to describe it.

The front door opened and a lovely gray-haired woman stepped out to greet Thorne. The older woman's gaze rested on Cindy, and although she revealed little emotion, Cindy had the impression the woman disapproved of her.

Thorne climbed out of the car and stepped around and kissed the woman on the cheek.

A rock settled in the pit of Cindy's stomach as Thorne opened her door and offered his hand to help her out.

"Cindy," he said, "I'd like you to meet my mother."

Chapter Nine

Cindy's introduction to Thorne's parents was strained at best. She was enraged that he would bring her to his family home without a word to prepare her. Even worse, he'd informed her that what she was wearing was perfectly fine. He couldn't have been more wrong. Jeans and a turtleneck sweater weren't the least bit acceptable if Gwendolyn Prince's look told Cindy anything. Cindy would have been more comfortable being unexpectedly granted an audience with the Pope.

Seated beside Thorne in the extravagant living room, Cindy rotated the stem of a crystal wineglass between her palms. Although Thorne's mother was subtle about it, Cindy could feel the other woman studying her. His father's gray eyes sparkled with undisguised delight. He, at least, seemed to be enjoying this farce.

"Where was it you said you met?" the elder Thorne asked.

"The company Christmas party."

Cindy let Thorne answer for her. Her mouth felt dry, and she wasn't sure her tongue would cooperate if she did try to speak.

"So you're employed by Oakes-Jenning?"

This time the question was shot directly at Cindy.

"Dad," Thorne interrupted smoothly. "I think I'll let you get me a refill." He held out his glass to his father, who stood and poured the clear wine.

The elder Prince silently offered Cindy a refill, but she refused with a short shake of her head. If there was ever a time she needed to keep her wits, it was now. Forget the audience with the Pope, she would have been more comfortable in a torture chamber. The minute she was alone with Thorne, she'd let him know what she thought of his "surprise."

"I don't believe I caught your last name?" His mother asked, eyeing Cindy.

"Territo. Cindy Territo." Her voice came out sounding like she was on her deathbed. Cindy felt as if she were.

"That sounds ethnic," Thorne's mother commented, not unkindly.

"It's . . ." Cindy began.

"Italian," Thorne finished.

"I see." His mother obviously didn't.

Cindy watched as the older woman downed the remainder of her wine. She appeared as uneasy as Cindy.

"Thorne tells me you're a student?" His father continued the inquisition.

"Yes, I'm studying computer programming."

This, too, was news to Thorne. He knew Cindy was uncomfortable answering all these questions. He'd asked his parents to make her feel welcome, but he should have known better than to suggest they not intimidate her with rounds of inquiries. His father was too cagey to let the opportunity pass. Thorne reached for Cindy's hand and was astonished to discover that her fingers were as cold as ice.

"I'm sure Cindy is just as curious about us," Thorne said, squeezing her hand reassuringly. "Why don't we let her ask what she'd like to know about us?"

"I... know everything I need to," she murmured with a feeble smile. The instant the words were out, Cindy wanted to grab them back, realizing she'd said the wrong thing. She'd made it sound as if all she cared about was Thorne's money. Nothing could be less true. She would have fallen in love with Thorne had he sold pencils on a street corner. Now, in addition to being ill at ease, she was acutely embarrassed.

Dinner did little to help. They sat at a long table with a crystal chandelier she suspected was worth more than her uncle's limousine. Thorne sat across from her, making her feel all the more alone. His parents dominated both ends of the long table.

A large glass of ice rested in front of Cindy, and her mouth was so uncomfortably dry that she reached for it, disappointed to find so little water inside. Thorne's mother gave her a pathetic glance and instantly Cindy realized that she'd committed some terrible faux pas. Her mortification reached a peak when the maid delivered a shrimp cocktail, placing the appetizer inside the glass of ice. Only then did Cindy realize the glass wasn't meant for water. Cindy died a little at that moment. If there had been a hole to hide in, she would have sought it, burying herself with blanket after blanket of humiliation. She dared not look at Thorne, certain he would find the entire incident amusing.

"What does your father do?" Gwendolyn asked, between bites of succulent shrimp.

Briefly Cindy closed her eyes to gather her composure. She'd already disgraced Thorne with her lack of finesse once, she'd be damned before she did so again. "I'm afraid I don't know...he deserted my mother and me shortly after I was born."

"Oh, my dear, how terrible for your mother."

"She's gone as well, isn't she?" Thorne asked almost absently, studying Cindy. His loving gaze caressed her, his brow distorted with concern.

"She died when I was five."

"Who raised you?" It was the elder Thorne who questioned her now. From the looks they were giving her, one would have thought she'd been beaten daily and survived on dry bread crumbs tossed under the table.

"My aunt and uncle were kind enough to raise me." Thorne's parents exchanged sympathetic glances. "Believe me," Cindy hurried to add. "There's no need to feel sorry for me. They loved me as they would their own daughter. We're a close-knit family with lots of cousins and assorted relatives." Her aunt and uncle, however, wouldn't dream of interrogating Thorne the way his parents were questioning her.... Then again maybe they would. Cindy felt slightly better musing about how her Uncle Sal would react to meeting

Thorne. The first hint of amusement touched the edges of her mouth. She raised her gaze to meet Thorne's and they shared a brief smile.

Dinner couldn't be over soon enough for Cindy. She ate only enough to assure that no one would comment. The prime rib rested like a lead weight in the pit of her stomach. Dessert, a frothy concoction of lime and whipped cream, was a cool respite, and she managed to consume a large portion of that.

"While the women have their coffee, let me show you my new nine iron." The elder Prince addressed his son.

Thorne's gaze met Cindy's. She nodded, assuring him that she'd be fine left alone with his mother. She was confident that Gwendolyn Prince had arranged this time so the two women could speak frankly, and Cindy was prepared to do exactly that.

The men left the table.

Cindy took a sip of her coffee and braced herself. She noted that Thorne's mother's hand shook slightly and she was reassured to realize that the old woman was equally nervous.

Neither spoke for a long moment.

"Mrs. Prince—"

"Cindy—"

They both began at the same instant and laughed, flustered and uneasy.

"You first, dear," Gwendolyn said.

Cindy straightened the linen napkin on her lap. "I wanted to apologize for drinking out of the wrong glass..." She paused, drew in a deep, steadying breath, deciding to do away with small talk and get to the point. "I believe I know what you want to say, and I couldn't agree with you more. You're absolutely right about me. It's perfectly obvious that Thorne and I are terribly ill suited."

If the older woman's hand had trembled before, now it positively shook. "Why, Cindy, what makes you suggest such a thing?"

"You mean other than my drinking from the shrimp boat?"

The first indication that Thorne's mother was capable of a smile showed on the older woman's ageless face. "My dear girl, shall I tell you about the time I drank too much wine and told Thorndike's mother that she was a cantankerous old biddy?"

Cindy raised the napkin to her mouth to disguise her laugh. "You honestly said that?"

"And he proposed the next day. He told me he needed a wife who would stand up to his mother. I'd been crazy about him for years, you see, and I didn't think he knew I was alive. We'd been dating off and on for months—mostly on—and our relationship seemed to be moving sideways. That Sunday dinner with his family was the turning point in our courtship."

"And you've enjoyed a happy marriage." Cindy made it a statement, confident that the Prince marriage had been a good one.

"Over forty years now."

Silence followed.

"I want you to know that little of what Thorndike and I say will influence our son. He's always been his own man, and he hasn't brought you here for our approval."

Cindy nodded, agreeing that Thorne wouldn't be intimidated by his family's reservations regarding her. "You don't need to say anything more, I understand."

"But I feel confident that you don't," Gwendolyn said hurriedly. "It's just that Thorne and Sheila were such an item that both Thorndike and I assumed...well, we naturally thought that he and Sheila...oh dear, I do seem to be making a mess of this."

"It would only seem natural that after all those months they would marry."

"And then out of the blue, Thorne mentioned meeting you." Gwendolyn looked flustered and reached for her coffee.

Cindy dropped her gaze. The Christmas Ball and her little charade did seem to have tossed a fly in the ointment.

"Thorne thinks highly of you."

"You and your husband must be special people to have raised a son as wonderful as Thorne." Cindy meant that sincerely. "He's touched my life in ways I'll always remember."

"I do believe you mean that."

"I do, but I realized early on that I'm not the woman for him. He needs a different type." Although she would have given anything in this world to be wrong, she knew she wasn't.

Gwendolyn's cup made a clanging sound when she set it in the saucer. "I don't suppose you've told Thorne that."

"Not yet."

"He won't give up on you easily."

Cindy agreed, remembering the detective. "He can be as stubborn as an ornery mule sometimes."

Gwendolyn laughed outright. "He's quite a bit like his father."

"I'm doing a poor job of expressing myself," Cindy said and her voice revealed her pain. "I want to reassure you that I won't upset you or your family by complicating Thorne's life."

"Oh dear," Gwendolyn looked stunned. "Now that I've met you, I was rather hoping you would."

The words were a soothing balm to Cindy. "Thank you."

"Oh, my," Gwendolyn touched her face with her fingertips. "I do wonder if I'm making an idiot of myself again. Thorndike swears I should never drink wine."

"He married you because of it," Cindy reminded the older woman, and they shared a smile.

"Thorne would never forgive me if I offended you."

"You haven't."

The men joined them a minute later and Thorne's searching gaze sought out Cindy's. She reassured him with a smile that everything had gone well between her and his mother and she saw him relax visibly. He'd been worried for nothing. She hadn't been raised in a large family without learning how to hold her own.

Thorne gave his parents a weak excuse and they left shortly afterward. Instead of heading toward the freeway, Thorne drove into a church parking lot and turned off the engine.

"My father was impressed with you."

"I can't imagine why," Cindy returned honestly.

He ignored that. "What did my mother have to say?"

"What I expected."

"Which was?" he probed.

Cindy shook her head. "We came to an understanding."

"Good or bad?"

"Good. I like her, Thorne, she's direct and honest."

He rubbed his hand along the back of her neck. "So are you, love," he said softly and directed her mouth to his, kissing her hungrily.

"So, Cindy Territo, it wasn't such a hard thing to reveal your name, was it?" He brushed his mouth over hers, his mouth nipping at her bottom lip with tiny, biting kisses.

"No." Nothing was difficult when she was in his arms. Since the Christmas Ball, she'd allowed his velvet touch to confuse the issue. She'd be so certain of what she had to do, and then he'd kiss her and she'd fall at his feet. It wasn't fair for him to have such an overwhelming effect on her. She wasn't weak-willed, nor was her character lacking. She hadn't once suspected that love would do this to a person.

Her aunt was knitting in front of the television set when Cindy let herself into the apartment. Cindy glanced at her aunt, said nothing and moved into the kitchen. Theresa put down the yarn and needles and followed her niece.

"So how was the Statue of Liberty?"

"We didn't go there." Her voice was strained with emotion.

"Oh." Her aunt opened the oven door and basted the turkey roasting inside. "So where'd you go?"

"Thorne took me to meet his family."

Surprised, Theresa let the oven door close with a bang. "His family? You must mean a great deal to him. So how did the introductions go?"

Cindy took a pitcher of orange juice from the refrigerator and poured herself a glass, but not because she was thirsty. She was merely looking for something, anything, to occupy her hands and her mind. "I met his mother and father and . . . nothing."

" 'Nothing,' you say?"

Her aunt knew her too well for Cindy to try to fool the older woman. She set the glass of juice on the kitchen table and slumped into the chair, burying her face in her hands. A sob escaped and Cindy ruthlessly bit down on her bottom lip, hoping to squelch the flood of pent-up tears that demanded release.

Theresa placed her hand on Cindy's shoulder and patted gently. "Love hurts, doesn't it, honey?"

"I've been fooling myself . . . it's just not going to work. I made such an idiot of myself . . . and everyone was so nice. Thorne pretended not to notice, and his mother assured me she'd done silly things in her life, and his father just looked at me like I was an alien from outer space. I could have died."

"I'm sure that whatever you did wasn't as bad as you think."

"It was worse!" she cried.

"Right now you think it is," Theresa stated calmly. "Give it a year or so and you'll look back and laugh at yourself."

Cindy couldn't visualize laughing about anything at the moment. She was hurting too much. She raised her head, sniffled and wiped the moisture from her face with the back of her hand.

"I've decided. I'm not going to see him again," Cindy said with iron determination, promising herself as well as informing her family of her resolution. "It isn't going to work, and confusing the issues with love won't change a thing."

"Did you tell Thorne that?"

Miserably, Cindy shook her head. "I didn't want to invite an argument." She couldn't bear to spend their last minutes together debating her decision. Thorne had taken her to meet his family to prove how easily she'd fit in, and the opposite had proven true. She'd enjoyed his parents. She couldn't imagine not liking the two people most influential in Thorne's upbringing. They were decent folks and his mother was a kick, but Cindy had known the minute she'd walked inside their home that the chasm that divided their life-styles was far too wide ever to bridge.

She glanced around the Territo family kitchen at the heavy mahogany dining-room table with plain wooden chairs that had once belonged to her grandmother. There were no plush Persian carpets or Oriental rugs beneath their table, only worn hardwood floors. Their furniture was simple, as were their lives. Comparing the two families would be like trying to mix spaghetti sauce with lobster.

Before they parted, Thorne had asked to meet her again. Distraught and too weak to argue with him, Cindy had agreed. Now she was sorry.

"The man's in love with you," Theresa said simply.

"But encouraging him will only hurt him more."

Theresa sadly shook her head. "Are you saying you don't love him?"

"Yes," Cindy cried, then bit her lower lip at the searing look her aunt gave her. "I love him," she admitted finally, "but that doesn't make everything right. Some things in life were meant to be; other relationships can never be right."

Her aunt gave her a troubled look. "You're old enough to know what you want. I'm not going to stand here and argue with you. Anything I say is unlikely to change your mind, since it's obvious you've thought about this a great deal. But I want you to know that you're a marvelous girl and a man like Thorndike Prince wouldn't fall in love with you if you weren't."

Cindy's head bobbed up and down. For now he may have convinced himself that he loved her, but later, after he knew her better, he'd regret his love. Because of the unusual circumstances of their relationship he looked upon her as a challenge. It hurt, but she'd made her decision, and although it was the most difficult thing she'd ever done in her life, she was determined to stick by it.

"Yes." Thorne flipped the intercom switch, his eyes remaining on the report he was studying. Interruptions were part of his day and he'd grown accustomed to doing several things at once when necessary.

Mrs. Hillard paused and cleared her throat. "Your mother is here."

Thorne released the button and groaned inwardly. He may be able to have Mrs. Hillard fend off unexpected and unwanted visits from Sheila, but his mother wouldn't easily be put off by his secretary's excuses. He pressed the button. "Go ahead and send her in."

"Thorne." His mother sauntered into the office, her face a cheerful facade.

He stood and kissed her on the cheek, already guessing that she was concerned about something. "To what do I owe this unexpected pleasure?" She wore her full-length fur coat, and absently Thorne thought about how Cindy would look in fox. No, he decided absently, with her blond hair, he'd buy her mink. He'd give it to her as an engagement present when they set their wedding date. He was anxious to give her all the things she deserved. She'd given him so much in such a little time that it would take a lifetime to repay her.

"I was in town and thought I'd let you take me to lunch."

His mother had obviously taught Sheila the same trick. "What about Dad?"

"He's tied up in a meeting."

"Ah." Understanding came.

"Besides, I wanted to talk to you."

Unexpectedly Thorne bristled, automatically suspicious of her intentions. His mother wanted to discuss Cindy. He knew it as clearly as if she'd stormed into his office and demanded they talk about the Italian woman he'd brought to their family home. He sighed, sensing an argument.

"What's the name of that nice little restaurant you like so well?" his mother asked, rearranging the small items on top of his desk, irritating him further.

"Tastings."

"Right. I made reservations at the Russian Tea Room."

Thorne managed to nod. It didn't matter where they ate or what they ate, as long as the air was clear when they'd finished.

Half an hour later, Thorne studied his mother as they sat in a plush booth in the Russian Tea Room. Methodically she removed her white gloves one finger at a time. He knew her well enough to realize she was stalling.

"You wanted to say something, Mother?" He had no desire to delay the confrontation. If she disapproved of Cindy, he'd prefer to have it in the open and over with quickly. Not that anything she said would alter his feelings toward the woman he loved. He'd prefer it if his family approved, but he wouldn't let them stand in his way.

"Sheila phoned me this morning and I'm afraid I may have done something you'd rather I hadn't." She tossed him an apologetic glance and reached for the menu, hiding behind it.

Thorne's fingers tightened around the water glass. "Perhaps it would be best if you started from the beginning."

"The beginning... Well, yes, I do suppose I should." She set the menu aside. "I think you already know that I've had my reservations about Cindy."

"Listen, Mother, let me assure you that your feelings about Cindy mean little to me. I love her and, God willing, I plan to marry her and . . ."

"Please, allow me to finish." She seared him with a look she hadn't used since his youth. Her words were sharp and clipped. "As it happens, I find your Cindy to be a delight."

"You do?"

"Don't be a ninny! She's marvelous; now quit acting so surprised." She shook her head lightly. "I thought at first that she might be too shy and retiring for you, which put me in a terrible position, since I sincerely doubted you'd care one way or the other what I thought of her. But as it happens, I like her. That girl's got pluck."

"Pluck?"

"Right. I'm pleased to hear you have the good sense to want to marry her."

Thorne was so astonished he nearly slid out of the booth and onto the floor. "I have every intention of making her my wife as soon as possible. She may put up a fight, but I'm not taking no for an answer."

His mother made an art of straightening the silverware, aligning each piece just so. "Well, dear, there may be a small problem."

"Yes?"

"Sheila seems quite broken up with the news that I happen to give my wholehearted approval of Cindy. Mentioning that you'd brought her by to meet your father and me may not have been my finest hour. I had no idea Sheila would react so negatively. I fear the girl may try to create problems for you."

"Let her." Thorne dealt with sensitive situations every day. He could handle Sheila. He'd calm her and end their relationship on a friendly note. "Don't worry, Mother, Sheila has been well aware of my feelings for Cindy for quite some time."

"She did seem to think you'd change your mind."

Thorne's mouth thinned with impatience. "She knows better."

"I'm worried about her, Thorne. I want you to talk to her."

Thorne's fingers smoothed the fork tines. "Okay. I'm not sure it will help. I regret any emotional trauma I may have caused her, but I'm not going to do anything more than talk to her."

"Do it soon."

Thorne agreed, elated with the information of his family's acceptance of Cindy. With clarity he recalled the look on her face when he'd last left her. She'd clung to him and kissed him with such fervor that it had been difficult to leave her. He thought about Cindy as his wife and the years that stretched before him like a golden pathway—a lifetime filled with happiness and love. Even though he'd considered marrying Sheila at one point, he'd never thought about their future the way he did with Cindy, plotting their happiness.

"I'm seeing her tomorrow."

"Sheila?" his mother inquired.

Irritated, he shook his head. "No, Cindy."

"But you will talk to Sheila; I'm afraid she may do something silly."

"I'll speak to her," Thorne promised, determined to put an end to his relationship with the other woman.

Thorne stared at the wall clock in the lobby of the American Museum of Natural History. Cindy was half an hour late. It wasn't like her not to be punctual and he was mildly surprised. He had every minute of their evening planned. Dinner. Drinks. Dancing. Then they'd take a walk in Central Park and he'd bring out the diamond. The Tiffany ring burned a hole in is pocket. Tonight was it. He'd waited thirty-three years to find Cindy and he wasn't ever going to let her go.

All day he'd rehearsed what he intended to say. First he'd tell her how knowing her had changed his life. It wasn't only singing in the shower and noticing the birds and blooming flowers, either. Before she'd sashayed into his life, he'd fallen into a deep-grooved rut. His work had become meaningless, merely occupying his time. He'd lost his direction.

But her laughter and her smile had lifted him to the heavens, given him hope. He'd tell her that he'd never thought he'd experience the love he did for her. It had caught him unawares.

Naturally she'd be surprised by the suddenness of this proposal. She might even insist on an extended engagement. Of course, he hoped she'd agree immediately so they could set the date and begin to make the necessary arrangements for their wedding—a church wedding. He didn't want any rushed affair; when he made his vows to Cindy he wanted them spoken before God, not some fly-by-night justice of the peace. He intended their vows to last a lifetime.

Growing impatient, Thorne pulled the newspaper from his briefcase. Maybe if he read the snail-pace minutes would go by faster. He scanned the business news and reached for the front page when the society section slipped to the floor.

Thorne retrieved it and was surprised to find Sheila's face smiling benignly back at him. Interested, he turned the page right side up and read the headlines. SHEILA MATHEWSON ANNOUNCES PLANS TO MARRY THORNDIKE PRINCE.

Thorne roared to his feet like a lion preparing to attack. The paper in his hand was crumpled into a wadded mass. So this was what his mother had come to prepare him for.... And worse, this was the reason Cindy hadn't arrived.

Chapter Ten

The minute Cindy walked into the apartment, her Aunt Theresa and Uncle Sal abruptly cut off their conversation. Cindy paused and studied their flushed faces; it wasn't difficult to ascertain that the two had been in the midst of a rousing argument. The instant Cindy arrived, they both seemed to find things to occupy their hands. Her aunt opened the refrigerator and brought out a head of lettuce and her uncle reached for a deck of cards, shuffling them again and again, his gaze centered on his hands.

"I'll be in my room," Cindy said, granting them privacy. She was sorry they were arguing, and although it was uncommon, she knew from experience it was best to let them resolve their differences without interference from her.

Sitting on the edge of her bed, Cindy eyed the clock. Thorne would be heading for the museum by now, anticipating their meeting. Only she wouldn't be there. She'd let him think she'd agreed to this date, but she hadn't confirmed anything.

Coward! her mind accused her harshly. But she had no option, Cindy argued back. Every time she was with Thorne, her objections melted like snow under a tropical sun. Her head was so boggled, so confused, she didn't know what she wanted anymore. Oh, she loved Thorne, she was convinced of that. But he was so easy to love. It would be far more difficult *not* to care for him.

Shaking her head vigorously, Cindy decided she couldn't leave Thorne waiting. That was childish and silly. It simply wasn't in her to let him waste his time worrying about her. She'd go to him and do her utmost to explain. All she wanted was some time apart. Some space to test their feelings. Everything had happened so quickly between them that it would be wrong to act impulsively now. True love can wait. A month was the amount of time she was going to suggest. That didn't seem so long. Thorne would have to promise not to see her until Valentine's Day. If he truly cared for her, he'd agree to that.

Once she'd made her decision—the third one in as many days—she acted purposefully. She had her scarf wrapped around her neck by the time she entered the kitchen. She paused to button her coat.

Her uncle took one look at her and asked, "Where are you headed?"

Sal so rarely questioned her about anything that his brusque inquiry now took her by surprise. "I'm...the museum."

"You're not meeting that Prince fellow, are you?"

Her aunt pinched her lips together tightly and slammed the kitchen drawer closed, obviously disapproving of Sal's interrogation.

Cindy's gaze flew from Theresa back to her uncle. "I had . . . yes, I planned to meet Thorne there."

"No."

"No? I don't understand."

"I said I don't want you to have anything to do with that rich, spoiled kid."

"But Uncle Sal—"

"The discussion is closed." Sal's hand slammed against the tabletop, upsetting the saltshaker.

Stunned, Cindy gasped and took a step backward. "I'm twenty-two years old. It's a little late to be telling me I can't meet someone."

"You are never to see that man again. Is that understood?"

"Cindy is old enough to make up her own mind," Theresa inserted calmly, her back to her husband.

"You keep out of this, woman."

"So the big Italian stallion thinks he can speak with all the authority of a supreme court judge," Theresa taunted, her face growing redder by the second. "And I say Cindy can meet her Prince anytime she wishes."

"And I say she can't!" Sal blared, turning around to face his wife.

"Uncle Sal, Aunt Theresa, please . . ."

"He's not good enough for you," Sal said, calmer this time, his eyes wide with appeal. "Not near good enough for our Cindy."

"Oh, Uncle Sal—"

"Cindy . . ."

The compassion in her aunt's eyes were so strong that Cindy forgot what she wanted to say.

The room went still, too quiet. Her uncle's gaze fell to the floor and the thick, dark lashes of Theresa's eyes glistened with moisture.

"Something happened." Cindy knew it as well as if they were shouting it at her. "It's Thorne, isn't it?"

Her Aunt Theresa nodded, her troubled gaze avoiding Cindy's.

"Is he hurt?" Alarm filled her, bordering on panic. "Oh, you must tell me if he's injured. I couldn't bear it if he—"

"The man's a no-good bum. You're best rid of him."

It was all so terribly confusing. Everyone seemed to be speaking in riddles. Her gaze drifted from her uncle back to her aunt, pleading with them both to tell her and put an end to this nightmare of fear.

"I think we'd better tell her," Theresa said softly.

"No," Sal raged.

"Tell me what?"

"It's in the paper," Theresa explained gently.

"I said she doesn't need to know," Sal shouted, taking the evening paper and stuffing it in the garbage.

"Uncle Sal!" Cindy pleaded. "What is it?"

Theresa crossed the room and reached for Cindy's hand. The last time Cindy could remember seeing her aunt look at her in exactly that way had been when she was a child and Theresa had come to tell the five-year-old that her mother had gone to live in Heaven.

"What is it?" Cindy asked, her voice so low and weak that it wobbled between two octaves. "He's not dead. Oh, dear God, don't tell me he's dead."

"No, love." Her aunt said softly.

Some of the terrible tension left Cindy's frozen limbs.

Theresa closed her eyes briefly and glanced over her shoulder to her husband. "She'll find out sooner or later. It's better she hear it from us."

It seemed for a moment that Sal was going to argue. His chest swelled as though to heartily disagree, then quickly deflated with defeat. He looked so unlike his robust, outgoing self that Cindy couldn't imagine what was troubling him so.

"Sal read the announcement in the paper and brought it to me."

"The announcement?" Cindy asked.

"Thorne's marrying—"

"—some high-society dame," Sal concluded sharply. Regret shouted from every part of him as though he would have done anything to have spared Cindy this.   "But I don't understand," Cindy murmured, uncertain what she was hearing.

"It was listed in the society page."

"Sheila?"

Her aunt nodded.

Cindy sank into a kitchen chair, her legs unable to support her. "I'm sure there's some mistake, I . . . he took me to meet his family."

"He was using you," Sal murmured, coming to stand behind her. Gently his hands patted her shoulders as he'd done when she was a little girl, giving solace. "He was probably using his family to give you the impression he was serious so he could get you into his bed."

"No," Cindy cried. "No, it was never like that. Thorne didn't even suggest . . . not once."

"Then thank God for that, that was where he was leading. He's a smart devil, I'll say that for him."

Theresa claimed the chair next to Cindy and reached for her numb fingers, rubbing them. "I refused to believe it myself until Sal showed me the article. But there it was, bold as can be. It's true, Cindy."

Cindy nodded, accepting what her family was telling her as truth. No tears burned for release. No hysterical sob brewed deep within her. She felt nothing. No pain. No sense of betrayal. No anger. Nothing.

"Are you going to be all right?" Theresa asked softly.

"I'll be fine. Don't worry. It was inevitable, you know. I think I accepted it from the beginning. Something deep inside me always realized he could never be mine."

"But . . . oh, Cindy, I can hardly believe it myself."

Cindy stood and hugged her aunt close. "You fell for the magic," she whispered gently. "So did I for a time. But you see, I'm not really Cinderella and Thorne isn't really a prince. It had to end sometime."

"But I hurt so much for you!" Theresa sobbed.

"Don't. I'm not nearly as upset as you think," Cindy murmured.

Theresa straightened and wiped her face free of tears.

"I'm going to study for a while." She was fighting off the terrible numbness, knowing she had to do something. Anything. Otherwise she'd go crazy.

Sal slipped an arm around his wife and Theresa pressed her head to his shoulder. "Okay," Sal told his niece softly. "You hit those books and you'll feel better."

Cindy walked back to her room and closed the door. It seemed so dingy inside. Dingy and gray. She didn't feel like studying, but she forced herself to sit on the mattress and open her textbook. The words blurred, swimming in and out of her focus, and Cindy was shocked to realize she was crying.

"I want a retraction and I want it printed in today's paper," Thorne raged at the society-page editor. The poor woman was red with indignation, but Thorne was beyond caring.

"I've already explained that we won't be able to do that until tomorrow's paper," the woman said patiently for the sixth time.

"But that could be too late."

"I apologize for any inconvenience this may have caused you, Mr. Prince, but we received Ms. Mathewson's announcement through the normal channels. I can assure you this kind of thing is most unusual."

"And you printed the wedding announcement without checking with the proposed groom?"

The woman sat at her desk, holding the pencil at each end with a grip so hard it threatened to snap it. "Let me assure you, Mr. Prince, that in all my years in the newspaper business, this is the first bogus wedding announcement that has ever crossed my desk. In the past there's never been any need to verify the event with the proposed groom—or bride for that matter."

"Then maybe you should start."

"Perhaps," she returned stiffly. "Now, if you'll excuse me, I've got work to do."

"You haven't heard the end of this," Thorne said heatedly.

"I don't doubt it," the editor returned with spirit.

Thorne did an abrupt about-face and left the newspaper office, unconcerned with the amount of attention his argument had caused.

On the street, he caught the first taxi he could flag down and headed back to the office. As it was, he was working on a tight schedule. He'd already attended an important meeting early that morning—one he'd tried to postpone and couldn't. The minute he was free, he'd had Mrs. Hillard contact Mike Williams, and he'd paced restlessly until he'd learned that Mike was out of town on a case and not expected back for another week.

The detective could well be his only chance of finding Cindy. Mike had gotten close to her once, but after Cindy had shown up outside his office building, Thorne had done as she requested and asked Mike to halt his investigation. After all, he'd gotten what he'd wanted—Cindy was back. Now he wished he'd pursued it further. She'd left him and he had no more chance of finding her now than when she'd left him the night of the Christmas Ball.

A feeling of desperation swamped Thorne. When Cindy hadn't shown at the museum, Thorne had spent the evening phoning every Territo in the telephone book—all fifty-seven—to no avail. By the time he'd finished, he was convinced Cindy had given him a phony name. From there he had no more leads.

Thorne dreaded returning to his office. No doubt there would be enough phone messages to occupy his afternoon—and he was supposed to be working on this merger! He had been placed in charge of an important business deal that meant great things for Oakes-Jenning and for his career. He couldn't let it slide—not when so many others were depending on him. This was not the week to be worrying about Cindy. He had neither the time nor the patience to be running around New York looking for her.

Mrs. Hillard came to a standing position when Thorne entered his office.

"Yes," he barked, and was instantly contrite.

"Mr. Jenning would like to talk to you when you have a spare moment." His secretary's gaze didn't meet his own and Thorne felt a twinge of guilt. He'd been abrupt with her, but it was tame in comparison to his treatment of Sheila. She'd been to see him first thing that morning and he'd hardly been able to look at her as the anger boiled within him. The woman had plotted to ruin his life. It was Sheila's fault that he couldn't locate Cindy. He'd said things to her that he'd never said to anyone. He regretted that now.

Perhaps he might have found it in his heart to forgive her, but she'd revealed no contrition. It almost seemed as if she were proud of what she'd done. He hadn't been the only one to lose his composure. Sheila had called Cindy the most disgusting names. Even now, hours later, Thorne burned with outrage.

In the end, he'd ruthlessly pointed at the door and asked her to leave. Apparently she'd realized her mistake. She began sobbing, ignoring his edict. Gently but firmly, he'd told her he planned to marry Cindy and nothing she could do would change his plans. Then, not knowing what else to do, Thorne had called for his secretary.

"Mrs. Hillard," he'd said, his eyes silently pleading with the older woman for assistance. "It seems Ms. Mathewson needs to powder her nose. Perhaps you could show her the way to the ladies' room."

"Of course."

Mentally Thorne made a note to give his secretary a raise. The older woman had handled the delicate situation with all the finesse of a United Nations ambassador. Tenderly she'd placed her arm around the weeping Sheila's shoulders, and with nothing more than a few whispered words she'd directed her away from Thorne's desk and out of his office.

In his office now, Thorne claimed his chair and unceremoniously looked over the phone messages. Having Paul Jenning ask to see him wasn't a good sign. Unless things went right with this merger, Thorne realized, it could set back his career five years. If only he knew how to contact Cindy....

"Have you been in *his* office yet?"

Cindy had no need to guess whose office Vanessa was referring to. Her co-worker hadn't stopped talking about Thorne from the moment Cindy had arrived for work. "Not yet."

"Will you go in there?"

"Vanessa, it's my job—nothing more and nothing less."

The other girl scooted her cleaning cart down the wide hallway, casting Cindy a worried glance now and then. "How can you be so calm? Aren't you tempted to plant a bomb in his top desk drawer or something? As far as I'm concerned, Prince is the lowest form of life. He's lower than low. Lower than scum. The pits of all mankind."

Cindy pressed her lips together and said nothing.

"You're taking this much too calmly."

"What do you want me to do?" Cindy said heatedly; she was quickly losing patience with her fellow worker.

"I don't know," Vanessa returned thoughtfully. "Cry, at least. Weep uncontrollably for a day or two and purge him from your system."

"It would take more than a good bout of crying to do that," Cindy mused. "What else?"

"I don't know what else." Vanessa looked confused. "I'd think you'd want to hate him."

Cindy wasn't allowed that luxury, either. "No, I can't hate him." Not when she loved him more than her very life. Not when she wished for his happiness with every breath she inhaled. Not when everything within her cried with thanksgiving for the short time they'd shared. "No," she repeated softly. "I could never hate him."

They paused outside Thorne's office. "You want me to clean it for you?"

"No." Cindy didn't need to think twice about the offer. From this night forward, this one office would be the only contact she had with Thorne. It was far too much—and not nearly enough.

"You're sure?"

"Positive."

The outer office, which Mrs. Hillard occupied, was neat as always, but Cindy brushed the feather duster over the top of the desk and around the edges of the typewriter. Next, she plugged in the vacuum cleaner. With a flip of the switch it roared to life, but she hadn't done more than a couple of swipes when it was abruptly switched off. Surprised, Cindy whirled around to discover Thorne holding the plug in his hand.

"Can't this wait?" he stormed, tossing the electric plug onto the carpet. "In case you hadn't noticed, I'm working in here."

Cindy was too stunned to react. It was obvious he hadn't looked at her. She was, after all, only the cleaning woman.

She turned, prepared to leave without another word, but in her rush, she bumped against the side of the desk and knocked over a stack of papers. They fluttered down to the carpet like autumn leaves caught in a gust of wind.

"Of all the, inept, stupid..."

Instantly, Cindy crouched down to pick them up, her shaking fingers working as quickly as she could make them cooperate.

"Get out before you do any more damage and I'm forced to fire you."

Cindy reared up, her eyes spitting fire. "How dare you speak to me or anyone else in that demeaning tone," she shouted. She had the satisfaction of watching Thorne's jaw sag open. "You think because you're Mr. Almighty Vice President that you can treat other people like they're your servants? Well, I've got news for you, Thorndike Prince. You can't fire me because—I quit!'' With that she removed the feather duster from her hip pocket, shoved it into his hand and stormed out of his office.

Chapter Eleven

Thorne moved quickly, throwing the feather duster
aside and hurrying out of his office. So this was Cindy's terrible secret. He had never been more relieved
about anything in his life. A flash of pinstriped coveralls and red bandana captured his attention in the
office across from his own and he rushed in.

"Cindy, you crazy idiot." He took her by the
shoulders, whirled her around and pressed her close to
hug the anger out of her.

She struggled, her arms ineffectively flailing right
and left, but Thorne wasn't about to set her free. Her
cries were muffled against his broad chest.

"Honey, don't fight me. I'm sorry—"

She gasped, braced her palms against him and
pushed with all her might until she broke free. If
Thorne had been surprised to find Cindy cleaning his

office, it was an even greater shock to discover the
woman he'd been holding wasn't Cindy.

"I'm not your 'honey,'" Vanessa howled.

"You're not Cindy?"

"Any idiot could see that." Disgruntled, she rear-
ranged her bandana and squared her shoulders. "Do
you always behave like an ape-man?"

"Where's Cindy?"

"And you're not exactly the love of my life, either," Vanessa continued sarcastically.

Thorne rushed from the office and down the hall,
stopping to search every room. Cindy was gone. Vanished. Frustration came at him like a charging bull.
This was the way it happened every time. Just when he
thought he'd found her, she disappeared, sending him
into agony until she happened to stumble into his life
again. No more. They were going to settle this craziness once and for all!

He rushed back to the other girl, braced his hands
against the doorway and shouted. "Where'd she go?"

"I don't know that I should tell you." Idly Vanessa
dusted the top of Rutherford Hayden's desk, obviously enjoying her moment of glory.

Thorne knotted his fists, growing more impatient by
the second. He wasn't going to let this saucy wench
keep him from his love. "Either you tell me where she
is or you're out of here."

"I wasn't all that keen to keep this job anyway,"
Vanessa claimed, and faked a yawn.

Thorne was inches from strangling her.

Vanessa sauntered to the other side of the office as
though she were a prima donna. "Do you love her?"

"Good Lord, yes!"

"If that's the case, then why was your engagement to another woman printed in the paper?"

"Sheila lied. Now, for God's sake, are you going to tell me where Cindy went?"

"You aren't going to marry this other woman?"

"That's what I just got through telling you. I want to marry Cindy."

Vanessa raised her index finger to her lips, as if giving the weighty matter consideration. "I suppose I *should* tell you, then."

If the woman valued her life, she would do so quickly.

"I was the one who brought Cindy your picture and told her you might be her prince."

"We'll name our first daughter after you," Thorne gritted the words between clenched teeth.

"Fair enough," Vanessa said with a sigh. "Take the elevator all the way to the basement, go to your left, then at the end of the corridor go left again, and it's the first room on your right. Have you got that?"

"Got it." Thorne took off, running. "Left, left, right; left, left, right," he mumbled over and over while he waited for the elevator. The ride to the basement had never seemed more sluggish, especially when he realized that he had to change elevators on the main floor. When he couldn't locate the service elevator, the security guard, Bob Knight, came to his aid.

Just before the heavy door glided shut, Thorne yelled, "We'll name one of our children after you, too!"

Cindy was too furious to think straight. She removed the coveralls and carelessly flung them into the laundry bin. "Can't you see I'm working in here," she muttered, sarcastically mimicking Thorne's words. The red bandana followed the coveralls, falling short of the bin, but Cindy couldn't have cared less.

"Cindy."

At the sound of Thorne calling her name, Cindy turned, closed the door and slid the lock into place.

Thorne tried the door, discovered it was locked, then pounded on it with both fists. "Cindy, I know you're in there!"

She pinched her lips together, refusing to answer him.

"Cindy, for God's sake at least hear me out."

"You don't need to say a word to me, Mr. Almighty Thorndike Prince." Dramatically she placed the back of her wrist to her forehead. "I suggest you leave before you do any more damage and I'm forced to fire you." She taunted him with his own threat.

"Cindy, please, I'm sorry, I had no idea that was you."

She reached for her jeans, sliding them over her hips and snapping them at the waist, her hands shaking in her hurry to dress. "I think you're . . . despicable. Vanessa was right. You are the lowest of the low."

"She'll have to change her mind. I just promised to name our first daughter after her."

"Oh, stop trying to be clever!"

"Cindy," he tried again, his voice low and coaxing, "hear me out. I've had a rotten day; I was convinced I'd never find you again and one thing after another has gone wrong. You're right, I shouldn't have shouted at you, but please understand, I didn't know you were the cleaning lady."

She rammed her arms into the long sleeves of her JETS sweatshirt and jerked it over her head. "It shouldn't have mattered who I was...you kept telling me that."

"And I meant it. If only you'd let me explain."

"You don't need to explain a thing to me...I'm only the charwoman."

"I love you, charwoman."

He was cheating, telling her that, knowing the effect it would have on her. Undaunted, Cindy threw open the door and faced him, arms akimbo and eyes flashing. "I suppose you love Sheila, too."

"No, I—"

"Don't give me that. Did you think I'm so socially inept, I wouldn't find out about your wedding announcement? I do happen to read the society page now and again."

"Sheila had that printed without my knowledge. I have no intention of ever marrying her. How could I when I'm crazy in love with you?"

That took some of the wind from her sails, and her temper went with it. She closed her eyes and bowed her head. "Don't tell me you love me, Thorne. I don't know that I'll be able to leave you if you do."

Thorne reached for her, astonished anew at how perfectly she fit into his arms and how right it felt to hold her. He held her close and sighed as a great relief moved through him. He had his Cindy, his princess, his love, and he wasn't ever going to release her again.

"That night was all a game," she mumbled. "I never dreamed...never hoped you'd come to care for me."

"The magic never stopped and it never will. You're mine, Cindy Territo."

"But, Thorne, surely you understand now why I couldn't let you know."

"Do you think it matters that you're employed by the janitorial department? I love you. I want you to share my life."

Cindy tensed. "Thorne, I'm frightened."

"There's no reason to be." His hand smoothed the curls at the back of her head in a reassuring motion.

"Are you crazy?" Cindy asked with a sobbing laugh. "Look at us."

Thorne blinked, not understanding.

"You're standing there in your five-hundred-dollar suit and I'm wearing bargain-basement blue jeans."

"So?"

"So! We're like oil and water: we don't mix."

Thorne smiled at that. "It just takes a little shaking up, is all. You can't doubt that we were meant to be together, Cindy, my very own princess."

"But, Thorne . . ."

He kissed her then, cutting off any further objection. His mouth settled firmly over hers; the kiss was both undeniably gentle and magically sweet. When he held her like this it was so easy to believe everything would always be this wonderful between them.

"I want to meet your family."

"Thorne, no." Cindy broke out of his arms, hugging her waist.

He looked stunned. "Why not?"

"Because—"

"I'll need to meet them sometime."

Her Uncle Sal's contorted, angry face flashed before Cindy. She knew he strongly disapproved of Thorne. If Cindy were to bring Thorne to the apartment, Sal would punch first and ask questions later. Any one of her uncles would behave the same way. Her family was highly protective of all their loved ones, and there would need to be a whole lot of explaining done before Cindy brought Thorne into their midst.

"Meet them?" Cindy repeated. "Why?"

"Cindy." He held her squarely by the shoulders. "I plan to marry you."

She blinked twice, overwhelmed with a flood of happiness and then immediately swamped with the backwash of doubts.

"You will be my wife, won't you?"

He asked with such tenderness that Cindy's eyes brimmed with tears. She bit her bottom lip and shook her head. "Yes..."

Thorne relaxed.

"No," she said quickly, then covered her face with both hands. "Oh, good grief, I don't know!"

"Do you love me?"

Her response was a vigorous nod.

"Then it's settled." He removed her hands from her face and kissed her eyes and her nose. Unable to stop, his lips descended slowly toward her mouth, nibbling along the way, pausing at her earlobe, working their way across the delicate line of her jaw....

"But, Thorne, nothing's settled. Not really. We...I need time."

"Okay, I'll give you time."

* * *

The organ music vibrated through the church. Cindy stood at the back of St. Anthony's and her heart went still as the first bridesmaid, holding a large bouquet of pink rosebuds, stepped forward. The second and the third followed. Cindy watched their progress, and her heart throbbed with happiness. This was her wedding day and within the hour she would experience the birth of her dreams. She would become Thorne's wife. Somehow they'd crossed every hurdle. She'd claimed she needed time. He'd given it to her. She was convinced her family would object, but with gentle patience Thorne had won over every member. Now it was June and almost six months had passed since the night of the Christmas Ball. Thorne had convinced her the magic of that night would last all through their lives, and finally Cindy could believe him. She hadn't thought it was possible to love anyone as much as she loved Thorne. There wasn't anything in this world their love couldn't overcome. They'd proved it.

Confident, Thorne stood at the altar, waiting for her. His eyes were filled with such a wondrous glow of tenderness that Cindy was forced to resist the urge to race into his arms.

His smile lent her assurance. He didn't look the least bit nervous, while Cindy felt as if a squad of bombers were about to invade her stomach. From the first, he'd been the confident one. Always so sure of what was right for them. Never doubting. Oh, dear Lord, how she loved him.

The signal for four-year-old Carla to join the procession came, and dressed in her long lavender gown, the little girl took one measured step after another.

Cindy stood at the back of the church and looked out over the seated guests. To her left were those who had loved and nurtured her most of her life. Her Aunt Theresa sat in the front row, a lace handkerchief clenched in her hand, and Cindy saw her dab away an escaped tear of happiness. Cousins abounded. Aunts, uncles, lifelong friends, Vanessa, Bob Knight and others who had come to share this glorious day of joy.

To her right was Thorne's family. Wealthy, cultured, sophisticated. St. Anthony's parking lot had never housed so many Cadillacs and Mercedes, nor had this humble sanctuary witnessed so many fur coats and expensive suits. But they'd come, filling the large church to capacity, wanting to meet the woman who was about to become Thorne's wife.

The organ music reached a climax of sound when Cindy stepped onto the trail of white linen that ran the length of the wide aisle. The train of the satin and lace dress that had been worn by both her mother and her aunt flowed behind her. The adrenaline pumped through Cindy's blood as she moved, each resounding note of the organ drawing her closer to Thorne, her prince, her love.

The congregation stood and Cindy experienced a throb of excitement as the faces of those she loved turned to watch her progress.

Thirty minutes later Cindy moved back down the same aisle as Thorne's wife. Family and friends spilled out of the church, crowding the steps. Cindy was repeatedly hugged and Thorne shook hand after hand.

The limousine arrived, and with his guiding hand at her elbow, Thorne led her down the steps and held open the car door for her.

Almost immediately, he climbed in after her.

"Hello, Mrs. Prince," he whispered, his voice filled with awe. "Have I told you today how much I love you?" he asked, and his eyes contained a tender glow.

"You just did that with a church full of witnesses," she reminded him softly. "I do love you, Thorne. There were so many times I didn't believe this day could ever happen, and now that it has, I know how right it is."

He gathered her in his arms and kissed her to the boisterous approval of their guests, who were still watching from the sidewalk.

"Did you see the banner?" Thorne asked, pointing to the outside of the church.

"No."

"I think Vanessa and the company had something to do with that."

Cindy laughed. There, above three double-width doors a banner was hung, the words bold and bright for all the world to read: CINDY AND HER PRINCE LIVED HAPPILY EVER AFTER.

* * * * *

SOME KIND OF
WONDERFUL

Debbie Macomber

To Dale Wayne Macomber,
who claims his mother never dedicates anything
to him.

What are little boys made of: Snails? Puppy dogs'
tails? Nope. Twelve-year-old boys are made of
football cards, dirty socks stuffed in a drawer, mag
bicycle wheels and stealing preteen girls' hearts.

Chapter One

"**O**nce upon a time in a land far away," Judy Lovin quoted in a still, reverent voice. The intent faces of the four-year-olds gathered at her feet stared up at her with wide-eyed curiosity. Hardly a whisper could be heard above her soft enunciation as Judy continued relating the fairy tale that had stirred her heart from the moment she'd first heard it as a youngster no older than these. It was the story of Beauty and the Beast.

Today, however, her thoughts weren't on the fairy tale, which she could recite from memory. As much as she'd tried to focus her attention on her job, Judy couldn't. She'd argued with her father earlier that morning and the angry exchange had greatly troubled her. To disagree with her father, a man she deeply loved and respected, was rare indeed. Charles Lovin was an outspoken, opinionated man who headed one of the world's most successful shipping companies. At the office he was regarded as a tyrant—demanding, but fair. At home, with his family, Charles Lovin was a kind and generous father to both Judy and her older brother, David.

Charles's Wedgwood teacup had clattered sharply when he'd placed it in the saucer that morning. "All those years of the best schooling and you prefer to work as a preschool teacher in a day-care center." He'd said it as though she were toiling among the lepers on a South Pacific island instead of the peaceful upper east side of Manhattan.

"I love what I do."

"You could have any job you wanted!" he'd flared.

His unprovoked outburst surprised Judy and she'd answered quietly. "I have exactly the job I do want."

His hand slapped the table, startling her. Such behavior was uncommon—indeed, unheard of—in the Lovin household. Even her brother couldn't disguise his shock.

"What good are my wealth and position to you there?" he roared. "Beauty, please..."

He used his affectionate name for her. She'd loved the fairy tale so much as a child that her father had given her the name of the princess in the timeless tale she'd read repeatedly. Today, however, she felt more like a servant than royalty. She couldn't recall a time when her father had looked at her in such a dictatorial manner. Swallowing a sip of tea, she took her time answering, hoping to divert the confrontation.

She was a gentle soul, like her mother, who had died unexpectedly when Judy was in her early teens. The relationship between father and daughter had grown warm and generous in the years that followed and even during her most rebellious teen years, Judy had rarely argued with him. And certainly not over something as trivial as her employment. When she'd graduated from the finest university in the country at the top of her class, she'd gone to work as a volunteer at a local day-care center in a poor section of town. She'd come to love her time with these precious preschoolers. Charles hadn't objected then, or when she'd been asked to join the staff full-time. Her pay was only a fraction of what she could make in any other job. After all these months, it seemed unfair that her father should object now.

"Father," she said, keeping calm. "Why are you concerned about the day-care center now?"

He'd looked tired and drawn out and so unlike himself that she'd immediately grown concerned.

"I'd assumed," he shouted, his expression angry, "that given time, you'd come to your senses!"

Judy attempted to disguise a smile.

"I don't find this subject the least bit amusing, young lady."

"Yes, Father."

"You have a degree from the finest learning institution this country has to offer. I expect you to use the brain the good Lord gave you and make something decent of yourself."

"Yes, Father."

"Try living off what you make taking care of other women's children and see how far you can get in this world."

She touched the edges of her mouth with her linen napkin and motioned with her head to Bently, who promptly removed her plate. The English butler had been with the family since long before Judy had been born. The servant gave her a sympathetic look. "Do we need the money, Father?" she asked quietly.

In retrospect, she realized she probably shouldn't have spoken in such a flippant tone. But to hear her father, it was as though they were about to be deported to the poorhouse or wherever it was people went when they became suddenly and unexpectedly destitute.

Charles Lovin completely lost his temper at that, hitting the table so forcefully that his spoon shot into the air and hit the crystal chandelier with a loud clatter startling them both.

"I demand that you resign today." And with that, he tossed his napkin onto his plate and stormed from the room.

Judy sat for a long moment as the shock settled over her. Gradually the numbness subsided and she pushed back her George II-style chair. All the furniture in the Lovin home had been in the family for generations. Many considered this a priceless antique; Judy considered it a dining-room chair.

Bently appeared then, a crisp linen towel folded over his forearm. He did so love ceremony. "I'm sure he didn't mean that, Miss." He spoke out of the corner of his mouth, barely moving his lips. It had always amused Judy that Bently could talk this way and she assumed he'd acquired his talent from years of directing help during dinner parties and other formal gatherings.

"Thank you, Bently," she said, grinning. "I'm sure you're right."

He winked then and Judy returned the gesture. By the time she arrived at the day-care center, she had put the thought of resigning out of her mind. Tonight when she returned home, her father would be his loving, kind self again. He would apologize for his outrageous temper tantrum and she would willingly forgive him.

"Miss Judy, Miss Judy!" Tammi, a lively youngster, jumped to her feet and effectively cut into Judy's thoughts. The four-year-old threw her arms around her teacher's neck and squeezed with all her might.

"That's a beautiful story."

Judy returned the whole-hearted hug. "I love it, too."

"Did Beauty and the Beast love each other forever and ever?"

"Oh, yes."

"Did they have lots of little beasts?"

"I'm sure they did, but remember that the Beast wasn't a beast any longer."

"Beauty's love turned him into a handsome prince," Jennifer exclaimed, exceedingly proud of herself.

Bobby, a blond preschooler with pale blue eyes, folded his arms across his chest and looked grim. "Do you know any stories about policemen? That's what I want to be when I grow up."

Judy affectionately rumpled the little boy's hair. "I'll see if I can find a story just for you tomorrow."

The youngster gifted her with a wide smile, and curtly nodded his head. "Good thing. A man can get tired of mushy stories."

"Now," Judy said, setting the book aside. "It's time to do some finger painting."

A chorus of cheers rose from the small group and they scurried to the tables and chairs. Judy stood and reached above her head to the tall cupboards for the necessary equipment.

"You know what I loved most about the Beast?" Jennifer said, lagging behind.

"What was that?" Judy withdrew an apron from the top shelf and tied it around her trim waist. Her brown hair fell in gentle curves, brushing the tops of her shoulders, and she pushed it back.

"I loved the way Beauty brought summer into the Beast's forest."

"It was her kindness and gentleness that accomplished that," Judy reminded the little girl.

"And her love," Jennifer added, sighing.

"And her love," Judy repeated.

"I have the report you requested."

John McFarland glanced up from the accounting sheets he was studying. "Put it here." He pointed to the corner of his beech desk and waited until his business manager, Avery Anderson, had left the room before reaching for the thick manila folder.

McFarland opened it, stared at the picture of the lovely brown-eyed woman that rested on the top and arched his brows appreciatively. Judy Lovin. He'd seen her pictures in the society pages of the *New York Times* several months ago, but the photo had done her fragile beauty little justice. As he recalled, the article had told about her efforts in a day-care center. He studied her photograph. She was lovely, but there were

far more beautiful women in the world. However, few
of them revealed such trusting innocence and subtle
grace. The women he dealt with possessed seductive
beauty, but were shockingly short of any heart. Seeing Judy's photograph, McFarland was struck anew
at the sharp contrast.

He continued to stare at the picture. Her doelike,
dark brown eyes smiled back at him and McFarland
wondered, for all that sweetness, if she had half the
backbone her father possessed. The thought of the
man caused his mouth to tighten with an odd mixture
of admiration and displeasure. He had liked Charles
Lovin when he'd first met him, and had been openly
challenged by him later. Few men had the courage to
tangle with McFarland, but the older man was stubborn, tenacious, ill-tempered . . . and, unfortunately,
a fool. A pity, McFarland mused, that anyone would
allow pride to stand in the way of common sense. The
U.S. shipping business had been swiftly losing ground
for over a decade. Others had seen it and diversified
or sold out. If McFarland hadn't bought them outright, he'd taken control by other channels. Charles
Lovin, and only Lovin, had steadfastly refused to relinquish his business, to his own detriment, it seemed,
McFarland mused. Apparently, leaving a dead and
dying company to his beloved son, David, was far
more important than giving him nothing.

McFarland's gaze hardened. Lovin was the last
holdout. The others had crumpled easily enough, giving in when McFarland had applied pressure in vary-
ing degrees. Miraculously, Lovin had managed to keep
his company. Word from the grapevine was that the
older man had been cashing in stocks, bonds and

anything else he could liquidate. Next, he supposed it would be priceless family heirlooms. It was a shame, but he experienced little sympathy for the proud man. McFarland was determined to own Lovin Shipping Lines and one stubborn old man wouldn't stand in his way. It was a pity, though; Lovin had guts and McFarland admired the man's tenacity.

Leafing through the report, he noted that Lovin had managed to take out a sizable loan from a New York bank. Satisfied, McFarland nodded and his lips twisted with wry humor. He was a major stockholder of that financial institution and several other Manhattan banks as well. He pushed the buzzer on his desk and Avery appeared, standing stiffly in front of the desk.

"You called, sir?"

"Sit down, Avery." McFarland motioned with his hand to an imposing leather wing chair. Avery had been with McFarland four years and he'd come to respect the other man's keen mind.

"Did you read the report?"

"Yes."

McFarland nodded, and absently flipped through the pages.

"It seems David Lovin is well thought of in New York circles," Avery added. "Serious, hard-working. Wealth doesn't appear to have spoiled the Lovin children."

"David?" McFarland repeated, surprised that he'd been so preoccupied that he'd missed something.

"The young man who will inherit the Lovin fortune."

"Yes, of course." McFarland had examined the Lovin girl's photograph and had been so taken with her that he hadn't gone on to read what was reported about her older brother. He did so now and was impressed with the young man's credentials.

"Many believe that if Lovin Shipping Lines can hold on for another year..."

"Yes, yes." McFarland knew all that. Congress was said to be considering new laws that would aid the faltering U.S. shipping business. McFarland was counting on the same legislation himself.

"Father and son are doing everything possible to manage until Washington makes a move."

"It's a shame," McFarland murmured, almost inaudibly.

"What's a shame?" Avery leaned forward to better hear his employer.

"To call in his loan."

"You're going to do it?"

McFarland studied his employee, amazed that the other man would openly reveal his disapproval. It wasn't often he was able to read Andersen's thoughts. To all the world, it would seem that McFarland was without conscience, without scruples, without heart. He was all those things and none of them. McFarland was an entity unto himself. People didn't know him because he refused to let anyone close. He had his faults, McFarland was the first to admit that, but he'd never cheated any man. His honesty couldn't be faulted... only his ethics.

He stood abruptly, placed his hands behind his back and paced the area in front of his desk. David Lovin was a fortunate man to have a heritage so richly blessed; McFarland knew nothing of his family. Orphaned at an early age, he'd been given up for adoption. No family had ever wanted him and he'd been raised in a long series of foster homes—some better than others.

McFarland had clawed his way to the top an inch at a time. He'd gotten a scholarship to college, started his first company at nineteen and been a millionaire by age twenty-one. At thirty-six, he was the one of the wealthiest men in the world. Surprisingly, money meant little to McFarland. He enjoyed the riches he'd accumulated, the island, his home, his Lear jet; money brought him whatever he desired. But wealth and position were only the by-products of success. Unlike those who had allowed their fortunes to become their all, McFarland's empire would die with him. The thought was a sobering one. Money had given him everything he'd ever wanted, but it couldn't give him what he yearned for most—love, acceptance, self-worth. A paradox, he realized somewhat sadly. Over the years, he'd grown hard. Bitter, too, he supposed. Everything in him demanded that he topple Lovin as he had a hundred other family businesses. Without regret. Without sentiment. The only thing stopping him was that damnable pride he'd recognized in Charles Lovin's eyes. The man was a slugger and he hated to take him down without giving the old boy a fighting chance.

"Sir, do you wish to think this matter through?"

McFarland had nearly forgotten Avery's presence. He nodded abruptly and the other man stood and quietly left the room.

Opening the doors that led to the veranda, McFarland stepped outside, braced his hands against the wrought-iron rail and looked out on the clear blue waves crashing against the shore far below. He'd purchased this Caribbean island three years earlier and named it St. Steven's Island. It granted him privacy and security. Several families still inhabited the far side of the island, and McFarland allowed them to continue living there. They were a gentle people and he'd never had a problem with any of them. On the rare occasions when he happened to meet the inhabitants, they ran from him in fear.

A brisk wind blew off the water, carrying with it the scent of seaweed. Briefly, he tasted salt on his tongue. Farther down the beach, he saw a lazy trail of foam that had left its mark on the sand, meandering without purpose into the distance. Sometimes that was the way McFarland thought of his life; he was without purpose and yet dominated by it. Another paradox, he mused, not unhappily, not really caring.

Unexpectedly, the decision came to him and he returned to his desk, again ringing for his assistant.

Avery was punctual as usual. "Sir?"

McFarland sat in his chair, rocked back and thoughtfully fingered his chin. "I've made a decision."

Avery nodded, reaching for his paper and pen.

McFarland hesitated. "I wonder how much that business means to that old man."

"By all accounts—everything."

McFarland grinned. "Then we shall see."

"Sir?"

"Contact Lovin as soon as possible and give him an ultimatum. Either I'll call in the loan—immediately—or he can send his daughter to me." He picked up the file. "I believe her name is Judy... yes, here it is. Judy."

Avery's pad dropped to the carpet. Flustered, he reached for the paper, and in the process lost his pen, which rolled under McFarland's desk. Hastily, he retrieved them both and, with nervous, jerky movements, reclaimed his place. "Sir, I'm... convinced I misunderstood you."

"Your hearing is fine."

"But... sir?"

"Naturally there will be several guarantees on my part. We can discuss those at a later date."

"Sir, such a... why, it's unheard of...I mean no man in his right mind..."

"I agree it's a bit unorthodox."

"A... bit, but surely... sir?" Avery stuttered, his jaw opening and closing like a fish out of water.

Watching, McFarland found him highly amusing. The man had turned three shades of red, each one deeper and richer than the one before. A full minute passed and he'd opened his mouth twice, closed it an equal number of times and opened it again. Yet he said nothing.

"What of the young lady? She may have a few objections," Avery managed finally.

"I'm confident that she will."

"But..."

"We'll keep her busy with whatever it is women like to do these days. I suppose she could redecorate the downstairs. When I tire of her, I'll set her free. Don't

look so concerned, Avery. I've yet to allow my baser
instincts to control me."

"Sir, I didn't mean to imply...it's just that..."

"I understand." McFarland was growing bored
with this. "Let me know when he gives you his decision."

"Right away, sir." But he looked as if he would have
preferred a trip to the dentist's office.

Judy returned home from work that afternoon,
weary in both body and spirit. She smiled at Bently,
who took her coat and purse from her.

"Is my father home?" Judy asked, eager to settle
this matter between them. If he felt as strongly as he
had that morning about her job at the day-care center, then she would do as he requested.

"Mr. Lovin is still at the office, Miss Judy."

Judy checked her watch, surprised that her father
was this late. He was almost always home an hour or
so before her. "I'll wait for him in the study," Judy
said. Something was worrying him; Judy was sure of
it. Now that she'd given pause, several matters didn't
set right. Whatever the problem was, Judy yearned to
assure him that she'd help him in any way possible. If
it meant her leaving the day-care center then she
would, without hesitation, but she was happy working with the children. Surely he wanted her happiness. Being a success shouldn't be judged by how
much money one happened to make. Contentment
was the most important factor and she was sure that
someone as wise and considerate as her father would
agree.

"In the study, miss? Very good. Shall I bring you tea?"

"That would be lovely. Thank you."

He bowed slightly and turned away.

Judy entered the library, which was connected to her father's study by huge sliding doors. She chose to wait among the leather-bound volumes and settled into the soft armchair, slipped off her pumps and placed her feet on the ottoman, crossing them at the ankles. The portrait of her mother, hanging over the marble fireplace, smiled down on her. Sometimes, when Judy had been much younger, she'd thought that Georgia Lovin could actually see her from that portrait. Judy would sometimes sneak into the room and talk with her mother. On occasion, she could have sworn, Georgia's eyes had moved. That was silly, of course, and Judy had long ago accepted that her mother was gone and the portrait was exactly that—a likeness of a lovely woman and nothing more.

Judy stared up at her now. "I can't imagine what got into Father this morning."

The soft, loving eyes appeared to caress Judy and plead with her to be patient.

"I've never known him to be in such an unreasonable and foul mood."

Her mother's look asked her to be more understanding and Judy quickly looked away. "All right, all right," she grumbled. "I'll be more patient."

Bently entered the study, carrying a silver tray. "Shall I pour?"

"I'll do it," she answered him with a smile, dismissing him. She reached for the pot. "Bently?"

"Yes, miss?" He turned back to her.

"Whatever happened to the Riordan sculpture that was on Father's desk?" The small bronze statue had been a prized piece that her father had loved. It had been on top of his desk for years.

Surprise rounded the butler's aged eyes. "I'm...not quite sure, miss."

"Did Father move it to his office?"

"That must be it."

"He'd never sell it." Judy was convinced of that. The Alice Riordan original had been a Christmas gift from her mother a few months before she died.

"I'm sure he didn't." The butler concurred and excused himself.

Now that she thought about it, there were other items missing from the house—a vase here and there; a painting that had disappeared. Judy hadn't given the matter much thought, but now she found it odd. Either her father had moved them to another location for safekeeping or they'd simply vanished into thin air. Even to entertain the notion that the staff would steal from the family was unthinkable. Bently, Cook and Anne had been with the Lovins for years.

Judy poured her tea and added a squeeze of fresh lemon. Bently had been thoughtful enough to bring two extra cups so that when her father and David arrived, she could pour for them.

She must have drifted off to sleep because the next thing Judy heard was the sound of gruff male voices. The door between the two rooms had been closed, but the raised impatient voices of her father and brother could be heard as effectively as if they were in the same room with her.

Judy sat upright and rubbed the stiffness from the back of her neck. She rotated her shoulders, intent on interrupting her father and brother and cajoling them into a cup of tea, but something held her back. Perhaps it was the emotion she heard in their voices—the anger; the outrage, the frustration. Judy paid little attention to business matters. The shipping line was her brother and father's domain, but it was apparent even to her that something was dreadfully wrong.

"You can't mean that you actually sold the Riordan?" David's astonished voice echoed off the paneled walls.

"Do you think I wanted to?" Charles Lovin returned, and the agony revealed in his voice nearly caused her heart to stop. "I was desperate for the money."

"But, Father..."

"You can't say anything to me that I haven't told myself a thousand times."

"What else?" David sounded worried and grim.

"Everything I could."

The announcement was followed by a shocked gasp, but Judy didn't know if it had sounded from her throat or her brother's.

"Everything?" David repeated, his voice choked.

"As much as humanly possible, without losing this house... and still it wasn't enough."

"What about Bently and the others?"

"They'll have to be let go."

"But, Father..."

"There's no other way," he cried. "As it is, we're still millions short."

Judy didn't know what was happening, but this had to be some mind-bending nightmare. Reality could never be this cruel. Her father was selling everything they owned. In addition to this estate, they owned homes all over the world. There were securities, bonds, properties, investments... Their family wealth went back for generations.

A fist slammed against the desk. "Why would McFarland call in the loan?"

"Who knows why that beast would do anything? He's ruined better men than I."

"For what reason?"

Her father paused. "Perhaps he enjoys it. God knows, I've been enough of a challenge for him. From everything I've been able to learn about the man, he has no conscience. He's a nobody; an orphan. I doubt that he had a mother. I've owned horses with better pedigrees than McFarland," he said bitterly. The next words were smothered, as though her father had buried his face in his hands. "...something I didn't tell you...something you should know...McFarland wants our Beauty."

"What?" David's shocked exclamation followed.

Judy bolted upright, her back rigid. It was apparent that neither her father nor David were aware she was in the other room.

"I heard from his business manager today. Avery Andersen spoke for McFarland and stated that either we come up with the amount of the loan plus the accumulated interest or send Judy to St. Steven's."

"St. Steven's?"

"That's the name of his private island."

"What does he want with... her?"

"Only God knows." The agony in her father's voice ripped at Judy's heart. "He swears he won't abuse her in any way, and that she'll have free run of the island, but..."

"Oh, Lord." David must have slumped into a chair. "So you were left to decide between a business that has been in our family for four generations and your daughter?"

"Those were exactly my choices."

"What... did you tell him?"

"You don't want to hear what I said to that man."

"No," David whispered, "I don't suppose I do."

"We have no option," Charles Lovin said through gritted teeth. "McFarland wins. I won't have Judy subjected to that beast." Heavy despair coated his words.

Numb, her whole body trembling, Judy leaned against the chair. Lovingly she ran her hand over the soft brown leather. This chair, like so much of what they owned, had been a part of a heritage that had been in their family for generations. Soon it would all be lost to them.

And only she could prevent it from happening.

Chapter Two

Judy's hand tightened around the suitcase handle as she stood on the deserted dock. The powerboat that had brought her to St. Steven's roared away behind her. She refused to look back, afraid that if she did, her courage would abandon her.

The island was a tropical paradise—blue skies, gentle breezes, virgin beaches and crystal clear water. Huge palm trees bordered the beach, swaying gently. The light scent of magnolias and orchids wafted invitingly toward her.

A tall man Judy guessed to be in his late forties purposefully approached her. He wore a crisp black suit that revealed the width of his muscular shoulders. His steps made deep indentations in the wet sand.

She'd only brought one suitcase, packing light with the prayer that her stay would be a short one. The single piece of luggage now felt ten times heavier than when she had left New York that morning.

Her father had driven her to the airport, where McFarland's private jet awaited her to take her to a secluded air strip. From there she was told it would be a short boat trip to the island. Tears had glistened in his faded blue eyes. He'd hardly spoken and when the moment came for Judy to leave, he'd hugged her so tightly she hadn't been able to breathe.

"Goodbye, Judy." His whispered words had been strangled by emotions. "If he hurts you..."

"He won't," she assured him and gently brushed the hair from his temple. "I'll be fine—and back home so soon you won't even know I've been gone."

A pinched, aged look had come over her father then and he'd whispered, "I'll know. Every minute you're away, I'll know."

Leaving her family hadn't been an easy task for Judy, especially when she felt as though she was being ripped from their arms.

After innocently eavesdropping on her father and David's conversation, Judy had openly confronted them. She would go to McFarland and they could do nothing to stop her. Her stubborn determination had stunned them both. She had refused to hear their arguments and had simply gone about packing. Within twenty-four hours she was on her way to St. Steven's.

She was here now, outwardly calm at least, and mentally prepared to do whatever she must.

"Miss Lovin?" The man asked politely, meeting her at the end of the pier.

Judy nodded, momentarily unable to find her voice.

"We've been expecting you." He reached for her suitcase, taking it from her hand. "Come this way, please."

Like a puppet on a string, Judy followed the muscle-bound stranger. He led her into the forest of trees to a waiting cart that reminded her of something she'd seen on the golf course. Only this one was far more powerful and surged ahead at the turn of a key.

When they came upon the house, Judy's breath became trapped within her lungs. The home was the most magnificent place she'd ever seen. It had been built on the edge of a cliff, nestled in foliage, and was adorned with Roman-style pillars and huge doors. Random clusters of tropical vines climbed the exterior walls, twisting their skeletal fingers upward.

"This way," the man said, standing on the walkway that led into the grand house.

Bemused, Judy climbed out of the cart and followed him through the massive doors. In the marble entryway she was met by a short, thin man. She identified him almost immediately as McFarland's assistant—the man she'd heard her father mention. He looked like an Avery—efficient, intelligent . . . bookish.

"Miss Lovin," he greeted her with an embarrassed smile. "I trust your journey was a pleasant one."

"Most pleasant." She returned his smile, although her knees felt like tapioca pudding. "You must be Mr. Andersen."

If he was surprised that she knew his name, he didn't reveal it. "Your rooms are ready if you'd like to freshen up before dinner."

"Please."

He rang a bell and a maid appeared as though by magic. The woman's gaze didn't meet Judy's as she silently escorted her up the stairs. The maid held open a pair of double doors that led to a parlorlike room complete with fireplace, television, bookshelves and two sofas. Off the parlor was a bedroom so lovely Judy stared in amazement at the lush blend of pastel colors. The view of the ocean from the balcony was magnificent. She stood at the railing, the wind whipping her hair about her face, and saw both a swimming pool and a tennis court. To her far right, she located another building that she assumed must be the stables. Her heart gladdened. She'd been riding almost from the time she could walk and thoroughly loved horses. Her cage was indeed a gilded one.

"Dinner will be in fifteen minutes," the maid informed her softly, speaking for the first time.

"Thank you," Judy answered formally. She squared her shoulders and her heart pounded faster. Soon she would be meeting the infamous McFarland—the man her father called the Beast.

But Judy was wrong. When she descended the stairs, armed with questions, to which she was determined to find the answers, she learned to her dismay, that she would be dining alone.

Mr. Andersen lived in a small house on the island and had departed for the day. McFarland had sent his regrets, but business prevailed. His brief note indicated he was looking forward to meeting her in the morning.

The dining-room table was set for eight with a service of the finest bone china. The butler seated Judy at the far end. The servants brought in one course after another, their footsteps echoing sharply in the silent chamber. Each course was delectable, but Judy ate little. Afterward, she returned to her room.

Her sleep was fitful as questions interrupted her dreams, each demanding an answer. Judy, unfortunately, had been given none. She wondered if McFarland was playing some kind of psychological game meant to intimidate her. If he was, then she had fallen an unwilling victim to his devilish plot. She knew little about McFarland—not even his given name. He was rarely seen in public and she had been unable to locate any pictures of him. Her father insisted he was arrogant, impudent, insolent, unorthodox and perhaps the worst insult—beastly.

What a strange place this was, she thought tiredly, staring up at the darkened ceiling. The house was built in a paradise of sun and sea and yet she felt a chill pervade her bones. It wasn't until early morning that she realized there was no joy here—no laughter, no fun.

By six, she couldn't bear to stay in bed any longer. Tossing back the covers, she rose and decided to head for the stables. She yearned to ride, to exorcise the fears that plagued her.

The house was like a tomb—silent, somber and gray—as Judy crept down the stairs. The front door opened without a problem and she slipped outside. The sun was rising, cloaking the island in golden threads of light.

A noise behind her caused her to twist around. A stranger on horseback was approaching her slowly. Even from a distance, Judy noticed that he sat tall in the saddle. A cowboy hat was pulled low over his eyes.

She hesitated. No doubt he was a security guard and from the way he regarded her, he either was looking for trouble or expecting it.

"Good morning," she called out tentatively.

He touched the brim of his hat in silent greeting. "Is there a problem?" His voice was deep and resonant.

"No...problem? Of course not."

His finely shaped mouth curved with amusement as he studied her from head to foot. A crooked grin slashed his handsome mouth.

Not knowing what else to do, Judy returned his look, staring back at those compelling blue eyes. She thought for a moment that he was silently laughing at her and she knotted her fists. Heated color worked its way up her neck, invading her cheeks. "It's a beautiful morning."

"Were you thinking of going for a walk?" He shifted his weight in the saddle and at the sound of creaking leather, Judy realized that he was dismounting. He took a step toward her, advancing in a pantherlike tread with inherent male power.

Before she was able to stop herself, Judy stepped backward in retreat. "No...I was heading for the stables. McFarland said I was to go anyplace I wanted on the island and...I thought I'd have someone choose a horse for me. Of course, I could saddle it myself."

Bold blue eyes looked straight into her startled, round ones. "I frighten you?"

"No...that's ridiculous." She felt like a stuttering fool. He didn't frighten her as much as he enthralled her. He radiated a dark energy with brooding eyes and the tall, lean build.

He grinned at her response and the movement crinkled the lines around his eyes, creasing his bronzed cheeks. "Relax, I'm not going to pounce on you."

She stiffened. "I didn't think for a moment that you would." Surely the help respected McFarland's guests—if she could call herself that.

"I'll walk you to the stables." He reached for the reins and the huge black stallion followed obediently behind them.

"Have you been on the island long?" she managed shakily, and attempted to smile.

"Three years."

She nodded, clenching her hands tightly together in front of her. This was the first person she had the opportunity to speak with and she was curious to find out as much as she could about McFarland before actually meeting him. In her mind she'd conjured up several pictures, none of them pleasant. She knew he had to be an unhappy, lonely man. Old, decrepit, cantankerous. "What's he like?"

"Who?"

"McFarland."

A muscle worked in his lean jaw and when he looked at her again, his eyes were dark and enigmatic. "Some say he's the devil incarnate."

Judy grinned and lowered her gaze to the ground. "My father calls him the beast."

"The beast," he repeated, seeming to find that amusing. "Some claim there's no compassion in him. Others insist he has no conscience, and still more believe he has no heart."

She glanced at the man's lathered, dusty horse and then at him. Pride shouted in the tilt of his strong chin and the set of his shoulders. Thoughtfully, she shook her head. "No," she said slowly, "I don't agree with that."

"You don't?"

"No," she repeated confidently. "He appreciates beauty too much. And if he didn't have a conscience he would have . . ." She hesitated for a second, and realized she was saying much more than she should to a mere security guard. McFarland could have ruined her father ten times over, but hadn't. The tycoon may not have a heart of gold, but he wasn't without conscience. Nor was he cruel.

"What do you think he's like? I take it you haven't met the man."

"I'm not sure how I feel about him. As you say, we haven't met, but from what I've seen, I'd guess that there's precious little joy in his life."

The man laughed outright. "Look around you," he said and snickered. "He's said to be one of the richest men in the world. How could any man have so much and not be happy?"

"Joy comes from within," she explained softly. "There's too much bitterness in him to have experienced true contentment."

"And who are you? Sigmund Freud?"

It was Judy's turn to laugh and she realized that she'd grown more at ease with this dark stranger. "No. I formed several opinions before I came to the island."

"Wait until you meet him, then. You may be pleasantly surprised."

"Perhaps." But Judy sincerely doubted it.

They arrived at the stables and were met by a burly fellow who ambled out to greet them.

"Good morning, Sam."

"'Morning," the other man grumbled, eyeing Judy curiously.

"Saddle Princess for Miss Lovin and see to it that Midnight is given extra oats. He deserves it after the ride I gave him this morning."

Judy turned abruptly. "How did you know my name?"

He ignored her, but his eyes softened slightly at her bemused, questioning look. "Tomorrow, saddle both horses at five-thirty. Miss Lovin and I will be riding together."

"Consider it done, Mr. McFarland."

Red-hot embarrassment washed over Judy. She dared not look at him.

"I'll see you at lunch, Miss Lovin."

It was all she could do to nod.

The morning passed with surprising speed. It had been months since Judy had last ridden and her body was unaccustomed to the rigors of the saddle. She hadn't gone far, preferring to investigate the island another day. A hot breakfast awaited her after she'd showered and she ate greedily. When she'd finished, she had written her father a long letter, then realized there was no place she could mail it. Presently, she lay back on the velvet sofa and closed her eyes, listening to music. The balcony doors were open and the fresh sea air swirled around her.

Someone knocked politely at her door. A maid had been sent to inform Judy that lunch would be served in ten minutes.

Experiencing both dread and excitement at once, Judy stood, repaired the damage to her hair and makeup and slowly descended the stairs. She paused at the bottom, gathered her resolve and painted a smile on her face, briefly wondering how long it would be before it cracked. She didn't expect to keep the cheerful facade long, but it was important to give McFarland the impression that she had been unruffled by their earlier encounter. She clasped her hands together and realized her palms were already damp in anticipation of the second meeting with the man who ruled an empire from this island.

He stood when she entered the dining room and recognized the determination in her eyes.

"I trust your morning was satisfactory," he said in polite, crisp tones.

Boldly, Judy met his probing gaze. "Why am I here?" She hadn't meant to hurl questions at him the instant she joined him, but his discerning look had unnerved her.

"I believe it's to eat lunch. Please sit down, Miss Lovin. I, for one, am hungry, and our meal will be served as soon as you're comfortable."

The butler held out the chair at the end of the table where she'd eaten the night before. With rebellion boiling in her blood, Judy sat on the brocade cushion of the mahogany chair.

A bowl of consommé was placed in front of her. When Judy lifted her spoon, she discovered that her hand was trembling and she tightened her grip.

"How long do you plan to keep me here against my will?" she said. Six place settings separated them; the distance could have been a football field for all the notice McFarland gave her.

"You'll be free to go shortly," he announced between courses, leaving her to wait a full five minutes before responding.

"I may leave?" She couldn't have been more surprised. "When?"

"Soon." He gauged her expression grimly. "Are you so miserable?"

"No," she admitted, smoothing the linen napkin across her lap. "The island is lovely."

"Good." His eyes gentled.

"Why do you hate my father?"

The question appeared to surprise him. "I don't. I find Charles Lovin to be a man of high moral character and principle."

Judy measured his words. "You like him then?"

"Let's say I respect him."

She hated to think what McFarland would do to a man he despised.

"Whose decision was it for you to come?" he asked unexpectedly.

"Mine."

He nodded and seemed to approve. "I imagine that your father and brother were opposed to your willingness to sacrifice yourself." He said this with more than a hint of sarcasm.

"Adamantly. I probably would never have been told of your...ultimatum, but I accidentally overheard them discussing it."

"You were wise to have come."

"How's that?"

"I wouldn't have hesitated to call in the loan."

"I don't doubt that for a second," she returned heatedly, disliking him. Her fingers gripped the smooth napkin in her lap, but that was the only outward sign of anger that she allowed herself.

His grin lacked amusement. "If you had refused, you'd have been burdened with a terrible guilt. In time, your peace and happiness would have been greatly affected."

The butler took away her untouched salad and served the main course. Judy stared down at the thin slices of roast beef, smothered in gravy and mushrooms, and knew she wouldn't be able to eat.

"Have you always been this dictatorial?" Judy demanded.

"Always." He sliced his meat slowly.

She thought of the class of four-year-olds she'd left behind. "You must have been one hell of a child." His teen years didn't bear contemplating.

Slowly, deliberately, McFarland lowered his knife and fork to the table. His eyes grew sober. "I was never a child."

Princess was saddled and ready for her early the following morning. Judy patted the horse's nose and produced a carrot from the hip pocket of her jeans.

"At great personal danger, I sneaked into the kitchen and got you this," she whispered, running her hand down the mare's brown face. "Now don't you dare tell Sam, or he'll box my ears." It hadn't taken Judy long to realize that Sam ruled the stables like his own castle and she could well be traipsing on the older man's toes.

"Do you have something for me as well?" The deep male voice spoke from behind her.

Judy whirled around to face McFarland. "No," she said, shaking her head. "I hope you don't mind..." She eyed the rapidly disappearing carrot.

He was dressed in black this morning, his expression brooding. Once again his hat brim shadowed his face. His mood was as dark and dangerous as his outfit. "You needn't worry about stealing vegetables."

Without another word, he mounted his horse with supple ease, causing the leather to creak and give with his weight. He hesitated long enough to reach for the reins and sent Judy a look that stated she was welcome to join him or go her own way.

Quickly, Judy placed her foot in the stirrup and swung her lithe frame onto Princess's back, grabbed the reins and cantered after him.

McFarland rode like the very devil, leading her deep into the jungle. The footpath was narrow and steep. Birds cawed angrily and flew out of their way, their wings beating against the underbrush. Leaves and branches slapped at Judy's face; mud spattered her boots and jeans. Still he didn't lessen the furious pace. It demanded all Judy's skill just to keep up with him. She barely managed. By the time he slowed, she was winded and her posterior was sorely bruised. He directed Midnight onto the beach and Judy gratefully followed, allowing Princess to trot along the sandy shoreline.

Judy stared at him. Panting, she was far too breathless to speak coherently. "Good—grief, Mc-

Farland—do you always tear—through the jungle like that?''

"No." He didn't look at her. "I wanted to see how well you rode."

"And?"

"Admirably well." he grinned, and his eyes sparkled with dry humor. Judy found herself involuntarily returning his smile.

"Next time," she said between breathless gasps, "I choose the route." Dark mud dotted her clothes and face. Her hair fell in wet tendrils around her cheeks and she felt as though they'd galloped through a swamp.

He, on the other hand, had barely splattered his shiny boots.

"Tell me about Judy Lovin," he demanded unexpectedly as they trotted side by side.

"On one condition. I want you to answer something for me."

"One question?"

"Only one," she promised, and raised her right hand as though giving an oath.

"All right."

She granted him a soft smile. "What do you want to know?"

"Details."

"All right," she said and nodded curtly. "I weighed just under seven pounds when I was born..."

"Perhaps current information would be more appropriate," he cut in.

Judy threw back her head and laughed. "All right. I'm twenty-four..."

"That old?"

She glowered at him. "How am I supposed to tell you anything if you keep interrupting?"

"Go on."

"Thank you," she muttered sarcastically. "Let me see—I suppose you want the vitals. I'm five five, short, I know, and I weigh about... No." She cast a look from the corner of her eye and slowly shook her head. "I don't think that's information a woman should give to a man."

He chuckled and Judy drew back on the reins, surprised at the deep rich sound of his amusement. His laugh was rusty, as if he didn't often give in to the urge.

He gave her an odd, half-accusing look. "Is something wrong?"

"No," she responded and shook her head, feeling self-conscious. He really should laugh more often, she thought. He looked young and carefree and less—she couldn't find the word—driven, she decided.

"What about men?"

"Men?"

"As in beaux, dating, courtship—that kind of thing."

"I date frequently." That was only a slight misrepresentation of the truth.

"Anyone special?"

"No—unless you consider Bobby; he's four and could steal my heart with a pout." She stopped Princess, swung her leg over the horse's back and slowly lowered her feet to the ground.

McFarland dismounted as well.

"My turn."

He shrugged. "Fire away."

"Your name." She thought it ridiculous that a man would be called McFarland—nothing less, nothing more.

"My name? You know that."

"I want to know your first name."

"Most people don't ask."

"I'm asking."

He hesitated long enough for her to become uneasy. "It's John."

She dropped her gaze to her mud-coated boots, testing the name on her tongue.

"Well?" he prompted, silently laughing at her. "Do you think it suits me?"

"It fits," she told him, her eyes serious.

"I'm glad to hear it," he said, mocking her.

"May I call you that?"

It seemed a lifetime passed before he finally answered. "If you wish."

"Thank you," she said humbly, and meant it. "You know, you really aren't a beast."

He frowned at that and brushed a wet strand of hair from her cheek. His fingers trailed across her face, causing the pit of her stomach to lurch at the unexpected contact.

"And you, my dear, are no Beauty."

Judy went cold, halting abruptly. "How did you know my father called me that?"

"I know everything there is about you. Right down to that Milquetoast you thought yourself in love with a couple of years back. What was his name again?

Richard. Yes, Richard. I am also aware that you've rarely dated since—disillusionment, I suppose.''

Judy felt the blood drain from her face.

"I know you fancy yourself a madonna of sorts to that group of four-year-olds. How very noble of you to squander yourself on their behalf, but I doubt that they appreciate it." His blue eyes were as cold as glacial ice.

Judy thought she might be sick.

He waited, his expression filled with grim amusement. "What, no comment?"

"None." She threw the reins over Princess's head. "Thank you for the ride, John, I found it quite exhilarating." Her chin held at a proud angle, she mounted and silently rode away, her back rigid.

McFarland watched her go and viciously slammed his boot against the sand. He didn't know what had made him speak to her like that. He'd known from the moment he'd seen her picture that she was like no other woman he'd ever encountered. Another woman would have spit angry words back at him for the unprovoked attack. Judy hadn't. She'd revealed courage and grace, a rare combination. McFarland didn't know if he'd ever seen the two qualities exemplified so beautifully in any one woman. Most females were interested in his power and his wealth. No one had cared enough to call him by his first name.

He didn't like the feelings Judy Lovin aroused in him. Studying her picture was one thing, but being close to her, feeling the vital energy she exuded, watching her overcome her natural reserve had all greatly affected him.

Judy was good—too good for the likes of him. He chewed up little girls like her and spit them out. He didn't want to see that happen to Judy.

What an odd position to be in, he mused darkly. He had to protect her from himself.

Chapter Three

Princess's hind feet kicked up sand as Judy trotted the horse along the virgin beach. Her thoughts were in turmoil. What a strange, complex man John Mc-Farland was. His eyes had been gentle and kind, almost laughing when he'd asked her to tell him about herself, and yet he'd obviously known everything there was to know about her. Her cheeks burned with hot humiliation that he'd discovered what a fool she'd made of herself over Richard. She'd been so trusting, so guileless with her affection and her heart ... so agonizingly stupid to have fallen in love with a married man. The pain of Richard's deception no longer hurt Judy, but her own flagrant stupidity continued to cause excruciating embarrassment.

Judy was so caught up in her thoughts that she didn't notice the children at first. Their laughter filled the cool morning air and she gently drew in her reins, slowing the roan's gait. As always, the gentle mare's response was quick and sure to Judy's lightest touch.

"Princess, look," she said, her voice filled with excitement. "Children." They were playing a game of hide-and-seek, darting in and out of the jungle and rushing to the water's edge. Judy counted seven children, all between the ages of eight and twelve, from what she could guess.

They didn't appear to notice her, which was just as well since she didn't want to disturb their game. The smallest, a boy, was apparently chosen as "it" and the others scattered, smothering their laughter as they ran across the sand.

Judy lowered herself from the saddle.

Her action must have drawn their attention because the laughter stopped abruptly. She turned around to find all the youngsters running to hide. Only the one small boy remained.

Judy smiled. "Good morning," she said cautiously, not wanting to frighten him.

He remained silent, his deep brown eyes serious and intense.

Digging deep into the pocket of her jodhpurs, Judy pulled out two sugar cubes. The first she fed to Princess, placing it in the palm of her hand and holding it out to the mare, who eagerly nibbled it up. The second sugar cube she held out to the youth.

He eyed it for a long moment before finally stepping forward and grabbing it out of her hand. Quickly, he jumped away from her. Holding it in his own palm, he carefully approached the horse. When Princess lowered her sleek head and ate the cube from his hand, he looked up and grinned broadly at Judy.

"She's really very gentle," Judy said softly. "Would you like to sit in the saddle?"

He nodded enthusiastically and Judy helped him mount the tall mare.

Astride Princess, the boy placed both hands on the saddle horn and sat up straight, as though he were a king surveying his kingdom. Gradually, one at a time, the other children walked out from their hiding places in the edge of the lush jungle.

"Good morning," Judy greeted each one. "My name is Judy."

"Peter."

"Jimmy."

"Philippe."

"Elizabeth."

"Margaret."

They all rushed toward her, eager to be her friend and perhaps get the chance to ride her beautiful horse.

Judy threw up her hands and laughed. "One at a time, or I'll never be able to remember." She laid her hand on the slim shoulder of one of the younger girls. "I'm pleased to make your acquaintance." She was rewarded with a toothless smile.

From the ridge high above the beach, McFarland looked down on the scene below, a silent witness to Judy's considerable charm. She was a natural with children, and although he shouldn't be surprised at the way they gravitated toward her, he was. More times than he could count, he'd come upon the island children playing in the surf or along the beach. Usually he saw little more than a fleeting glimpse of one or two running away as though he were the devil incarnate. To them, he probably was.

Until he'd watched Judy weave her magic over these simple children, McFarland hadn't given a second thought to the few families who made this island their home. He allowed them to remain on St. Steven's, not for any humanitarian reasons, but simply because his feelings toward them were indifferent. They could stay or leave as they wished.

Unfortunately, he couldn't say the same thing about Judy Lovin. The sound of her laughter swirled like early morning mist around him. As he watched her now with these children, an unwilling smile touched the hard edges of his mouth. He, too, was a victim of the magic she wove so carelessly across his island.

He didn't like it, not one damn bit.

Sharply pulling back Midnight's reins, McFarland turned the horse and rode toward the other side of the island as if the fires of hell were licking at his heels.

By the time Judy returned to the house, McFarland had already eaten breakfast and sequestered himself in his offices. Judy wasn't disappointed. She'd purposely stayed away in an effort to avoid clashing with him a second time that morning. The man greatly puzzled her and she didn't know how to react to him.

Feeling increasingly unsettled as the morning turned to midday, she ordered a light lunch and ate in her room. In the afternoon, she swam in the Olympic-sized pool, forcing herself to swim lap after lap as she worked out her confusion and frustration. She had no clue as to why McFarland had sent for her other than to torment her family, and she hated to think that he would purposely do so. If she'd understood him better, she might be able to read his motive.

Breathless from the workout, Judy climbed out of the pool and reached for her towel, burying her face in the plush thickness. As she drew the material over her arms and legs, goose bumps pricked her skin and she realized that she was being watched. A chill shivered up her spine and she paused to glance around. She could see no one, but the feeling persisted and she hurriedly gathered her things.

In her own rooms, Judy paced, uncertain and unsettled. Deciding what she would do, she sat at the large desk and wrote a long, chatty letter to her father and brother. The hallway was silent when she came out of her room. She hesitated only a moment before making her way down the stairs and into the wing of the house from where she suspected McFarland ruled his empire.

"Miss Lovin?"

Avery Andersen's voice stopped her short when she turned a corner and happened upon a large foyer. "Hello," she said with feigned brightness. "I apologize if I'm intruding."

Avery stood, his hands pressing against the top of his desk as he leaned forward. "It's no intrusion," he said, obviously ill at ease at her unexpected appearance.

Judy hated to fluster the dear man. "I have some letters I'd like to mail."

"Of course."

Judy raised questioning eyes to his. "They're to my family?" She made the statement a question, asking if there would be any objection. "Is there regular mail delivery to the island?"

"All correspondence is handled by courier."

"Then there wouldn't be any objection to my writing my father?"

"None whatsoever."

Judy hated to be suspicious, but Avery didn't sound all that confident, and it would be so easy for him to deceive her.

"I'll see to it personally if that will reassure you, Miss Lovin." McFarland's voice behind her was brisk and businesslike.

Judy blushed painfully as she turned to face him. "I'd appreciate that," she said, stammering slightly. The potent virility of his smile caused her to catch her breath. That morning, when riding, he'd been sneering at her and now she could feel her pulse react to a simple twist of his mouth.

"Thank you, John," she said softly.

"John?" Avery Andersen echoed, perplexed, but his voice sounded as though it had come from another room—another world.

"Would you care to see my office?" McFarland asked, but the sparkle in his deep blue eyes made Judy wonder if he was silently taunting her. She felt the same way the fly must have when the spider issued a similar invitation.

"I don't want to interrupt your day." Already she was retreating from him, taking small, even steps as she backed away from Avery Andersen's desk. "Perhaps another time."

"As you wish." His eyes gentled perceptively at her bemused look. "We'll talk tonight at dinner."

The words were as much a command as an invitation. Without question it was understood that she would be in the dining room when called.

Judy nodded. "At dinner."

By the time she closed the doors to her suite, her heart was thumping wildly. She attempted to tell herself she feared John McFarland, but that wasn't entirely true—the man was an enigma. Instead of gauging her responses by his mood, Judy decided she could only be herself.

She dressed for dinner in a skirt and blouse that had been favorites of her father's. Charles had claimed that the lovely pink and maroon stripes enhanced the brown of her eyes, reminding him of her mother.

At the top of the stairs, Judy placed her hand on the railing and paused. She was eager for this dinner, yet apprehensive. Her stomach turned over at the thought of food, but she yearned to know the man, "the Beast." Why he'd brought her to St. Steven's had yet to be answered. She had a right to know; she needed to know. Surely it wasn't too much to ask.

He was standing by the fireplace, sipping wine, when she entered the dining room. Once again she was struck by his virility. He, too, had dressed formally, in a pin-striped suit that revealed broad, muscular shoulders and narrow hips.

"Good evening, Judy."

She smiled and noted that he'd used her given name for the first time. A little of the tension drained out of her.

"John."

"Would you care for a glass of white wine before dinner?"

"Please." The inside of her mouth felt as though a field of cotton had taken root. The wine would help or it could possibly drown her sadly lacking wit. As he approached her with a full goblet, Judy was unsure if she should take it. His burning blue eyes had the power to sear her soul and they burned into her now. Without realizing what she was doing, Judy reached for the wine, gripping the slim base of the glass as though it were a life ring in a storm-tossed sea.

"Why do you hate my father?" she asked, the demanding words slipping from her mouth without warning as she met his bold gaze.

"On the contrary, I hold him in high regard."

Judy's eyes widened with disbelief.

"Charles Lovin has more grit than twenty men half his age."

"You mean because he's managed to hold you off against impossible odds?"

"Not so impossible," McFarland countered, before taking a sip of wine. "I did allow him a means of escape."

Judy digested his statement, baffled by his reasoning. "You wanted me on the island," she said softly.

"Yes, you."

It wasn't as though he coveted her company. In the two long days since her arrival, he'd barely spoken to her, indeed he seemed to avoid doing so.

"But why? What possible good am I to you?"

"None at all. I require no one." A hardness descended over his features then, and his eyes narrowed, steely and withdrawn, effectively shutting her out. His face revealed his arrogance and an overwhelming pride. A troubled frown creased Judy's brow. Pain filled her breast and she yearned with every womanly part of her to ease the hurt from his life. She longed to understand what made him the way he was.

Somehow, somewhere, someone cruel and heartless had mortally wounded John McFarland's tender spirit. From the torment revealed in his eyes, she knew the scars hadn't healed.

"Am I to be your slave?" she asked, without anger, her voice smooth and even.

"No."

"Y-your pet?"

"Don't be ridiculous," he shouted. "You're free to do as you wish."

"Can I leave?"

He gave a curt laugh then and took a sip of his wine. "You are here to amuse me."

"For how long?"

He shrugged. "Until you no longer do so."

Muted footsteps distracted Judy's attention to the manservant who stood just inside the dining room. He nodded once in McFarland's direction.

"I believe our dinner is ready. Chicken Béarnaise." He moved to her end of the table and held out her chair for her. Judy was grateful for the opportunity to sit down. Her legs felt as wobbly as cooked spaghetti. No man had ever affected her the way John did. He claimed he needed no one, and by all outward appearances he was right.

Once she was seated, John claimed the chair at the opposite end of the long table.

Without ceremony, Judy spread the soft linen napkin in her lap. "I happened upon some children today," she said conversationally after several tense moments.

"There are a number of families who live on the island."

"They're quite friendly. At first I wasn't sure they spoke English, but I soon realized that they speak it so fast that it sounds like a foreign language."

John smiled at that. "I haven't had the opportunity to talk to them myself, but I'll keep that in mind when I do."

"They asked about you."

"The children?"

"Yes, they call you the Dark Prince."

A brief smile flickered over his face. "The natives prefer to hide from me."

"I know."

Good humor flashed in his eyes as he studied her. Once again, she'd surprised him. He'd expected her to be outraged, spitting angry tirades at him, ruining his meal. Instead, she sat at the end of his table with the subtle grace of royalty when he knew she must be dying on the inside at his callousness.

"Since they call me the Dark Prince, did they give you a name?"

Judy hesitated and shifted her gaze. "I asked them to call me Judy."

"But they didn't."

"No." A dark color invaded her already flushed face. Swallowing became difficult.

"Tell me what they decided to call you."

"I—I'd prefer not to."

"Finding out would be a simple matter," he said in low, nonthreatening tones.

Judy found little amusement in her predicament. "They called me 'the Dark Prince's woman.' I tried to explain that I was only a friend, but it didn't seem to do any good. I know this probably embarrasses you, but I couldn't seem to change their minds."

The laughter drained from McFarland's eyes. He'd meant to tease her, mock her innocence, but she was concerned that these people, these nonentities who occupied his land, had offended him by suggesting she was his woman. He felt as though someone had delivered him a swift kick in the behind. He raised his eyes to her, studying her to be certain she wasn't taunting him, and knew in his heart it wasn't in her to insult man or beast. And he was both.

Their meal arrived and McFarland realized he had little appetite. "Do you like the island?" he asked, wanting to hear her speak again. The sound of her voice was soothing to him.

"It's lovely."

"If there's anything you wish, you need only ask."

"There's nothing." Judy felt unsure. His tone, his look, everything about him had changed. His mocking arrogance had vanished, evaporated into the heavy night air. No longer did he look as though he meant to admonish her for some imagined wrong, or punish her for being her father's daughter. She found it impossible to eat.

"Do you dislike the solitude?"

She searched his face, wondering why he cared. "It's not Manhattan, but I don't mind. To be honest, I needed a vacation and this is as close to paradise as I'm likely to find."

"You've napped."

She nodded, chagrined.

"You're to have complete run of the house and island."

"Thank you, John," she said humbly, "you've been very kind."

Kind? He'd been kind to trap her into staying on the island? Kind to have blackmailed her into leaving everything familiar in her life? He stared at her, not understanding how she could even suggest such a thing. Abruptly, he pushed his plate aside and stood. "If you'll excuse me, I have some business matters that require my attention."

"Of course."

He stormed out of the room then, as though she had greatly offended him. For a full minute, Judy sat frozen, uncertain of what had transpired between them. He had seemed to want her company, then despised it.

She, too, had no desire to finish her meal, and feeling at odds with herself, she stood. The evening was young and she had no intention of returning to her rooms. John had claimed that she could freely explore the house and she had yet to see half of it.

Judy never made it beyond the center hall. The doors were what had attracted her most. The huge mahogany panels stretched from the ceiling to the polished floor, reminding her of ancient castles. Unable to resist, she twisted both handles, pushed open the massive doors and entered the dimly lit room.

She paused just inside, and a sigh of pure pleasure slipped from her throat. A library, elegantly decorated with a handful of comfortable leather chairs, two desks and a variety of tables and lamps. Every available wall was filled with books. If she'd inadvertently stumbled upon a treasure, Judy couldn't have been more pleased. A turn of the switch bathed the room in light and she hurried forward to investigate.

An hour later, when the clock chimed, Judy was astonished to realize that she'd been longer than a few minutes. Reverently, she folded back the pages of a first edition of Charles Dickens's *A Christmas Carol*. Each book produced a feeling a respect and awe. Mingled with the classics were volumes of modern literature; one entire wall was dedicated to nonfiction.

With such a wide variety to choose from, Judy finally selected a science fiction novel by Isaac Asimov. She sat in the high-backed leather chair and read for an hour before slipping off her shoes and curling her feet beneath her. Suddenly thirsty, she went to the meticulous stainless-steel kitchen and made herself a cup of tea. Carrying it into the library, Judy returned to her chair.

McFarland found her there after midnight, sleeping contentedly in the chair, her legs curled beneath her. Her head was nestled against the upholstery with one arm carelessly tossed over her face. The other arm dangled limply at her side so that the tips of her fingers barely touched the Persian carpet. Transfixed, he stood there for a long moment studying her, unable to look away.

A tender feeling weakened him, and he sat in the chair opposite hers. For a long time, he was content to do nothing but watch her sleep. He wondered at the wealth of emotion she aroused in him. He knew it wasn't love; it wasn't even close. He felt protective toward her, and yearned to take away the troubles that plagued this young woman's life. Surprisingly, he wanted her to be happy.

She looked as innocent as a child, but was very much a woman. She was gentle and kind, angelic without being saintly. Honorable without being lofty. Generous without being benign. He'd never known a woman like her, and was suddenly shocked to find himself consumed with fear. He could hurt Judy Lovin, hurt her beyond anything she'd known in her life, hurt her more than Richard, who had stolen her trust and wounded her heart with his greed.

McFarland knew she would fall in love with him at the slightest encouragement. His conjecture wasn't based on ego, but on the knowledge that Judy, by nature, was giving and loving. If he were to ask, she would deny him nothing. His power over her frightened him, but that wasn't what stopped him from using her love. He wasn't any knight in shining armor. No, the simple truth was that Judy's control of him was more terrifying than any pleasure he would obtain in gaining her heart.

He thought about waking her and it seemed only natural to lean over and kiss her. Her lips would be soft and nimble under his. In his mind, he pictured her raising her arms and hugging his neck. She would smile at him and they'd stare at each other, uncertain of what to say. She'd blush in that special way she had that made her all the more beautiful, and her thick lashes would fan her cheek as she struggled to hide her feelings from him.

Forcefully, McFarland's fingers clenched the arm of the leather chair. He'd have a maid wake her and see her to her room. At this rate, he'd end up spending the night with her if he didn't leave.

She was just a woman, he reminded himself, and no doubt there were like a million others just like her. Who needed her? Not John McFarland.

* * *

"Midnight," Judy urged, standing on the bottom rung of the corral fence. "If you want it, you'll have to come to me." She held out the carrot to the prancing black stallion who snorted at her and pawed the ground.

"It's yours for the taking," she said soothingly. Winning the trust of the sleek, black horse had become paramount in the four days that had passed since the night she'd fallen asleep in the library. John had purposely been avoiding her; Judy was convinced of that. The only times they were together were at dinner, and he was always preoccupied with business, avoiding conversation and generally ignoring her.

Judy wasn't offended as much as bemused. At any moment, she half expected to receive word that he no longer required her presence on St. Steven's, or some other stiffly worded decree. She wouldn't mind leaving, although she would miss the children who had fast become her friends. She'd been on the island a week now and surely that was enough time to serve whatever purpose he warranted.

But she would miss the children. She met them daily now on the beach. They brought her small, homemade gifts; a flower pot and a hat woven from palm leaves, both cleverly done. A huge conch shell and a hundred smaller ones had been given to her with great ceremony. In return she told them stories, laughed at their antics and played their games. She met their mothers and visited their homes. She would miss them, but she wouldn't forget them.

"Midnight," she coaxed anew. "I know you want this carrot." If John wouldn't allow her to be his friend, then she'd work on the horse. Judy found several comparisons between the two; both were angry, arrogant and devilishly proud.

The horse remained in the farthest corner of the corral, determined to ignore her, just as John seemed determined to ignore her existence.

"I suppose all the women tell you how good-looking you are?" she said with a soft laugh. "But I'm not going to say that. As it is, you're much too conceited."

Midnight bowed his powerful head and snorted angrily.

"I thought that would get you." Jumping down from the fence, Judy approached the gate. "You're really going to make me come to you, aren't you?"

The stallion pranced around the yard, his tail arched and proud.

"You devil," Judy said, with a loud sigh. "All this time together and you're more stubborn now than when I started."

The horse continued to ignore her.

"What if I told you I had a handful of sugar cubes in my pocket?" She patted her hip. "Sweet, sweet sugar cubes that will melt in your mouth." As she spoke, she released the clasp to the gate and let herself inside the corral.

Midnight paused and stared at her, throwing his head to and fro. "You'll have to come to me, though," she said softly.

His hoof dug at the hard dirt.

"Honestly, horse, you're more stubborn than your master."

She took three steps toward the huge black stallion, who paused to study her. He jerked his neck, tossing his thick black mane into the air.

With one hand on her hip, Judy shook her head. "You don't fool me one bit."

Someone approached from behind her, but Judy ignored the sound of footsteps, suspecting Sam. He was bound to be angry with her. He'd told her repeatedly not to get inside the corral, but since Midnight refused to come to her, she had no choice.

"Don't move." John's steel-edged words cut through her. "If you value your life, don't move."

Chapter Four

Judy went still, her heart pounding wildly. She wanted to turn and assure John that Midnight wouldn't hurt her. She longed to tell him that she'd been working for days, gaining the stallion's trust. All her life she'd had a way with animals and children. Her father claimed she could make a wounded bear her friend. Midnight had a fiery nature; it was what made him such a magnificent horse. He'd been a challenge, but he would never purposely injure her. But Judy said none of these things. She couldn't. John's voice had been so cold, so cutting, that she dared not defy him.

The clicking sound behind her told Judy that Midnight's master had entered the corral. He walked past her and his clipped, even stride revealed his fierce anger. He didn't spare her a glance and from the hard, pinched look around his eyes, she was glad.

Midnight pranced around the corral, his eyes on the two invaders in his private world. His satiny black head was held high and proud, his tail arched, his feet kicking up loose dirt.

McFarland gave one shrill whistle to which the stallion responded without delay. Midnight cocked his head and galloped past Judy to his master's side, coming to an abrupt halt. He kicked the dirt once and lowered his head. With one smooth movement, McFarland gripped the horse's mane and swung his weight onto the stallion's back. Midnight violently protested against the unexpected action and reared, kicking his powerful front legs.

Judy sucked in her breath, afraid that McFarland hadn't time to gain control of the animal. She was wrong; when the horse planted his feet on the ground, John was in charge.

"Get out."

The words were sharp enough to slice through metal. He didn't so much as look at her, but then he didn't need to for her to feel his contempt and anger. Judy did as he requested.

McFarland circled the paddock a few times before swinging off the stallion's back and joining her at the corral gate.

"You stupid idiot," he hissed. He grabbed her by the shoulders and gave her one vicious jerk. "You could have been killed."

When he released her, Judy stumbled backward. Her eyes were wide with fear. No one in all her life had ever spoken to her in such a menacing tone. No one had dared to raise a hand to her. Now she faced the wounded bear, and was forced to admit that Charles

Lovin had been wrong; John McFarland was a beast no woman could tame.

"Who the hell let you inside the corral?"

Her throat had thickened, making speech impossible. Even if she had been able to answer him, she wouldn't have. Sam had no idea she'd ever been near Midnight.

"Sam!" McFarland barked the stable man's name with marked impatience.

The older man rushed out of the barn, limping. His face was red and a sheen of perspiration broke out over his forehead.

McFarland attacked him with a barrage of swear words. He ended by ordering the man to pack his bags.

Sam went pale.

"No," Judy cried.

McFarland turned on her then, his eyes as cutting as his words. He stood no more than a foot from her, his whole being bearing down on her as he shouted, using language that made her pale. Her eyes widened as she searched his face, attempting to hide her fear. She squared her shoulders with some difficulty. Her chin trembled with the effort to maintain her composure as she squarely met his cold gaze, unwilling for him to know how much he intimidated her.

McFarland couldn't make himself stop shouting at her. The boiling anger erupted like a volcano spitting fire. By chance, he'd happened to look out his window and seen Judy as she opened the corral gate. The fear had nearly paralyzed him. All he could think of was getting to her, warning her. A picture of Midnight's powerful legs striking out at her had driven him insane. He hadn't been angry then, but now he burned with it.

From her pale features, McFarland could see the shock running through Judy's veins as the pulse at the base of her throat pounded frantically. Still, the words came and he hated himself for subjecting her to his uncontrollable tantrum.

"Anyone who pulls an asinine trick like this doesn't deserve to be around good horseflesh," he shouted. "You're a hazard to everyone here. I don't want you near my stables again. Is that understood?"

Her head jerked back as though he'd slapped her. Glistening tears filled her eyes.

"Yes." She nodded weakly, signaling that she would abide by his edict.

She left him then, with such dignity that it took all his strength not to run after her and beg her forgiveness.

The air was electrified and McFarland rammed his hand through his thick hair. Sam stood there, accusing him, silently reprimanding him with every breath. The older man had once been a friend; now his censure scorched McFarland.

"I'll be out of here by morning," Sam muttered, and with a look of disgust, he turned away.

The remainder of the day was a waste. McFarland couldn't stop thinking of what he'd said to Judy and experienced more than a twinge of conscience. Lord, that woman had eyes that could tear apart a man's soul. When he'd ordered her to stay away from the horses, she'd returned his look with confused pain, as though that was the last thing she'd expected. He had wanted to pull her into his arms, hold her against his

chest and feel the assurance of her heart beating close
to his. Instead, he'd lashed out at her, attacked her
with words, unmercifully striking at her pride when all
he'd really wanted to do was protect her.

His vehement feelings shocked him most. He tried
to tell himself that Judy deserved every word he'd said.
She must have been crazy to get into a pen with an
animal as unpredictable as Midnight. He'd warned her
about him; so had Sam. Anyone with a brain in his
head would have known better. There were times when
even he couldn't handle that stallion.

Damn! McFarland slammed his fist against the
desktop. He couldn't afford to feel like this toward a
woman. Any woman, and most particularly Judy
Lovin.

As she came down the stairs for dinner that evening, Judy's stomach tightened and fluttered with raw
nerves. Her face continued to burn with humiliation.
She would have much preferred to have dinner sent to
her room and completely avoid John, but she had to
face the beast for Sam's sake.

"Good evening, John," she said softly, as she entered the dining room.

He stood with his back to her, staring out the window. He turned abruptly, his eyes unable to disguise
the surprise. From all appearances, he hadn't expected to see her.

"Judy."

They stood staring at each other before taking their
places at the elegant table.

Not a word was exchanged during the entire meal.
In all her memory, Judy couldn't recall a more awk-

ward dinner. Neither had much appetite; eating was a pretense. Only after their plates had been removed and their coffee poured did she dare to appeal to the man across the table from her.

"Although I would prefer never to speak of what happened this afternoon, I feel I must talk to you about Sam."

John took a sip of his coffee. His eyes narrowed slightly, affronted that she would approach him on a matter he was sure to consider none of her business.

She clenched her napkin and forced herself to continue. "If you make Sam leave the island you might as well cut off both his legs. St. Steven's is his home; the horses are his family. What happened wasn't his fault. He'd told me repeatedly to stay away from Midnight. If he'd known I'd gone into that corral he would have had my hide. I snuck in there when Sam wasn't looking. He doesn't deserve to lose everything because of me."

John lowered his cup to the saucer without speaking.

"You may be a lot of things, John McFarland, but I trust you to be fair."

He arched his brows at that comment. This woman had played havoc with his afternoon, caused him to alienate a man he'd once considered a friend, and now she seemed to believe that by pleading softly she could wrap him around her little finger.

"Sam leaves in the morning, as scheduled."

Without ceremony, she rose from her chair. Her eyes held his, round with disbelief. "I see now that I misread you. My judgment is usually better, but that isn't important now." With nothing more to say, she turned to leave the room. After only a few steps, she paused and looked back. "My father once told me something, but I didn't fully appreciate his wisdom until this moment. He's right. No man is so weak as one who cannot admit he's wrong."

By the time she reached her rooms, Judy discovered she was shaking. She sat on the edge of her mattress and closed her eyes. The disillusionment was almost more than she could bear. She'd been wrong, very wrong about John McFarland. He was a wild, untamable beast—the most dangerous kind of animal...one without a heart.

Several hours passed, and although John had forbidden her to go near the stables again, Judy couldn't stay away. She had to talk to Sam, tell him how deeply sorry she was.

She changed from her dress into shorts and a light T-shirt. As usual the house was silent as she slipped down the stairs and out the front door.

Even the night seemed sullen and disenchanted. The air was still and heavy, oppressive. The area around the house was well lit, but the stable was far enough away to be enveloped in heavy shadows. The moon shone dimly.

As Judy walked along the path that led to the stables, she felt a chill invade her limbs. She longed for home and the comfort of familiarity. Folding her arms around her middle, she sighed. She tried not to think about how long John intended to keep her on the island. Surely he would send her away soon. After the incident with Midnight, he would be eager to be rid of her. She was a thorn in his side—a festering one.

Not for the first time did she feel like an unwelcome stranger to the island. Although she'd done everything possible to make the best of the situation, she was still John's prisoner. In the days since her arrival, she'd struggled to create some normalcy in her life. She had begun to feel at ease. Now that had changed. Without access to Princess, she wouldn't be able to see the children as frequently and with Sam's dismissal, the servants would avoid her, fearing they, too, would lose their positions. Loneliness would soon overwhelm her.

The door to the stable was open, revealing the silhouette of Sam's elongated shadow. His actions were quick and sure and Judy strained her ears, thinking she heard the soft trill of his whistle.

"Evening, Sam," she said, pausing just inside the open doorway."

"Miss Lovin." His eyes brightened with delight, then quickly faded as he glanced around. "Miss Lovin, you shouldn't be here . . ."

"I know," she said gently, interrupting him. "I came to tell you how sorry I am."

He shrugged his thick shoulders, seemingly unconcerned. "Don't you bear that any mind. It's all taken care of now."

The words took a moment to sink into Judy's bemused mind. "You mean you aren't leaving?"

Sam rubbed the side of his jaw and cocked his head. "I've never known Mr. McFarland to change his mind. A man doesn't become as wealthy as that one without being decisive. I knew I'd done wrong to let you get close to that stallion—I figured I deserved what I got. Can't say that I agree with the way he flayed into you, though, you being a lady and all, but you took it well."

"You aren't leaving the island?" Judy repeated, still not convinced she could believe what she was hearing.

"No. Mr. McFarland came to me, claimed he was wrong and that he'd overreacted. He asked me personally to stay on. I don't mind telling you I was surprised."

If Sam was surprised, Judy was astonished. She felt warm and wonderful. The sensation was so strong that she briefly closed her eyes. She hadn't misjudged John. He was everything she believed and a thousand times more.

"Mr. McFarland's here now," Sam continued, his voice low. "Midnight's still in the corral and he went out there. I don't suppose you saw him or you wouldn't be here." The man who ruled the stables removed his hat and wiped his forehead with the back of his hand, then he gave Judy a sheepish grin. "He didn't say anything to me about letting you in the stables again."

"I'll leave," she said, unable to hold back a smile. Sam was back in John's good graces, and she had become a threat.

The older man paused and looked around him before whispering, "You come see me anytime you want. Princess will miss you if you don't bring her a carrot every now and again."

Judy laughed and gently laid her hand upon his forearm. "Thank you, Sam."

His grin was off center, but she was grateful that she could count him as her friend.

Judy left the barn, intent on escaping before John discovered her presence. Her world had righted itself and there was no reason to topple it again so soon.

She was halfway to the house when she changed her mind, realizing how much she wanted to thank John. Like his stallion, John was dangerous and unpredictable. He was different from any man she'd ever known, and it frightened her how much she wanted to be with him. How much she wanted to thank him for not firing Sam.

John's shadow moved in and out of the dim moonlight as she approached. As Sam had claimed, he stood by the corral, one booted foot braced against the bottom rung, his arms looped over the top. The red tip of his cigarette glowed in the night, which surprised Judy since she'd never seen him smoke.

A moment later she joined him. "It's a lovely night, isn't it?" she said, tentatively leaning against the fence, searching for something to say.

McFarland tensed, his face hard and unyielding. He avoided looking at her. "There's a storm brewing."

"No," she countered with a soft smile. "The storm has passed."

He gave a low, self-mocking laugh. "I asked you to stay away from here."

"I won't come again if you wish."

What he did wish would have shocked her all the way to those dainty feet of hers, just as it had shocked him. He liked his women spicy and hot; Judy Lovin was sweet and warm.

"I'd like to show you something," she said, breaking into his thoughts. "But I need your trust."

He didn't answer her one way or the other. All evening he'd been toying with the idea of sending her back to her family and he was at a loss to understand why the idea no longer appealed to him. The woman had become a damn nuisance. She forced him to look deep within himself; she plagued his dreams and haunted his days. He hadn't had a moment's peace since she'd stepped onto the island.

"John, will you trust me for one moment?"

He tossed the half-smoked cigarette on the ground and smashed it with his boot. A muscle locked in his jaw and he turned his head slightly.

Standing on the bottom rung of the corral, she gave a shrill whistle that was an imitation of the one John had used earlier that day to attract Midnight's attention.

The stallion snorted once, jerked his head and casually walked over to her.

"Here, boy," she said, patting his nose and rubbing her hands and face over his as he nuzzled her with the affection of a lifelong friend. "No, I don't have any sugar cubes with me now, but I will another day. I wanted to show your master that we're friends."

Midnight gave a soft whinny and seemed to object when she stepped down and moved away.

McFarland wouldn't have been any more shocked if she'd pulled out a six-shooter and fired on him. She'd made Midnight look as tame as a child's pony. His throat tightened.

"I was never in any real danger," she explained in a low, gentle voice. "Midnight and I are friends. Most of his stubborn arrogance is show. It's expected of him and he likes to live up to his reputation."

"When?" McFarland growled.

"I've been working with him in the afternoons. We made our peace two days ago. He would even let me ride him if I wished, but he's your horse and I wouldn't infringe."

Why the hell not? She had infringed on everything else in his life! His peace of mind had been shot from the minute she'd turned those incredible eyes on him. She'd accused him of weakness in a voice as soft as an angel's, and condemned him with the noble tilt of her chin. She'd faced his angry tirade with a grace that had wounded his heart.

Without a word, he left her standing at the corral, not trusting himself to speak.

Hours later, unable to sleep, McFarland looked around his still bedroom. He didn't know what to make of Judy Lovin; she could be either demon or angel. She tamed wild animals, was beloved by children and caused his cynical heart to pound with desires that were only a little short of pure lust.

The maid woke Judy early the next morning just as dawn dappled the countryside.

"Mr. McFarland is waiting for you, miss."

Judy sat up in bed and rubbed the sleep from her eyes. "Mr. McFarland?"

"He's at the stables, miss."

"He wants me to go riding with him?"

"I believe so, miss."

With a surge of energy, Judy tossed back the covers and climbed out of bed. "Could you please tell him I'll be there in ten minutes?"

"Right away, miss."

Judy was breathless by the time she arrived at the stables. Princess was saddled and waiting for her; Midnight stood at the roan's side. John appeared from inside the barn.

"Good morning," she said brightly. He was dressed in black again, his eyes a deep indigo blue. "It's a glorious morning, isn't it?"

"Glorious," he echoed mockingly.

She decided to ignore his derision. The earth smelled fresh in the aftermath of the night's storm. The dew-drops beaded like sparkling emeralds on the lush foliage.

"Are you ready?" McFarland asked as he mounted.

"Any time." She swung her weight onto Princess's back.

As he had the first time she'd ridden with him, John rode like the very devil. Judy was able to keep pace with him, but by the time they reached the far side of the island, she was exhausted from the workout.

He slowed their pace and they trotted side by side on the flawless beach.

"You never cease to amaze me," he said, studying her. He'd ridden hard and long, half expecting her to fall behind, almost wishing she had.

"Me? I find you astonishing. Do you always ride like that?"

"No," he admitted sheepishly.

"You must have been born in the saddle."

"Hardly. I'd made my first million before I ever owned a horse."

"When was that?"

A slow, sensual smile formed as he glanced in her direction. "You're full of questions today, aren't you?"

"Does it bother you?"

He stared at her, bemused. "No, I suppose not."

"I imagine you had a colorful youth."

He laughed outright at that. "I'd been arrested twice before I was thirteen."

"Arrested?" Her eyes rounded.

"I thought that would shock you."

"But why?"

"I was a thief." He threw back his head and laughed. "Some say I still am."

Judy dismissed his joking with a hard shake of her head. "I don't believe that. You're an honorable man. You wouldn't take anything that didn't belong to you without a reason."

Her automatic defense of him produced a curious ache deep in his chest. There had been a reason—a damn good one. Someone had tried to cheat him. In like circumstances, he would respond identically. He wasn't bad, but in all his life, only one man had ever believed in him. From grade school, he'd been branded a renegade, a hellion. He'd been all that and more. He wouldn't be where he was today if he hadn't been willing to gamble. He had had to be tough, and God knew he was.

When he didn't respond, Judy sought his gaze. The look in his eyes made her ache inside. He wore the wounds of his past like medals of valor, but the scars were etched deep in his heart.

"What about you?" he taunted. "Haven't you ever done anything wrong?"

"You mean other than falling in love with a married man?"

The pain was so clear in her eyes that McFarland was ashamed to have asked the question.

"Actually, I have," she returned, recovering quickly. "I may not have been arrested but I could have been."

He arched both brows.

"Actually, I'm a thief, too, but I was smart enough not to get caught." She laughed outright, slapped the reins against Princess's neck and sped off, leaving a cloud of sand in her wake.

McFarland caught up with her easily.

She turned and smiled at him, her brown eyes sparkling. Dismounting, she brushed the wind-tossed hair from her face and stared into the sun. "I love this island. I love the seclusion and the peacefulness. No wonder you had to have it."

McFarland joined her on the beach. He knew he was going to kiss her, knew he'd regret it later, but he was past caring. He touched her shoulder and turned her so that she faced him, giving her ample opportunity to stop him if she wished.

Judy didn't. Her pulse surged as his mouth moved to cover hers.

His arms went around her, bringing her close as one hand moved up and down her spine, molding her to him. Her breasts grazed his chest and he groaned and dragged his mouth away. She tasted like paradise and now that he'd sampled her sweetness he didn't know how he could avoid wanting more. "I wish I hadn't done that," he said with a moan.

"I'm glad you did," she whispered.

"Dear God, don't tell me that."

"Yes..."

She wasn't allowed to finish as he cupped her face and kissed her again hungrily, unable to get enough of her. Sensuously, he rubbed his mouth back and forth over her moist lips until she groaned and leaned against him, letting him absorb her weight. He drew her so close their bodies were pressed full length against each other. He could feel the rise and fall of her softness against him as he lowered his hands and restlessly explored her back.

His fingers became tangled in her hair as he kissed her hard, his tongue greedily invading her mouth. He felt the tremor work its way through her at the unexpected intimacy and heard the soft sounds of passion that slid from her throat.

Instantly, he sobered, breaking off the kiss.

Judy sagged against him and released a long breath, pressing her forehead against his hard chest. "You kiss the same way you ride."

McFarland slowly rubbed his chin against the top of her head as a lazy smile touched the corners of his mouth. She made him tremble from the inside out. He'd been right the first time, he shouldn't have let this happen. He should have found the strength to resist. Now that he'd held her, now that he'd tasted her, there was no turning back.

"John?"

He wanted to blame her for what she did to him, punish her for dominating his thoughts and making him hunger for her touch, but his rage was directed solely at himself. It wasn't in him to lash out at her again, not for something she didn't deserve.

"I shouldn't have said those things."

"I know," she whispered, intuitively knowing he was talking about Midnight. "I understand."

"Why didn't you say something?"

"I couldn't—you were too angry. I'd frightened you."

He looped his arm around her shoulder. He should be begging for forgiveness, but all she seemed to do was offer excuses for him. "I want to make it up to you."

"There's no need. It's forgotten."

"No," he said forcefully. "I won't pass it off as lightly as that. Anything you want is yours. Just name it."

She went still.

"Except leaving the island." There must be a thousand things she longed to own, he thought. Jewels, land, maybe stocks and bonds. He would give them to her, he'd give her anything she asked for.

"John, please, there's no need. I . . ."

"Name it." His eyes hardened.

She bit the corner of her lower lip, realizing it would do little good to argue. He was making amends the only way he knew how—with money. "Anything?"

He nodded sharply.

"Then I want the school on the island remodeled. It's run down and badly in need of repairs and unsafe for the children."

Chapter Five

Paulo, a gleeful year-old baby, rested on Judy's hip as though he'd been permanently attached. Other children followed her around the cluster of homes as though she were royalty. The small party walked to the outskirts of the school yard, where the workers were busily constructing the new schoolhouse.

"Mr. McFarland told me the school will be ready by the end of the month," Judy told the children. The building had gone up so quickly that it had astonished Judy and the islanders. The day after she had made her request, a construction crew had arrived, followed quickly by several shiploads of building supplies. Judy shuddered to think of the expense, but John hadn't so much as blinked when she said she wanted a school. And when John McFarland ordered something constructed, there were no delays.

Paulo's mother joined Judy and the other children. The baby gurgled excitedly, stretched out his arms and leaned toward his mother. Judy gave him a kiss and handed him over.

"Paulo likes you."

"As long as his mother isn't around," Judy responded with a soft laugh.

"The children are very happy," the shy mother added, looking toward the school.

"Don't thank me. Mr. McFarland is having it built, not me."

"But you're his woman and you're the one who told him of our need."

Judy had long since given up explaining that she wasn't John's "woman," although the thought wasn't as objectionable as when she'd first arrived. In the weeks since she'd first come to St. Steven's, her attitude toward John had altered dramatically. He was the beast her father claimed; Judy had seen that side of him on more than one occasion. But he possessed a gentleness, too, a loving-kindness, that had touched her heart.

Now that she knew him better, she hoped to understand his idiosyncrasies. He'd told her so little of his life, but from what she'd gleaned, he'd been abandoned at an early age and raised in a series of foster homes. A high-school teacher had befriended him, encouraged his talents and helped him start his first business. Although the teacher had died before John had achieved his financial empire, the island had been named after him—Steven Fischer.

Since the kiss they'd shared that early morning, Judy's relationship with John had altered subtly. As before, he didn't seek out her company and the only time that she could count on being with him was at dinner. She was allowed to take Princess whenever she wished, but the invitation to ride with John had come only twice. He treated her with the politeness due a houseguest, but avoided any physical contact, which told her that he regretted having kissed her.

Judy didn't regret it. She thought about that morning often, relived it again and again, fantasizing, wishing it hadn't ended so quickly.

Letters from her family arrived regularly now. Both her father and her brother worried about her, but Judy frequently assured them she was happy, and to her surprise, realized it was the truth. She missed her old life, her family and her home, but she kept them close in her heart and didn't dwell on the separation.

John had given no indication as to when she could return and she hadn't asked. For now she was content.

After spending the morning with the children, Judy returned to the house, wearing a wreath of flowers on her head like a crown. The children and Paulo's mother had woven it especially for her and she'd been touched by their generosity.

Since it was an hour until lunch, Judy decided to write her family and give John the letter at lunch. The library doors were open and beckoned her inside. Judy walked into the room.

McFarland sat at the desk, writing.

"John," she whispered, surprised. "I'm sorry, I didn't mean to intrude."

He glanced up and the heavy frown that creased his forehead relaxed at the sight of her. She wore a simple yellow sundress with a halo of flowers upon her thick, dark hair, and looked so much like a visitation of some heavenly being that he couldn't pull his eyes away from her.

"You didn't disturb me," he assured her.

"It's a fantastic morning," she said eagerly, seeking a topic to carry the conversation.

In the weeks since her arrival, Judy had acquired a rich, golden tan. Her healthy glow mesmerized him. "Beauty" did little to describe this woman, whose charm and winsome elegance had appealed so strongly to his heart. McFarland had never known anyone like her. Her gentle goodness wasn't a sugar coating that disguised a greedy heart. Judy Lovin was pure and good; her simple presence humbled him.

The memory of the one kiss they'd shared played havoc with his senses. He'd avoided touching her since, doing his utmost to appear the congenial host. The sweetest torment he'd ever endured was having her close and not making love to her. He feared what would happen if he kissed her again, and yet the dream of doing so plagued his sleep.

He had planned to return Judy to her family before now, but couldn't bring himself to do so. He was at odds with himself, realizing that it was inadvisable to continue to keep her on the island with him. If she'd revealed some signs of being unhappy and asked to return to New York, he would allow it, but Judy showed no desire to leave and he selfishly wished to keep her with him despite her family's constant pleading.

"I spent the morning with the children," Judy said, still only a few steps inside the room. "They're excited about the school."

John nodded, unconcerned. "Did they give you the flowers?"

She raised tentative fingers to her head, having forgotten about the orchid wreath. "Yes, the children are clever, aren't they?" Out of the corner of her eye, she caught sight of an elaborate chess set. When he didn't respond to her first question, she asked another. "Do you play?"

McFarland's gaze followed her own. "On occasion."

"Are you busy now?"

He glanced at his watch, more for show than anything. He was always busy, but not too busy to torture himself with her. "Not overly so."

"Shall we play a game, then?" She longed for his company. "That is, if it wouldn't be an intrusion."

His gaze held hers and it wasn't in him to refuse her anything. "All right," he agreed.

Her warm smiled rivaled the most glorious sunrise. "Good," she said, and brought the chess set to the desk and pulled up a chair to sit opposite him.

"Shall we make it interesting?" McFarland asked, leaning forward.

"Money?"

He grinned. "No."

"What then?"

"Let the winner decide."

"But..."

"How good are you?"

Judy dropped her gaze to the board. "Fair. If I lose, what would you want from me?"

Oh, Lord, what a question. The possibilities sent his blood pressure soaring. He wanted her heart and her soul, but not nearly half as much as he wanted to feel her sweet body beneath his own. The image clawed at his mind and nagged at his senses. He'd be her first lover; that alone was enough to force him to rein his desire.

"John?"

"What would I want?" he repeated hurriedly. "I don't know. Something simple. What about you; what would you want?"

Her bubbly laughter echoed off the book-lined walls in dulcet tones. "Something simple."

His eyes softened as he studied her. Afraid that he would be caught staring, McFarland tried to look away and discovered her eyes held his as effectively as a vise. A man would be tempted to sell his soul for her smile.

"It's your move."

McFarland forced his attention to the board, unaware that she'd placed her pawn into play. "Right." He responded automatically, sliding his own man forward.

By the sheer force of his will, he was able to concentrate on the game. Her technique was straightforward and uncomplicated and a few moves later, he determined that she revealed a weak strategy. He should be able to put her in checkmate within ten to fifteen minutes, but he wasn't sure he wanted to. If he were to lose, albeit deliberately, then he'd be obligated to give her "something simple." He thought about how she'd look in a diamond necklace and doubted that the jewels could compete with her smile. Emeralds would draw out the rich color of her deep brown eyes, but no necklace could do her eyes justice. A sapphire broach perhaps. No, not jewels. Furs...

"John? It's your turn."

Slightly embarrassed to be caught dreaming, he slipped his bishop forward with the intent of capturing her knight, which was in a vulnerable position.

Judy hesitated. "That wasn't a good move, John. Would you like to take it over?"

She was right, it wasn't a brilliant play, but adequate. "No, I released my hand from the bishop."

"You're sure?"

He studied the pieces again. He wasn't in any imminent danger of losing his king or the match. If he did forfeit the game it would be on his terms. "Even if this were a bad move, which it isn't," he added hastily, "I wouldn't change it."

Her eyes fairly danced with clever excitement. "So be it, then." She lifted her rook, raised her eyes to his before setting it beside his undefended king, and announced, "Checkmate."

Tight-lipped, John analyzed the play and was astonished to discover she was right. So much for her being straightforward and uncomplicated! The woman had duped him with as much skill as a double agent. The first couple of plays had been executed to give him a sense of false security while she set him up for the kill.

"I won," she reminded him. "And according to our agreement, I am entitled to something simple."

McFarland still hadn't taken his eyes off the chess board. The little schemer. Now that he'd seen how she'd done it, he was impressed with her cunning and skill. All right. He'd lost in a fair game; he was ready for her to name her price.

"Okay," he said a bit stiffly. "What would you like? A diamond necklace?"

She shook her head. "Oh, no, nothing like that."

"What then? A car?"

For an instant she was too stunned to reply. "Good heavens, no. It seems your idea of something simple and mine are entirely different."

"What do you want then?"

"Your time."

His expression grew puzzled. "My what?"

"Time," she repeated. "You work much too hard. I don't even recall an afternoon when you weren't cooped up in that stuffy office. You own a small piece of paradise; you should enjoy it much more often."

"So what's that got to do with anything?"

"For my prize I want us to pack a lunch and take it to the beach. It'll be a relaxing afternoon for us both."

He grinned at the idea that she would assume he had the time to do nothing but laze on the beach. Surely she wasn't so naive not to know he ruled a financial empire. Offices around the globe were awaiting his decisions. "I don't have time for that nonsense," he said finally with a crooked half smile. Sometimes he forgot how uncomplicated she was.

"That's a shame," Judy said, looping a dark strand of hair around her ear. "Unfortunately, you were the one who decided to place a wager on the match. You should never have made the suggestion if you weren't willing to follow through with it."

"I'll buy you something instead. I know just the thing."

Judy shook her head adamantly. "I would have sworn you were a man of your word. The only thing I want is this afternoon."

"Damn it, Judy," he shouted, and slapped his hand against the surface of the desk. "I can't afford to waste precious time lollygagging around the beach.

"Yes, John."

"There are cost sheets, reports, financial statements . . . that all must be reviewed this afternoon."

"Yes, John."

"Decisions to be made." His voice rose in volume with every word. "Offers to be considered."

Judy let neither his tone nor his words intimidate her. "I'll be at the door in one half hour and leave with or without you. But I honestly believe that you are a man of honor."

She left the room and McFarland continued to sit at the desk, hot with frustration. She had tricked him; she'd set him up, patiently waited and then waltzed in for the kill while he sat across from her like a lamb with its throat exposed. His laugh was filled with bitterness. Damn innocent woman. Tokyo Rose was more subtle than Judy Lovin!

At the appointed time, Judy stood in the foyer waiting for John. When he didn't come, she lingered for an additional five minutes. Deeply disappointed, she lifted the large wicker picnic basket and walked out of the house alone.

In his suite of offices, McFarland stood at the balcony door staring into space, thinking. It wasn't that he didn't have the time to spend lazing on the beach. If he truly wanted, he could have joined her. The problem was Judy. Every time he was with her, the need for her, his burning desire, dug deep talons into his chest. A curious ache tore at his heart. Perhaps his upbringing—or lack of one—was the problem. At no other time in his life had he wanted to know a woman the way he did Judy. He yearned to hold her in his arms and hear tales from her childhood, and tell her of his own. From the little bit she'd described, he'd recognized how close she'd been to her mother. She rarely spoke of her brother or father and McFarland didn't encourage it, fearing she missed them and would ask to be released.

For his own part, McFarland had told her more of his life than he'd ever revealed to anyone. Being with her made him weak in ways he couldn't explain. That kiss was a good example. He'd promised himself he wouldn't do it and then... His heart sneered at the simple memory of holding her in his arms and tasting her willing response. A low groan of frustration worked its way up the back of his throat and he momentarily closed his eyes.

Pivoting, he walked over to the liquor cabinet, poured himself a stiff drink and downed it in two swallows. He wanted her. This gut-wrenching soul-searching led to one thing and one thing only. He hungered to take Judy in his arms and kiss her senseless until she knew a fraction of his desire. And when the moment came, she would smile up at him with those incredible eyes of hers and give him her very soul and ask nothing in return. His power was so frightening that he trembled.

"Mr. McFarland?" Avery Andersen stepped into the office.

"Yes," he snapped.

"I'm sorry to disturb you."

McFarland shook his head, dismissing the apology. "What is it?"

Avery shifted his feet and squared his shoulders. "It's Miss Lovin."

"Yes. Is there a problem? Is she hurt?" He strove to keep his voice unemotional, although his heart was hammering anxiously against his ribs.

"No... no. Nothing like that."

"Then what?" he asked, losing his patience.

Avery ran a finger inside his stiff white collar. "She's been on the island nearly a month now."

"I'm aware of that."

"I was wondering how much longer her family can expect to be kept waiting before she's returned."

"Have they been pestering you again?" Grim resolve tightened his features. Judy enjoyed the island; he could see no reason to rush her departure.

Avery gave one short, barely perceptible shake of his head and dropped his gaze. "No..."

"Then who's doing the asking?"

Avery squared his shoulders and slowly raised his gaze to his employer's. His lips parted and quivered slightly. "I am, sir."

"You?"

"That's right, Mr. McFarland."

"How long Miss Lovin stays or doesn't stay is none of your concern." His tone was cold and calculated.

"But, sir . . ."

"That'll be all, Avery."

He hesitated for a long moment before turning, white-lipped, and walking out of the room.

McFarland watched his assistant leave. Even his staff had been cast under her spell. Sam, who could be as mean as a saddle sore, rushed to do her bidding. Princess had never been groomed more frequently or better. When asked about the extra attention paid to the mare, Sam had actually blushed and claimed it was for Miss Lovin.

The maids fought to serve her. The chef somehow managed to learn her favorite dishes and cooked them to the exclusion of all else. Pleased by his efforts, Judy had personally gone to thank him and kissed the top of his shining bald head. The island children followed her like a pied piper. Even Midnight had succumbed to her considerable charm. McFarland wiped a hand over his face. The entire island rushed to fulfill her every command. Why the hell should he be exempt from yearning to please her?

"Avery," he barked.

"Sir." The other man rushed into the room.

"Cancel my afternoon commitments."

"Excuse me?" Incredulous disbelief widened the older man's eyes.

"I said wipe out any commitments I have for the remainder of the day."

Avery checked his watch. "Are you feeling ill, Mr. McFarland? Should I contact a doctor?"

"No. I'm going swimming."

Avery's eyes narrowed in disbelief. "Swimming?"

"In the ocean," McFarland explained, grinning.

"The one outside—the one here?"

"That's right." Purposefully, he closed the folder on his desktop lest he be tempted to stay. "Avery, when was the last afternoon you had free?"

"I'm not sure."

"Take this one off as well. That's an order."

An instantaneous smile lit up the fastidious man's face. "Right away, Mr. McFarland."

McFarland felt as young as springtime and as excited as a lover on Valentine Day as he walked through the house to his quarters and changed clothes. With a beach towel wrapped around his neck, he walked down the front lawn and searched the outskirts of the beach. He found Judy lying under the shadow of a tall palm tree. A large blanket was spread out in the grass and the picnic basket was opened. He glanced inside and there was enough food to hold off a siege.

Judy lay on her back with her eyes closed, soaking up the sun's golden rays. She appeared tranquil, but her thoughts were spinning. She shouldn't be on St. Steven's. She should be demanding to know when John intended to release her so she could return to her family. Instead she was lazing on the beach feeling sorry for herself because she'd misjudged John McFarland. Her pride was hurt that he would refuse such a simple request. She liked being with John; the highlight of her day was spending time with him. She savored those minutes, and was keenly disappointed when he chose to leave her. The kiss they'd shared had changed everything; nothing could be the same anymore. They had only come to trust each other enough to be friends; now they feared each other. The kiss hadn't satisfied their curiosity; it had left them yearning for more.

A soft protest sounded from her throat. She was falling in love with John. She didn't want to love him. He would hurt her and send her away when he tired of her. Nor did he want her love. It would embarrass him—and her—if he were ever to guess.

"You knew I'd come, didn't you?" McFarland said, standing above her.

Judy's eyes shot open, blinked at the bright sunlight and closed again. Shielding her eyes with her hand, she braced herself on one elbow and looked at him again. "John." She sat upright.

He didn't look pleased to be there, but she was too happy to care.

"Sit down." She patted the blanket beside her. "And no, I didn't know you were coming, but I'm happy that you did."

He snickered softly in disbelief and joined her. Looping an arm around his bent knee, he stared into the rolling blue surf. "I'll have you know I left McDonnell Douglas on the wire to fulfill this wager."

"They'll contact you tomorrow."

"You hope."

"I know," she said, hiding a smile. "Now don't be angry with me. You were the one who suggested we make things interesting."

"Hell, why can't you be like every other woman in the world and request diamonds?"

"Because some things are worth more than jewels."

"What's the problem? Do you have so many that more don't interest you?" His face was hard and unyielding, but his anger was directed more at himself than Judy.

"My mother left me three or four lovely pieces." She slowly trailed her finger in the sand. "But I seldom wear jewelry." He wouldn't understand and it would be embarrassing to her if she were to explain that being with him was worth more to her than rubies and pearls.

A strained moment followed. "I shouldn't have snapped at you."

She turned to face him and was caught once again in his tortured gaze. Her breath froze in her lungs as her chest tightened. Not knowing what drove her, she raised her hand to his face, yearning to wipe away the hurt. John's eyes closed as her fingers lightly brushed his cheek. His beard nipped at her fingertips. He caught her hand, then, and raised his eyes to hers, kissing the sensitive inside of her hand.

The sensation of his tongue against her palm produced a soft gasp from Judy.

"I shouldn't do this," he said and groaned, directing her face to his. He kissed her cheek, her temple and her eyes.

They broke apart momentarily, and when he reached for her again, Judy met him halfway. This time the kiss was much deeper, and when he raised his head they were both dazed and more than a little shocked. The kiss was better, far better than either had anticipated.

McFarland rose to his knees, pulling Judy with him. Her look of innocent desire tore at his conscience. He hadn't meant to kiss her again; he feared hurting her more than he feared losing his wealth. But the soft, feminine feel of her as she brushed her breasts over his torso caused his blood to boil. And in the end, he kissed her again and again, slanting his mouth over hers until his heart thundered and roared. He lost himself in the unequaled taste of her. Her sweetness melted away years of loneliness. When she placed her trembling hand over his chest, it seared his flesh as thoroughly as a branding iron. At the moment, it wasn't in McFarland to protest.

John's kisses made Judy light-headed. The finest wine couldn't produce a sensation as potent as this. She trembled in his arms and when her gaze met his, her eyes were wide.

He dragged his gaze away from her, afraid of her angelic innocence.

"Let's swim."

Judy nodded and he helped her to her feet.

The turquoise water was only a few feet away and they stepped into the rolling surf together. The cool spray against her heated flesh took Judy's breath away.

John dove into an oncoming wave and Judy followed him. He broke the surface several feet from her, turned and waited for her to swim to him.

"Have you ever body surfed?" He shouted to be heard above the sound of the churning sea.

"No, but I'd like to."

"Good." He reached out and gripped her waist. "We'll take this wave together."

With no option, Judy closed her eyes and was thrust into the swelling wall of water. Her hold on John tightened as they were cast under the surface by a giant surge of unleashed power. The tide tossed them about as effortlessly as a grain of wheat caught in the wind.

Judy threw back her head and laughed once the wave passed them to wash up on the beach. "That was wonderful." She wrapped her arms around John's neck.

"You're slippery," McFarland said, using the excuse to draw her closer. His hand held her firmly against him, creating another kind of torture. His fingers brushed the wet strands of hair away from her face. Her pulse went wild at his gentle touch.

His eyes held hers and darkened just before his mouth crushed hers. Judy gave herself to the kiss, responding with all the love stored in her heart. The water took then again, but neither seemed concerned. When they broke the surface, Judy was breathless and weak.

McFarland's chest heaved. He had thought he could escape his need for her in the water, but it hadn't worked that way. "You're even better in the water."

"Pardon?"

"Nothing," he grumbled.

She threw back her head and laughed. "You taste like salt water."

And she tasted like heaven. Good God, how was he ever going to let her go? "Judy?"

She wound her arms around his neck and smiled shyly. Maybe he would admit that he loved her. Her heart beat anxiously. It was a fanciful dream. Earning John's love would take more than a few playful moments in the surf. He had to learn to trust.

"Listen," he said in a low voice that sounded strangely like a groan. "I have to tell you something."

She lifted her head, fearing that the time had come for him to send her away.

"I'm leaving."

Her heart slammed against her breast. "When?"

"In the morning."

"How long?"

"A few days," he said, and continued to brush the wet hair from her face, although it had long since been smoothed into place. "Four, possibly five."

Perhaps he had decided to send her away. Her eyes must have revealed her distress.

"Will you wait for me here, Beauty?"

She nodded, overcome with relief.

"Good," he whispered, and greedily sought her mouth once again.

Not until he kissed her did she realize he hadn't called her Judy.

Chapter Six

John left just after dawn the next morning. Judy was awake and at the sound of muted voices from downstairs, she reached for her robe and rushed down the winding stairway. By the time she arrived, John had already left, but she could see his Jeep in the distance. She stood on the huge porch, leaning dejectedly against the thick marble column. She would have liked to have wished him well.

"Morning, Miss Lovin."

Judy straightened and turned toward Avery Andersen.

"Morning. I see John got off without a hitch."

"He should be away only a few days."

"Four at the most." She quoted what John had told her. Her gaze followed his disappearing figure until he was out of sight. "It won't be so bad."

"He's instructed me to see to your every wish."

She smiled. If she were to have a silly craving for pastrami from her favorite New York deli, Judy didn't doubt that speedy arrangements would be made.

"He doesn't go away often," Avery went on to explain as he straightened his bow tie. "He wouldn't now if it wasn't necessary."

Judy nodded. John hadn't wanted to leave her. She'd seen the regret in his eyes as they pleaded softly with her for understanding.

"Some claim McFarland's a recluse," Avery commented thoughtfully, studying Judy.

"No," she countered, and gently shook her head. "Not in the true sense of the word, but he cares a great deal for his privacy."

"He does at that," the older man agreed.

They turned to go back inside then, each walking through the wide doors and parting at the foot of the stairs.

Four days didn't seem long, Judy told herself as she dressed. The time would fly. She glanced at her watch; already fifteen minutes had gone.

Slumping onto the edge of the bed, Judy released a long, slow breath. She loved John and was only beginning to realize the full ramifications of blithely handing him her heart. Caring for him excited her, and made her afraid. John wouldn't be an easy man to love; he knew so little about it. Judy had been surrounded by it, smothered in it. Her love for John gave him an awesome power to hurt her and she wasn't convinced that telling him of her feelings would be in her best interests—or his.

The first day passed without incident. The second was equally dull. Mealtimes were the loneliest hours.

She sat at the end of the table and experienced such an overwhelming sense of privation that she scolded herself for being so painfully dramatic.

Nothing seemed right without John. Not riding Princess around the island; not visiting the children; not letters to her family, not swimming.

She was lonely and bored, fidgety and at odds with herself. One man had toppled her world and a few days without him taxed the balance of her humdrum existence.

The night of the third day, Judy tossed and turned in her bed, unable to sleep. She missed John dreadfully and was angry with herself for feeling such a loss without him.

At midnight, she threw aside the blankets and silently crept down the stairs for a glass of milk, hoping that would help her insomnia. John's office was on the opposite side of the house from the kitchen, and Judy carried her milk with her to the opulently paneled suite, flipping on the lights. She silently slipped into his desk chair, tucking her bare feet under her. Briefly she closed her eyes, inhaling the scent of him. A smile curved her mouth. She could almost feel his presence and some of the ache eased from her heart.

Weary to the bone, McFarland entered the house and paused in the foyer, resisting the urge to climb the stairs and wake Judy. The thought of holding her sleepy head against his chest was almost more than he could bear.

The business meetings hadn't gone well and in part he blamed himself. Negotiations had come to an impasse and, in his impatience to return to the island, he had asked that the meeting be adjourned while both parties considered the lengthy proposals. He would have stayed in Dallas if he'd felt it would have done any good, but he figured it would be better to return to St. Steven's rather than buckle under to United Petroleum's unreasonable demands.

He paused, rubbed a hand over his face and smiled. He didn't need to wake Judy to feel her presence in his home. She was like the sweet breath of spring that brought the promise of summer. He had only to shut his eyes to see her bouncing down the stairs with a vitality that rivaled life itself. The sound of her laughter was like sparkling water bubbling over a short waterfall. Her smile could blot out the sun.

His heart constricted with emotion. He would surprise her first thing in the morning. Until then he would have to be content.

With that thought in mind, he headed toward his rooms, until a light in his office attracted his attention. It was unlike Avery to work this late unless there was a major problem. Frowning, McFarland decided he'd best check into the matter.

One step into his office and he stopped cold. Judy was curled up in the chair behind his desk, sound asleep. She was the picture of innocence with her head cocked to one side, the thick coffee-colored hair falling over her cheek. She wore a plain nightgown beneath an equally unfeminine robe. Neither did much to reveal the womanly curves beneath. However, McFarland had never experienced a stronger stab of desire. It cut through him, sharp and keen, and trapped the breath in his lungs.

Had it been any other woman, he would have kissed her until she was warm and willing in his arms, carried her into his room and satisfied his yearning with her lush body. He couldn't do that with Judy; her sweet innocence prevented that.

He hesitated, debating on how he should wake her. His impulse was to bend over and kiss her, but he feared that would never satisfy him and the potency of his desire would only shock her. Shaking her awake or calling her name might frighten her.

Of her own accord, Judy stirred and stretched her arms high above her head, arching her back and yawning loudly. She hadn't meant to fall asleep. When she opened her eyes, she discovered John standing on the other side of the desk from her. She blinked. At first she was convinced he wasn't real but the embodiment of her deepest desires. When she realized that he was indeed very much alive, she leaped from the chair, nearly tripping on the hem of her nightgown.

"John." She slapped her hand over her breast. "I'm so sorry... I don't know what came over me to come into your office. It must have shocked you to find me here. I... do apologize."

"My home is yours. No apology is necessary," he said softly as his gaze fell on the empty glass.

"I couldn't sleep." She brushed the array of hair from her face, still flustered and more than a little embarrassed. "When did you get in?"

A smile twitched at the corners of his mouth. She looked like a guilty child who had been caught with her hand in the cookie jar. "Only a few minutes ago."

She clenched her hands together and smiled brightly, genuinely pleased that he had returned. "Welcome home."

"It's good to be here."

Judy tightened her hands to restrain the urge to run into his arms, hold onto him and beg him never to leave her again. Her heart continued to pound, but she didn't know if it was from being caught in his office or just the virile sight of him.

"Did anything happen while I was away?" he asked, reaching for his mail and idly flipping through it.

"Nothing important." She stood across from him, drinking in his presence as though he would disappear at any moment. "Are you hungry? I'd be happy to fix you something." She prayed he was famished, just so she would have an excuse to stay with him longer.

"Don't go to any trouble."

"I won't. Will a sandwich do?" She smiled then, inordinately pleased to be able to do this one small thing for him.

"A sandwich would be fine."

He followed her into the kitchen and pulled up a stool to a stainless-steel table while Judy opened the refrigerator and took out the necessary ingredients.

"How was the trip?" she asked, liberally slathering the bread with butter and mayonnaise before placing slices of turkey and tomato over it.

McFarland had never discussed his business matters with anyone outside of his office. The temptation to do so now was strong, but he didn't. "Everything went as expected," he said matter-of-factly, which was only half true.

Judy cut the sandwich into halves, set it on a plate and handed it to him. Then she poured them each a glass of milk and sat on a stool across from him.

Elbows braced against the tabletop, she cupped her face in her hands and studied him while he ate. Her brow creased with concern as she noted the lines of fatigue around his eyes and mouth. "You look exhausted."

"I am. I didn't make it to bed last night."

"The meetings didn't go well, did they?"

Her intuition surprised him; he hadn't thought he was that easy to read. "I didn't expect them to."

"What happened?"

McFarland shrugged. "I made an offer, they rejected it and came back with a counteroffer."

"And you rejected that?"

He paused, the glass halfway to his mouth. "Not exactly. Not yet, anyway," he elaborated.

"But you will?"

Again he shrugged, and his eyes met hers. "I'm not sure."

Judy continued to study John. He was physically exhausted, but the mental defeat weighed far heavier on him. As a young girl, she had often watched her mother soothe the tension from her father. Georgia Lovin hadn't offered suggestions; she had had no expertise in business, but she possessed the uncanny ability to get her husband to relax and talk out the problem so that he found the solution. Judy prayed that she could do the same for John.

"You want this deal, don't you?" she asked him softly.

McFarland nodded. "I've been working on it for over a year now. The offer I made United Petroleum is a fair one—hell, it was more than fair. But I'm at a disadvantage."

"Why?"

He set the glass down hard. "Because they damn well know I want this."

"I see."

"Now that you mention it, I may have appeared too anxious to settle." He couldn't deny his eagerness. He had wanted to get those papers signed so he could get back to the island and Judy, his mission accomplished. He'd thought he'd been more subtle, but perhaps not. "Let me explain," he said, taking a napkin and scribbling down a series of figures.

He spoke nonstop for fifteen minutes. Most everything he said was far beyond Judy's comprehension, although she pretended to understand every bit of it. She nodded at the appropriate times and smiled when he finished.

"You're right," he said with a wide grin. "Damn, why didn't I think of that?"

Judy hadn't a clue as to what he was talking about, but it didn't seem to matter. The weariness was gone from his eyes. He stood and paced the kitchen.

"That's it," he said, and paused in front of her. "Has anyone ever told you what a marvel you are?" His hands cupped her face and he kissed her soundly.

Judy's breath lodged in her chest. "What was that for?" she asked in a voice that sounded strangely unlike her own.

"To thank you." He checked his watch. "It's late, but I think I'll contact my attorney and talk this latest strategy over with him."

"John," she protested. "It's one o'clock in the morning!"

"For the money I pay that man it shouldn't matter what time I call him."

Before she could protest further, John was at the kitchen door. He opened it, paused and turned back. "Will you ride with me in the morning?"

She smiled and nodded eagerly, grateful that he'd thought to ask.

In his office, McFarland emptied his briefcase and set the file for United Petroleum on his desktop. It struck him then, sharply. Without him knowing how, Judy had gotten him to reveal the minute details of this buy out. He'd told her everything without the least bit of hesitation. He didn't fear what she'd do with the information; there was nothing she could do.

What shocked him was that she had so completely gained his confidence that he cheerfully gave out industry secrets without a second thought. This woman tied knots a sailor couldn't untangle, and every one of them was strung around his heart, choking off his independence. She was quickly making herself essential.

He paused and rubbed his hand over his face as he analyzed the situation. McFarland didn't like the thought of a woman, any woman, controlling his life. Not one damn bit. Something had to be done to put an end to it.

* * *

At dawn Judy rushed to meet John at the stables. She had slept like a baby after leaving him. When the maid had come to wake her, she'd resisted climbing out of the warm bed, preferring to hold on to the memory of John's arms around her. It took her a moment to realize she'd been dreaming.

Midnight and Princess were saddled and waiting.

"Morning," she called to Sam and smiled at John, who immediately swung onto Midnight's back.

The burly trainer waved and Judy took a moment to stroke Princess's smooth neck before mounting. John's look remained stoic.

"How'd you sleep?" she asked when they'd gone only a couple of hundred feet. He was quiet, withdrawn and taciturn—nothing like the warm, gentle man he'd been when they'd parted.

"I didn't get to bed," he answered crisply.

"Oh, John, again? You must be ready to fall out of the saddle."

"No. After you left last night, I got to analyzing the proposal and decided there were still more things I wanted to change before I talked to Butterman."

Judy assumed Butterman was his attorney. "What did he have to say?"

John's look remained thoughtful, intense. "Not much." But he seemed to think the idea would work. "Unless United Petroleum wants to play games, I should hear back sometime this afternoon." He tipped back the rim of his hat and glanced down at his watch. "The fact is, I should probably call this morning's ride short and get back to the office in case they contact me this morning."

Judy was aghast. "You don't honestly intend to work, do you? Good heavens, you've been away on an exhausting business trip."

"So?"

"You haven't slept in who knows how long."

McFarland's mouth thinned with impatience. "What's that got to do with anything?"

"Everything," she cried, losing control of her own even temper. She didn't know what was wrong with him this morning, but she had a hunch that a few hours of rest would cure it.

"Just what am I supposed to do?"

"Sleep."

"I'm expecting a phone call."

"Avery will wake you."

"What are you? My nurse?"

Judy's gloved hands tightened around the reins at the unnecessarily harsh edge to his voice. "Someone needs to look after you."

"And I suppose you're volunteering for the job?" McFarland didn't want to shout at her, but he couldn't seem to make himself stop. She was right. God knew he hadn't seen a bed in over forty-eight hours, but he sure as hell didn't want a woman dictating his actions.

Judy clamped her mouth together so tightly that her jaw ached. She refused to rise to the bait of his acid tongue.

They rode together for a half hour without saying a word. McFarland derived little pleasure from the outing. He regretted having snapped at Judy, especially when he would much rather have taken her in his arms and kissed her. He searched his mind for a way to apologize without it costing him his pride, and found none.

When they returned to the stable, Judy lowered herself from Princess's back and turned toward John. "As I recall, only a few hours ago you considered me wise and insightful. I don't know what happened since then, but I really do wish you'd rest."

"Why?"

She clenched her fists. "You're killing yourself working day and night for no reason."

"I call ten million dollars a damn good reason."

"Is it worth your health?" she cried, tears glistening in her eyes. "Is it worth becoming so unreasonable no one can talk to you? Is it worth saying something you don't mean?"

"You seem to be doing a good job of exactly that."

"I care about you."

"Is that supposed to excite me?" he asked. "You care about everything—horses, children . . . bugs. It would be hard to find something that you didn't care about. Listen, Miss Bleeding Heart, I can do without your mollycoddling. Got that?"

"No," she said with incredible pride, her face pale and grim.

"You've been nothing but a damn nuisance since you came to the island. There isn't a man or woman here who doesn't bend to your every wish. Well, I refuse to be one of them. You'll do what I tell you. It won't be the other way around. Have you got that?"

If possible, her face went even paler. Her eyes rounded with pain and shock. She opened her mouth to say something, then closed it again. The effort to restrain the tears drained her of energy. Still, she refused to look away.

"I won't bother you again, John McFarland," she whispered with quiet dignity and turned from him, nearly blinded now by her tears. How quickly everything had changed. She'd missed John until her heart had ached. She'd longed to savor this morning's outing with him and instead had found herself the object of a tongue-lashing she had yet to fully understand.

In her rooms, she sat and stared at the wall as the tears flowed freely down her ashen cheeks. She was in love with a beast. The possibility of ever gaining his heart struck her as ludicrous. In his own words, she was a damn nuisance and, with that, Judy realized that he would probably never have it in him to love her.

At lunchtime, she sent word that she wouldn't be joining him and requested that all her meals be sent to her room. If John found her company so taxing, there was no need to punish him with her presence. She refused to trouble him again and was determined to avoid him until he saw fit to summon her.

A day passed.

A night.

Another day.

Another long, sleepless night.

A third day came and went and still John didn't ask for her. She thought about him, yearned for him. Judy was convinced that she could wilt away in her rooms and he would have cared less. She loved him and he considered her an annoyance. All these weeks when she had treasured every moment with him, he'd found her a bothersome pest.

Still, he didn't summon her. To escape her room, Judy walked along the beach in the early morning light. For the first time she entertained thoughts of leaving and regretfully rejected them. They had struck a bargain, and although it grew increasingly difficult, she would stay on the island until he sent her away.

Countless times Judy wondered why he bothered to keep her there. She yearned to be with her family.

McFarland was growing less amused by the day at Judy's stubbornness. Perhaps he had been a bit unreasonable, but it certainly shouldn't have amounted to this. For four days, she had refused to have anything to do with him. That had been her choice, but enough was enough. The entire house was in an uproar.

McFarland had discovered the chef arguing with Avery. French insults rushed like water out of a spigot while the four-star chef gestured freely with his hands. The entire time, the man sent accusing glances in McFarland's direction.

"What was that all about?" he had asked his assistant later, having found the display only a little short of comical.

"He—ah—is concerned," Avery commented, looking embarrassed and red-faced.

"Concerned? Is it the kitchen help again?"

"No." Avery busied himself with shifting papers around his desk.

"Then what is it?" McFarland pressed.

"He's concerned about Miss Lovin."

McFarland's grin faded and his eyes grew cold. "Judy? What's wrong?"

"He claims she isn't eating properly and that she sends back her meals untouched. He's tempted her with his most famous recipes and nothing seems to work. He fears she is making herself ill."

A muscle jerked convulsively in McFarland's clenched jaw.

"I realize this isn't any of my concern, Mr. McFarland, but..."

"You're right, it isn't your business."

Avery squared his shoulders, his own jaw tightening. "I've been with you for several years now, but these last three days have been more difficult than ever. You have been impatient, and unreasonably demanding, and I can find no excuse for it. You have my notice, Mr. McFarland."

McFarland was stunned. Perhaps he had been a bit more demanding in the past few days, but that wasn't any reason for Avery to resign. "As you wish," he answered with some reluctance.

The afternoon went smoothly after that, but when they'd finished, Avery presented him with a brief but precise letter of resignation.

McFarland read it over twice, convinced there must have been some mistake. There wasn't; Avery was leaving him.

In an effort to think through this unexpected turn of events, McFarland took two cold beers from his cooler and decided to visit Sam. To his additional shock, he discovered that the stable man regarded him with a black scowl.

"Don't tell me she's got you on her side as well?" McFarland barked, angry because he should have known better. Judy had had Sam twisted around her little finger from the minute she'd tamed Midnight. "Doesn't a one of you recognize the hand that feeds you? Good Lord, I don't believe it. Not you, too?"

In response, Sam chuckled, ambled to the back of the barn and brought out two rickety chairs.

"Women are a pain in the backside," McFarland said, pulling the tab from the aluminum top and guzzling a long swallow.

Sam joined him in the toast. "Can't say I blame you. You'll do well to be rid of her."

McFarland wiped his mouth with the back of his hand as his bemusement faded. "What do you mean?"

"You don't plan to keep her on the island? Not with the way she's been acting."

McFarland planned exactly that. He had no intention of letting her leave. This thing between them was a spat, nothing more. She'd infringed on his private life and he wouldn't stand for it. Given time, she would recognize the error of her ways and come to him, gushing with apologies. And being the good-hearted soul he was, he would forgive her.

"She's a damn busybody, that one," Sam added. "Why, look at the way she stuck her nose in your affairs, dictating the way you should run your business. No man should be expected to put up with that kind of feminist assertiveness."

"Have you been watching Donohue again?" McFarland felt obligated to ask.

"Look at the way she's constantly needling you, asking for one thing or another, making selfish demands. I hear how she's constantly seeking gifts."

Mcfarland's face tightened. "She's never asked for a damn thing."

Sam took another long swallow of beer. "If I were you, I'd put her in a rowboat and cast her out of my life. Let her fend for herself. As you said, she's a damn nuisance; she isn't worth the trouble."

McFarland mumbled something unintelligible under his breath. "Who said she was a nuisance?"

"You did, heard you tell her so myself. Should have seen the look in her eyes." Sam's laugh was loud and boisterous. "She's plump full of pride and spirit, that one. You'd best break it if you intend to keep her around here."

It seemed the entire barn had gone still. "What else did I say to her?"

"Oh, lots of things."

"What things?"

The blood drained from McFarland's face as Sam told him. He'd been so exhausted that he didn't remember the half of it. Now, every word, every syllable was a vicious punch to his abdomen.

McFarland crushed the aluminum can with his hands and stood. He felt sick.

"Where are you going?"

McFarland didn't answer.

"You're going to get rid of her, aren't you?" Sam asked, and noting the look on McFarland's face, he chuckled, pleased with himself.

Chapter Seven

Once again McFarland was in the uncomfortable position of needing to seek Judy's forgiveness. It gnawed at his conscience, and clawed at his sleep until he rolled over and stared at the darkened ceiling. His heart constricted and the first doubts concerning what he was doing with Judy surfaced. He'd seen her picture in some newspaper and his interest had been awakened. He had yet to understand what craziness had driven him to force her to come to his island. In the weeks since her arrival his life had been drastically affected. She'd been open, happy, guileless and unbelievably gentle when she had every excuse to hate him. He had berated her, lashed out at her, and still she turned those incredible eyes on him and found it within her to smile.

By everything that was right, he should release her and send her back to her family. His heart pounded slowly, painfully, at the thought of never hearing the sound of her laughter again, or having those incredible round eyes smile into his, or seeing her ride across his land with her hair in careless disarray. A heaviness pressed against his chest.

He couldn't do it—sending her away was unthinkable. The tenderness in her eyes and her gentle smile filled him with an exhilaration he couldn't begin to analyze. He wasn't entirely sure he wanted to. She was an angel who caused him to feel things he'd never experienced, emotions he'd fought against most of his life. All he knew was that he needed her on St. Steven's for now. He'd deal with tomorrow later.

Judy pounded the feather pillow and battled with another wave of depression. She was wide awake. In another hour it would be dawn and she could escape the self-imposed prison of her room. With nothing better to do, she climbed out of bed, dressed and crept out of the house, heading for the stables.

Her heart felt incredibly weary.

The sky remained dark, but the promise of dawn lay just over the horizon. She could hear Sam stirring in the back of the barn as she saddled Princess and rode toward the beach.

Sam's features were twisted in a dark scowl as he searched McFarland's face in the half light of early dawn.

"She's gone," he announced harshly.

"Who?"

"Princess."

McFarland's eyes widened. No one would dare steal the mare. Only Judy rode her. "Has anyone checked the house to see..."

"The maid says there's no one in her room. Her bed barely looks slept in."

McFarland's own features hardened with sharp determination, and in a single motion, he swung his weight onto Midnight's back. He braced his knees against the stallion's powerful sides and pulled tightly on the reins. "In which direction does she usually ride?"

Sam gestured widely with both hands. "North. Sometimes east."

"I'll head west."

Sam's nod was curt, his eyes boring into McFarland's. "You bring her back; she belongs here."

The words were shouted as McFarland raced out of the yard. He wouldn't come back until he found her. By God, he would horsewhip the one who had helped her in this underhanded scheme. What the hell good was security if she could carry out her own escape? He'd fire the whole damn lot of them, but first he had to find Judy.

McFarland would have ridden from one side of the island to the other, torn down the entire jungle to stop her. To his utter astonishment, all it took was a wild fifteen-minute ride. He came upon her with such shocking ease that his heart begun to slam against his chest. He paused, his frantic heartbeat stilling as he raised his eyes to the sky in eternal gratitude.

She was walking on the beach with Princess following two steps behind. Her head drooped lackadaisically; the reins were draped over her shoulders as she ambled along. Although McFarland was positioned high on the ridge above, he could see how distressed Judy was. Her head hung low, her shoulders were hunched and it looked as though a steel mantle were weighing heavily upon her shoulders. He didn't need to see her tear-streaked face to know that she had been crying. The realization had the oddest effect upon him. Guilt tore at him and his chest tightened, constricting with a pain that was razor sharp. He couldn't take his eyes off her. Witnessing her pain brought out such an overwhelming desire to protect her that he could hardly breathe.

Since the night Sam had set him straight about the things he'd said to Judy, McFarland had sought for a means of salvaging his pride. He admitted he owed her an apology, but he yearned to give it without denting his considerable pride. He could present her with a token gift, perhaps. Something that would convey his message and cost him little emotionally. Watching her now, a sick feeling settled into the pit of his stomach and he realized he would gladly fall to his knees and beg her forgiveness. He was a selfish bastard and Beauty—his Beauty—deserved far better.

Judy wiped the moisture from her cheek, angry with herself for being so melancholy. From the first, she had known it would be difficult to love John. She'd thought she'd accepted that. In the long days since their ride together, she had come to understand far better the cost love demanded. But she had her pride, too—in some ways it was as considerable as John's—and she would die before she would let him know that he held her heart in the palm of his hand.

A flash of ebony caught her attention and she turned and spotted John on the ridge above her. Judy's heart rushed to her throat. He pulled on the reins and she realized with a start that he was planning on meeting her. It was one thing to realize he had found her, and another to allow him to see her tears.

Desperate to escape, she mounted Princess and slapped the reins hard against the mare's flanks. Princess shot across the beach, her powerful hind feet kicking up a flurry of sand. Judy realized her best chance of escape was in the jungle and headed in that direction. Chancing a look behind her, she was astonished to see that John had already reached the beach.

"Hurry, Princess," she cried, frantically whipping the reins back and forth across her neck.

Judy didn't see what it was that darted across the beach, but Princess reared, her legs kicking in terror. Unable to stop herself, Judy slipped sideways in the saddle. In a desperate effort to regain her balance, she groped for the saddle horn, but it was too difficult to keep atop the bucking horse. A sense of unreality filled her. She hadn't been unseated by a horse since she was a child. She refused to believe it, but the ground that rushed up to meet her was more than real. A cry of panic froze in her lungs as she lifted her arms to break the fall. Then the impact of her torso against the solid beach brutally drove the air from her lungs and for a moment everything went black.

McFarland saw Princess buck and watched helplessly as Judy teetered while frantically trying to regain her seat. He saw her fall and knew she'd landed hard. A score of swear words scorched the morning mist and his heart thundered with alarm. The thoughts that flashed through his mind were completely illogical. He'd sell his business interests around the world if she were unhurt. If that didn't satisfy the powers that be, he offered his life, his heart, his soul—anything—just as long as Judy wasn't hurt.

He pulled Midnight to an abrupt halt, vaulted from the stallion's back and ran across the sand, more frightened than he could remember being in his life.

Falling to his knees at Judy's side, he gently rolled her over. The steady, even pulsing at the side of her neck caused him to go weak with relief. He ripped the jacket from his arms and placed it under her head. Then, not knowing what else to do, he lifted her limp hand into his own, frantically rubbing the inside of her wrist.

Judy's eyes fluttered open to discover John leaning over her, looking sickly pale. "Princess?" she whispered, and tried to sit up.

It took McFarland a moment to realize she was worried about the mare. He was astonished; Judy could have been maimed, or worse, killed, and she seemed to care nothing for her own well-being.

"Is she hurt?"

McFarland shook his head and responded in a husky voice. "She's fine. What about you?"

Her smile was little more than a slight trembling of her lips. It was too soon to tell. She felt like she was going to throw up and the world spun crazily. "I'm all right," she said weakly, putting up a brave front.

"You're sure?" His intense gaze burned over her face.

"The only thing bruised is my pride." With some difficulty she stood, stumbled and swayed toward him.

Her ribs hurt like crazy, but she successfully hid the pain.

McFarland caught her, gently wrapping his arms around her, holding her against him, grateful for the excuse to bring her into the shelter of his embrace. He brushed the hair away from her face, and Judy noted that he was shaking as much as she was.

"I'm fine, John. Something must have spooked Princess. I think it was a rabbit." She tilted her head back and saw the torment in his eyes as he relived the moment of her fall.

Their gazes met. Neither moved; neither breathed. Slowly, he lowered his mouth to hers. The kiss was gentle and savage at the same time. Judy could find no way to describe the turbulent sensation that jolted her. It was as though she realized she could have been killed and forever denied the feel of John's arms again. Judy wanted to cherish this moment forever, and forget the pain.

They remained locked in each other's arms long after the kiss had ended. Timeless seconds passed, each more precious that the one before.

"I've got to get you to a doctor," he said at last.

"John, I'll be all right."

"You're shaking."

She smiled, unable to tell him his kisses contributed to the trembling as much as the pain.

His low whistle brought Midnight to their side. "You'll ride with me."

"But..."

One look effectively cut off any argument. McFarland climbed onto Midnight's back first.

Judy stared at the stallion and felt her knees go weak. The last thing she wanted to do was get back on a horse. Although she strove to reassure John that she was unhurt, she felt as though someone had taken a baseball bat to her ribs. It hurt to breathe and she ached everywhere. Nothing seemed broken, but something wasn't right, either. "What if he won't seat me?" she asked shakily.

John dismissed that suggestion with a curious smile. "You said yourself Midnight was your friend."

"So I did," she grumbled, staring at the hand he offered her. She accepted it, and his strong fingers closed over her own, prepared to lift her onto the stallion's back. However, the simple action of raising her arm caused her to gasp with pain.

Hurriedly, she drew it back to her side, closed her eyes and pressed her forehead against John's leg. The next thing she knew, she was on her knees in the sand, clenching her side.

"You idiot," he shouted, dismounting, "why didn't you say something?"

Tears welled in her eyes as she lifted her pain-riddled gaze to his. "Why do you always yell at me?" she asked in a hoarse whisper.

"Beauty, I'm sorry."

She held her arm protectively across her ribs. "Only my father calls me that."

"It's true, you know," he said gently, kneeling beside her, holding her with such tenderness that she couldn't identify the greater pain—loving John or the ache in her ribs.

"I'm not beautiful," she countered.

"Yes, love, you are. You're the most beautiful woman I know. Now, don't argue with me, understand?"

She offered him a weak smile.

The trip back to the house seemed to take torturous hours. She pleaded with him to leave her and send someone back for her. The injury wasn't so bad that she couldn't stand to be alone for a half hour or more. John adamantly refused and, in the end, she did ride Midnight, cradled in John's arms so that he absorbed every jolt and shock.

She rode sidesaddle, her head resting against his chest, her arms around his middle. Their progress was slow and by the time they arrived she was hazy with pain and incredibly sleepy.

Sam and several others rushed out to greet them.

"Send for a doctor," John barked urgently.

With some effort, Judy lifted her head. "I thought you said you weren't going to yell anymore."

"I said that?" He pretended to be amazed.

She frowned and drew in a slow, painful breath. "Maybe you didn't, at that."

His fingers found the back of her neck and he buried them deep in her hair. "If it will make the hurt go away, I'll promise never to raise my voice again."

The ache in her side immediately lessened.

He issued other orders, but in a subdued voice that swelled Judy's heart, not because she found his shouting objectionable, but because he cared enough about her to try to please her. After the last four days of the bitter cold war that had raged between them, this sweet attention was bliss.

John helped her off Midnight's back and carried her into the house. She protested when he started up the stairs to her room, but it didn't stop him.

"I'm too heavy," she cried.

"Now look who's yelling."

"John, please, you're the one who'll need the doctor if you insist on hauling me up these stairs."

"I'll risk it."

"But I wish you wouldn't." It was useless to protest. Besides, he was already halfway up the staircase.

When he reached the hallway outside her room, he kicked her door open, crossed the room and gently laid her on the bed. It took Judy only an instant to realize that lying down wasn't the thing to do and kicking out her feet, she struggled to a sitting position.

"What's wrong?" McFarland saw the flash of pain in her eyes and felt it as strongly as if the agony were his own.

She shook her head and closed her eyes. "Nothing. Just go away, will you? I'll be fine in a minute."

To her surprise he did leave her, but two maids were in her room within a matter of seconds. They were followed by the security guard who had met her the day of her arrival.

Judy grinned. "So we meet again."

"I have some medical training," he explained. "Mr. McFarland asked that I check you over before the doctor arrives."

Judy nodded and slumped onto the end of her bed.

McFarland was pacing in the hallway outside her room when Wilson returned. "Well?" he asked anxiously.

"My guess is that she's cracked a couple of ribs."

"She's in considerable pain, isn't she?" Although Judy tried to hide it from him, McFarland could tell that she wanted to scream and her agony burned in his veins, scorching his conscience and searing his tormented soul.

"She's pretending it doesn't hurt, but I know better," Wilson commented wryly.

"Give her something for the pain," McFarland demanded gruffly.

The other man looked uncertain for the first time. "I don't know that I should, Mr. McFarland. The doctor might want to..."

"It could be hours before he arrives. Give her something and do it now. That's an order."

Wilson nodded, swallowing any argument. "Right away."

He returned a few minutes later with two capsules, instructing Judy to take them both. Within minutes she drifted into a troubled sleep. She curled into a tight ball, taking shallow breaths in an effort to minimize the pain.

When she woke, she discovered that John was sitting at her bedside, staring at his hands, his face bleak, his eyes lifeless.

"John?"

He straightened and turned toward her. "Yes, love?"

"The island needs...something. A medical facility. What if one of the children were to get hurt? Then...what? There's nowhere..." She felt so sluggish, so miserable. The pills hadn't taken the pain way; only her mind was numb.

"The doctor will be here soon," he hurried to assure her.

She nodded and moistened her lips with her tongue. "I'm thirsty."

"Here." He lifted her head and held a glass of cool water to her lips. She managed to take several sips. When she had finished drinking, he gently kissed her forehead.

"John?" He voice was little more than a slurred whisper. She struggled to keep her eyes open and gave up the effort.

The soft catch in her voice stabbed at his heart. "Yes, love."

"I'm sorry to be such a nuisance."

The words burned him like a red-hot iron. "You were never that."

"But you said..."

He gripped her hand in his own and raised it to his lips, tenderly kissing her knuckles. "I was wrong." McFarland couldn't remember ever admitting that to anyone.

He stayed at her bedside until the medical team arrived. Then he lingered outside her room until the physician had finished the examination, which seemed to take hours. McFarland paced the area in front of her room so long that he grew dizzy. He smoked rarely, but desperately needed a cigarette.

His thoughts ran into each other until they flashed through his mind in a muddled sequence. Judy running away from him, Judy falling, Judy in pain. It was all his fault. Lord knew he had never meant to hurt her. She was too delicate, too sweet to bear the brunt of his brutality.

When the physician finally did appear, McFarland found himself studying the other man, fearing what he would soon learn. "Will she be all right?" His eyes pleaded with the white-haired man for assurance.

"I believe so. We brought along a portable X-ray machine. She's cracked two ribs and has a slight concussion."

"Any internal damage?" That was McFarland's greatest fear.

"Not that we can detect."

He ran his fingers through his hair. "Should she be hospitalized?"

The middle-aged physician with the stocky build shook his head. "I can't see where that would do any good. What she needs now more than anything is rest. For the time being she isn't going to feel much like getting out of bed. However, that's for the best. Let her sleep."

"How long?"

"Keep her down a couple of days, then gradually increase her activity."

"What about the pain? I don't want her to suffer." He couldn't bear to see her face twisted in agony.

"I've left a prescription and instructions with my nurse, Miss Reinholt. Miss Lovin is sleeping comfortably now."

McFarland let out his breath in a long, slow sigh. "Good. Thank you, doctor." He offered the physician his hand and had Wilson escort the medical team to the waiting helicopter.

McFarland checked on Judy one last time before heading toward his office. He was stalled in the foyer by several of the staff members. They raised questioning eyes to him, their concern evident.

"How is Miss Lovin, sir?" the chef asked as he bravely stepped forward.

Only a day before McFarland would have bitten off the pompous man's head for daring to approach him on a subject that was none of his concern. Now he patiently explained the extent of Judy's injuries and answered his and the others' legion of questions.

From there McFarland went to his offices. Avery stood when he entered the room.

Before his assistant could ask, he rattled off his now rehearsed report. "Cracked ribs, bruises and a mild concussion. She'll be confined to her bed for a few days and good as new in a couple of months. Or so the doctor claims.

Avery nodded. "How about you?"

"Me?"

"It doesn't appear to me that you're going to recover in a couple of months," he said boldly.

McFarland paled and glared at his assistant before walking into his office and soundly closing the door. Avery was right; McFarland doubted that he'd ever be the same again. He had been shaken to the very roots of his existence. He buried his face in his hands and sat, unmoving, for what seemed like hours.

Somehow he made it through the day, dictating memos, making decisions, charting the course of financial institutions, but for the little emotion he put into it, he could have been playing Monopoly. Nothing seemed real; nothing seemed right.

The mere thought of food nauseated him; he couldn't eat; he couldn't work. And when night came, he discovered he couldn't sleep, either. He'd tried to stay away, to let her rest, and realized it was impossible.

The nurse in the stiff white uniform answered his knock on Judy's door.

"She's sleeping."

McFarland nodded, feeling foolish. "Go ahead and take a break, I'll stay with her."

The woman looked grateful, and left soon afterward.

McFarland was thankful to spend the time alone with Judy. Her face was relaxed now and revealed no signs of pain. That eased the load of guilt that had burdened him from the moment he had watched Judy slide helplessly from the mare's back.

He couldn't tolerate the thought of her in pain. He wasn't squeamish, never had been, but Judy's whimper had had the most curious effect upon him. He had gone weak. With others, McFarland had often battled feelings of rage; with Judy he could only blame himself. He felt sick with his guilt.

"John." His name was little more than a faint whisper.

"I'm here." Anxiously, he scooted the chair to her bedside.

The clock on the nightstand said it was near midnight. Or was it noon? Judy didn't know anymore. Everything remained so fuzzy and unclear in her mind. "Have you been here all this time?"

"No." He shook his head. "The nurse needed a break."

"The nurse?"

"Yes, the doctor felt you needed around-the-clock attention."

"That's ridiculous." She tried to laugh and sucked in a harsh breath, her ribs heartily protesting.

"Sh, you're suppose to keep quiet."

She ignored that and pushed herself up on one elbow. "Help me sit up, would you?"

"No."

"John, please, I need to talk to you."

"No, you don't."

"I'm on my deathbed, remember? Humor me."

He grudgingly helped her into a sitting position. Next he fluffed up her pillow and securely tucked the sheets around her waist.

A smile lit up her eyes and for the life of him, McFarland couldn't tear his gaze away. "There," he said, proudly, brushing his palms against each other several times as though he had accomplished some amazing feat.

"What's that?" Judy pointed toward a small crate on the floor next to the dresser.

"A gift."

"From whom?"

"Me."

Although it required some effort, she managed a smile. "Well, for heaven's sake, bring it to me."

He lifted it from the crate after breaking away the rugged strips of wood. It was cradled in a thick blanket. "I meant to have it wrapped, all frilly with bows, the way you'd like."

"Oh, John, it doesn't matter. As it is, I don't understand why you'd want to buy me anything."

The room went quiet as McFarland reclaimed his chair. "Go ahead and open it."

The object was heavy and awkward in her lap. With infinite care, Judy unrolled the blanket, her excitement growing. As the bronze figure became recognizable, she paused and raised her eyes to his. "John? Oh, John, could it be what I think it is?"

He arched both eyebrows playfully. "I don't know."

Tears filled her eyes and Judy bit her bottom lip, too overcome to speak.

"Judy?"

She pressed her fingers to her mouth as she blinked back the tears. "It's the Riordan sculpture Mother gave Father. He was forced to sell it . . . recently."

"Yes."

"You knew?" Her hand lovingly traced the bronze piece, stroking it as though she hadn't believed that she would ever hold it in her hands again.

Reverently, she set the sculpture aside and lifted her arms to John. Tears glistened in her eyes. "Come here," she whispered brokenly. "I want to thank you."

Chapter Eight

McFarland made excuses to visit Judy. Ten times a day he found reasons that demanded he go to her. He discovered it was necessary to confer with her nurse at least twice a day, sometimes three times. He delivered Judy's lunch along with his own so they could share their meals together. In the evening, he felt Miss Reinholt, the nurse, should have some time off, so McFarland took it upon himself to stay with the patient. Seldom did he come empty-handed. Judy's injury was the perfect excuse for him to give her the things he felt she deserved.

Judy's eyes would light up with such happiness at his arrival that each day his excuses became all the more flimsy. The Riordan sculpture rested on the nightstand and more than once McFarland had caught Judy gazing at it longingly. He knew the piece reminded her of her life in New York, but she never mentioned leaving the island. Nor did he.

"John," Judy whispered the third day of her convalescence. "You have got to get rid of that woman." She bobbed her head in the direction of the stiff-backed nurse who sat knitting in the opposite corner of the room.

"Why?" He lowered his voice conspiratorially, his eyes twinkling.

"I'm not joking, so quit laughing at me! Miss Reinholt is driving me batty. Every time I turn around she's flashing a light in my eyes or placing a thermometer under my tongue. When I complained, she suggested there were other areas where she could stick the blasted thing."

Despite himself, McFarland burst into laughter.

Judy's eyes narrowed and she whispered gruffly, "I'm pleased you find this so amusing."

"I'm sorry," he said, but he didn't feel the least bit contrite.

In a huff, Judy crossed her arms over her chest and tried to be angry with him. She couldn't. He'd been so wonderful, so attentive, that it wasn't in her to find fault with him. It was as though he yearned to make up to her for his harshness since her arrival on the island.

"I'm sick of sitting in bed." She tried to appear stern, but the edges of her mouth quivered with suppressed laughter.

He grinned and nodded.

"You'd think I was the only woman ever to survive two cracked ribs—the way everyone's acting. I've got news for you. I am not a medical marvel."

"I realize that."

"You don't," she countered, struggling to keep her voice low and unemotional. "Otherwise you'd let me up."

"You're allowed to get up."

"Sure, for five minutes every hour. Big deal." She stuck out her arm. "I'm losing my tan! I'll have you know I worked hard for this."

He chuckled and Judy resisted the urge to stick her elbow into his ribs. He seemed to find the entire situation comical.

"You aren't taking me seriously, John, and it's driving me crazy!"

"All right, all right. I'll tell Miss Reinholt that you're allowed to get up more often."

"I want to sit in the sun," she pleaded.

"Perhaps tomorrow."

It would do little good to argue. "Promise?"

He nodded. His eyes held hers and were so warm and caressing that Judy wondered why she ever longed for sunshine when she had John.

"And . . ."

"Hmm?"

"No more gifts." Her room was filled to overflowing with everything he'd given her. There was hardly available space for all the flowers—roses, orchids, daisies. In addition, he'd given her bottle upon bottle of expensive French perfumes, and jewelry until she swore she could open her own franchise. Her slightest wish had been fulfilled ten times over.

"I like giving you things."

Her hand reached for his. Intuitively Judy recognized that John was soothing his conscience. A troubled frown lined her forehead. It was important that he know she didn't blame him. "The accident wasn't your fault."

His fingers grasped hers and his face tightened. "I caused you to fall..."

"John, no." Her free hand caressed his clenched jaw. "I was the one who ran from you. It was an accident." In her heart, the pain of her cracked ribs was a small price to pay for an end to the hostility between them.

Miss Reinholt set her needlework aside and checked her watch. "It's time to take Miss Lovin's temperature," she announced in a crisp, professional tone.

"See what I mean?" Judy said out of the side of her mouth.

"I'd better get back to the office." John leaned over and lightly brushed his lips over hers, then stood and left the room.

Obediently, Judy opened her mouth as the nurse approached. She lay back and closed her eyes, savoring the memory of those few minutes with John. Although he came often, he seldom stayed more than ten or fifteen minutes. Judy was so pleased to see him for any amount of time that she didn't complain.

John wasn't her only visitor. Avery Andersen arrived shortly after noon, pulled up a chair and talked for an hour. He was such a fuddy-duddy that Judy had to struggle to keep from laughing. He wasn't any taller than she and couldn't seem to finish a sentence without stuttering. Toward the end of their conversation, he seemed to relax.

Ten minutes after Avery's visit, John reappeared, looking perplexed. He ran his fingers through his hair and studied her. "What did you say to Avery?"

"When?"

"Just now. He was here, wasn't he?"

Judy nodded. "I didn't say anything special. He came to see how I was doing. You didn't mind, did you? I mean, if he should have been doing something else, I apologize."

John's look was absent as he shook his head. "We'd finished for the day."

"Is something wrong?"

John smiled then, a rich, rare smile. "He's decided to stay."

"Avery? I didn't know he was leaving."

"He isn't," he muttered, bemused. "At least, not anymore."

"Well, I'm pleased if you are."

He stared at her. "You're sure you didn't say anything?"

"I said a lot of things."

His gaze returned to her. "Like what?"

"John, honestly. I don't know . . . I mentioned the weather and we talked about the stock market—he was far more knowledgeable about the subject than I'll ever be. We talked about you some, but only a little bit. Now that you mention it, he did seem overly nervous at first."

"Avery's always nervous."

"Then there was nothing out of the ordinary."

McFarland sat on the edge of the bed and braced his hands on either side of her head. "It appears I'm in your debt again."

"Good, I like it that way."

He looked as though he wanted to kiss her. He even bent his head closer to her own, his gaze centered on her lips. Judy wished he would and tried to beckon him with her eyes, but he didn't and left soon afterward, leaving her frustrated and more than a little disappointed. He had kissed her several times since the accident, light kisses that teased her with the memory of other more potent ones. He treated her more like an indulgent older brother. Infuriated, she was powerless to change his attitude until she was out of bed.

Disappointed, Judy crossed her arms over her chest and sighed dejectedly. She couldn't blame John for not finding her tempting; she must look a sight with her plain nightgowns. What she wouldn't give for a skimpy piece of silk!

Feeling tired, Judy slept for the next hour and woke to distant hammering, at least that was what it sounded like. The tap, tap, tap was so faint that she was astonished that she even heard it.

"What's that noise?" She sat upright, looking toward her nurse.

"Is it troubling you? Mr. McFarland instructed me to let him know if the construction disturbed your rest."

"Construction?"

"Yes, Mr. McFarland is having a medical clinic built. I'll be staying on the island full-time following your recovery."

"He's building a clinic?"

"Yes, I've already seen several of the children for physical examinations. Arrangements are being made to fly a doctor in twice a week from now on."

Judy was too astonished to make a sound. Stinging tears filled her eyes. Grimacing at the pain, Judy tossed aside the sheets and climbed out of bed. She reached for the robe that lay at the foot of her bed.

"Miss Lovin, what are you doing?"

She wiped the tears from her face and tried to speak, but couldn't. Instead, she shook her head, and, holding her hand against her side, walked out of her room.

"Just where do you think you're going?" Virginia Reinholt demanded, hands pressed against her overly round hips.

It was all Judy could do to point down the stairs.

"Miss Lovin, I must insist that you return to your room immediately. Mr. McFarland will be most displeased."

Judy ignored the woman and carefully moved down the stairs, taking one step at a time. It hurt to walk, but she discovered that pressing her arm against her side lessened the ache.

The middle-aged nurse ran ahead of Judy and was waiting for her at the bottom of the stairs. "I must insist you return to your room this instant."

"No," Judy said with as much resolve as she could muster.

"Then you leave me no option but to inform my employer." The nurse marched toward McFarland's suite of offices.

The flustered woman was standing in front of Avery's desk, visibly displeased when Judy appeared. Avery wiped his forehead with his handkerchief, straightened his bow tie and nodded now and again.

Judy sidestepped them both, knocked politely on John's door and let herself into his office.

"Judy?" He rose to his feet immediately. "Good God, woman, what are you trying to do? Kill yourself?" He noted her tears then, and lowered his voice sufficiently. "Love, what is it?" He walked around his desk and pulled her into his arms.

Judy tried to tell him, but her voice refused to cooperate. Whimpering softly, she framed his face with her hands and spread a foray of kisses over his jaw and cheeks, quick, random kisses. Unerringly, she found his eyes, his nose, his ear. She kissed him again and again, ignoring his weak protests.

"Judy," he said thickly, his hands on her upper arms.

He continued to speak, but Judy effectively cut him off by slanting her mouth over his, thanking him silently for his thoughtfulness. Eagerly, her lips parted moist under his, and the first sensuous taste of his mouth stilled her.

Gently, McFarland forced her mouth open wider. The intensity of the kiss rocked them both and, feeling weak, he found a chair and sat with her nestled in his lap.

He drew her closer and teased her with feathery strokes of his tongue. Judy moaned, lost in the whirling sensation.

McFarland had restrained from holding or touching her like this. Her innocence humbled him, and he feared he would frighten her with the fierce passion she aroused in him.

Since the accident, he'd kissed her a handful of times, but each gentle kiss had only created more of a need than it satisfied. Now her tongue boldly met his own, dueling, probing deeper and deeper, stroking and exploring. McFarland trembled uncontrollably like a leaf trapped in the wind. His need for her mounted with such intensity that it sapped the strength from him. Her unrestrained breasts were full and ripe against his chest and it was another torture not to fill his hands with them and know for himself the feel of her silken skin against his own. Emotions that had been hiding just below the surface gushed forth, nearly overpowering him with their intensity.

Groaning, McFarland tore his mouth free and nuzzled his face in her neck, holding her as close as he dared, afraid of causing her further pain. Her tenderness enveloped him, and with it a desire so overwhelming that he couldn't hold her much longer and remain sane.

"John," she pleaded, "don't stop."

"Oh, Lord..." He kissed her again because refusing her anything was beyond him. His mouth ardently claimed hers, and when he'd finished, their breathing was staggered and weak.

Gently, he held her face and wiped the tears from her cheek with the side of his thumb, still aghast at the power she held over him. "What happened?"

She shook her head. "I heard pounding... or what I thought was... pounding."

McFarland nodded, encouraging her to continue.

"You're building a medical clinic?"

"Yes."

She brushed her hands over his face, stroking, savoring every inch of his beloved features while she gathered her composure. "Thank you," she said in a small, broken voice.

McFarland studied her, more perplexed than ever. He'd given her a host of gifts, but nothing had evoked this response. Not even the sculpture. A simple medical clinic had reduced her to tears.

A hard knock forced them apart.

"I must apologize for this rude interruption, Mr. McFarland," the nurse said, standing just inside the door, looking angry and frustrated. "There was no stopping her—I did try."

"I flew the coop," Judy whispered, and was rewarded with a quick smile from John.

"I really must insist that she return to bed immediately."

"Oh, do I have to?" Judy asked with a ragged sigh.

McFarland stood, bringing Judy with him. "Yes, you must."

"Another day of this and you might as well bury me in my jammies." Playfully, she pressed the back of her hand to her forehead and rolled her eyes.

"Another kiss like that," McFarland said, low enough for only Judy to hear, "and you can bury me, too."

Virginia Reinholt led the way back to Judy's room, clucking as she went, listing Judy's myriad faults with each step.

Judy looked into John's eyes as he carried her, letting him know who was really the injured party as far as her nurse went.

McFarland followed Miss Reinholt into the room and gently lowered Judy to the bed. She didn't release her arms from around his neck, but held him a moment longer while she whispered, "Just wait until you get sick!"

* * *

"Are you sure you're up to this?" McFarland asked for the fifth time in as many minutes. The thought of her on another horse made him wince.

"If you ask me that one more time I think I'll scream," Judy told him with a scathing look that added credence to her threat. "It's been three weeks since the accident. I'm not recovering from brain surgery, you know!"

"But horseback riding . . ."

"If Miss Reinholt approved, so can you. Besides, I want to ride again before I lose my nerve."

"To hell with yours," McFarland muttered, "mine is shot."

Sam brought both Princess and Midnight around to the front of the stables and held Princess while Judy slipped her foot into the stirrup and mounted the mare.

The effort caused a painful twinge, but nothing she wasn't able to readily disguise. "There," she said triumphantly.

"Right." McFarland swung his weight atop Midnight and circled the yard. She hadn't fooled him; she was hurting and he was furious that she wouldn't put this off longer until she'd had the time to heal completely.

"Are you coming or not?" She tossed the question over her shoulder as she trotted ahead of him toward the beach.

"Judy, for God's sake, slow down," he shouted, racing after her.

"No."

The wind carried her laughter and McFarland relaxed in his saddle as the sound washed over him like a healing balm. The last few weeks had drastically altered their relationship.

He had never had a time like this with a woman. A shared look could mean more than an hour's conversation; a kiss in the moonlight could fill him with longing for her. She might have been innocent, but she aroused in him a sensual awareness far stronger than anything he'd ever known. When she laughed, he laughed; when she ached, he ached; when she was happy, he was happy.

He spent as much of his day with her as his business would allow. For the first time, he delegated his duties freely. He'd known that Avery Andersen was a competent manager, but in the past three weeks, he'd learned to fully utilize and appreciate the man's instinctive talents.

If McFarland needed to read over papers regarding his business interests, he would often do it in the evenings. Content simply to be at his side, Judy would sit across from him in the library reading, a book propped in front of her, while he handled his affairs. Oftentimes he found his interest wavering. Watching her was by far the greater joy.

There had been a time when he would have despaired of taking off an afternoon; now he dedicated days to Judy. She was like a multifaceted jewel that sparkled with each twist and turn. Judy Lovin was his jewel, his light . . . his Beauty.

McFarland couldn't imagine his life without her now. Her laughter filled his days; her smile touched his soul. Some inner, spiritual part of himself must have known this would happen—that was the only possible explanation for why he had forced her to come to the island. For the first time in his life he was utterly content. There were no more mountains to conquer, no more bridges to cross. There was nothing he desired more than what he possessed right at that moment.

"I've missed this," Judy said happily, breaking into his thoughts.

He'd ridden only five or six times himself, preferring to spend any free time with her.

"John," she said, her voice softening, "I thought I specifically asked you to stop buying me gifts."

"I vaguely recall something to that effect," he said, feeling glib.

"If you think you've fooled me, you're wrong. I know exactly what's been going on."

"I wouldn't dream of disregarding your wishes." He did his best to disguise a smile.

"I suppose you don't think I've noticed the way Sam's been walking around like a peacock. You've bought another horse."

The woman was a marvel. Shaking his head, McFarland chuckled. "She's a beauty. You're going to love her."

"Oh, John, honestly. What am I going to do with you?" *Love me. Marry me. Give me children. Fill my life with joy and laughter.* The possibilities were endless.

"Oh, John, look," Judy cried. "The children are playing in the surf."

McFarland paused, watched their antics and laughed.

"They haven't seen you in a couple of weeks," he said after a moment. "I'll wait for you here."

"Wait for me?" She turned questioning eyes to him.

"I'll frighten them away."

Judy frowned. She understood what he meant, but it was time the children got to know him the way she did, the way he really was. "But you're with me," she explained, climbing down from Princess. "Come on." She held her hand out to him.

McFarland felt a twinge of nervousness as he joined her. He hadn't been around children much and if he were to admit it, he would tell her that he felt as apprehensive as they did.

"Philippe. Elizabeth." Judy called their names and watched as they turned, paused only a moment, then raced toward her.

"Judy!"

Arms went flying around her amidst a chorus of happy cries.

Judy fell to her knees and joyously hugged each one.

"We heard you nearly died."

"There's a nurse on the island now. Did you know that?"

"Paulo got a new tooth."

"It'll take more than a fall to do me in," she told them with a light laugh, dismissing their concern. She raised her eyes to John's, daring him to contradict her. "Children, I have someone I want you to meet." She rose to her feet and slipped her arm around John's waist. "This is Mr. McFarland. He owns the island."

All the children froze until Elizabeth and Margaret curtsied formally, their young faces serious as they confronted John McFarland. The boys bowed then, tucking their arms around their waists.

McFarland frowned, raised his brows at Judy and followed the boys' example, bending in half. "I'm most pleased to make your acquaintance."

"Did you build us the school?"

"The nurse stuck a needle in my arm, but I didn't cry."

"The doctor said I have to eat my vegetables."

The flurry of activity took him by surprise. Patiently, he was introduced to each child.

"Judy. Judy." Jimmy came running from the edge of the jungle, carrying a huge cage. "Did you see my bird?"

The youth was so obviously proud of his catch that Judy paid undue attention to the large blue parrot. "He's lovely."

"I caught him myself," Jimmy went on to explain. "He was trapped in the brush and I grabbed him and put him inside the cage."

The square box had been woven from palm leaves. "You did an excellent job.".

"He sings, too. Every morning."

"I think you should set him free," Margaret said, slipping her hand into Judy's. "No one's happy in a cage."

"But he sings," Jimmy countered.

"He's such a pretty bird," Philippe said, sticking his finger into the holes, hoping the parrot would jump on it. Instead, his wings fluttered madly in an effort to escape.

"I give him food. He'll even let me hold him."

"But how do you know that he's happy?" Margaret persisted.

"Because I just do!"

"But how do you know he'll be happy tomorrow?"

"Because he will!"

Judy felt the blood drain from her face. The happy chatter of the children sharply abated. Even the ocean appeared to hold back the surf. Judy couldn't take her eyes from the blue parrot. Her throat clogged with emotion. She was like that bird. Against her will, she had been trapped into coming to the island. John had forced her into leaving everything she loved behind. He had given her gift upon gift, petted her, held her in high regard, but it had changed nothing. She was still in a cage, a gilded one, but nevertheless a cage. She could flutter her wings, wanting to escape, but she was trapped as effectively as the parrot.

"I...think I should get back to the house," she said, her voice shaky and weak.

"It was too much for you," John grumbled, taking her by the elbow and leading her back to Princess. "You've gone pale," he said gently, studying her.

Judy felt as though someone had robbed her of her happiness. She'd been playing a fool's game to believe that she could ever be more than a plaything to John. He had told her when she first arrived that she had been brought to St. Steven's to amuse him. She'd fulfilled that expectation well, so content was she with her surroundings.

The ride back to the house seemed to require all her energy.

"I'm contacting the doctor," McFarland announced the minute they had dismounted and the horses had been led away. "I knew it was too soon, but I went against my better judgment."

"No," Judy said, hardly able to look at him. "I'll go lie down for a moment. Then I'll be fine." She knew that wasn't true, but she needed an excuse to get away from him and think. She doubted that she'd ever be the same again.

A letter was waiting for her on the dresser in her room. She stared at the familiar handwriting and felt overwhelmingly homesick. Tears burned for release as she held the envelope to her breast and closed her eyes. Home. Her father. David. New York had never seemed so far from her, or so unattainable.

The content of the letter had an even more curious effect upon her. Suddenly in control of herself again, she marched out of her room and down the stairs to confront John.

He was in his office dictating letters to Avery when she approached him. He looked up, surprised to find her standing here. "Judy," he said softly. "Are you feeling better?"

"I'm fine." She noted how he smiled blithely, unaware of the change in her spirit. "John, I need to talk to you."

He dismissed Avery with a shake of his head. Judy closed the door after his assistant and turned to face him, pressing her hands against the door. Her lack of emotion surprised even her.

"There was a letter from my family in my room when I returned."

"I'd heard one had been delivered."

She dropped her hands to her side. "My brother is getting married."

McFarland grinned, pleased the other man had found someone who would share his life. "It seems the shipping business has improved." With a little subtle help from him. The Lovins need never know, and it eased his conscience to repay them in small measure for sending Judy to him.

"My father is happy with his choice and so am I. David has loved Marie for several years now, but delayed the wedding because ... well, you know why."

For having received such good news, Judy didn't appear happy.

"John," she said, boldly meeting his gaze. "I've been here nearly three months now."

"Yes."

"You asked me and I came without question. I've never asked to go free."

A sense of dread filled McFarland. "What are you saying?"

"John, please, I want to go home."

Chapter Nine

"I won't let you go," McFarland answered thickly.

Judy closed her eyes to the bittersweet pain. "I haven't amused you enough?" At his blank stare, she continued. "That was the reason you brought me to the island, or so you claimed."

"That has nothing to do with it."

"Then what does?"

McFarland's control was slipping and rather than argue, he reached for his pen and scribbled instructions across the top of a sheet. If he ignored her, maybe she would forget her request and drop the entire matter.

"John," she said softly. "I'm not going away until you answer me."

"I've already said everything I intend to. The subject is closed."

"The subject is standing in front of you demanding an answer!"

"You're my guest."

"But you won't allow me to leave."

A strained, heavy silence fell between them. Judy's breathing was fast and shallow. Her throat burned as she struggled to hold back her emotions.

"John, please."

"You are my guest."

"I may leave?"

"No!" His rage was palpable. He didn't know why, after all these weeks, she would ask him to release her. His heart felt like a stone in his chest.

The ugly silence returned.

When Judy spoke again, her voice was incredibly soft, yet tortured. "Then I'm your prisoner."

She turned and left him, feeling as though she were living out her worst nightmare. She dared not look back; the tears nearly blinded her as she stepped out of his office.

McFarland watched her go, overcome by an unidentifiable, raw emotion. She claimed to be his prisoner, but there were chains that bound him just as strongly. She'd come to him and within a matter of weeks had altered the course of his life. He couldn't afford to lose Judy—she was his sunshine, his joy. She'd brought summer to the dark winter of his existence. Dear God, how could he ever let her go?

Judy returned to her suite. Dark clouds weighted her heart. She'd been happy with John and the island life. Everything had been good—until she had seen the cell. Now she stood in front of her own set of bars, her hands gripping the steel of her gilded cage. Like the bird wildly seeking escape, her wings were frantically beating, seeking freedom.

When her eyes were empty of tears, she took her brother's letter and withdrew it from the envelope. For the third time, she read it. Every word was a more painful form of torture. Things she'd taken for granted returned to haunt her. Bently and the funny way he had of speaking out of the corner of his mouth; the dining-room chairs that were a family heritage; the Priscilla drapes that hung over her bedroom windows.

Her beloved brother was getting married. Some of the weight lifted from her heart as she thought of David as a husband and someday a father. Marie would make him a good wife. His excitement and joy were evident in the letter. She could almost see him with his eyes sparkling and his arm around Marie's shoulder. How Judy wished she could be with him to share in this special moment.

At noon, although she had no appetite, Judy left her rooms and paused just inside the dining room. John was waiting for her, standing at his end of the table, his hands braced against the back of his chair.

"Are you feeling better?" he asked cordially.

"No." She dropped her gaze to the table. A small, beautifully wrapped gift rested beside her water glass. She raised questioning eyes to John, unsure of what to make of this.

"Go ahead and open it."

She wanted to tell him that she wouldn't accept any more gifts. He couldn't buy her as he'd done everything else in his life. She wasn't for sale. The only thing she sought from John McFarland was the freedom to return home, and he wouldn't allow that.

Dutifully, she sat down and peeled away the paper. Inside was a diamond bracelet of such elegance and beauty that her breath caught in her lungs. "It's beautiful."

John looked exceedingly pleased. "I was saving it for just the right moment."

Judy gently closed the velvet box and set it aside. "Why now? Did you want to prove that my shackles are indeed jewel-encrusted? You needn't have bothered, John. I've always known that."

His face convulsed and, as he stared at her, his eyes grew dark and hot.

Neither spoke another word during their meal, and when Judy left the dining room, she pointedly left the bracelet behind.

A week passed, the longest, most difficult week of Judy's life. She didn't ask John to release her again, but her desire to leave the island hung between them at every meeting. Although she avoided him, he seemed to create excuses to be with her. He chatted easily, telling her little things, pretending nothing had changed. Judy wasn't that good an actress; she spoke only when he directed a question to her. Although she strove to remain distant and aloof, it was difficult.

To work out her frustration, she rode long hours across the island. The sweltering heat of late summer was oppressive. One afternoon toward dusk, she changed from her riding clothes into her swimming suit.

The pool was blissfully cool when she dove in. She hoped the refreshing water would help alleviate the discomfort of the merciless sun and her own restlessness. She swam lazy laps, drawing comfort from the effort of mundane exercise.

She hadn't been in the water ten minutes when John joined her. As he approached the pool, Judy swam to the shallow end, stood up and shakily brushed the wet hair from her face. She defied him with her eyes, demanding that he leave and give her some privacy.

He ignored her silent pleas and jumped into the pool. At first he did little more than laps. Somewhat relieved, Judy continued her exercise. When he suddenly appeared beside her, it was a surprise.

"Remember the last time we were in the water together?" he asked, his voice husky and low.

In an effort to get away from him, Judy swam to the deep end and treaded water. She remembered that afternoon on the beach all too well; he'd held her in his arms while the rolling surf plunged them underwater. He had kissed her and held her body close to his as the powerful surf had tossed them about.

Now his presence trapped her. She refused to meet his commanding look.

"You remember, don't you?" He demanded an answer.

"Yes," she cried, and swallowed hard.

His face tightened and he lowered his voice, each syllable more seductive than the last. "So do I, Judy. I remember the way you slid your arms around my neck and buried your face in my chest."

She shook her head in silent denial.

"You trembled when I kissed you and you clung to me as though I were your life. I remember everything. You tasted of sunshine and honey."

Judy closed her eyes. "And salt," she whispered involuntarily. "You claimed I tasted like salt."

"That, too."

"Don't." She desperately wanted him to leave her and pleaded in a hoarse whisper for him to do exactly that.

"I'm not going." He noted that her eyes were overly bright and that she was struggling to hold back the tears. "I miss you. I want things to go back to the way they were."

Her chin rose and the blood drained from her face. "It can't," she cried, her mouth trembling. "It never can again."

As much as he tried, McFarland couldn't understand what had changed. Why had she all of a sudden come to him and asked to return to New York? He had tried—God knew he'd tried—to understand, but she'd made it impossible. In a week, she hadn't spoken more than a few times to him. He'd attempted to draw her out, to discover what was troubling her. All she did was look at him with her large, soulful eyes as though she would burst into tears at any moment. After a week, he was quickly losing his patience.

"Why can't it be the same?" he asked.

"I'm your prisoner."

"You aren't," he shouted.

"You brought me here as an amusement."

"In the beginning, perhaps, but that's all changed."

"But it hasn't," she said flatly. "Nothing has. I'm your pawn."

"But you were happy."

She flinched at the truth. "Yes, for a time I was."

"What changed?"

"The walls," she said in a tormented voice. "I could see the walls closing in around me."

McFarland hadn't a clue as to what she was talking about. Walls? What walls? She had more freedom now than she recognized. She ruled his heart; he was hers to do with as she wished.

"Judy," he said, trapping her against the bright blue tile of the pool. His face was only inches from hers. "You're talking nonsense."

"To you, maybe... you don't understand."

"I only understand this," he said, weaving his fingers into her wet hair. He kissed her then, pressing his body against her own as he hungrily claimed her mouth, branding her as his.

Judy fought him, bunching her fists and hitting him where she could. Her frantic blows didn't faze him and, with a whimper, she pressed her hands against his broad chest and pushed with all her might.

"Don't fight me," he moaned, holding her tighter. He rubbed his mouth seductively over hers, lightly teasing her, testing her. "It was good with us. You can't have forgotten how good."

"Yes, I remember," she wept. Instinctively, her body arched toward him and she slipped her arms tightly around his neck. She was trembling when he kissed her again and she arched intimately against him. Her mouth opened eagerly to him, giving him everything he wanted. His senses reeled and he nearly lost his grip on the pool's edge.

"I can't let you go," he whispered, and kissed her gently, slowly, again and again until she was weak and clinging in his arms. His body burned with need for her. Raising his head, he looked into her eyes. "I'll give you anything."

Tears scorched a trail down her face. "I only want one thing."

Knowing what she was about to say, McFarland closed his eyes to the pain that lacerated his heart.

"I want my freedom," she sobbed. Her shoulders shook uncontrollably as she climbed out of the pool. "I want to go home."

Guilt tore at him. He could deal with anything but her pain. Judy was using his twisted conscience against him and in that moment, McFarland was convinced he hated her.

Then, seeing her tear-streaked face as she reached for the towel and ran from him, McFarland realized something more—he hated himself twice as much.

Her tears didn't abate, even when Judy returned to her room. The power John had to bend her will to his own shook her to the core of her being. How easily he had manipulated her. His kisses were more potent than her desire to return to her family. Within minutes she had become weak, willing to give him anything he desired.

When McFarland returned to his office, his mood was dark. He was short-tempered with anyone who had the misfortune of being within earshot. It was as though he wanted to punish the world for trying to take the only woman he'd ever cared about from him.

"Mr. McFarland," Avery said, late that same afternoon. He stood just inside the office, not daring to approach his employer's desk.

"What is it?" McFarland barked. "I haven't got all day."

"It's Miss Lovin, sir."

The pencil McFarland was holding snapped in half. "She's staying, Avery, and there's not a damn thing you can say that will change my mind."

"But, sir..."

"In time, she'll accept matters as they are."

"But her family..."

"What about them?"

"They've personally appealed for your mercy. It seems the Lovin boy is getting married and requests his sister's presence at the wedding."

"They appealed for mercy! I hope you told them I have none." McFarland shuffled through some papers, paying unnecessary attention to them.

"The family's requesting some indication of when you plan to release Miss Lovin. The wedding can be delayed at... at your convenience."

"Mine," he snickered loudly. "I hope you told them I have no plans of releasing her."

"You won't let her off the island even to attend her brother's wedding?"

"No."

"But, sir..."

"That will be all, Avery."

McFarland's assistant squared his shoulders and paused as though gathering his courage before speaking.

"Listen, Avery," McFarland barked, unwilling to listen to anyone's opinion regarding Judy. His mind was set. "Feel free to submit your resignation. Only next time I may not be so willing to give it back when you change your mind."

That evening, McFarland sat alone in the library. Over the years since he'd been on the island, he'd spent countless nights in this room. Now it felt as cold and unwelcoming as an unmarked grave. When he couldn't tolerate it any longer, he rose and stepped outside, heading toward the stables. A beer with Sam would ease his mind. He was halfway there when he saw Judy, silhouetted in the moonlight, sitting on the patio by the pool. Her head was slightly bowed, the soft folds of her summer dress pleated evenly around her. The pale light of the moon shone like a halo for the angel she was. Her soft gentleness had never been more apparent.

The scene affected him more than all her pleas. He remembered standing on the ridge and watching her play with the island children on the beach below. He recalled how her eyes would light up just before his mouth met hers; he recalled how she clung to him. With vivid clarity, he remembered the fall from the horse's back and how he would have given everything he had owned not to see her hurt or taken from him. Now, although she wasn't permanently injured, he was losing her.

His presence must have disturbed her, because she turned and her eyes found his. McFarland's stomach knotted at the doubt and uncertainty he saw in her gaze. With everything that was in him, he yearned to

ease her pain, but in doing so he would only increase
his own. He needed her now. The beast who had once
claimed he needed no one was dependent upon a mere
woman.

The sudden thunder and lightning barely registered
in McFarland's mind. The drenching rain soaked him
in minutes, and still he didn't move.

Judy came to him, her gaze concerned.

"Go inside," he rasped.

Her face was bloodless and strained. "Not without
you."

He nearly laughed at her concern. It shouldn't
matter to her what became of him; she was the one
who wanted to walk out of his life.

"John." She urged him again a moment later.

"I find your solicitude a little short of amusing."

The flatness of his voice sent a chill through her
veins. Judy hesitated.

He noted then that she was as drenched as he. "Go
inside," he murmured. "I'll be in after a few minutes."

"If you stay out here, you'll catch a chill."

Raw emotion fueled his anger and he shouted loudly
enough to be heard over the furious clap of thunder.
"Leave me!"

Her eyes welled with tears.

McFarland couldn't bear to see her cry. He stepped
close and cupped her sweet face. His heart ached with
all the emotion he felt for her. He could make her stay,
force her to live on the island and ignore her desire to
leave. In time she would forget her family, accept her
position on St. Steven's and in his life. He would give

her everything a woman would possibly want; everything he owned would be hers.

In that moment, McFarland knew that everything he possessed, all his wealth, all that he was, would never be enough for Judy. He dropped his hands and turned toward the house.

When they reached the front door, John opened it for her. Judy paused and looked up at him. If she were unhappy, she was barely upset compared to the misery she witnessed in his eyes.

"John," she whispered brokenly. Even now his unhappiness greatly affected her. Even now she loved him. "I . . ."

His face tightened as a dark mask descended over his features, a mask she recognized readily. He'd worn it often the first weeks after her arrival. She had forgotten how cold and cruel he could look, how ruthless he could be.

"Don't say it," he interrupted harshly. "Don't say one damn thing. Not a word." He turned and abruptly left her standing alone. Without looking back once, he moved out of the foyer.

Princess was saddled and ready for Judy early the next morning. She hadn't slept well and looked forward to the rigorous exercise.

"Morning, Sam," she said, without much enthusiasm.

The groom ignored her, cupping a stallion's hoof in his lap and running a file across the underside.

"Sam?"

"Morning," he grumbled, not looking at her.

"Is something wrong?" Sam had been her ally and friend from the first.

"Wrong? he repeated. "What could be wrong?"

"I don't know."

"For nearly two weeks now this place has been like a battlefield."

Judy opened her mouth to deny it.

"But does ol' Sam question it? No." He answered his own inquiry and raised his head to glare at her. "I figured whatever was wrong would right itself in time. Looks like I was wrong."

"I wish it were that simple," Judy murmured, stroking Princess's neck.

Sam continued to run the file back and forth across the stallion's hoof. "McFarland bites my head off and you walk around here looking like you spent half the night crying your eyes out. You get any paler and someone could mistake you for a ghost!"

Judy raised her hands to her cheeks, embarrassed.

Sam lowered the stallion's leg to the ground and slowly straightened. "McFarland's been shouting at you again?"

"No."

"Has he been unfair?"

"That's not what this is about."

"Did he get after you for something you didn't do?"

"No."

Hands on his hips, Sam took a step toward her. "Do you love him or not?"

Judy felt the blood rush through her veins.

"Well?" he demanded.

"Yes," she answered, her voice shaking uncontrollably.

"I thought so."

She pushed the hair out of her face. "Loving someone doesn't make everything right."

"Then do whatever it is you have to do to make it that way."

Judy swallowed down the hard lump that had formed in her throat. Sam made everything sound so uncomplicated.

"For heaven's sake, woman, put an end to this infernal bickering. And do it soon, while there's still a man or woman who's willing to remain in McFarland's employ."

Judy rode for hours. When she returned, a maid announced that McFarland wished to see her at her earliest convenience. With her heart pounding, Judy rushed up the stairs for a quick shower.

By the time she appeared in John's office Avery looked greatly relieved to see her.

"You're to go right in," he instructed.

"Thank you, Avery," she said as he opened the door for her.

John was writing, his head bent, and although she was fairly certain he knew she was there, he chose to ignore her.

After the longest minute of her life, he raised his gaze to hers and gestured for her to take a seat. His look was cool and distant.

Judy shivered as she sat down. "I've been in communication with New York this morning," he said evenly.

She nodded, not knowing exactly what he was leading up to. He could be referring to her family, but he hadn't said as much.

"The launch will leave the island at five tomorrow morning. However, the copter is at your disposal."

Judy blinked. "Are you saying I'm free to leave?"

"That's exactly what I'm saying."

It took a minute for the full realization to hit Judy. She sighed as the great burden was lifted from her shoulders. "John..."

He ignored her. "From what I understand, you'll be home in plenty of time for your brother's wedding."

Her smile was tremulous. "Thank you."

He nodded abruptly. "Is tomorrow soon enough, or would you prefer to leave now?"

"Tomorrow is fine."

He returned to his paperwork.

"John..."

"If you'll excuse me, I have work to do," he said pointedly.

The icy harshness in his voice was a slap in the face. Judy stood, clasping her fingers tightly in front of her. "I'll never forget you, John McFarland, or this island."

He continued with his work as though she hadn't spoken.

"If I don't see you again..."

John glanced at his watch and while she was speaking, reached for his phone and punched out a number.

Judy blinked back stinging tears of anger and embarrassment.

"Goodbye, John," she said softly, and with great dignity, turned and left his office.

That evening Judy ate alone. The dining-room table had never seemed so big or the room so empty. She'd spent the afternoon preparing for her departure. Her suitcase was packed, her room bare of the items that had marked it as hers. She'd visited the children one last time and had stopped at the stables to feed Princess and Midnight. Sam had grumbled disapprovingly when he heard she was leaving and when she hugged him goodbye, the gruff old man's eyes glistened.

"I didn't think you'd fix things up this way," he barked.

After all the excitement, Judy had expected to sleep that evening. To her surprise, she couldn't.

At midnight, she silently made her way down the stairs for a glass of milk. The light from under the library door surprised her. She cracked it open to investigate and found John sitting at the oak desk, a half-full whiskey bottle in one hand and a shot glass in the other.

He raised his gaze to study her when she entered the room. His eyes widened in disbelief, then narrowed. "What are you doing here?"

The words were slurred and barely discernible. Judy shook her head, hardly able to believe what she was seeing. In all the weeks that she'd been on the island, John had never abused alcohol. "You're drunk."

He lifted the bottle in mocking salute. "You're damn right I am."

"Oh, John." She nervously tucked her hair behind her ear, feeling wretched.

"You think too highly of yourself if you believe I did this because you're leaving."

"I..."

He refilled his glass, the whiskey sloshing over the sides of the glass. He downed the contents in one swallow and glared at her maliciously. "You were a damn nuisance."

Judy swallowed a heated response.

"I would have done well to be rid of you weeks ago."

Ten excellent excuses to turn and walk away presented themselves. Judy ignored each one. For some perverse reason she wanted to hear what he had to say.

"You're such a damn goody-goody."

She clasped her fingers more tightly together.

Again he filled the shot glass. "I could have had you several different times. You know that, don't you? God knows, you were willing enough." His eyes challenged her to defy him. "But I didn't take what you so generously offered me." His short laugh lacked humor. He bent forward and glared at her. "You know why? I like my women hot and spicy. You're sweet, but you'd soon grow tasteless."

Judy felt as though her face were red enough to guide lost ships into harbor. Each word was a lash across her tender back, salt to the wound, alcohol poured over the festering sore.

His eyes grew cold as he glared at her. He took a drink straight from the bottle. "Why are you still standing there?"

Judy couldn't answer him. She shook her head and wiped the moisture from her face.

"Get out," he roared. "Out of my house! Out of my life!"

A part of Judy yearned to wrap her arms around him and absorb his anger. The battle raged within her.

"Go on," he shouted forcefully. "Get out of here before I do something we'll both regret."

"Goodbye, John," she whispered tightly. She closed the massive doors when she left and flinched at the unexpected sound of breaking glass.

"Goodbye, Beauty."

The words were so faint that Judy wasn't convinced she had heard them.

Judy sat in her room, waiting for the sun to rise. She hadn't slept after the confrontation in the library; she hadn't even tried.

At four, the maid came to wake her and was surprised to find her already up. "Mr. Andersen will escort you to the dock," the girl informed her.

"Thank you."

Avery was waiting for Judy at the bottom of the stairs. He took the lone suitcase from her hand and gave her a sympathetic look. Judy paused and glanced in the direction of the library.

"Take care of him for me, will you?" she asked.

Avery cleared his throat and looked doubtful. "I'll do my best."

The launch was waiting for them at the dock. Judy hugged John's assistant and Sam, who arrived at the last minute, looking flustered and upset.

Only when the boat had sped away did Judy dare to glance back to the island. In the distance she saw a third figure standing separate from the others.

John McFarland watched the only woman he had ever loved vanish from him life. In releasing her, he had committed the ultimate sacrifice. It was probably the only completely unselfish deed of his lonely life.

Chapter Ten

The sound was what astonished Judy most. Street noise: buses, taxis, traffic, shouts, raised voices, laughter, televisions, radios. The clamor wasn't as irritating as it was distracting. The island had taught her to appreciate the wonders of silence.

But this was Manhattan, not St. Steven's Island, Judy had to repeatedly remind herself. The first few days following her arrival home, she'd felt as though she had returned to another planet. The life that had once been familiar and comfortable felt strangely out of sync and appallingly loud. In time, she realized, she would adjust, just as she had adapted to life on the island.

"It's McFarland, isn't it?" her father asked her over breakfast the first week she was home.

"John?"

Charles Lovin's features were tight with anxiety. Their months apart had taken their toll on the elder Lovin. It showed in the way his eyes followed her, his gaze sad and greatly troubled. "McFarland treated you abominably, didn't he?"

"Of course not," Judy answered, dismissing her father's fears with a generous smile. "John Mc-Farland was the perfect gentleman."

"From the beginning?"

Judy lowered her gaze to her plate as an unexpected twinge of loneliness brought tears to her eyes. "In his own way, yes. He's an unusual person."

"You think I don't know that? I died a thousand deaths worrying about you alone on that island with that...that animal."

"I wasn't alone with John and, Father, really, he isn't a beast."

Charles Lovin's instant denial faded quickly in Judy's ears. She pretended to be listening while her father listed John's many faults in a loud, haranguing voice. Her thoughts were a thousand miles away on a Caribbean island where orchids grew in abundance and children laughed and a man ruled his own kingdom.

"Judy, are you listening to me? Judy?"

"I'm sorry," she said contritely, looking to her father. "What was it you were saying?"

Father and son exchanged meaningful glances.

"I'm sure you can appreciate that Dad and I were concerned about you," David said, studying his sister thoughtfully.

"Naturally, I would have been worried myself had the circumstances been reversed," Judy murmured, feeling wretched. She wanted to defend John, but both her father and her brother were filled with bitterness toward him.

"He never spoke to us personally," David continued. "I can't begin to tell you how frustrated Dad and I were. We must have contacted McFarland a hundred times and never got past that harebrained assistant of his. By the way, what's this Andersen fellow like?"

"Avery?"

"Yes. I tell you, he's an expert at sidestepping questions. No matter how much Dad and I hounded him, we never could get a straight answer."

At the memory of Avery Andersen, Judy brightened and spent the next five minutes describing John's assistant. "He really is a funny little man. So polite and..."

"Polite!" Her father nearly choked on his coffee. "The next thing I know you'll be telling me McFarland is a saint."

Judy blushed at the memory of all the times he could have made love to her, and hadn't. "In some ways he was a saint."

Her announcement was followed by a stunned silence.

"Any man who pulls the kind of stunts John McFarland does will burn in hell," Charles Lovin stated emphatically.

"Father!"

"I mean it. That man is a demon."

Judy pushed her plate aside and valiantly managed not to defend John. "And just what did he do that was so terrible?"

"Why, he . . . he nearly destroyed our business."

"It's thriving now; you told me so yourself."

"Now!" The elder Lovin spat. "But McFarland drove us to the bring of disaster, then took delight in toying with us."

"He told me once that he held you in high regard," Judy informed him.

"Then Lord help us if he ever covets my friendship!"

With great difficulty, Judy kept her own counsel. Neither her father nor her brother could understand John the way she did. Given their position, she would probably feel differently, but that didn't change her opinion of him, her love for him.

"Does he do this sort of thing often?" David asked, as he sliced into his ham.

Judy blinked, not understanding.

"Were there other women on the island?" he elaborated.

"A few. But I was the only one he . . ." She paused and searched for the right word.

"You were the only woman he blackmailed into coming?" her father finished for her.

"The only one he sent for," Judy corrected calmly.

"That man is a menace to society," Charles muttered angrily as he sipped his coffee.

Judy couldn't tolerate their insults any longer. She sighed and shook her head. "I hate to disappoint you both, but John McFarland is kind and good. He treated me with the utmost respect the entire time I was on the island."

"He held you like a prisoner of war."

"He released me when I asked," she told them, stretching the truth only a bit."

"He did?"

"Of course." She dabbed the corner of her mouth with her napkin, ignoring the way both family members were staring at her with their mouths gaping open.

"He held you for three months, Judy," David said, watching her keenly. "You mean to say that in all that time you never asked to leave?"

"That's right."

Again father and son exchanged looks.

"I don't expect you to understand," she told them lamely. "The island is a tropical paradise. I didn't think to ask to leave until ... until the end."

The dining room grew silent.

Her father hugged Judy before she left the room. "It's good to have you home, Beauty."

"It's good to be home."

In her bedroom, Judy ran her fingers over the brocade-covered headboard and experienced none of the homecoming sensations she'd expected. She loved this room; it was a part of her youth, a part of her existence before she had met John McFarland.

Sitting on her mattress now, Judy experienced a poignant sense of loss. She'd changed on the island, blossomed. John had taught her what it was to be a woman and no matter how much she would have wished it, she couldn't go back to being the frightened girl who had left New York destined for a Caribbean island.

A letdown was only natural, Judy tried to reason with herself. When she'd been on the island, home had seemed ideal. Everything was perfect in New York. There were no problems, no difficulties, no heartache. To her dismay, she was learning that reality falls far short of memory.

A polite knock at her door diverted her attention from her troubled thoughts. "Come in."

Marie Ashley, David's fiancé, walked into the room. "Are you ready?"

"I've been ready for weeks," Judy said, rising from the bed. She slipped on a pair of comfortable shoes. "I plan to shop till I drop."

"Me, too," Marie said, her eyes shining. "David and I need so many things. Oh, Judy, we're going to be so happy." She hugged her arms around her middle and sighed with ecstasy. "Did he tell you that I broke into tears when he proposed? I couldn't even answer him. Poor David, I'm sure he didn't know what to make of me, blubbering and carrying on like that."

"I imagine he got the message when you threw your arms around his neck and started kissing him."

Marie's hands flew to her hips. "He told you!"

"Ten times the first day I was home," Judy informed her cheerfully. "I don't know who is more excited, you or my brother."

"Me," Marie said unequivocally.

Laughing, the two hurried down the stairs to the sports car Marie had parked out front.

The day was a busy one. True to their word, both women shopped until their feet ached and they couldn't carry another package. They ended up back at the Lovin family home, bringing take-out Chinese food with them.

Judy deposited her shopping bags in the polished entryway. "Bently," she called, "we're home."

A quick grin cracked the butler's stiff facade as he regarded the pair of them. He already treated Marie like a family member. "Several wedding gifts arrived this afternoon," he informed them primly.

"Here?" Marie asked, surprised.

"I can assure you, Miss Ashley, I did not haul them from your family's home."

"Where are they, Bently?" Judy asked, sharing a smile with Marie.

"I placed them in the library."

"Come on," Marie said eagerly, "let's go check out the loot."

Judy followed her soon-to-be sister-in-law into the book-lined room.

"I took the liberty of unwrapping them for you," Bently said.

Both Judy and Marie paused in the doorway and gasped at the rich display of paintings and sculptures. The room went still and Judy's hand flew to her heart. Each piece was lovingly familiar; they were the items her father had sold in a desperate attempt to save the shipping line. The ones he had surrendered piece by piece, prolonging the agony.

"All this?" Marie gasped. "Who? Who would possibly give us so much?"

Judy knew the answer even before Bently spoke.

"The card says John McFarland."

Judy's eyes drifted shut. John, her John.

"Why, he's the man..." Marie stopped short. "Judy?" Her voice was low and hesitant. "Are you all right?"

Judy forced her eyes open. "Of course. Why shouldn't I be?"

"You look like you're about to faint."

"It's from lack of nourishment," Judy explained, her voice shaking. "You dragged me through half the department stores in Manhattan and didn't feed me lunch. What do you expect?"

"I want you to tell me everything. Now sit down."

Judy followed the order because she wasn't convinced she could remain upright for much longer.

"Bently, bring us some coffee."

"Right away, Miss Ashley."

Despite her misery, Judy smiled, finding a new respect for her brother's fiancé. "I swear, within a year you'll be the one running the family business."

"I'll have my hands full managing David," Marie returned matter-of-factly.

The coffee arrived and Marie poured, handing Judy the first cup. "You don't need to say much," she began gently. "It's obvious to me that you love him."

Judy dropped her gaze. "I do. Unfortunately, my family hates him. They think he's some kind of monster."

"But you know better?"

"I do, Marie. He frightened me in the beginning; he can be terrifying. Believe me, I know he's arrogant and stubborn, but as the weeks passed, I discovered that underneath he was a man like every other man. One with hurts and doubts and fears. I learned how kind and generous he can be."

"But, Judy, he forced you to live on that island."

"It's beautiful there. Paradise."

"David and your father were convinced he was mistreating you."

"Never. Not intentionally. Once I had an accident—my fault, actually, although John seemed to blame himself and..."

Marie gasped.

"I didn't let my family know," Judy explained patiently. "They would have only worried and I couldn't see any point in increasing their anxiety."

"What happened?"

"I fell—it doesn't matter. What is important is that John was so wonderful to me. I've never seen anyone more concerned. He spent hours taking care of me. I think he slept in my room for at least two nights. Every time I woke up, he was there. I...I didn't know any man could be so gentle."

Marie smiled faintly. "What are you planning to do now?"

Judy held the coffee cup in both hands. "I...don't know."

"Do you want to go back to the island?"

Judy hung her head and whispered. "Yes. Nothing's the same without John. I loved St. Steven's, but more importantly I love John."

"Oh, Judy, your father..."

"I know." She managed to keep her voice steady. "I think he'd rather die than see me go back to the island. John will always be the beast in his eyes."

"Give him time," Marie suggested softly. "Look what happened with David and me."

Judy wasn't sure she understood. "I know that David hasn't seen anyone but you for a couple of years."

"Five years, Judy, I waited five long years for that man."

Judy had no idea the romance between them had been brewing all that time.

"With all the financial problems with the business, David told me it could be years before he saw his way clear to marry me or anyone. He told me it was useless for me to wait."

"How painful for you."

"Oh, it gets worse. He broke off our relationship and suggested I marry someone else. When I refused, he insisted that I start seeing other men. He made a point of introducing me to his friends and when that didn't work..." She hedged, and her eyes grew dull with pain.

"What happened?" Judy asked gently.

"I wouldn't give up on him. I loved him too much. If he didn't want to marry me, then I was destined to die an old maid. There's never been anyone else for me. Only David."

"What did he do?"

Marie's smile revealed a great sadness. "He said some cruel things to me in an effort to keep me from—what he called—wasting my life."

Judy recalled her last night on the island and the horrible things John had said to her. He loved her; she was sure of it. But he had never asked her to stay, never told her he loved her. Still, she knew he loved her, just as he must have known.

"Of course, all his angry insults didn't work," Marie continued. "I knew what he was doing. He couldn't have gotten rid of me to save his soul."

"I take it he tried."

Marie's mouth quivered. "Oh, yes, for months. Inventive schemes, too, I might add, but I'm more stubborn than he took into account."

Judy gripped her friend's hand. "I hope he appreciates how lucky he is."

"Are you kidding? I plan to remind him every day for the next fifty years. Now," she said forcefully, sucking in a huge breath. "It's your turn, Judy Lovin, to prove to a man that you mean business."

Judy's gaze rested on their clasped hands. "The night before I left the island, I found John...drinking. He told me he was glad to see me go."

"What did you say?"

"Nothing."

"Good."

"Good?"

"Right. He didn't mean it."

"I know. He was hurting."

Marie smiled then, knowingly. "The guilt is probably driving him crazy about now."

Judy studied her brother's fiancé. "What makes you say that?"

Marie gestured with her hand toward the array of wedding gifts that filled the library. "Look around you, Judy Lovin."

"But..."

"No buts, girl," Marie interrupted. "You're going back to the island. And when you do he'll so happy to see you there won't be a single doubt."

Judy went pale.

"It's what you want, isn't it?"

"Yes, but Father and David..."

"Just who are you planning to spend the rest of your life with, anyway? Do you presume to believe they'll appreciate your sacrifice? Do you think my family was overjoyed with me hanging around year after year?" Marie asked. "Good grief, no! They were convinced that unless I married David, I was going to become a permanent fixture in the old homestead."

Judy laughed, despite her misery.

"My dad was so desperate to get rid of me that he started bringing home strangers off the streets to introduce to his spinster daughter. I'm telling you, between David and my father, I turned down two neurosurgeons, a dentist, three attorneys and a construction tycoon."

The thought was so ridiculous that Judy couldn't stop laughing. Soon Marie joined her and the two kept it up until their sides hurt and tears rolled down their faces.

That one talk with her future sister-in-law gave Judy all the fortitude she needed to face an army of Charles Lovins. She chose her moment well—the reception following David and Marie's wedding.

"Father," she said, standing beside him in the receiving line. "I have something to tell you."

He shook hands with a family friend before turning his attention to his daughter. "Yes, Beauty."

"I love John McFarland."

She expected a bellow of outrage, anger... something other than his acceptance and love. "I suspected as much. Are you going back to him?"

Tears brimmed in Judy's eyes. "Yes."

"When?" His own voice sounded choked.

"Soon."

"He'll marry you?"

Judy chuckled and winked at her sister-in-law. "He'd better."

Charles Lovin arched thick eyebrows. "Why's that?"

"I'm not taking no for an answer. Marie and I have a bet on which one of us is going to present you with your first grandchild."

The older man's eyes sparkled with unshed tears at the prospect. "Then what are you doing sticking around here?" He turned her in his arms and hugged her fiercely. "Be very, very happy."

"I know I will. You'll come visit?"

"If he'll allow it."

Her arms tightened around him. "He will, I promise."

The launch slowed to a crawl as it approached the dock of St. Steven's Island. Two formidable security guards were waiting to intercept the unannounced intruders.

"Miss Lovin?"

"Hello, Wilson," Judy said, handing him her luggage. "Is Mr. McFarland available?"

The guard looked uncertain. "I believe he is. Does he know you're coming?"

"No."

He winced at that, but didn't hesitate to help her climb out of the boat.

"Will you see to it that my things are delivered to my room?" Judy asked.

"Right away."

"Thank you, Wilson."

By the time Judy arrived at the house, there was a small army of McFarland employees following her, all talking excitedly.

Sam arrived, breathless from the stables. "Hot dog," he cried and slapped his knee. "It's about time you got here."

"I was only gone two weeks."

"That's about thirteen days too long!"

"How has he been?"

Sam shook his head. "Meaner than a saddle sore."

Judy glanced around to note that several of the other employees were nodding their heads, agreeing with Sam's assessment.

"He's fired me three times in the last week alone," Wilson volunteered.

"Moi aussi," the chef added, ceremoniously crossing his arms over his chest and pointing his nose toward the sky, greatly insulted. "He had zee nerve to suggest I return to cooking school."

"Everything will be better now that Miss Lovin's back," Sam assured the irate staff. "Next time you leave, though," the groom warned Judy, "we'll all be on that boat with you."

"I won't be leaving," she told them confidently.

A small cheer arose and when Judy entered the house, she was met with a red-faced Avery.

"Miss Lovin!" He looked stunned, flustered, then greatly relieved. "Oh, thank God you're back."

"Where is he?" she asked, resisting the urge to hug her friend.

"The library." He pointed in the direction of the closed doors as though he'd expected her to have forgotten. "I tried to take care of him like you wanted," Avery said, his words coming out in a rush. "Only, Mr. McFarland, well, he didn't exactly take kindly to my solicitude."

"I can imagine," Judy said, grateful for such loyal friends.

Gathering her courage, she stood in front of the library doors. She found it fitting that he would be there. The last time she had confronted him had been in the paneled, book-lined room. Only this time, she planned to do all the talking.

She didn't knock, but gently opened the doors and stepped inside.

"I said I wasn't to be disturbed," John shouted.

Judy's heart constricted at the sight he made, hunched behind a desk. He looked hard, his blue eyes void of any emotion except anger and regret. She noted the lines of fatigue around his eyes and the flatness of his hard mouth.

"John, it's me," she said softly, loving him so much that only her strong will prevented her from walking into his arms.

His head snapped up. His eyes went wide with questioning disbelief and he half rose from his chair. "Beauty." He froze as though he couldn't decide what to do.

"Don't, John."

"Don't?" he repeated, puzzled.

"Don't ask me to leave. I won't, you know."

McFarland heard the catch in her voice and sank back into the leather chair. How well she knew him; the words had dangled on the tip of his tongue to demand that she march back where she came from. It wasn't what he wanted, but he had to protect her from himself.

Judy moved farther into the room. "David's wedding was beautiful, and ours is going to be just as special."

"Ours?" he mocked.

"Yes, ours! You're marrying me, John McFarland."

"You're sure as hell taking a lot for granted."

"Perhaps."

"Judy, no." He wiped his hand over his face, thinking this all could be a dream. It wasn't. "Don't do this. You're making sending you away damn difficult."

She boldly met his glare. "I plan on making it impossible."

He closed his eyes and said nothing for the longest moment. "Judy, there's someone better for you in New York. Some man who will give you the kind of life you deserve. Some man your father will approve of. He's right—I am a beast."

She planted her hands on his desktop, remembering everything Marie had gone through for David. "I only want you."

"Forcing you to live on the island was a mistake."

His face revealed nothing, but she felt the powerful undertow of his emotions.

"It's right for me to love you, John."

He flinched as though she'd struck him.

"I'm not good enough for you," he told her in a hard, implacable voice. "The things I did to your family... the things I did to you."

"Coming to this island was right for me. You're right for me. I love you. All I ask is that you love me in return."

Again he flinched, and his jaw tightened. He reached out and gently stroked her cheek. "I've loved you from the moment you showed me how you'd tamed Midnight."

Her gaze holding his, Judy walked around the desk. McFarland stood.

She slipped her arms around his neck and leaned her weight into him. "Oh, John, life isn't right without you. I had to leave you to learn that there's no one for me anyplace else but right here."

"Judy." He groaned and sought her mouth with a hunger that had been fed with self-hatred and weeks of loneliness. His fingers plowed through her hair as he slanted his mouth over hers. He kissed her again and again, as though it would take a hundred years to make up for the two weeks without her.

"I live in a tropical paradise and it was winter without you," he breathed into her hair.

"It's summer now," she answered, her eyes glistening.

"Yes," he said, his voice raw. His hand was gentle on her hair. "I love you, Beauty. God knows why you want to marry a beast."

"I have my reasons," she said as she lovingly pushed him back into his chair. "There's a small wager I need to tell you about."

"Oh?" He pulled her into his lap and she leaned forward and whispered it in his ear.

The sound of McFarland's laughter drifted through the library doors and the seven who had gathered there sighed contentedly.

Winter had left St. Steven's never to return.

From that moment, the islanders liked to tell how the Beast was gone forever.

Beauty had tamed him.

*   *   *   *   *

ALMOST PARADISE

Debbie Macomber

Chapter One

"Mirror, mirror on the wall—who's the fairest of us all?" Sherry White propped one eye open and gazed into the small bathroom mirror. She grimaced and quickly squeezed both eyes shut. "Not me," she answered and blindly reached for her toothbrush.

Morning had never been her favorite time of day. She agreed with the old adage claiming that if God had intended people to see the sun rise, He would have caused it to happen later in the day. Unfortunately, Jeff Roarke, the director of Camp Gitche Gumee, didn't agree. He demanded his staff meet early each morning. No excuses. No reprieves. No pardons.

Fine, Sherry mused. Then he'd have to take what he got, and heaven knew she wasn't her best at this ungodly hour.

After running a brush through her long, dark curls, Sherry wrapped a scarf around her head to keep the

hair away from her face and returned to her room
where she reached for a sweater to ward off a chill.
Then she hurried across the lush green grass of the
campgrounds to the staff meeting room. Once there,
a hasty glance around told her she was already late.

"Good morning, Miss White," Jeff Roarke called,
when she took the last available seat.

"Morning," she mumbled under her breath, crossing her arms to disguise her embarrassment. He'd
purposely called attention to her, letting the others
know she was five minutes late.

His sober gaze had followed her as she'd maneu-
vered herself between the narrow row of chairs. Now
his intense eyes remained on her until her heart hammered and indignation rose in her breast. She experienced a perverse desire to shatter Jeff Roarke's
pompous attitude, but the feeling died a quiet death as
she raised her gaze to meet his. Was she imagining a
hint of amusement lurking there? At any rate, he was
regarding her with a speculative gleam that was dis-
tinctly unsettling. Evidently satisfied that he'd unnerved her, he began to speak again.

Although she knew she should be taking notes,
Sherry was having trouble tearing her gaze away from
the imperious camp director, now that his attention
was off her. Jeff Roarke was tall, easily over six feet,
and superbly fit. His jaw was lean and well defined—
okay, he was absurdly good-looking, she'd grant him
that. But Sherry sensed an arrogance in him, an un-
compromising authority, an aggressive virility that
really got under her skin.

She'd known a month earlier when she'd met Mr. Almighty Roarke for the job interview that they weren't going to get along. She'd flown to Sacramento from Seattle and met him in his office, praying she hadn't made the long trip in vain. She'd wanted this job so badly... and then she'd blown it.

"I think it's a marvelous idea to name the camp after a cute children's song," she'd said cheerfully.

Roarke looked shocked. "Song? What song? The camp's name is taken from the poem 'Song of Hiawatha' by Henry Wadsworth Longfellow."

"Oh—uh, I mean, of course," Sherry said, her face flaming.

From there the interview seemed shaky, and Sherry was convinced she'd ruined her chances as Roarke continued to ask what seemed like a hundred questions. But although he didn't appear overly impressed with her qualifications, he handed her several forms to complete.

"You mean I'm hired?" she asked, confused. "I...I have the job?"

"I'd hardly have you fill out the paperwork if you didn't," he returned, his face impassive but those hazel eyes of his brimming with amusement.

"Right." Sherry's heart raced with excitement. She was going to escape her wacky stepmother, Phyliss. For one glorious summer no one need know where she was. But as Sherry began to complete the myriad forms her enthusiasm for her plan dwindled. She couldn't possibly put down references—anyone she'd list would be someone who'd have contact with her father and stepmother. The instant her family discovered where Sherry was hiding, it would be over.

Roarke seemed to note Sherry's hesitancy as she studied the forms. "Is there something you disagree with, Miss White?"

"No," she said, hurriedly filling out the names and addresses of family friends and former employers, but doing her best to make them unreadable, running the letters together and transposing numbers.

Nibbling anxiously on her bottom lip, Sherry finished and handed over the completed paperwork.

From that first meeting with Jeff Roarke, things had gone swiftly downhill. Sherry found him... she searched for the right word. Dictatorial, she decided. He'd let it be known as director of Camp Gitche Gumee that he expected her to abide by all the rules and regulations—which was only fair—but then he'd proceeded to give her a Michener-length manual of rules and regulations, with the understanding that she would have it read by the time camp opened. Good grief! She'd been hired as a counselor for seven little girls, not as a brain surgeon.

"Are there any questions?"

Jeff Roarke's words to the early-morning assembly broke into her consciousness, startling Sherry into the present. Worried, she glanced around her, hoping no one had noticed that she'd casually slipped into her memories.

"Most of the children will arrive today," Roarke was saying.

He'd gotten her up at this time of day to tell her that? They'd have to be a bunch of numskulls not to know when the children were coming. All week the entire staff had been working to prepare the cottages and campgrounds for the children's arrival. Sherry glared at him for all she was worth, then squirmed when he paused and stared back at her.

"Is there a problem, Miss White?"

Sherry froze as the others directed their attention to her. "N-no."

"Good—then I'll continue."

The man never smiled, Sherry mused. Not once in the past week had she seen him joke or laugh or kid around. He was like a man driven, but for what cause she could only speculate. The camp was important to him, that much she'd gleaned immediately, but why a university professor would find such purpose in a children's camp was beyond Sherry's understanding. There seemed to be an underlying sadness in Jeff Roarke, too, one that robbed his life of joy, stole the pleasure of simple things from his perception.

But none of the counselors seemed to think of Jeff Roarke the same way she did. Oh, the other female staff members certainly noticed him, Sherry admitted grudgingly. From the goo-goo eyes some of the women counselors were giving him, they too were impressed with his dark good looks. But he was so stiff, so dry, so serious that Sherry considered him a lost cause. And she had enough on her mind without complicating her life worrying about someone like the camp director.

Sherry expected to have fun this summer. She needed it. The last three years of college, living near home, had left her mentally drained and physically exhausted. School was only partly to blame for her condition. Phyliss was responsible for the rest. Phyliss and her father had married when Sherry was a college freshman and Phyliss, bless her heart, had never had children. Seeing Sherry as her one and only opportunity to be a mother, she'd attacked the project with such gusto that Sherry was still reeling from the effects three years later. Phyliss worried that Sherry wasn't eating well enough. Phyliss worried about the hours she kept. Phyliss worried that she studied too hard. To state the problem simply—Phyliss worried.

As a dedicated health nut, her stepmother made certain that Sherry ate correctly. There were days Sherry would have killed for a pizza or a hot dog, but Phyliss wouldn't hear of it. Then there was the matter of clothes. Phyliss loved bright colors—and so did Sherry, in moderation. Unfortunately, her stepmother considered it her duty to shop with Sherry and "help" her choose the proper clothes for college. As a result, her closet was full of purples, army greens, sunshine yellows and hot, sizzling pinks.

So she'd planned this summer as an escape from her wonderful but wacky stepmother. Sherry wasn't exactly proud of the way she'd slipped away in the middle of the night, but she'd thought it best to avoid the multitude of questions Phyliss would ply her with had she known Sherry was leaving. She'd managed to escape with a note mailed from the airport that stated in vague terms that she was going to camp for the summer. She hated to be so underhanded, but knowing Phyliss, the woman would arrive with a new wardrobe of coordinated shades of chartreuse—and order Sherry's meals catered when she learned that her beloved stepdaughter was eating camp food.

Sherry had chosen Camp Gitche Gumee because it had intrigued her. Being counselor to a group of intellectually gifted children in the heart of the majestic California redwoods sounded like the perfect escape. And Phyliss would never think to search California.

"Within the next few hours, fifty children will be arriving from all around the country," Roarke continued.

Sherry childishly rolled her eyes toward the ceiling. He could just as well have given them this information at seven—the birds weren't even awake yet! Expecting her to retain vital information at this unreasonable hour was going beyond the call of duty.

"Each cottage will house seven children; Fred Spencer's cabin will house eight. Counselors, see me following the meeting for the names of your charges. Wherever possible, I've attempted to match the child with a friend in an effort to cut down on homesickness."

That made sense to Sherry, but little else did.

As Roarke continued speaking, Sherry's thoughts drifted again. In addition to Jeff Roarke, their fearless leader, Sherry knew she was going to have problems getting along with Fred Spencer, who was counselor for the nine- and ten-year-old boys. Fred had been a counselor at Camp Gitche Gumee for several summers and was solidly set in the way he handled his charges.

Sherry had come up with some ideas she'd wanted to talk over in the first few days following her arrival. Since Fred was the counselor for the same age group as hers, it had seemed natural to go to him. But Fred had found a reason to reject every suggestion. Five minutes with him and Sherry discovered that he didn't possess a creative bone in his body and frowned dutifully upon anyone who deviated from the norm. But more than disagreeing with her, Sherry had gotten the impression that Fred highly disapproved of her. She wasn't sure what she'd done to invoke his ire, but his resentment toward her was strong enough to cause her to feel uneasy whenever they were in the room together.

With a sigh, Sherry forced her attention back to Roarke. He continued speaking for several minutes, but most of what he had to say was directed to the housekeepers, cooks and grounds keepers. The classroom teachers had been briefed the day before.

A half hour later the staff was dismissed for breakfast—and not a minute too soon, Sherry mused as she walked toward the large dining hall. Blindly she headed for the coffeepot. If Jeff Roarke was going to call staff meetings when the moon was still out, the least he could do was provide coffee.

"Miss White," Roarke called, stopping her.

Sherry glanced longingly toward the coffeepot. "Yes?"

"Could I speak to you a minute?"

"Sure." She headed toward the back of the dining hall, where he was waiting for her.

Roarke watched the newest staff member of Camp Gitche Gumee make her way toward him, walking between the long tables, and he smiled inwardly. That Sherry White wasn't a morning person was obvious. During the staff meeting, her eyes had drooped half-closed and she'd stifled more than one yawn. For part of that time her features had been frozen into a far-away look, as though she were caught in some day-dream.

Thinking about her, Roarke felt his brow crease into a slight frown. He'd hired her on impulse, something he rarely acted upon. He'd liked her smile and her spirit and had gotten a chuckle out of her misunder-standing about the name of the camp. He found her appealing, yet she made him nervous, too, in a way he couldn't explain even to himself. All he knew was that she'd shown up for the interview, and before he'd re-alized what he was doing, he'd hired her. In analyzing his actions later, Roarke had been astonished. Liking the way she smiled and the way her eyes softened when she spoke of children were not good enough reasons to hire her as a counselor. Yet he felt he hadn't made an impossible choice. In spite of her apparent dislike of his methods, Roarke felt she would do an excellent job with the children, and more than a good person-ality match with him, the youngsters were what was most important.

"Yes?" Sherry asked, joining him. Her gaze remained a little too obviously on the coffeepot on the other side of the room.

Opening his briefcase, Roarke withdrew a camp reference sheet and handed it to her. "I'm sorry to bother you, but your application form must have gotten smeared across the top—I wasn't able to read the names of your references."

Sherry swallowed uncomfortably. She should have known scribbled letters and numbers wouldn't work.

"Could you fill this out and have it back to me later this afternoon?"

"Sure—no problem," she said, her smile forced.

"Well," he said, puzzled by the frown that worried her brow, "I'll see you later, then."

"Later," she agreed distractedly. Her gaze fell to the form. If worst came to worst she could always give him false telephone numbers and phony addresses. But that could lead to future problems. Of course if she didn't, it could lead to problems right now!

Depressed, Sherry folded the form, then made a beeline for the coffee. Claiming her seat, she propped her elbows on the table and held the thick ceramic mug with both hands, letting the aroma stir her senses to life. She might not function well in the mornings, but she'd manage for this one summer. She'd have to if Roarke intended to keep holding these merciless 5:00 a.m. staff meetings.

"Morning," Lynn Duffy called out as she approached. Lynn, who had been assigned as housekeeper to Sherry's cabin, claimed the chair next to Sherry's. She set her tray on the table and unloaded her plate, which was heaped with scrambled eggs, bacon and toast. "Aren't you eating?"

Sherry shook her head. "Not this morning."

"Hey, this camp has a reputation for wonderful food."

"I'm not hungry. Thanks anyway." Sherry rested her chin in her hands, worrying about the references and what she could put down that would satisfy Jeff Roarke. "I wonder what kind of stupid rule he's going to come up with next," she muttered, setting the paper beside her mug.

"Jeff Roarke?"

"Yes, Roarke." Somehow Sherry couldn't think of the camp director as "Jeff." She associated that name with someone who was kind and considerate, like Lassie's owner or an affectionate uncle.

"You have to admit he's got a grip on matters."

"Sure," Sherry admitted reluctantly. Roarke ran this camp with the efficiency of a Marine boot camp. "But I have yet to see a hint of originality. For instance, I can't imagine children's cottages named Cabin One, Cabin Two and so on."

"It's less confusing that way."

"These kids are supposed to be geniuses, I strongly suspect they could keep track of a real name as easily as a boring, unadorned number."

"Maybe so," Lynn said and shook her head. "No one's ever said anything before."

"But surely the other counselors have offered suggestions."

"Not that I've heard."

Sherry raised her eyebrows. "I'd have thought the staff would want something more creative than numbers for their cabins."

"I'm sure Mr. Roarke thought the kids would be more comfortable with numbers. Several of the children are said to be mathematical wizards."

"I suppose," Sherry agreed. Roarke was totally committed to the children and the camp—Sherry didn't question that—but to her way of thinking his intentions were misdirected. Every part of camp life was geared toward academia, with little emphasis, from what she could see, on fun and games.

Lynn's deep blue eyes took on a dreamy look. She shook her head. "I think the whole idea of a special camp like this is such a good one. From what I understand, Mr. Roarke is solely responsible for organizing it. He worked years for these summer sessions. For the past four summers, he hasn't taken a penny for all his efforts. He does it for the kids."

The news surprised Sherry, and she found herself revising her opinion of the camp director once again. The man intrigued her, she had to admit. He angered and confused her, but he fascinated her, too. Sherry didn't know what to think anymore. If only he weren't such a stick-in-the-mud. She remembered that Lynn was one of those who had been making sheep's eyes at Roarke earlier. "I have the feeling you think Jeff Roarke is wonderful," she suggested.

Lynn nodded and released a heavy sigh. "Does it show that much?"

"Not really."

"He's so handsome," Lynn continued. "Surely you've noticed?"

Sherry took another sip of her coffee to delay answering. "I suppose."

"And so successful. Rumors flew around here last summer when Mr. Roarke became the head of the economics department for Cal Tech."

Again Sherry paid close attention to her coffee. "I'm impressed."

"From what I understand he's written a book."

A smile touched the corners of Sherry's mouth. She could well imagine what dry reading anything Roarke had written would be.

"Apparently his book caused quite a stir in Washington. The director of the Federal Reserve recommended it to the President."

"Wow!" Sherry was impressed.

"And he's handsome to boot."

"That much is fairly obvious," Sherry allowed. All right, Jeff Roarke was lean and muscular with eyes that could make a woman go all soft inside, but she wasn't the only one to have noticed that, and she certainly wasn't interested in becoming a groupie.

"He really gets to me," Lynn said with a sigh.

"He does have nice eyes," Sherry admitted reluctantly.

Lynn nodded and continued. "They're so unusual. Yesterday when we were talking I would have sworn they were green, but when I first met him they were an incredible hazel color."

"I guess I hadn't noticed," Sherry commented. Okay, so she lied!

Carefully Lynn set her fork beside her plate, her look thoughtful. "You don't like him much, do you?"

"Oh, I like him—it's just that I figured a camp for children would be fun. This place is going to be about as lively as a prison. There are classes scheduled day and night. From the look of things, all the kids are going to do is study. There isn't any time left for fun."

Evidently Lynn found her observations humorous. A smile created twin dimples in her smooth cheeks. "Just wait until the kids get here. Then you'll be grateful for Mr. Roarke's high sense of order."

Maybe so, Sherry thought, but that remained to be seen. "You worked here last summer?"

Lynn nodded as she swallowed a mouthful of eggs. "I was a housekeeper then, too. Several of us are back for a second go-around, but Mr. Roarke's the real reason I came back." She hesitated. "How old do you think he is?"

"Roarke? I don't know. Close to thirty, I'd guess."

"Oh dear, that's probably much too old for someone nineteen."

Lynn's look of abject misery caused Sherry to laugh outright. "I've heard of greater age differences."

"How old are you?"

"Twenty-one," Sherry answered.

Lynn wrinkled her nose, as though she envied Sherry those years. "Don't get me wrong. There's no chance of a romance developing between Mr. Roarke and me, or me and anyone else for that matter—at least not until camp is dismissed."

"Why not?"

"Mr. Roarke is death on camp romances," Lynn explained. "Last year two of the counselors fell in love, and when Mr. Roarke found them kissing he threatened to dismiss them both." Lynn sighed expressively and a dreamy look came over her. "You know what I think?"

Sherry could only speculate. "What?"

"I think Mr. Roarke's been burned. His tender heart was shattered by a careless affair that left him bleeding and raw. And now—years later—he's afraid to love again, afraid to offer his heart to another woman." Dramatically, Lynn placed her hand over her own heart as though to protect it from the fate of love turned sour. She gazed somberly into the distance.

The strains of a Righteous Brothers song hummed softly in the distance, and it was all Sherry could do to swallow down a laugh. "You know this for a fact?"

"Heavens, no. That's just what I think must have happened to him. It makes sense, doesn't it?"

"Ah—I'm not sure." Sherry hedged.

"Mr. Roarke is really against camp romances. You should have been here last year. I don't think I've ever seen him more upset. He claimed romance and camp just don't mix."

"He's right about that." To find herself agreeing with Roarke was a surprise, but Sherry could see the pitfalls of a group of counselors more interested in one another than in their charges.

Lynn shrugged again. "I don't think there's anything wrong with a light flirtation, but Mr. Roarke has other ideas. There are even rules and regulations on how male and female counselors should behave in each other's company. But I suppose you've already read that."

When Sherry didn't respond, Lynn eyed her speculatively. "You did read the manual, didn't you?"

Sherry dropped her gaze to the tabletop. "Sort of."

"You'd better, because if he catches you going against the rules, your neck will be on the chopping block."

A lump developed in Sherry's throat as she remembered the problem with her references. She'd need to keep a low profile. And from the sound of things, she had best be a good little counselor and keep her opinions to herself. What Lynn had said about studying the manual made sense. Sherry vowed inwardly to read it all the way through and do her utmost to follow the rules, no matter what she thought.

"You'll do fine," Lynn said confidently. "And the kids are going to really like you."

"I hope so." Unexpected doubts were jumping up and down inside Sherry like youngsters on pogo sticks. She had thought she'd be a natural for this position. Her major was education, and with her flair for originality, she hoped to be a good teacher. The kids she'd come here to counsel weren't everyday run-of-the-mill nine- and ten-year-olds, they were bona fide geniuses. Each child had an IQ in the ninety-eight percentile. She lifted her chin in sudden determination. She'd always appreciated a challenge. She'd been looking forward to this summer, and she wasn't about to let Jeff Roarke and his rules and regulations ruin it for her.

"The only time you need to worry is if Mr. Roarke calls you to his office after breakfast," Lynn said, interrupting Sherry's thoughts.

Sherry digested this information. "Why then?"

Lynn paused long enough to peel back the aluminum tab on a small container of strawberry jam. "The only time anyone is ever fired is in the morning. The couple I mentioned earlier, who fell in love last summer—their names were Sue and Mark—they talked to Mr. Roarke on three separate occasions. Each time in the afternoon. Every time Sue heard her name read from the daily bulletin she became a nervous wreck until she heard the time of the scheduled meeting. Mark didn't fare much better. They both expected to get the ax at any minute.''

"Roarke didn't fire them?''

"No, but he threatened to. They weren't even allowed to hold hands.''

"I bet they were miserable.'' Sherry could sympathize with both sides. She was young enough to appreciate the temptations of wanting to be with a boy at camp but old enough to recognize the pitfalls of such a romance.

"But worse than a camp romance, Mr. Roarke is a stickler for honesty. He won't tolerate anyone who so much as stretches the truth.''

"Really?'' Sherry murmured. Suddenly swallowing became difficult.

"Last year a guy came to camp who fibbed about his age. He was one of three Mr. Roarke fired. It's true Danny had lied, but only by a few months. He was out of here so fast it made my head spin. Of course, he got called in to Roarke's office in the morning,'' she added.

"My goodness.'' Sherry's mouth had gone dry. If Roarke decided to check her references her days at Camp Gitche Gumee were surely numbered.

"Well, I'd best go plug in my vacuum.''

"Yeah—" Sherry raised her hand "—I'll talk to you later."

The younger girl stood and scooted her chair back into position. "Good luck."

Sherry watched the lanky teenager leave the mess hall, and for the first time she considered that maybe escaping Phyliss at summer camp hadn't been such a brilliant idea after all.

Chapter Two

Three hours later the first bus load of children pulled into Camp Gitche Gumee. The bus was from nearby Sacramento and the surrounding area, but Roarke had announced at their morning get-together that there were children traveling from as far away as Maine and Vermont. The sum these parents paid for two months of camp had shocked Sherry, but who was she to quibble? She had a summer job, and in spite of her misgivings about the camp director, she was pleased to be here.

Standing inside her cabin, Sherry breathed in the clean scent of the forest and waited anxiously for her charges to be escorted to her cabin. When she chanced a peek out the door, she noted Peter Towne, the camp lifeguard, leading a forlorn-looking girl with long, dark braids toward her.

Sherry stepped onto the porch to meet the pair. She tried to get the little girl to meet her gaze so she could smile at her, but the youngster seemed determined to study the grass.

"Miss White, this is Pamela Reynolds."

"Hello, Pamela."

"Hi."

Peter handed Sherry Pamela's suitcase.

Thanking him with a smile, Sherry placed her free hand on the shy girl's shoulder and led her into the cabin.

The youngster's eyes narrowed suspiciously as she sat on the nearest bunk. "You're not scared of animals are you?"

"Nope." That wasn't entirely true, but Sherry didn't consider it a good idea to let any of her charges know she wasn't especially fond of snakes. Not when the woods were ripe for the picking.

"Good."

"Good?" Sherry repeated suspiciously.

With a nervous movement, Pamela nodded, placed her suitcase on the thin mattress and opened it. From inside, she lifted a shoe box with holes punched in the top. "I brought along my hamster. I can keep him, can't I?" Blue eyes pleaded with her.

Sherry didn't know what to say. According to the camp manual, pets weren't allowed. But a hamster wasn't like a dog or a cat or a horse, for heaven's sake. Sherry hedged. "What's his name?"

"Ralph."

"That's a nice name." Her brain was frantically working.

"He won't make any noise and he barely eats anything and I couldn't leave him at home because my parents are going to Europe and I know we aren't supposed to bring along animals, but Ralph is the very best friend I have and I'd miss him too much if he had to stay with Mrs. Murphy like my little brother."

Appealing tears glistened in the little girl's eyes and Sherry felt herself weaken. It shouldn't be that difficult to keep one tiny hamster from Roarke's attention.

"But will Ralph be happy living in a cabin full of girls?"

"Oh, sure," Pam said, the words rushing out, "he likes girls, and he's really a wonderful hamster. Do you want to hold him?"

"No thanks," Sherry answered brightly. The manual might have a full page dedicated to pets, but it didn't say anything about adopting a mascot. "If the others agree, I feel we can keep Ralph as our mascot—as long as we don't let any of the other cabins find out about him." Sherry cringed inwardly at the thought of Jeff Roarke's reaction to her decision. The thought of his finding a pet, even something as unobtrusive as a hamster, wasn't a pleasant one, but from the looks of it the little girl was strongly attached to the rodent. Housing Ralph seemed such a little thing to keep a child happy. Surely what Ironjaw didn't know wouldn't hurt him....

Three ten-year-olds, Sally, Wendy and Diane, were escorted to the cabin when the next bus load arrived. Although they were different in looks and size, the three shared a serious, somber nature. Sherry had ex-

pected rambunctious children. Instead, she had been
assigned miniature adults.

Sally had brought along her microscope and several specimens she planned to examine before dinner.
Sherry didn't ask to see them, but from the contents
of the jars that lined Sally's headboard, she didn't
want to know what the child planned to study. Sherry's social circle didn't include many nine- and ten-
year-olds, but she wasn't acquainted with a single child
who kept pig embryos in jars of formaldehyde as
companions.

Wendy, at least, appeared to be a halfway normal
preteen. She collected dolls and had brought along an
assortment of her prize Barbies and Kens, including
designer outfits for each. She arranged them across the
head of her bed and introduced Sherry to Barbie-
Samantha, Barbie-Jana and Barbie-Brenda. The Kens
were also distinguished with their own names, and by
the time Wendy had finished, Sherry's head was
swimming.

Sherry didn't know what to make of Diane. The ten-
year-old barely said a word. She chose her bunk, unpacked and then immediately started to read. Sherry
noted that Diane's suitcases contained a bare minimum of clothes and were filled to capacity with books.
Scanning the academic titles caused Sherry to grim-
ace; she didn't see a single Nancy Drew.

Twins, Jan and Jill, were the next to make their entrance. They were blond replicas of each other and
impossible to tell apart until they smiled. Jan was
lacking both upper front teeth. Jill was lacking only
one. Sherry felt a little smug until she discovered Jill

wiggling her lone front tooth back and forth in an effort to extract it. Before the day was over, Sherry realized, she would be at their mercy. Fine, she decided, the two knew who they were—she'd let them sort it out.

The last child assigned to Cabin Four was Gretchen. Sherry recognized the minute the ten-year-old showed up that this child was trouble.

"This camp gets dumpier every summer," Gretchen grumbled, folding her arms around her middle as she surveyed the cabin. She paused and glanced at the last remaining cot. "I refuse to sleep near the window. I'll get a nosebleed and a headache if I'm near a breeze."

"Okay," Sherry said. "Is there anyone here who would like to trade with Gretchen?"

Pam suddenly found it necessary to feed Ralph.

Sally brought out her microscope.

Wendy twisted Barbie-Brenda into Ken-Brian's arms and placed them in a position Sherry preferred not to question. Soon, no fewer than three Barbies and an equal number of Kens were in a tangled mess of arms and legs.

Jan and Jill sat on the end of their bunks staring blindly into space while Jill worked furiously on extracting her front tooth.

Diane kept a book of mathematical brainteasers propped open in front of her face and didn't give any indication that she'd heard the request.

"It doesn't look like anyone wants to trade," Sherry told the youngster, whose mouth was twisted with a sour look. "Since you've been to camp before, you knew that the first to arrive claim the beds they want.

I saw you lingering outside earlier this afternoon. You should have checked in here first."

"I refuse to sleep near the window," Gretchen announced for the second time.

"In that case, I'll place the mattress on the floor in my room and you can bunk there, although I feel you should know, I sometimes sleep with my window open."

"I sincerely hope you're teasing," Gretchen returned, eyes wide and incredulous. "There are things crawling around down there." She studiously pointed to the wood floor.

"Where?" Sally cried, immediately interested. Her hand curled around the base of her microscope.

"I believe she was speaking hypothetically," Sherry mumbled.

"Oh."

"All right, I'll sleep by the window and ignore the medical risk," Gretchen said heatedly. She carelessly tossed her suitcase on top of the mattress. "But I'm writing my mother and telling her about this. She's paying good money for me to attend this camp and she expects me to receive the very best of care. There's no excuse for me to be mistreated in this manner."

"Let's see how it goes, shall we?" Sherry suggested, biting her tongue. This kid was a medical risk all right, but the only thing in danger was Sherry's mental health. Already she could feel a pounding headache coming on. By sheer force of will, she managed to keep her fingers from massaging her temples. First Roarke and now Gretchen. No doubt they were related.

"My uncle is a congressman," Gretchen said, to no one in particular. "I may write him instead."

The entire cabin pretended not to hear, which only seemed to infuriate Gretchen. She paused smugly. "Is Mr. Roarke the camp director again this year?"

"Yes," Sherry answered cheerfully. She knew it! Roarke was most likely another of this pest's uncles. "Would you like me to make an appointment for you to speak to him?"

"Yes. I'll let him handle this unfortunate situation." Gretchen removed her suitcase from the bunk and gingerly set it aside, seemingly assured that the camp director would assign her a cot anywhere she wanted.

"I'll see if I can arrange it when you're in the computer class," Sherry said.

By afternoon Camp Gitche Gumee was in full swing. Cabins were filled to capacity and the clamor of children sounded throughout the compound.

After the girls had unpacked and stored their luggage, Sherry led them into the dining hall. Counselors were expected to eat their meals with their charges, but after lunch Sherry's time was basically free. On occasion she would be given the opportunity to schedule outdoor activities such as canoeing and hiking expeditions, but those were left for her to organize. Most of the camp was centered around challenging academic pursuits. Sessions were offered in biochemistry, computer skills and propositional calculus. Sherry wondered what ever happened to stringing beads and basket weaving!

When the girls were dismissed for their afternoon activities, Sherry made her way to the director's office, which was on the other side of the camp-grounds, far from the maddening crowd, she noted. It was all too apparent that Roarke liked his privacy.

Tall redwoods outlined the camp outskirts. Wild-flowers grew in abundance. Goldthreads, red bane-berry and the northern inside-out flower were just a few that Sherry recognized readily. She had a passion for wildflowers and could name those most common to the West Coast. Some flowers were unknown to her, but she had a sneaky suspicion that if she picked a few, either Sally or Diane would be able to tell her the spe-cies and Latin title.

When she could delay the inevitable no longer, Sherry approached Roarke's office. She knocked po-litely twice and waited.

"Come in," came the gruff voice.

Squaring her shoulders, preparing to face the lion in his den, Sherry entered the office. As she expected, his room was meticulously neat. Bookshelves lined the walls, and where there weren't books the space was covered with certificates. His desk was an oversize mahogany one that rested in the center of the large room. The leather high-backed chair was one Sherry would have expected to find a bank president using—not a camp director.

"Miss White."

"Mr. Roarke."

They greeted each other stiffly.

"Sit down." He motioned toward the two low-backed upholstered chairs.

Sherry sat and briefly studied the man behind the desk. He looked to be a young thirty although there were lines faintly etched around his eyes and on both sides of his mouth. But instead of detracting from his good looks, the lines added another dimension to his appeal. Lynn's words about Roarke suffering from a lost love played back in Sherry's mind. Again she sensed an underlying sadness in him, but nothing that could readily be seen in the square, determined lines of his jaw. And again it was his piercing gaze that captured her.

"You brought back the reference sheet?" Roarke prompted.

"Yes." Sherry sat at the edge of her seat as though she expected to blurt out what she had to say and make a mad dash for the door. She'd reprinted the names and addresses more clearly this time, transposing the numbers and hoping that it would look unintentional when the letters were delayed.

"I have it with me," she answered, and set the form on his desk. "But there's something else I'd like to discuss. I've been assigned Gretchen Hamburg."

"Ah, yes, Gretchen."

Apparently the girl was known to him. "I'm afraid I'm having a small problem with her," Sherry said, carefully choosing her words. "It seems Gretchen prefers to sleep away from the window, but she dawdled around outside while the others chose bunks, and now she's complaining. She's asked that I make an appointment for her to plead her case with you. She . . . insinuated that you'd correct this situation for her."

"I'm—"

Sherry didn't allow him to finish. "It's my opinion that giving in to Gretchen's demands would set a precedent that would cause problems among the other girls later."

His wide brow furrowed. "I can understand your concerns."

Sherry relaxed, scooting back in her chair.

"However, Gretchen's family is an influential one."

Sherry bolted forward. "That's favoritism."

"Won't any of the other girls trade with her?"

"I've already suggested that. But the others shouldn't be forced into giving up their beds simply because Gretchen Hamburg—"

"Have you sought a compromise?" he interrupted.

Sherry's hands were clenched in such tight fists that her punch would have challenged Muhammad Ali's powerful right hand. "I suggested that we place the mattress on the floor in my room, but I did mention that I sometimes sleep with my window open."

"And?"

"And Gretchen insisted on speaking to you personally."

Roarke drummed his fingers on the desktop. "If you haven't already noticed, Gretchen is a complainer."

"No!" Sherry feigned wide-eyed shock.

Roarke studied the fiery flash in Sherry's dark brown eyes and again experienced an unfamiliar tug on his emotions. She made him want to laugh at the most inappropriate times. And when he wasn't amused by her, she infuriated him. There didn't seem to be any in-between in the emotions he felt for her. Sherry White could be a problem, Roarke mused, although he was convinced she'd be a terrific counselor. The trouble was within himself. He was attracted to her—strongly. He would have been better off not to have hired her than to wage battle with his emotions all summer. He'd need to keep a cool head with her— keep his distance, avoid her whenever possible, bury whatever it was in her that he found so appealing.

Sherry was convinced she saw a brief smile touch Roarke's mouth, so faint that it was gone before it completely registered with her. If only he'd really smile or joke or kid, she would find it infinitely more pleasant to meet with him. A lock of hair fell across his brow and he brushed it back only to have it immediately return to its former position. Sherry found her gaze mesmerized by that single lock. Except for those few strands of cocky hair Roarke was impeccable in every way. She sincerely doubted that as a child his jeans had ever been torn or grass stained.

"Well?" Sherry prompted. "Should I send Gretchen in to see you?"

"No."

"No?"

"That's what I said, Miss White. I can't be bothered with these minor details. Handle the situation as you see fit."

Using the arms of the chair for leverage, Sherry rose. She was pleased because she didn't want Ms. Miserable to use Roarke to manipulate her and the other girls in the cabin. Sherry was halfway out the door when Roarke spoke next.

"However, if this matter isn't settled promptly, I'll be forced to handle the situation myself. Dorothy Hamburg has been a faithful supporter of this camp for several years."

Well, she might as well jerk Pamela and Ralph from the center cot, Sherry thought irritably. One way or another Gretchen was bound to have her own way.

Chapter Three

Dressed in their pajamas, the seven preteens sat Indian fashion on their cots, listening wide-eyed and intent as Sherry read.

"And they lived happily ever after," Sherry murmured, slowly closing the large book.

"You don't really believe that garbage, do you?" Gretchen demanded.

Sherry smiled softly to herself. Gretchen found fault with everything, she'd discovered over the course of the first week of camp. Even when the little girl enjoyed something, it was her nature to complain, quibble and frown. During the fairy tale, Gretchen had been the child most enraptured, yet she seemed to feel it was her duty to nitpick.

"How do you mean?" Sherry asked, deciding to play innocent. The proud tilt of Gretchen's chin tore at her heart.

"It's only a stupid fairy tale."

"But it was so lovely," Wendy chimed in softly.

"And the Prince..."

"...was so handsome." Jan and Jill added in unison.

"But none of it is true." Gretchen crossed her arms and pressed her lips tightly together. "My mother claims that she's suffering from the Cinderella syndrome, and here you are telling us the same goofy story and expecting us to believe it."

"Oh no," Sherry whispered, bending forward as though to share a special secret. "Fairy tales don't have to be true; but it's romantic to pretend. That's what makes them so special."

"But fairy tales couldn't possibly be real."

"All fiction is make-believe," Sherry softly assured her chronic complainer.

"I don't care if it's true or not, I like it when you read us stories," Diane volunteered. The child had set aside Proust in favor of listening to the bedtime story. Sherry felt a sense of pride that she'd been able to interest Diane in something beyond the heavy reading material she devoured at all hours of the night and day.

"Tell us another one," Wendy begged. Her Barbie and Ken dolls sat in a circle in front of her, their arms twisting around one another.

Sherry closed the book. "I will tomorrow night."

"Another fairy tale, okay?" Pamela insisted. "Even though he's a boy, Ralph liked it." She petted the hamster and reverently kissed him good-night before placing him back inside his shoe-box home.

Sherry had serious doubts about Ralph's environment, but Pamela had repeatedly assured her that the box was the only home Ralph had ever known and that he'd never run away. All the time the child spent grooming and training him lent Sherry confidence. But then, she hadn't known that many trick hamsters in her time.

"Will you read *Snow White and the Seven Dwarfs* next?" Sally wanted to know. She climbed into her cot and tucked the microscope underneath her pillow.

"Snow White it is."

"You're sort of like Snow White, aren't you?" Diane asked. "I mean, your name is White and you live in a cottage in the forest with seven dwarfs."

"Yeah!" Jan and Jill chimed together.

"I, for one, resent being referred to as a dwarf," Gretchen muttered.

"Wizards then," Wendy offered. "We're all smart."

"Snow White and the Seven Wizards," Sally commented, obviously pleased with herself. "Hey, we all live in Snow White's cottage."

"Right!" Jan and Jill said, with identical nods.

"But who's Prince Charming?"

"I don't think that this particular Snow White has a Prince Charming," Sherry said, feigning a sad sigh. "But—" she pointed her index finger toward the ceiling "—some day my prince will come."

"Mr. Roarke," Gretchen piped in excitedly. "He's the handsomest, noblest, nicest man I know. He'll be your prince."

Sherry nearly swallowed her tongue in her rush to disagree. Jeff Roarke! Impossible! He was more like the evil huntsman intent on doing away with the unsuspecting Snow White. If he ever checked her references, doing away with her would be exactly what happened! In the past week, Sherry had done her utmost to be the most accommodating counselor at camp. She hadn't given Roarke a single reason to notice or disapprove of her. Other than an occasional gruff hello, she'd been able to avoid speaking to him.

"Lights out everyone," Sherry said, determined to kill the conversation before it got out of hand. The less said about Roarke as Prince Charming, the better. The girls were much too young to understand that to be called princely a man must possess certain character traits. Sherry hesitated and drew in a shaky breath. All right, she'd admit it—Jeff Roarke's character was sterling. He was dedicated, hardworking and seemed to genuinely love the children. And then there were those incredible eyes of his. Sherry sharply shook herself back into reality. A single week with her charges and already she was going bongos. Roarke was much too dictatorial and inflexible to be a prince. At least to be *her* Prince Charming.

With a flip of the switch the room went dark. The only illumination was a shallow path of golden moonlight across the polished wood of the cabin floor.

Sherry moved into her own room and left the door ajar in order to hear her seven wizards in case of bad dreams or nighttime troubles. The girls never ceased to surprise her. It was as though they didn't realize they were children. When Sherry suggested reading a fairy tale, they'd moaned and claimed that was *kids'* stuff! Sherry had persisted, and now she was exceptionally pleased that she had. They'd loved *Cinderella* and eaten up *Little Red Riding Hood*. Diane, the reader, who had teethed on Ibsen, Maupassant and Emerson, wasn't sure who the Brothers Grimm were. But she sat night after night, her hands cupping her face as she listened to a different type of classic—and loved it.

Sally, at ten, knew more about biochemistry than Sherry ever hoped to understand in her lifetime. Yet Sally couldn't name a single record in the top ten and hadn't thought to bring a radio to camp. Her microscope was far more important!

These little geniuses were still children, and if no one else was going to remind them of that fact, Sherry was! If she could, she would have liked to scream that in Jeff Roarke's face. He had to realize there was more to life than academia; yet the entire camp seemed centered around challenging the mind and leaving the heart empty.

Sitting on the edge of her cot, Sherry's gaze fell on the seven girls in the room outside her own. She had been given charge of these little ones for the next two months, and by golly she was going to teach these children to have fun if it killed her!

"Ralph!"

The shrill cry pierced Sherry's peaceful slumber. She managed to open one eye and peek toward the clock radio. Four-thirteen. She had a full seventeen minutes before her alarm was set to ring.

"Miss White," Pamela cried, frantically stumbling into Sherry's room. "Ralph is gone!"

"What!" Holding a sheet to her breast, Sherry jerked upright, eyes wide. "Gone? What do you mean gone?"

"He's run away," the little girl sobbed. "I woke up and found the lid from the shoe box off kilter, and when I looked he was...m-missing." She burst into tears and threw her arms around Sherry's neck, weeping pathetically.

"He didn't run away," Sherry said, thinking fast as she hugged the thin child.

"He didn't?" Pamela raised her tear-streaked face and battled down a fresh wave of emotion. "Then where is he?"

"He's exploring. Remember what I said about Ralph getting tired of his shoe-box home? He just went on an adventure into the woods to find some friends."

Pamela nodded, her dark braids bouncing.

"I suppose he woke up in the middle of the night and decided that he'd like to see who else was living around the cabin." The thought was a chilling one to Sherry. She squelched it quickly.

"But where is he?"

"I...I'm not exactly sure. He may need some guidance finding his way home."

"Then we should help him."

"Right." Stretching across the bed, Sherry turned on the bedside lamp. "Ralph," she called softly. "Allie, allie oxen free." It wouldn't be that easy, but it was worth a shot.

"There he is," Sally cried, sitting up in her cot. She pointed to the dresser on the far side of the outer room. "He ran under there."

"Get him," Pamela screamed and raced out of Sherry's quarters.

Soon all seven girls were crawling around the floor in their long flannel nightgowns looking for Ralph. He was still at large when Sherry's alarm clock buzzed.

"Damn," she muttered under her breath. She looked up to find seven pairs of eyes accusing her. "I mean darn," she muttered back. The search party returned to their rescue mission.

"I've got to get to the staff meeting," Sherry announced dejectedly five minutes later when Ginny, the high-school girl who was working in hopes of being hired as a counselor next summer, arrived to replace her. "Listen, don't say a word to anyone about Ralph. I'll be back as quickly as I can."

"Okay," Jan and Jill answered for the group.

Because she knew what Roarke would say once she asked him about the hamster, Sherry had yet to mention Ralph's presence in their happy little cabin. To be honest, she hadn't figured on doing so. However, having the entire cabin turned upside down in an effort to locate the Dr. Livingstone of the animal kingdom was another matter.

Dressing as quickly as possible, Sherry hopped around on one foot in an effort to tie her shoelace, then switched legs and continued hopping across her pine floor.

"That's working," Diane cried, glancing in Sherry's direction. "Keep doing it."

"I see him. I see him. Ralph, come home. Ralph come home," Pamela begged, charging in the flannel nightgown over the cold floor.

A minute later, Sherry was out the door, leaving her charges to the mercy of one fickle-hearted hamster. By the time she reached the staff meeting she was panting and breathless. Roarke had already opened the meeting, and when Sherry entered, he paused and waited for her to take a seat.

"I'm pleased you saw fit to join us, Miss White," Roarke commented coolly.

"Sorry. I overslept," she mumbled as she claimed the last available chair in the front row. Rich color blossomed in her already flushed cheeks, reminding her once again why she'd come to dislike Jeff Roarke. The man went out of his way to cause her embarrassment—seemed to thrive on it.

Roarke read the list of activities for the day, listing possible educational ventures for each cabin's nightly get-togethers. Then, by turn, he had the counselors tell the others how they'd chosen to close another camping day.

"We discussed how to split an atom," the first counselor, a college freshman, told the group.

This appeared to please Roarke. "Excellent," he said, nodding his head approvingly.

"We dissected a frog," the second counselor added.

As each spoke, Sherry grew more uncomfortable. The neckline of her thin sweater felt exceptionally tight, and when it was her turn, her voice came out sounding thin and low. "I read them the Cinderella story," she said.

"Excuse me." Roarke took a step closer. "Would you kindly repeat that?"

"Yes, of course." Sherry paused and cleared her throat. "I read my girls 'Cinderella.'"

A needle dropping against the floor would have sounded like a sonic boom in the thick silence that followed.

"Cinderella," Roarke repeated, as though he was convinced he hadn't heard her correctly.

"That's right."

"Perhaps she could explain why anyone would choose to read a useless fairy tale over a worthwhile learning experience?"

The voice behind Sherry was familiar. She turned to find Fred Spencer glaring at her with undisguised disapproval. Since their first disagreement over Sherry's ideas, they hadn't exchanged more than a few words.

Sherry turned her head around and tucked her hands under her thighs, shifting her weight back and forth over her knuckles. "I consider fairy tales a valuable learning tool."

"You do?" This time it was Roarke who questioned her.

From the way he was looking at her, Sherry could tell that he was having a difficult time accepting her reasoning.

"And what particular lesson did you hope to convey in the reading of this tale?"

"Hope."

"Hope?"

The other counselors were all still staring at her as though she was an apple in a barrel full of oranges.

"You see, sometimes life can seem so bleak that we don't see all the good things around us. In addition, the story is a romantic, fun one."

Roarke couldn't believe what he was hearing. Sherry was making a mockery of the goals he'd set for this year's camp session. Romance! She wanted to teach her girls about some fickle female notion. The word alone was enough to make his blood run cold.

"Unfortunately, I disagree," Roarke said. "In the rational world there's no need for romantic nonsense." Although he tried to avoid looking at Sherry, his gaze refused to leave her. She looked flustered and embarrassed, and a fetching shade of pink had invaded her cheeks. Her gaze darted nervously to those around her, as if hoping to find someone who would agree with her. None would, Roarke could have told her that. His gaze fell to her lips, which were slightly moist and parted. Roarke's stomach muscles tightened and he hurriedly looked away. Love clouded the brain, he reminded himself sternly. The important things in life were found in education. Learning was the challenge. He should know. By age fifteen, he'd been a college student, graduating with full honors three years later. There'd been no time or need for trivial romance.

Sherry had seen Roarke's lips compress at the mention of romance, as though he associated the word with sucking lemons. "People need a little love in their lives," Sherry asserted boldly, although she was shaking on the inside.

"I see," he said, when it was obvious that he didn't.

The meeting continued then, and the staff was dismissed fifteen minutes later. Sherry was the first one to vacate her chair, popping up like hot bread out of a toaster the second the meeting was adjourned. She had to get back to the cabin to see if Ralph had been caught and peace had once again been restored to the seven wizards' cabin.

"Miss White." Roarke stopped her.

"Yes." Sherry's heart bounded to her throat. Damn, she'd hoped to make a clean getaway.

"Would it be possible for you to drop by my office later this afternoon?" The references—she knew it; he'd discovered they'd been falsified.

Their eyes met. Sherry's own befuddled brown clashed with Roarke's tawny-hazel. His open challenge stared down her hint of defiance, and Sherry dropped her gaze first. "This afternoon? S-sure," she answered finally, with false cheerfulness. At least he'd said afternoon rather than morning, so if Lynn was right she didn't need to start packing her bags yet. She released a grateful sigh and smiled. "I'll be there directly after lunch."

"Good."

He turned and Sherry charged from the meeting room and sprinted across the grounds with the skill of an Olympic runner. Oh heavens, she prayed Ralph had returned to his home. Life wouldn't be so cruel as to break Pamela's heart—would it?

Back at the cabin, Sherry discovered Pamela sitting on her bunk, crying softly.

"No Ralph?"

All seven children shook their heads simultaneously.

Sherry's heart constricted. "Please don't worry."

"I want Ralph," Pamela chanted, holding the pillow to her stomach and rocking back and forth. "Ralph's the only friend I ever had."

Sherry glanced around, hoping for a miracle. Where was Sherlock Holmes when she really needed him?

"He popped his head up between the floorboards a while ago," Sally explained, doubling over to peek underneath her bunk on the off chance he was there now.

"He's afraid of her microscope," Gretchen said accusingly. "I'm convinced that sweet hamster was worried sick that he'd end up in a jar like those...those pigs."

"He knows I wouldn't do that," Sally shouted, placing her hands defiantly on her hips, her eyes a scant inch from Gretchen's.

"Girls, please," Sherry pleaded. "We're due in the mess hall in five minutes."

A shriek arose as they scrambled for their clothes. Only Pamela remained on her bed, unmoved by the thought of being late for breakfast.

Sherry joined the little girl and folded her arm across the small shoulders. "We'll find him."

Tears glistened in the bright blue eyes. "Do you promise?"

Sherry didn't know what to say. She couldn't guarantee something like that. Pamela was a mathematical genius, so Sherry explained in terms the child would understand. "I can't make it a hundred per cent. Let's say seventy-five/twenty-five." For heaven's sake just how far could one hamster get? "Now, get dressed and go into the dining room with dry eyes."

Pamela nodded and climbed off her cot.

"Girls!" Sherry raised her hand to gain their attention. The loud chatter died to a low hum. "Remember, Ralph is our little secret!" The campers knew the rules better than Sherry. Each one was well aware that keeping Ralph was an infraction against camp policy.

"Our lips are sealed." Jan and Jill pantomimed zipping their mouths closed.

"After breakfast, when you've gone to your first class, I'll come back here and look for Ralph. In the meantime I think we'd best pretend nothing's unusual." Her questioning eyes met Pamela's, and Sherry gave her a reassuring hug.

With a gallant effort, Pamela sniffed and nodded. "I just want my Ralphie to come home."

After the frenzied search that had resulted from his disappearance, Sherry couldn't have agreed with the little girl more.

Before they left the cabin for the dining room, Sherry set the open shoe box in the middle of the cabin floor in the desperate hope that the runaway would find his own way home. She paused to close the door behind her charges and glanced over her shoulder with the fervent wish: *Ralph, please come home!*

In the dining hall, seated around the large circular table for eight, Sherry noted that none of her girls showed much of an appetite. French toast should have been a popular breakfast, but for all the interest her group showed, the cook could have served mush!

As the meal was wearing down, Mr. Roarke stepped forward.

"Isn't he handsome?" Gretchen said, looking toward Sherry. "My mother could really go for a man like him."

After what had happened that morning, Sherry was more than willing to let Gretchen's mother take Jeff Roarke. Good luck to her. With his views on romance she'd be lucky if she made it to first base.

"He does sort of look like a Prince Charming," Sally agreed.

"Mr. Roarke?" Sherry squinted, narrowing her gaze, wondering what kind of magic Roarke used on women. Young and old seemed to find him overwhelmingly attractive.

"Oh, yes," Sally repeated with a dreamy look clouding her eyes. "He's just like the prince you read about in the story last night."

Sherry squinted her eyes again in an effort to convince the girls she couldn't possibly be interested in him as a romantic lead in her life.

Standing in front of the room, his voice loud and clear without a microphone, Roarke made the announcements for the day. The highlight of the first week of camp was a special guest speaker who would be giving a talk on the subject of fungus and mold. Roarke was sure the campers would all enjoy hearing Dr. Waldorf speak. From the eager nods around the room, Sherry knew he was right.

Fungus? Mold? Sally looked as excited as if he'd announced a tour of a candy factory that would be handing out free samples. Maybe Sherry was wrong. Maybe her charges weren't really children. Perhaps they really were dwarfs. Because if they were children, they certainly didn't act like any she'd ever known.

Following breakfast, all fifty wizards emptied the dining room and headed for their assigned classes. Sherry wasted little time in returning to her cottage.

The shoe box stood forlornly in the middle of the room. Empty. No Ralph.

Kneeling beside the box, Sherry took a piece of squished French toast from her jeans pocket and ripped it into tiny pieces, piling them around the shoe box. "Ralph," she called out softly. "You love Pamela, don't you? Surely you don't want to break the sweet little girl's heart."

An eerie sensation ran down her spine, as though someone were watching her. Slowly Sherry turned to find a large calico cat sitting on the ledge of the open window. His almond eyes narrowed into thin slits as he surveyed the room.

A cat!

"Shoo!" Sherry screamed, shooting to her feet. She whipped out her hands in an effort to chase the monster away. She didn't know where in the devil he'd come from, but he certainly wasn't welcome around here. Not with Ralph on the loose. When the cat ran off, and with her heart pounding, Sherry shut and latched the window.

By noon, she was tired of looking for Ralph—tired of trying to find a hole or a crack large enough to hide a hamster. An expedition into the deepest, darkest jungles of Africa would have been preferable to this. She joined the girls in the dining room and sadly shook her head when seven pairs of hope-filled eyes silently questioned her on the fate of the hamster. Pamela's bottom lip trembled and tears brimmed in her clear blue eyes, but she didn't say anything.

The luncheon menu didn't fare much better than breakfast. The girls barely ate. Sherry knew she'd made a terrible mistake in allowing Pamela to keep the hamster. She'd gone against camp policy and now was paying the price. Rules were rules. She should have known better.

After lunch, the girls once again went their separate ways. With a heavy heart, Sherry headed for Roarke's office. He answered her knock and motioned for her to sit down. Sherry moistened her dry lips as the girls' comment about Roarke being a prince came to mind. At the time, she'd staunchly denied any attraction she felt for him. To the girls and to herself. Now, alone with him in his office, Sherry's reaction to him was decidedly positive. If she were looking for someone to fill the role of Prince Charming in her life, only one man need apply. She found it amusing, even touching, that somehow even in glasses, this man was devastating. He apparently wore them for reading, but he hadn't allowed the staff to see him in them before now.

"Before I forget, how did you settle the problem with Gretchen Hamburg?"

"Ah yes, Gretchen." Proud of herself, Sherry leaned back in the chair and crossed her legs. "It was simple actually. I repositioned her cot away from the wall. That was all she really wanted."

"And she's satisfied with that?"

"Relatively. The mattress is too flat, the pillow's too soft and the blanket's too thin, but other than that, the bed is fine."

"You handled that well."

Sherry considered that high praise coming from her fearless director. He, too, leaned back in his chair. He hesitated and seemed to be considering his words as he rolled a pencil between his palms. "I feel that I may have misled you when you applied for the position at Camp Gitche Gumee," he said after a long pause.

"Oh?" Her heart was thundering at an alarming rate.

"We're not a Camp Fire Girl camp."

Sherry didn't breathe, fearing what was coming next. "I beg your pardon?"

"This isn't the usual summer camp."

Sherry couldn't argue with that—canoeing and hiking were offered, but there was little else in the way of fun camping experiences.

"Camp Gitche Gumee aspires to academic excellence," he explained, with a thoughtful frown. "We take the brightest young minds in this country and challenge them to excel in a wide variety of subjects. As you probably noted from the announcements made this morning, we strive toward bringing in top educators to lecture on stimulating subjects."

"Like *fungus and mold*?"

"Yes. Dr. Waldorf is a world-renowned lecturer. Fascinating subject." Roarke tried to ignore her sarcastic tone. From the way she was staring back at him, he realized she strongly disapproved, and he was surprised at how much her puckered frown affected him. Something deep inside him yearned to please her, to draw the light of her smile back into her eyes, to be bathed in the glow of her approval. The thought froze him. Something was drastically wrong with him. With restrained anger, he pushed his glasses up the bridge of his nose.

Her lack of appreciation for the goals he'd set for this summer put him in an uncomfortable position. She saw him as a stuffed shirt, that much was obvious, but he couldn't allow Sherry's feelings to cloud his better judgment. He didn't want to destroy her enthusiasm, but it was necessary to guide it into the proper channels. He liked Sherry's spirit, even though she'd made it obvious she didn't agree with his methods. He hesitated once more. He didn't often talk about his youth, saw no reason to do so, but it was important to him that Sherry understand.

"I would have loved a camp such as this when I was ten," he said thoughtfully.

"You?"

"It might astonish you to know that I was once considered a child prodigy."

It didn't surprise her, now that she thought about it.

"I was attending high-school classes when most boys my age were trying out for Little League. I was in college at fifteen and had my master's by the time I was twenty."

Sherry didn't know how to comment. The stark loneliness in his voice said it all. He'd probably had few friends and little or no contact with other children like himself. The pressures on him would have crumpled anyone else. Jeff Roarke's empty childhood had led him to establish Camp Gitche Gumee. His own bleak experiences were what made the camp so important to him. A surge of compassion rose within Sherry and she gripped her hands together.

"Learning can be fun," she suggested softly, after a long moment. "What about an exploration into the forests in search of such exotic animals as the salamander and tree frog?"

"Yes, well, that is something to consider."

"And how about camp songs?"

"We sing."

"In Latin!"

"Languages are considered a worthy pursuit."

"Okay, games," Sherry challenged next. Her voice was raised as she warmed to her subject. She knew she wouldn't be able to hold her tongue long. It was better to get her feelings into the open than to try to bury them. "And I don't mean Camp Gitche Gumee's afternoon quiz teams, either."

"There are plenty of scheduled free times."

"But not organized fun ones," Sherry cried. "As you said, these children are some of the brightest in the country, but they have one major problem." She was all the way to the edge of her cushion by now, liberally using her hands for emphasis. "They have never been allowed to be children."

Once again, Roarke shoved his glasses up the bridge of his nose, strangely unsettled by her comments. She did make a strong case, but there simply wasn't enough time in a day to do all that she suggested. "Learning in and of itself should offer plenty of fun."

"But—"

Sherry wasn't allowed to finish.

"But you consider fairy tales of value?" he asked, recalling the reason he'd called her into his office.

"You're darn right I do. The girls loved them. Do you know Diane Miller? She's read Milton and Wilde and hasn't a clue who Dr. Seuss is."

"Who?" He blinked.

"Dr. Seuss." It wasn't until then that Sherry realized that Roarke knew nothing of Horton and the Grinch. He'd probably never tasted green eggs with ham or known about Sam.

Roarke struggled to disguise his ignorance. "I'm convinced your intentions are excellent, Miss White, but these parents have paid good money for their children to attend this camp with the express understanding that the children would learn. Unfortunately, fairy tales weren't listed as an elective on our brochure."

"Maybe they should have been," Sherry said firmly. "From everything I've seen, this camp is so academically minded that the entire purpose of sending a child away for the summer has been lost."

Roarke's mouth compressed and his eyes glinted coldly. Sherry could see she'd overstepped her bounds.

"After one week you consider yourself an expert on the subject?"

"I know children."

His hands shuffled the papers on his desk. "It was my understanding that you were a college senior."

"With a major in education."

"And a minor in partying?"

"That's not true," Sherry cried, coming to her feet.

Roarke rose as well, planted his hands on the desk-top, and leaned forward. "Fairy tales are out, Miss White. In the evening you will prepare a study plan and have it approved by me. Is that understood?"

Sherry could feel the hot color fill her face. "Yes, sir," she responded crisply, and mocked him with a salute. If he was going to act like a marine sergeant then she'd respond like a lowly recruit.

"That was unnecessary!"

Sherry opened her mouth to argue with him when the calico cat she'd witnessed earlier in her cabin win-dow suddenly appeared. A gasp rose in her throat at the tiny figure dangling from the cat's mouth.

"Ralph!" she cried, near hysteria.

Chapter Four

"Ralph?" Roarke demanded. "Who the hell is Ralph?"

"Pamela's hamster. For heaven's sake do something!" Sherry cried. "He's still alive."

Slowly, Roarke advanced toward the cat. "Buttercup," he said softly. "Nice Buttercup. Put down..." He paused, twisting his head to look at Sherry.

"Ralph," Sherry supplied.

Roarke turned back to the cat. "I thought you said the name was Pamela."

"No, Ralph is Pamela's hamster."

"Right." He wiped a hand across his brow and momentarily closed his eyes. This just wasn't his day. Cautiously, he lowered himself to his knees.

Sherry followed suit, shaking with anxiety. Poor Ralph! Trapped in the jaws of death.

"Buttercup," Roarke encouraged softly. "Put down Ralph."

The absurdity of Roarke's naming a cat "Buttercup" unexpectedly struck Sherry, and a laugh oddly mingled with hysteria worked its way up her throat and escaped with the words, "The cat's name is Buttercup?"

This wasn't the time to explain that his mother had named the cat. "Buttercup isn't any more unusual than a hamster named Ralph!" Roarke said through gritted teeth.

Sherry snickered. "Wanna bet?"

Proud of her catch, Buttercup sat with the squirming rodent in her mouth, seeming to wait for the praise due her. Roarke, down on all fours, slowly advanced toward the feline.

"Will she eat him?" That was Sherry's worst fear. In her mind she could see herself as a helpless witness to the slaughter.

"I don't know what she'll do to him," Roarke whispered impatiently.

By now they were both down on all fours, in front of the sleek calico.

"I'll try to take him out of her mouth."

"What if she won't give him up?" Sherry was about an inch away from pressing the panic button.

Lifting his hand so slowly that it was difficult to tell that Roarke was moving, he gently patted the top of Buttercup's head.

"For heaven's sake don't praise her," Sherry hissed. "That's Pamela's hamster your cat is torturing."

"Here, Buttercup," he said soothingly, "give me Ralph."

The cat didn't so much as blink.

"I see she's well trained." Sherry couldn't resist the remark.

Roarke flashed her an irritated glance.

Just then the phone rang. Startled, Sherry bolted upright and her hand slapped her heart. A gasp died on her lips as Buttercup dropped Ralph and shot across the room. Roarke dived for the hamster, falling forward so that his elbow hit the floor with a solid thud. His glasses went flying.

"Got him," Roarke shouted triumphantly.

The phone pealed a second time.

"Here."

Without warning or option, Roarke handed Sherry the hamster. Her heart was hammering in her throat as the furry critter burrowed deep into her cupped hands. "Poor baby," she murmured, holding him against her chest.

"Camp Gitche Gumee," Roarke spoke crisply into the telephone receiver. "Just one moment and I'll transfer your call to the kitchen."

Sherry heard him punch a couple of buttons and hang up. In a sitting position on the floor, she released a long, ragged breath and slumped against the side of the desk, needing its support. At the rate her heart was pumping, she felt as if she had just completed the hundred-yard dash.

Roarke moved away from her and she saw him reach down and retrieve his glasses.

"How is he?" he asked, concerned.

"Other than being frightened half to death, he appears to be unscathed."

Silence.

"I...I suppose I should get Ralph back to the cabin," she said, feeling self-conscious and silly.

"Here, let me help you up." He gave her his hand, firmly clasping her elbow, and hauled her to her feet. Sherry found his touch secure and warm. And surprisingly pleasant. Very pleasant. As she stood she discovered that they were separated by only a few inches. "Yes...well," she said and swallowed awkwardly. "Thank you for your help."

His eyes held hers. Lynn was right, Sherry noted. They weren't hazel but green, a deep cool shade of green that she associated with emeralds. Another surprise was how dark and expressive his eyes were. But the signals he was sending were strong and conflicting. Sherry read confusion and a touch of shock, as though she'd unexpectedly thrown him off balance.

Roarke's gaze dropped from her eyes to her mouth and Sherry's breath seemed to jam in her lungs.

She knew what Roarke wanted. The muscles of her stomach tightened and a sinking sensation attacked her with the knowledge that she would like it if he kissed her. The thought of his mouth fitting over hers was powerfully appealing. His lips would be like his hand, warm and firm. Sherry pulled herself up short. She was flabbergasted to be entertaining such thoughts. Jeff Roarke. Dictator! Marine sergeant! Stuffed shirt!

"Thank you for your help," she muttered in a voice hardly like her own. Hurriedly, she took a step in retreat, unable to escape fast enough.

Roarke stood stunned as Sherry backed away from him. He was shaking from the inside out. He'd nearly kissed her! And in the process gone against his own policy, and worse, his better judgment. Fortunately, whatever had been happening to him hadn't seemed to affect her. She'd jumped away from him as though she'd been burned, as if the thought of his kissing her was repulsive to her. Even then, it had taken all the strength of his will not to reach out and bring her into his arms.

Sherry watched as Roarke's mouth twisted into a mocking smile. "When you return to your cottage, Miss White, I suggest you read page 36 of the camp manual."

Without looking, Sherry already knew what it said: no pets! Well, anyone with half a brain in his head would recognize that Ralph wasn't a pet—he was a mascot. In her opinion every cabin should have one, but Sherry already knew what Roarke thought of her ideas.

"Miss White." He stopped her at the office door.

The softness in his accusing voice filled her with dread. "Yes?"

"I'd like to review your lesson plans for the evening sessions for the next week at your earliest convenience."

"I'll... I'll have them to you by tomorrow morning."

"Thank you."

"N-no," she stammered. "Thank you. I thought we'd lost Ralph for sure."

Sherry didn't remember walking across the camp-grounds. The next thing she knew, she was inside the cabin and Ralph was safely tucked inside his shoe-box home.

Her heart continued to pound frantically and she sank onto the closest available bunk, grateful that Ralph had been found unscathed. And even more grateful that the issue of her application form and the references had been pushed to the side.

As much as she'd like to attribute her shaky knees and battering heart to Buttercup's merciless attack on Ralph, Sherry knew otherwise. It was Roarke. Like every other female in this camp, she had fallen under his magical spell. For one timeless moment she'd seen him as the others did. Attractive. Compelling. Dynamic. Jeff Roarke! There in his office, with Ralph in her hand, they'd gazed at each other and Sherry had been stunned into breathlessness. She wiped a hand over her eyes to shake the vivid image of the man from her mind. Her tongue moistened her lips as she imagined Roarke's mouth over hers. She felt herself melting inside and closed her eyes. It would have been good. Very, very good.

It took Sherry at least ten minutes to gather her composure, and she was grateful she'd kept her wits about her. It wasn't so unusual to be physically attracted to a man, she reassured herself. She had been plenty of times before; this wasn't really something new, and it was only an isolated incident. Wasn't it? As a mature adult, she was surely capable of keeping her hormones under control. For the remainder of the summer she would respond to Roarke with cool politeness, she decided. If he were to guess her feelings, she would be at his mercy.

Somehow, Sherry got through the rest of the day. Peace reigned in the cabin, and when the evening session came, Sherry read her young charges the story of Snow White and the Seven Dwarfs. She'd promised them she would, and she wouldn't go back on her word. But to be on the safe side, she also decided to teach them a song.

"Okay, everyone stand," she instructed, when she'd finished the story.

Simultaneously, seven pajama-clad preteens rose to their feet.

"What are we going to do now?" Gretchen cried. "I want to talk about Snow White."

"We'll discuss the story later." Sherry put off the youngster, and extended her hands. "Okay, everyone, this is a fun song, so listen up."

When she had their attention, she swayed her hips and pointed to her feet, singing at the top of her lungs how the anklebone was connected to the legbone and the legbone was connected to the hipbone. Seven small hips did an imitation of Sherry's gyrating action. Then the girls dissolved into helpless giggles. Soon the entire cabin was filled with the sounds of joy and laughter.

To satisfy her young charges, Sherry was forced into repeating the silly song no less than three times. At least if she were asked to report tomorrow on their evening activity, Sherry would honestly be able to say that they'd studied the human skeleton. It felt good to have outsmarted Roarke.

"Five minutes until lights-out," Sherry called, making a show of checking her watch. From the corner of her eye, she saw the girls scurry across the room and back to their cots.

"I still want to talk about Snow White," Gretchen cried, above the chaos. "You told me we'd have time to discuss the story."

"I'm sorry," Sherry admitted contritely, sitting on the edge of the young girl's mattress. "We really don't—not tonight."

"But when the lights go out, that doesn't mean we have to go to sleep."

"Yeah," another voice shouted out. Sherry thought it came from Diane, the reader.

"Someone—anyone, turn out the lights," Sally cried. "Then we can talk."

The room went dark.

Gretchen's bed was closest to the cabin entrance. The room felt stuffy, so Sherry opened the door to allow in the cool evening breeze. A soft ribbon of golden light from the full moon followed the whispering wind inside the cabin.

"Did any of you know that Camp Gitche Gumee is haunted?" Sherry whispered. The girls' attention was instant and rapt.

"There's no such thing as ghosts," Gretchen countered, but her tone lacked conviction.

"Oh, but there are." Sherry whispered, her own voice dipping to an eerie low. "The one who roams around here is named Longfellow."

"Oh, I get it," Diane said with a short laugh. "He was the author of the poem—"

"Shh." Sherry placed her index finger over her lips. Dramatically, she cupped her hands over her ears. "I think I hear him now."

The cabin went still.

"I hear something," Wendy whispered. In the moonlight, Sherry could see the ten-year-old had all ten of her Barbies and Kens in bed with her.

"You needn't worry." Sherry was quick to assure the girls. "Longfellow is a friendly ghost. He only does fun, good things."

"What kind of things?"

"Hmm, let me think."

"I bet Longfellow brought Ralph back."

Sherry hadn't told Pamela how Buttercup had captured the hamster. Her pet's narrow escape from the jaws of death would only terrorize the softhearted little girl.

"Now that I think about it, Pamela, you're right. Longfellow must have had a hand in finding Ralph."

"What other kinds of things does Longfellow do?" Jan and Jill wanted to know. As always, they spoke in unison. Jill's front tooth was still intact, but it wouldn't last much longer with the furious way she worked at extracting it.

"He finds missing items like socks and hair clips. And sometimes, late at night when it's stone quiet, if you listen real, real hard, you can hear him sing."

"You can?"

"Actually, he whistles," Sherry improvised.

The still room went even quieter as seven pairs of ears strained to listen to the wind whisper through the forest of redwoods outside their door.

"I hear him," Diane said excitedly. "He's real close."

"When I was a little kid," Sally told the group excitedly, "I used to be afraid of ghosts, but Longfellow sounds like a good ghost."

"Oh, he is."

"Can you tell us another story?" Gretchen pleaded. "They're fun."

For the chronic grumbler to ask for a fairy tale and admit anything was fun was almost more than Sherry could comprehend. "I think one more story wouldn't hurt," she said. "But that has to be all." Remembering the conversation with Roarke earlier that afternoon, Sherry felt a fleeting sadness. After tonight, her stories would have to come from more acceptable classics. She thought her girls were missing a wonderful part of their heritage as children by skipping fairy tales. If she didn't want this job so badly, Sherry would have battled Roarke more strenuously.

Leaning back against the wall, she brought her knees up to her chin, sighed audibly while she chose the tale, and started. "Once upon a time in a land far, far away..."

By the time she announced that "they lived happily ever after" the cabin was filled with the even, measured breathing of sleeping children. If the girls weren't all asleep they were close to it.

Gretchen snored softly, and taking care not to wake the slumbering child, Sherry climbed off her cot and checked on the others. She pulled a blanket around Jan's and Jill's shoulders and removed inanimate objects from the cots, placing Sally's microscope on the headboard and rescuing the Barbies and Kens from being crushed during the night. Ralph was firmly secured in his weathered home, and Sherry gently slid the shoe box from underneath Pamela's arm.

"Sleep tight," she whispered to the much-loved rodent. "Or else I'll call Buttercup back."

As she moved to close the cabin door, Sherry was struck by how peaceful the evening was. Drawn outside, she sat on the top step of the large front porch and gazed at the stars. They were out in brilliant display this evening, scattered diamonds tossed on thick folds of black velvet. How close they seemed. Sparkling. Radiant.

Sherry's hands cupped her chin as she rested her elbows on her knees and studied the heavens.

"Good evening, Miss White." Roarke had heard their singing earlier, had come to investigate and had been amused by her efforts to outwit him.

The sound of Roarke's voice broke into Sherry's thoughts. "Good evening, Mr. Roarke," she responded crisply, and straightened. "What brings you out tonight?" Lordy, she hoped he hadn't been around to hear the last fairy tale, or worse, her mention of Longfellow.

He paused, braced one foot against the bottom step and looked over the grounds. "I like to give the camp a final check before turning in for the night."

"Oh." For the life of her, she couldn't think of a single thing more to say. Her reaction to him was immediate. Her heart pounded like a jackhammer and the blood shot through her veins. She'd like to fool herself into believing the cause was the unexpectedness of his arrival, but she knew better.

"How's Ralph?" Roarke questioned.

"Fully recovered. How's Buttercup?"

"Exceptionally proud." The soft laugh that followed was so pleasant sounding that it caused Sherry to smile just listening to him.

"You have a nice laugh." She hadn't meant to tell him that, but it slipped out before she could stop herself. As often was the case when she spoke to Jeff Roarke, the filter between her brain and her mouth malfunctioned and whatever she was thinking slid out without forethought.

"I was about to tell you how effervescent *your* laugh sounds."

Sherry couldn't remember a time she'd ever given him the opportunity to hear her laugh. The circumstances in which they were together prohibited it. Staff meetings were intensely serious. No one dared show any amusement.

"When—"

"Tonight. I suppose you plan to tell me that the legbone connected to the hipbone is a study of the human skeleton?"

Words ran together and tripped over the tip of her tongue. "Of course not . . . well, yes, but . . ."

He laughed again. "The girls thoroughly enjoyed it, didn't they?"

"Yes."

"That sort of education wasn't exactly what I had in mind, but anything is better than those blasted fairy tales."

Sherry was forced into sitting on her hands to keep from elbowing him. Fairy tales weren't silly or senseless. They served a purpose! But she managed to keep her thoughts to herself—with some effort.

Silence again.

"I have my lesson plan if you'd like to see it," she said, and started to get up, but his hand on her forearm stopped her.

"Tomorrow morning is soon enough."

He surprised her even more by climbing the three steps and taking a seat beside her. He paused and raised his eyes to the sky.

"Lovely, isn't it?" he asked.

"Yes." The one word seemed to strangle in her throat. Roarke was close enough to touch. All Sherry would have had to do was shift her weight for her shoulder to gently graze his. Less than an inch separated their thighs. Although she strove to keep from experiencing the physical impact of brushing against him, there was little she could do about the soft scent of the after-shave Roarke wore, which was so masculinely appealing. Every breath she drew in was more tantalizing than the one before. Spice and man—a lethal combination.

It was the night, Sherry decided, not the man. Oh, please, not the man, she begged. She didn't want to be so strongly attracted to Jeff Roarke. She didn't want to be like all the others. The two of them were so different. They couldn't agree on anything. Not him. Not her.

Neither spoke, but the silence wasn't a serene one. The darkness seemed charged with static electricity. Twice Sherry opened her mouth, ready to start some banal conversation simply to break the silence. Both times she found herself incapable of speaking. When she chanced a look in his direction she discovered his thick eyebrows arched bewilderedly over a storm cloud of sea-green eyes.

Naturally, neither one of them had the courage to introduce the phenomenon occurring between them into casual conversation. But Sherry was convinced Roarke felt the tug of physical attraction as strongly and powerfully as she did. And from the look of him, he was as baffled as she.

"Well, I suppose I should turn in," she said, after the longest minute of her life.

"I suppose I should, too."

But neither of them moved.

"It really is a lovely night," Sherry said, looking to the heavens, struck once again by the simple beauty of the starlit sky.

"Yes, lovely," Roarke repeated softly, but he wasn't gazing at the heavens, he was looking at Sherry. He'd believed everything he'd said to her about romance being nonsense, but now the words came back to haunt him. Right now, this moment with her seemed more important than life itself. He felt trapped in a whirlpool of awareness. The sensations that churned inside him were lethal to his mental health and he wouldn't alter a one. This woman had completely thrown him off balance with the unexpected flaring need he felt to hold her in his arms. Slipping his arm around her shoulder seemed the most natural act in the world...and strictly against his own camp policy. The urge to do so was so strong that he crossed his arms across his chest in an effort to keep them still. He was stunned at how close he'd come to giving in to temptation. Stunned and appalled.

Whatever caused Sherry to turn to meet his gaze, she didn't know. Fate, possibly. But she did rotate her head so that her eyes were caught by his as effectively as if trapped in a vise. Mesmerized, their gazes locked in the faint light of the glorious moon. It was as though Sherry were looking at him for the first time— through a love-struck teen's adoring eyes. He was devastatingly handsome. Dark, and compellingly masculine.

Unable to stop herself, she raised her hand, prepared to outline his thick eyebrows with her fingertips, and paused halfway to his face. His troubled eyes were a mirror of her own doubtful expression, Sherry realized. Yet his were charged with curiosity. He seemed to want to hold her in his arms as much as she yearned to let him. His mouth appeared to hunger for the taste of hers just as she longed to sample his. His shallow breath mingled with her labored one. Deep grooves formed at the sides of his mouth, and when his lips parted, Sherry noted that his breathing was hesitant.

Driven by something stronger than her own common sense, Sherry slowly, inch by inch, lowered her lashes, silently bending to his unspoken demand. Her own lips parted in welcome as her pulse fluttered wildly at the base of her throat.

Roarke lowered his mouth to a scant inch above hers.

Sherry was never sure what happened. A sound perhaps. A tree branch scraping against the roof of the cabin—perhaps an owl's screeching cry as it flew overhead. Whatever it was instantly brought her to her senses, and she was eternally grateful. She jerked her head back and willfully checked her watch.

"My goodness," she cried in a wobbly, weak voice, "will you look at the time?"

"Time?" he rasped.

"It's nearly eleven. I really must get inside." Already she was on her feet, rushing toward the front door as though being chased by a mad dog.

Not waiting for a response from Roarke, Sherry closed the door and weakly leaned against it. Her heart was thumping like a locomotive gone out of control. Her mouth felt dry and scratchy. Filled with purpose, she walked over to the small sink and turned on the cold water faucet. She gulped down the first glass in huge swallows and automatically poured herself a second. In different circumstances, she would have taken her temperature. There was something in the air. Sherry almost wished it was a virus.

The next morning, Sherry was on time for the staff meeting. She hadn't slept well and was awake even before the alarm sounded. At least when she was a few minutes early she could choose her own seat. The back of the room all but invited her and she claimed a seat there.

Lynn Duffy scooted in beside her.

"Morning," Sherry greeted her.

"Hi. How's it going?"

Sherry pushed the cuticle back on her longest fingernail. "Just fine. The kids are great."

"You got Gretchen Hamburg—don't tell me everything's fine. I know better."

"She's a cute kid!"

"Gretchen?" Lynn grumbled. "You've got to be teasing. The kid's a royal pain in the rear end!"

Two days ago, Sherry would have agreed with her, but from the minute Gretchen had announced that fairy tales were "fun" she'd won Sherry's heart.

Roarke stepped to the podium, and the small gathering of staff went silent. Sherry noted that he took pains not to glance in her direction, which was fine by her. She preferred that he didn't. This morning the memory of those few stolen moments alone under the stars was nothing short of embarrassing. She'd rather forget the entire episode. Chalk it up to the decreased layer of ozone in outer space. Or the way the planets were aligned. The moon was in its seventh house. Aquarius and Mars. A fluke certainly. She could look at him this morning and feel nothing...well, that wasn't exactly true. The irritation was gone, replaced by a lingering fascination.

After only a minimum of announcements, the staff were dismissed. Sherry stood, eager to make her escape.

"Sherry," Lynn said, following her out of the meeting room, "do you have some free time later?"

"After breakfast."

Her friend looked a bit chagrined. "I have to run into town. Would you like to come along?"

"Sure, I'll come over to your cabin after I get my wizards off to their first class."

Lynn brightened. "I'll look for you around eight, then."

Her friend took off in the opposite direction and Sherry's gaze followed the younger girl. Now that she thought about it, Lynn didn't seem to be her normal, cheerful self. Sherry had the impression that this jaunt into town was an excuse to talk.

It was.

The minute Sherry got into Lynn's car she could feel the other girl's coiled tension. Sherry was uncertain. She didn't know if she should wait until Lynn mentioned what was troubling her, or if she should say something to start Lynn talking. She chose the latter.

"Are you enjoying the camp this summer?" Sherry asked.

Lynn shrugged. "It's different."

"How's that?"

Again her shoulders went up and down in a dismissive gesture. The long country road that led to the small city of Arrow Flats twisted and turned as it came down off the rugged hillside.

"Have you noticed Peter Towne?" Lynn said quietly.

"The lifeguard?"

"Yeah . . . it's his second year here, too. Last summer we were good friends. We even managed a few letters since then, Christmas, Easter and the like."

As Sherry recalled Peter was a handsome sunbleached blonde who patrolled the beaches during the afternoons and worked in the kitchen after dinner. "How old is he?"

"Nineteen—the same age as me."

Whatever was troubling Lynn obviously had to do with Peter. "He seems to be nice enough," Sherry prodded.

"Peter is more than nice," Lynn said dreamily. "He's wonderful."

Sherry wouldn't have gone quite that far to describe him. "So you two worked together last year?"

"Right."

The teenager focused her attention on the roadway, which was just as well since it looked treacherous enough to Sherry.

"What makes you bring up his name?" Sherry ventured.

"Peter's?"

"Yes, Peter's."

"Did I bring him up?"

"Lynn, honestly, you know you did."

The other girl bit the corner of her bottom lip. "Yeah, I suppose his name did casually pop into the conversation."

It seemed to Sherry that Lynn regretted having said anything so she let the matter drop. "I had my first run-in with ol' Ironjaw."

"You mean Mr. Roarke?"

"He and I had a difference of opinion about the evening sessions. He'd prefer for me to discuss the intricacies of U.S. foreign policy. I'd rather tell ghost stories. I imagine we'll agree on a subject somewhere in between."

"I saw you put something on the podium for him this morning."

"Lesson plans."

"He's making you do that?"

"As a precaution."

"Oh."

Lynn eased the car to a stop at the crossroads before turning onto the main thoroughfare. Arrow Flats was about ten miles north of the camp. Sherry noticed the way Lynn's hands tightened around the steering wheel at the intersection.

"Two nights ago, I couldn't sleep," she said in a strained, soft voice. "I decided to take a walk down to the lake. There was an old piece of driftwood there so I sat down. Peter... couldn't sleep, either. He happened to come by, and we sat and talked."

"From everything I've seen, Peter's got a good head on his shoulders."

"It was nearly one before we went back to camp. He kissed me, Sherry. I never wanted anyone to kiss me more than Peter that night in the moonlight. It was so romantic and... I don't know... I've never felt this strongly about any boy before."

Sherry could identify with that from her own surprising experience with Roarke, the night before on the porch. Maybe there really was something in the air, she thought hopefully.

"Now every time I look at Peter I see the same longing in his eyes. We want to be together. I...I think we may be falling in love."

Sherry thought it was wonderful that the friendship between the two had blossomed into something more, but she understood her friend's dilemma. The camp was no place for a romance.

"Oh, Sherry, what am I going to do?" Lynn cried. "If Mr. Roarke finds out, both Peter and I will be fired."

Chapter Five

"**G**ood morning, Miss White."

Roarke's voice rose to greet her when Sherry slipped into the back row of chairs in the staff room. She muttered something appropriate, embarrassed once again to be caught coming in tardy for yet another early-morning session. On this particular day, her only excuse was laziness. The alarm had gone off and she simply hadn't been able to force herself out of bed.

As always, Roarke waited until she'd settled in her seat before continuing.

Sherry tried her best to listen to the day's announcements, but her mind drifted to Lynn and Peter and their predicament. It felt peculiar to side with Roarke, but Sherry agreed that a romance at camp could be a source of problems for the teenagers and everyone else. Lynn's attraction to Peter was a natural response for a nineteen-year-old girl, and Peter was a fine boy, but camp simply wasn't the place for their courtship. Sherry had advised her friend to "cool it" as much as possible. In a couple of months, once camp had been dismissed, the two could freely date each other.

Sherry's gaze skidded from the tall blond youth back to Lynn. They were doing their best to hide their growing affection for each other, but from the not-so-secret glances they shared, their feelings were all too obvious to Sherry. And if she could see how they felt, then it probably wouldn't be long before Roarke did, too.

A chill ran up Sherry's arms, and she bundled her sweater more tightly around her. She yawned and rubbed the sleep from her eyes, forcing herself to pay attention to what Roarke was saying.

The others were beginning to stand and move about before she realized that the session had come to a close. Still she didn't move. Standing, walking about, thinking, seemed almost more than she could manage. What she needed was some kind soul to intravenously feed her coffee a half hour before the alarm went off.

"Is there a problem, Miss White?"

Sherry glanced up to find Roarke looming above her.

"No," she mumbled and shook her head for emphasis.

"Then shouldn't you be getting back to your cabin?"

She nodded, although that, too, required some effort. A giant yawn escaped, and she cupped her hand over her mouth. "I suppose."

"You really aren't a morning person, are you?"

Her smile was weak. "It just takes a while for my heart to start working."

Roarke straddled a seat in the row in front of her and looped his arm over the chair back as he studied her. She looked as though she could curl up right there and without much effort go back to sleep. The urge to wrap her in his arms and press her head against his shoulder was a powerful one. He could almost feel her softness yield against his muscled strength. Forcibly, he shook the image from his mind. His gaze softened as he studied her. "Did you hear anything of what I said?"

"A...little," she admitted sheepishly. He grinned at that, and she discovered that his smile completely disarmed her. Speaking of getting her heart revved up! One smile from Jeff Roarke worked wonders. No man had the right to look that good this early in the day. Her mind had come up with a list of concrete arguments for him to postpone these sessions to a more decent time of day, but one charming look shot them down like darts tossed at fat balloons. "I don't know what it is about mornings, but I think I may be allergic to them."

"Perhaps if you tried going to bed earlier."

"It doesn't work," she said, and yawned again. "I wish I could, but at about ten every night, I come alive. My best work is done then."

Roarke glanced at his watch, nodded and stood. "Your cabin is due in the mess hall in fifteen minutes."

Sherry groaned and dropped her feet. Her hand crisply touched her forehead. "Aye, aye, Commandant, we'll be there."

Roarke chuckled and returned her mock salute.

When Sherry entered the cabin, she discovered the girls in a frenzy. Pamela had climbed to the top of the dresser and was huddled into a tight ball clutching Ralph, her knees drawn up against her chest. Gretchen faced the open door, a broom raised above her head, prepared for attack, while Jan and Jill were nearby, holding their shoes in their fists like lethal weapons.

Ginny, the high-school girl who had been assigned to stay in the cabin while Sherry was at the morning meeting, was in as much of a tizzy as the girls.

"What happened?" Sherry demanded.

"He tried to kill Ralph," Pamela screamed hysterically.

"Who?"

"I read about things like this," Diane inserted calmly. "It's a natural instinct."

"What is?" Sherry cried, hurriedly glancing from girl to girl.

"The cat," Jan and Jill said together.

"Ralph was nearly eaten," Pamela cried.

Sherry sagged with relief. "That's only Buttercup."

"Buttercup!"

"He belongs to Mr. Roarke."

"Mr. Roarke has a cat named Buttercup?" Gretchen said, lowering her broom to the floor. A look of astonishment relaxed her mouth into a giant O.

"Apparently so."

"But he tried to get Ralph." Pamela opened her hands and the rodent squirmed his head out between two fingers and looked around anxiously.

"We need a cage," Sherry said decisively. "That shoe box is an open invitation to Buttercup."

"Can't Mr. Roarke keep his cat chained up or something?" Wendy suggested. The Barbies and Kens were scattered freely across the top of her mattress.

"I thought we weren't supposed to have pets," Gretchen complained. "I find Mr. Roarke's actions highly contradictory."

"Since we're keeping Ralph, mentioning Buttercup to Mr. Roarke wouldn't be wise," Sherry informed them all with a tight upper lip.

"But we've got to do something."

"Agreed." One glance at her watch confirmed that her troop was already late for breakfast. "Hurry now, girls. I'll take care of everything."

"Everything?" Pam's bold eyes studied her counselor.

"Everything," Sherry promised.

By the time Sherry and her cabin arrived at the mess hall, the meal was already half over. The stacks of pancakes had cooled and the butter wouldn't melt on them properly. Gretchen complained loudly enough for the cooks in the kitchen to hear.

In the middle of breakfast, Sally produced a huge tannish-gold hawk moth she'd trapped the night before and passed it around the table for the others to admire, momentarily distracting Sherry.

"Girls, manners. Please," she cried, when Wendy stuffed a whole pancake into her mouth. Sticky syrup oozed down the preteen's chin.

"But we have to hurry," Diane complained.

"You'll talk to Mr. Roarke about his cat, won't you?" Pam wanted to know as she climbed out of her chair, her meal untouched.

"I'll see what I can do."

When the last girl had left the dining room, rushing to her class, Sherry sighed with relief. She hadn't so much as had her first cup of coffee and already the morning was a disaster.

"Problems, Miss White?" Again Roarke joined her. He handed her a steaming mug of coffee.

She cupped it in her hands and savored the first sip. "Bless you."

Roarke pulled out a chair and sat down across the table from her.

"Buttercup paid us another visit," she said after a long moment.

"Ralph?"

"Is fine. . . ."

His jaw tightened. "May I remind you, Miss White, that it is against camp policy to have a pet?"

"Ralph is a mascot, not a pet."

"He's a damn nuisance."

"You're a fine one to talk," she returned heatedly and took another sip of coffee in an effort to fortify her courage. "As for camp policy—what do you call Buttercup?"

"The camp cat."

"She's not a pet?"

"Definitely not."

"My foot!"

"If there are problems with Ralph, then the solution is simple—get rid of him."

"No way! Pamela's strongly attached to that animal." Surely Roarke wasn't heartless enough to take away a child's only friend. "This is the first time Pamela's spent more than a few days away from home and family. That hamster's helping her through the long separation from her brother and parents."

"If I allow Ralph to stay, then next year someone is likely to bring a boa constrictor and claim it's not a pet, either."

Sherry twisted her head from side to side, glancing around her. Lowering her voice, she leaned forward and whispered, "No one knows about Ralph. I'm not telling, the girls aren't telling. That only leaves you."

"Buttercup knows."

"She's the problem," Sherry gritted between clenched teeth.

"No," Roarke countered heatedly. "Ralph is."

From the hard set of the director's mouth, Sherry could see that discussing this matter would solve nothing. She held up both palms in a gesture of defeat. "Fine."

"Fine what? You'll get rid of Ralph?"

"No! I'll take care of the problem."

"How?" He eyed her dubiously.

"I haven't figured that out yet, but I will."

"That I don't doubt. Just make sure I don't know a thing about it."

"Right." Playfully, she winked at him, stood, reached for a small pancake, popped it into her mouth and left the dining hall. She understood Roarke's concerns, but occasional exceptions to rules had to be made. Life was filled with too many variables for him to be so hard-nosed and stringent. Ralph had to be kept a secret, and more than that, the rodent couldn't continue to rule the lives of her seven charges. A cage was one solution, but knowing Buttercup, that wouldn't be enough to distract the cat from her daily raids.

She found the answer in town. That night after the evening meal, Sherry carried in the solution for the girls to examine.

"What's it for?" Sally wanted to know when Sherry held the weapon up for their inspection.

Bracing her feet like a trained commando, Sherry looped the strap over her shoulder and positioned the machine gun between her side and her elbow. "One shot from this and Buttercup won't be troubling Ralph again."

"You aren't going to..." Jan began.

"...shoot him?" Jill finished her twin's worried query.

The girls' eyes widened as Sherry's mouth twisted into a dark scowl. "You bet. I'm going to shoot him—right between the eyes."

A startled gasp rose.

"Miss White," Pamela pleaded, "I don't want you to hurt Buttercup."

Sherry relaxed and lowered the machine gun, grinning. "Oh, I wouldn't do that. This is a battery-operated water gun."

"Really?"

"A water gun?" Diane asked, lowering her book long enough to examine Sherry's weapon.

"I knew that all along," Gretchen said.

"I'll show you how it works." Sherry aimed it at her bedroom door and fingered the trigger. Instantly, a piercing blast of water slammed against the pine door ten feet away.

"Hey, not bad," Diane said excitedly.

"It's as accurate as a real gun," Sherry explained further. "After a shot or two from this beauty, Buttercup won't come within fifty feet of this cabin."

The spontaneous applause gladdened Sherry's heart. She accepted the praise of her charges with a deep bow and placed the weapon in her bedroom. Returning a moment later, she entered the room with a dark visor pulled down low over her eyes. She held out a deck of cards toward them.

"Okay, girls, gather 'round," she called. "Tonight's lesson is about statistics." Grinning, she playfully shuffled the cards from one hand to the other. "Anyone here ever played gin rummy?"

If Sherry had thought her charges enjoyed the fairy tales, they were even more ecstatic about cards. Their ability to pick up the rules and the theory behind the games astonished her. It shouldn't, she mused. After all they were real live wizards! After she'd taught them the finer point of gin rummy, the seven had eagerly learned hearts and canasta. At nine-thirty, their scheduled bedtime, the girls didn't want to quit. Cards were fun, and there was precious little time for that commodity at Camp Gitche Gumee.

When the lights were out, Sherry lay in her own bed, wishing she could convince Jeff Roarke that camp, no matter what its specialty, was meant to be fun.

No longer did Sherry think of Roarke in negative terms. They still disagreed on most subjects, but the wall of annoyance and frustration she'd felt toward him had been a means of hiding the sensual awareness she experienced the minute he walked into the room. It pricked her pride to admit that she was like every other female over the age of ten at Camp Gitche Gumee. Jeff Roarke was as sexy as the day was long. And since this was June, the days were lengthy enough to weave into the nights.

Sherry expelled her breath and sat upright in the darkened room. It wasn't only thoughts of Roarke that were keeping her awake. Guilt played a hand in her troubled musings. Her father and Phyliss were probably worried sick about her. Leaving the way she had hadn't been one of her most brilliant schemes. By this time, no doubt, her stepmother had hired a detective agency to track her down.

Contrite feelings about her evening sessions with the girls also played a role in her sleeplessness. She'd handed in the lesson plans to Roarke knowing that she'd misled him a little. It was stretching even her vivid imagination to link canasta and gin rummy with statistics.

This summer had been meant to be carefree and fun, and Sherry was discovering that it was neither.

Tossing aside the blankets, she reached for her jeans. The pay phone was situated on the campgrounds, directly across from her cabin. If she talked to her father, she'd feel better. There wasn't any need to let Phyliss know where she was, but it couldn't hurt to keep in touch.

Pulling her sweatshirt over her head, Sherry tiptoed between the bunks and quietly slipped out the front door. The night was filled with stars. A light breeze hummed across the treetops, their melody singing in the wind. Cotton-puff clouds roamed across the full moon, and the sweet scent of virgin forest filled the air. Tucking the tips of her fingers in her hip pockets, Sherry paused to examine the beauty of the world around her. It was lovely enough to take her breath away.

The pay phone was well lit, and Sherry slipped her quarters into the appropriate slot. Her father's groggy voice greeted her on the fourth ring.

"Hello?"

"Hi, Dad."

"Sherry?"

"How many other girls call you Dad?"

Virgil White chuckled. "You give me as much trouble as ten daughters."

"Honestly, Dad!"

"Sherry, where—"

Her father's voice was interrupted by a frenzied, eager one. "Oh, thank God," a female voice came over the line. "Sherry, darling, is that you?"

"Hello, Phyliss. Listen, I'm in a pay phone and I've only got a few quarters—"

"Virgil, do something.... Sherry's nearly penniless."

"Phyliss, I've got money, it's just quarters I'm short of at the moment. Please listen, I wanted you to know I'm fine."

"Are you eating properly?"

"Three meals a day," Sherry assured her.

"Liver once a week? Fresh fruit and vegetables?"

"Every day, scout's honor."

The sound of her father's muffled laugh came over the wire. "You were never a Girl Scout."

Phyliss gasped and started to weep silently.

"Dad, now look what you've done. Phyliss, I'm eating better than ever, and I have all the clothes I could possibly need."

"Money?"

"I'm doing just great. Wonderful, in fact. I don't need anything."

"Are you happy, baby?"

"Very happy," Sherry assured them both.

"Where are you—at least tell me where you are," her stepmother cried.

Before she could answer, the operator came back on the line. "It will be another $1.25 for the next three minutes."

"I've got to go."

"Sherry," Phyliss pleaded. "Remember to eat your garlic."

"I'll remember," she promised. "Goodbye, Dad. Goodbye, Phyliss." At age twenty-one she didn't require a baby-sitter, although Phyliss seemed convinced otherwise. As the good daughter, Sherry had done her duty.

Gently she replaced the telephone receiver, feeling much relieved. Looking up she discovered Roarke advancing toward her across the lawn in long, angry strides. Just the way he moved alerted her to his mood. She stiffened with apprehension and waited.

"Miss White." His gaze traveled from the telephone to her and then back again. "Who's staying with the girls?"

"I . . . they're all asleep. I didn't think it would matter if I slipped out for a couple of minutes. I'd be able to hear them if there was a problem," she went on hurriedly, trying to cover her guilty conscience. She really hadn't been gone more than a few minutes.

The anger left Roarke as quickly as it came. He knew he was being unreasonable. The source of his irritation wasn't that Sherry had stepped outside her cabin. It was the fact that she'd made a phone call, and he strongly suspected she'd contacted a male friend.

Self-consciously, Sherry lowered her head. "You're right, I shouldn't have left the girls. I'll make sure it doesn't happen again."

"It's a pleasure to have you agree to something I say," Roarke said, his face relaxing into a lazy smile.

Sherry's heart lifted in a strange, weightless way. She'd been tense, conscious once more that she'd done something to irritate him.

"I'll walk you back to your cabin," he suggested softly.

"Thank you." It wasn't necessary, for the cabin was within sight, but she was pleased Roarke chose to keep her company.

"I saw you on the phone," he commented, without emotion, a few minutes later. "I suppose you were talking to one of your boyfriends."

"No," she corrected, "that was my family."

Roarke cleared his throat and straightened. "Is there a boyfriend waiting for you back . . . where was it again?"

"Seattle, and no, not anyone I'm serious about." Sherry went still, her heart thundering against her breast. "And you? Do y-you have someone waiting in Berkeley?"

Roarke shook his head. There was Fiona, another professor whom he saw socially. They'd seen each other in a friendly sort of way for a couple of years, but he hadn't experienced any of the physical response with Fiona that he did with Sherry. Come to think of it, Fiona's views on romance were much like his own. "There's no one special," he said after a moment.

"I see." From the length of time that it took him to tell her that, Sherry suspected that there was someone. Her spirits dipped a little. Good grief, did she think he lived like a hermit? He couldn't! He was too damn good-looking.

Roarke's gaze studied her then, and in the veiled shadows of the moon, Sherry noted that it was impossible to make out the exact color of his eyes. Green or tawny, it didn't seem to matter now that they were focused directly on her. Her breathing became shallow and she couldn't draw her gaze away from him. Finally, she dragged her eyes from his and looked up at the stars.

Neither spoke for several minutes, and Sherry found the quiet disarming.

"You seem to have adjusted well to the camp," Roarke commented. "Other than a few problems with mornings, that is."

"Thank you."

"How did the lessons go this evening? Wasn't it statistics you told me you were planning to discuss?"

Sherry swallowed down her apprehension and answered in a small, quiet voice. "Everything went well."

Roarke's eyes narrowed as he watched her struggle to keep the color from invading her cheeks. She might think herself clever, but he wasn't completely ignorant of her creative efforts.

"I may have deviated a little," she admitted finally.

"A little?" Roarke taunted. "Then let me ask you something."

"Sure." She tried to make her voice light and airy, belying her nervousness.

"Who got stuck with the queen of spades?"

"Gretchen," she returned automatically, then slapped her hand over her mouth. "You know?"

"I had a fair idea. A little friendly game of hearts, I take it?"

She nodded, studying him. "And canasta and gin rummy, while I was at it."

He did nothing more than shake his head in a gesture of defeat.

"Are you going to lecture me?"

"Will it do any good?"

Sherry laughed softly. "Probably not."

"That's what I thought."

She relaxed, liking him more by the minute. "Then you don't mind?"

Roarke sighed. "As long as you don't fill their minds with romantic tales, I can live with it. But I'd like to ask about the lesson plans you handed in to me."

"Oh, I was planning to do everything I wrote down . . . I'm just using kind of . . . unorthodox methods."

"I figured as much." His face relaxed into a languorous smile. "I'd guess that the night you intend a study on finances is really a game of Monopoly."

"Yes . . . how'd you know?" He didn't sound irritated, and that lent Sherry confidence.

"I have my ways."

"Do you know everything that goes on in this camp?" She'd never met anyone like him. Roarke seemed to be aware of every facet of his organization. How he managed to keep tabs on each area, each cabin, was beyond her.

"I don't know everything," he countered, "but I try. . . ."

As his voice trailed off the beauty of the night demanded their attention. Neither spoke for a long moment, but neither was inclined to leave, either.

"I find it surprising that you don't have someone special waiting for you." Roarke's voice was low, slightly bewildered.

"It's not so amazing." A few men had been attracted to her—before Phyliss had drilled them on their intentions, invited them to dinner and driven them crazy with her wackiness. A smile touched the corner of Sherry's mouth. If there was anyone she wished to discourage, all she need do was introduce him to her loony stepmother. "I'm attending Seattle Pacific full-time, and I'm involved in volunteer work. There isn't much opportunity to date."

While she was speaking, Roarke couldn't stop looking at her. Her profile was cast against the moon shadows of the dark violet sky. The light breeze flirted with her hair, picking up the wispy strands at her temple and puffing them out and away from her face. Her dark hair was thick and inviting. He thought about lifting it in his hands, running the silky length through his fingers, burying his face in it and breathing in its fresh, clean scent. From the moment she'd first entered his office he'd thought she was pretty. Now, Roarke studied her and saw much more than the outward loveliness that had first appealed to him. Her spirit was what attracted him, her love of life, her enthusiasm.

He'd never seen a cabin enjoy their counselor more. Sherry was a natural with the children. Inventive. Clever. Fun. A hundred times since she'd arrived at camp, he'd been angered enough to question the wisdom of having hired her. But not tonight, not when he was standing in the moonlight with her at his side. Not now, when he would have given a month's wages to taste her lips and feel her softness pressed against him. She was a counselor and he was the camp director, but tonight that would be so easy to forget. He was a man so strongly attracted to a woman that his heart beat with the energy of a callow youth's.

Sherry turned and her gaze was trapped in Roarke's. At the tender look in his eyes, her breath wedged in her lungs, tightening her chest. Her heart thudded nervously.

"I guess I should go inside," she said, hardly recognizing her own voice.

Roarke nodded, willing her to leave him while he had the strength to resist her.

Sherry didn't move; her legs felt like mush and she sincerely doubted that they'd support her. If she budged at all, it was to lean closer to Roarke. Never in all her life had she wanted a man to hold her more. His gaze fell to her mouth and she moistened her lips in invitation, yearning for his kiss.

Roarke groaned inwardly and closed his eyes, but that only served to increase his awareness of her. She smelled of flowers, fresh and unbelievably sweet. Warmth radiated from her and he yearned to wrap his arms around her and feel for himself her incredible softness.

"Good night, Sherry," he said forcefully, bounding to his feet. "I'll see you in the morning."

Sherry sagged with relief and watched as Roarke marched away with the purposeful strides of a marine drill sergeant, his hands bunched into tight fists at his side.

Chapter Six

"**I** demand that we form a search party," Wendy cried, crossing her arms over her chest and glaring at Sherry. "You did when Ralph was missing."

"Wendy, sweetheart," Sherry said, doing her best to keep calm. "Ralph is a living, breathing animal."

"A *rodent hamustro* actually," Sally informed them knowingly.

"Whatever. The thing is—a misplaced Ken doll doesn't take on the urgency of a missing rodent."

"But someone stole him."

Sherry refused to believe that any of the girls would want Ken badly enough to pilfer him from their cabin mate. "We'll keep looking, Wendy, but for now that's the best we can do."

Hands placed on her hips, the youngster surveyed the room, her eyes zeroing in on her peers. "All right, which one of you crooks kidnapped Ken-Richie?"

"Wendy!"

"I refuse to live in a den of thieves!"

"No one stole your doll," Sherry said for the tenth time. "I'm sure you misplaced him."

Wendy gave her a look of utter disgust. "No one in their right mind would misplace the one and only love of Barbie-Brenda's life."

"Oh, brother," Sherry muttered under her breath.

"I think Longfellow might have done it," Pamela inserted cautiously. "It's just the kind of thing a ghost would do."

"Longfellow?"

"Right," Jan and Jill chimed in eagerly. "Longfellow."

Wendy considered that for a moment, then agreed with an abrupt nod of her head and appeared to relax somewhat. "You know, I bet that's exactly what did happen."

Over the next two days the standard response to any problem was that Longfellow was responsible. Soon the entire camp was buzzing with tales of the make-believe ghost Sherry had invented.

"My mattress has more bumps than a camel," Gretchen claimed one morning.

Six preteens glanced at the chronic complainer and shouted in unison, "Longfellow did it!"

Ralph's cage door was left open to Pamela's dismay. "Longfellow," the girls informed her.

At breakfast, the Cream of Wheat had lumps. The girls looked at one another across the table, nodded once and cried, "Longfellow."

Every time Sherry heard Longfellow's name, she cringed inwardly. That Roarke hadn't heard about the friendly ghost was a miracle in itself. Sherry had already decided that when he did, she would give an Academy Award performance of innocence. By now, news of the spirit had infiltrated most of the cabins, although Sherry couldn't be certain which counselors had heard about him and who hadn't. She did notice, however, that the boys from Fred Spencer's cabin were unusually quiet about the ghost.

Since the night she'd met Roarke at the pay phone, their relationship had gone from a rocky, rut-filled road to a smooth-surfaced freeway. He'd shocked her by ordering coffee served at their early-morning meetings. Although he hadn't specifically said it was for her benefit, Sherry realized it was.

"I don't think I ever thanked you," she told him one morning early in the week, when the staff had been dismissed from their dawn session.

"Thanked me?" He looked up from reading over his notes.

"For the coffee." She gestured with the foam cup, her gaze holding his.

Roarke grinned and his smile alone had the power to set sail to her heart.

"If you'll notice, I haven't been late for a single meeting since the coffee arrived. Fact is, I don't even need to open my eyes. The alarm goes off, I dress in the dark and follow my nose to the staff room."

"I thought that would induce you to get here on time," he said, his gaze holding hers.

Actually, the coffee hadn't a single thing to do with it. She came because it was the only time of day she could count on seeing Roarke. Generally, they didn't have much cause to spend time with each other, because Roarke was busy with the running of the camp and Sherry had her hands full with her seven charges. That he'd become so important to her was something of a quandary for Sherry. The minute he discovered she'd falsified her references, she'd be discharged from Camp Gitche Gumee. More than once Lynn had specifically told her that Mr. Roarke could forgive anything but dishonesty. Sherry had trouble being truthful with herself about her feelings for Roarke for fear of what she'd discover.

"I'm pleased the coffee helped." Dragging his eyes away from her, Roarke closed his notebook and walked out of the building with her. "Have you spent much time stargazing lately?"

She shook her head and yawned. "Too tired."

"Pity," he mumbled softly.

It would have been so easy for Sherry to forget where they were and who they were. She hadn't ever felt so strongly attracted to a man. It was crazy! Sometimes she wasn't completely sure she even liked him. Yet at all hours of the day and night, she found herself fantasizing about him. She imagined him taking her in his arms and kissing her, and how firm and warm his mouth would feel over her own. She dreamed about how good it would be to press her head against his shoulder and lean on him, letting his strength support her. She entertained fleeting fantasies even while she was doing everything in her power to battle the unreasonable desires.

"By the way," Roarke said, clearing his throat, "one of the references you gave me came back marked 'no such address.'"

"It did?" Sherry's heart pounded, stone-cold. She'd prayed he wouldn't check, but knowing how thorough Roarke was made that wish nothing short of stupid. She was going to have to think of something, and quick.

"You must have listed the wrong address."

"Yes ... I must have."

"When you've got a minute, stop off at the office and you can check it over. I'll mail it out later."

"Okay."

They parted at the pay phone, Sherry heading toward her cabin and Roarke toward the mess hall.

The cabin was buzzing with activity when Sherry stepped inside, but when the girls spied their counselor the noise level dropped to a fading hum and the seven returned to their tasks much too smoothly.

Suspicious, Sherry paused and looked around not knowing exactly what she expected to find. The girls maintained a look of innocence until Sherry demanded, "What's going on here?"

"Nothing," Sally said, but she was smiling gleefully.

Sherry didn't believe it for a moment. "I don't trust you girls. What are you up to?" Her gaze swept the room. Never in her life had she seen more innocent-looking faces. "Ginny?" Sherry turned her questions to the teenager who replaced her in the early mornings when she attended the staff meetings.

"Don't look at me." The teenager slapped her sides, looking as blameless as the girls.

"Something's going on." Sherry didn't need to be a psychic to feel the vibrations in the air. The seven wizards were up to something, and whatever it was seemed to have drawn them together. All through breakfast they were congenial and friendly, leaning over to whisper secrets to one another. Not a single girl found fault with another. Not even Gretchen! Their eyes fairly sparkled with mischief.

Sherry studied them as they left the mess hall for their classes. Her group stayed together, looking at one another and giggling with impish delight without provocation.

"Hi." Lynn pulled out a bench and sat across the table from Sherry.

Sherry pulled her gaze away from her wizards. "How's it going?"

Lynn shrugged. "I'm not sure."

"Have you been seeing Peter?"

"Are you kidding?" Lynn asked and snorted softly. "We know better. Oh, we see each other all the time, but never alone."

"That's wise."

"Maybe, but it sure is boring." Lynn lifted her mug to her lips and downed her hot chocolate. "It's getting so bad that the eighth-grade boys are beginning to look good to me."

Despite the seriousness of her friend's expression, Sherry chuckled. "Now that's desperate."

"Peter and I know the minute we sneak off, we'll get caught—besides we aren't that stupid." She sagged against the back of her chair. "I don't know what it is, but Mr. Roarke has this sixth sense about these things. He always seems to know what's happening. Peter's convinced that Mr. Roarke is aware of everything that goes on between us."

"How could he be?"

Lynn shrugged. "Who knows? I swear that man is clairvoyant."

"I'm sure you're exaggerating." Sherry's stomach reacted with dread. She was living with a time bomb ticking away—she'd been a fool to have tried to slip something as important as references past Roarke.

"Since Peter and I haven't seen a lot of each other," Lynn continued, "we've been writing notes. It's not the same as being alone with each other, but it's been...I don't know...kind of neat to have his thoughts there to read over and over again."

Sherry's nod was absent.

"Well, I suppose I'd best get to work." Lynn swung her leg over the bench and stood.

"Right," Sherry returned, "work."

"By the way, I think the signs are cute."

Sherry's head shot up. "Signs? What signs?"

"The ones posted outside the cabins. How'd you ever get Mr. Roarke to agree to it? Knowing the way he feels about fairy tales, it's a wonder—"

Rarely had Sherry moved more quickly. She'd known her girls were up to something. Signs. Oh, good heavens! By the time she was outside the mess hall, she was able to view exactly what Lynn had been talking about. In front of each cabin a large picket had been driven into the ground that gave the cabin a name. The older boys' quarters was dubbed Pinocchio's Parlor, the younger Captain Hook's Hangout. Cinderella's Castle was saved for the older girls. But by far the largest and most ornate sign was in front of her own quarters. It read: The Home of Sherry White and the Seven Wizards.

The quality of the workmanship amazed Sherry. Each letter was perfectly shaped and printed in bright, bold colors. There wasn't any question that her girls were responsible, but she hadn't a clue as to when they'd had the time. It came to her then—they hadn't painted the markers themselves, but ordered them. Gretchen had claimed more than once that her father had given her her own American Express card. She'd flashed it a couple of times, wanting to impress the others. Of all the girls, Gretchen had taken hold of the tales of fantasy with rare enthusiasm. She loved them, and had devoured all the books Sherry had given her.

"Miss White," Roarke's voice boomed from across the lawn.

Her blood ran cold, but she did her best not to show her apprehension. "Yes?"

He pointed in the direction of his headquarters. "In my office. Now!"

The sharp tone of his voice stiffened Sherry's spine. If she'd been in a less vulnerable position, she would have clicked her heels, saluted crisply and marched toward him with her arms stiffly swinging at her sides. Now, however, was not the time to display any signs of resistance. She could recognize hot water when she saw it!

It seemed the entire camp came to a halt. Several children lingered outside the classrooms, gazing her way anxiously. Teachers found excuses to wander around the grounds, a few were in a cluster, pointing in Sherry's direction. Fred Spencer, the counselor who had made his opinion of Sherry's ideas well-known, looked on with a sardonic grin. Each group paused to view the unfolding scene with keen interest.

Before Sherry had a chance to move, Roarke was at her side. Over the past few weeks, she'd provoked the stubborn camp director more times than she could count, but never anything like what he suspected she'd done this time. A muscle worked its way along the side of Roarke's stern jaw, tightening his already harsh features.

"M-maybe it would be best to talk about this after you've had the opportunity to cool down and think matters through. I realize it looks bad, but—"

"We'll discuss it *now*."

"Roarke, I know you're going to have trouble believing this, but I honestly didn't have anything to do with those signs."

His lip curled sardonically. "Then who did?"

Sally and Gretchen hurried up behind the couple. "Don't be angry with Miss White," Gretchen called out righteously. "She told you the truth. In fact, the signs are a surprise to her, too."

"Then just who is responsible?" Roarke demanded.

The two youngsters looked at each other, grinned and shouted their announcement. "Longfellow!"

"Who?"

Sherry wished the ground would open so she could dive out of sight and escape before anyone noticed. If Roarke had frowned upon her filling the girls' heads with fairy tales as "romantic nonsense," then he was sure to disapprove of her creating a friendly spook.

"Longfellow's our ghost," Sally explained, looking surprised that the camp director wouldn't know about him. "Longfellow, you know—he lives here."

"Your what? Who lives where?" Roarke managed to keep his voice even, but the look he gave Sherry could have forced the world into another ice age.

"The ghost who lives at Camp Gitche Gumee," Sally continued patiently. "You mean, no one's ever told you about Longfellow?"

"Apparently not," Roarke returned calmly. "Who told *you* about him?"

"Miss White," the girls answered in unison, sealing Sherry's fate.

"I see."

Sherry winced at the sharpness in his voice, but the girls appeared undaunted—or else they hadn't noticed.

"You aren't upset with Miss White, are you?" Sally asked, her young voice laced with concern. "She's the best counselor we ever had."

"The signs really were Longfellow's idea," Gretchen added dryly.

Roarke made a show of looking at his watch. "Isn't it about time for your first class? Miss White and I will discuss this matter in private."

The children scurried off to their class, leaving Sherry to face Roarke's displeasure alone. Having two of her charges defend her gave her ego a boost. Roarke was so tall and overpowering that she realized, not for the first time, how easily he could intimidate her. A sense of consequence seemed to emanate from him, and something about his presence caused her to square her shoulders, thrust out her chin and face him head-on.

She turned to look at him, hands on her hips, feet braced. "I have other plans this morning. If you'll excuse me, I would—"

"The only place you're going is my office."

"So you can shout at me?"

"So we can discuss this senselessness," he said through gritted teeth.

It wouldn't do any good to argue. He turned and left her to follow him, and because she had no choice, she did as he requested, dreading the coming confrontation. For the past few days at camp, Sherry had come to hope that things would be better between her and Roarke. The night he'd walked her back from the pay phone had blinded her to the truth. They simply didn't view these children in the same way. Roarke saw them as miniature adults and preferred to treat them as such. Sherry wanted them to be children. The clash was instinctive and intense.

Roarke held the office door open for her and motioned with his hand for her to precede him. Sherry remembered what Lynn had said about Roarke firing people in the mornings. Well here she was, but she wasn't going down without an argument. Of all the things she had expected to be dismissed over—falsified references, misleading lesson plans, ghost stories—now it looked as if she was going to get the shaft for something she hadn't even done.

"I already told you I had nothing to do with the signs," she spoke first.

"Directly, that may be true, but indirectly there's no one more to blame."

Sherry couldn't argue with him there. She was the one who had introduced the subject to her seven wizards.

"If you recall, I specifically requested that you stop filling the children's heads with flights of fancy."

"I did," she cried.

"It's all too obvious that you didn't." His shoulders stiff, he marched around the desk and faced her. Leaning forward, he placed his hands on the desktop and glared in her direction. "You're one of those people who request an inch and take a mile."

"I..."

"In an effort to compromise, I've given you a free hand with the nine- and ten-year-old girls. Against my better judgment, I turned my head and ignored gin rummy taught in place of statistics classes. I looked the other way while you claimed to be studying frozen molecules when in reality you were sampling homemade ice cream."

"Don't you think I know that? Don't you think I appreciate it?"

"Obviously, you don't," he shouted, his voice gaining volume with each word. "Not if you stir up more problems by conjuring up a...a ghost. Of all the insane ideas you've come up with, this one takes the cake."

"Longfellow's not that kind of spook."

His eyes narrowed with a dark, furious frown. "I suppose you're going to tell me—"

"He's a friendly spirit."

Roarke muttered something she couldn't hear and raked a hand through his hair. "I can't believe I'm listening to this."

"The girls have a hundred complaints a day. Wendy's Ken-Richie doll is missing—one of the ten she brought to camp."

"Ken who?"

"Her Ken doll that she named Ken-Richie."

"What the hell is a Ken doll?"

"Never mind, that's not important."

"Anything you do is important because it leads to disaster."

"All right," Sherry cried, losing patience. "You want to know. Fine. Ken-Richie is the mate for Barbie-Brenda. Understand that?"

Roarke was growing more frustrated by the minute. There had been a time when he felt he had a grip on what was happening at camp, but from the minute Sherry had arrived with her loony ideas, everything had slid downhill.

"Anyway," Sherry continued, "it's so much easier to blame Longfellow for stealing Ken-Richie than to have a showdown among the girls."

"Who actually took the . . . doll?"

"Oh, I don't know—no one does. That's the point. But I'm sure he'll turn up sooner or later."

"Do you actually believe this . . . Longfellow will bring him back?" Roarke taunted.

"Exactly."

"That's pure nonsense."

"To you, maybe, but you're not a kid and you're not a counselor."

"No, I'm the director of this camp, and I want this stupidity stopped. Now."

Sherry clamped her mouth closed.

"Is that understood, Miss White?"

"I can't."

"What do you mean you can't? You have my direct order."

She lifted her palms and shrugged her shoulders. "It's gone too far. Almost everyone in the entire camp knows about Longfellow now. I can't put a stop to the children talking about him."

Roarke momentarily closed his eyes. "Do you realize what you've done?"

"But it was all in fun."

He ignored that. "This camp has a reputation for academic excellence."

"How can a make-believe ghost ruin that?"

"If you have to ask, then we're in worse trouble than I thought."

Sherry threw up her hands in disgust. "Oh, honestly!"

"This is serious."

Now it was Sherry's turn to close her eyes and gain control of her temper. She released a drawn-out sigh. "What is it you want me to do?" she asked, keeping her voice as unemotional as possible. "I realize that within a few weeks, I've managed to ruin the reputation for excellence of this camp—"

"I didn't say that," he countered sharply.

"By all rights I should be tossed out of here on my ear...."

Roarke raised both hands to stop her. They glared at each other, each daring the other to speak first. "Before this conversation heats up any more, I think we should both take time to cool down," Roarke said stiffly.

Sherry met his gaze defiantly, her heart slamming against her breast with dread. "Do you want me to leave?"

He hesitated, then nodded. "Maybe that would be best."

Tears burned the backs of her eyes and her throat grew tight with emotion. "I'll...pick up my check this afternoon."

Roarke frowned. "I want us to cool our tempers— I'm not firing you."

Sherry's head snapped up and her heart soared with hopeful expectation. Roarke wasn't letting her go! She felt like a prisoner who'd been granted a death row pardon by the governor at the last minute. "But it's morning—you mean, you don't want me to leave Camp Gitche Gumee?"

Roarke looked confused. "Of course not. What are you talking about?"

The flood of relief that washed over her submerged her in happiness. It took everything within Sherry not to toss her arms around his neck and thank him.

With as much aplomb as she could muster, she nodded, turned around and walked across the floor, but paused when she reached the door. "Thank you," she whispered, sincerely grateful.

It seemed the entire camp was waiting for her. A hush fell across the campus when she appeared. Faces turned in her direction and Lynn gestured with her hands, wanting to know the outcome.

Sherry smiled in response, and it seemed that everyone around released an elongated sigh. All except Fred Spencer, who Sherry suspected would be glad to see her leave. Until that moment, Sherry hadn't realized how many friends she'd made in her short stay at Camp Gitche Gumee. Her legs felt weak, her arms heavy. Although she'd been fortunate enough to hold on to her job, Roarke was still furious with her. More than anything she wanted to remain here for the entire camp session. And not because she was running away from Phyliss, either. She'd left Seattle because of her crazy, wonderful stepmother, seeking a respite from the woman she loved and didn't wish to offend. But Sherry wanted to stay in California for entirely different reasons. Some of which she sensed she didn't fully understand herself.

At break time, Sally, Gretchen and two other girls came storming into the cabin.

"Hi," Sherry said cheerfully. "What are you guys doing here?"

The girls exchanged meaningful glances. "Nothing," Wendy said, swinging her arms and taking small steps backward.

"We just wanted to be sure everything was okay."

Sherry's answering grin was wide. She winked and whispered, "Things couldn't be better."

"Good!" A breathless Jan and Jill arrived to chime in unison.

Producing a stern look was difficult, but Sherry managed. She pinched her lips together and frowned at her young charges. The last thing she needed was to do something else to irritate Roarke. "Aren't you girls supposed to be in class?"

"Yes, but..."

"But we wanted to see what happened to you."

"It's too hot to sit inside a classroom, anyway," Gretchen grumbled.

"Gretchen's right," Sally added, looking surprised to agree with the complainer.

"Scat," Sherry cried, "before I reach for my machine gun."

The girls let loose with a shriek of mock terror and ran from the cabin, down the steps and across the lawn. Sherry grinned as she watched them scatter like field mice before a prowling cat.

It was then that she noticed the signs in front of each cabin had been removed. She crossed her arms, leaned against the doorjamb and experienced a twinge of regret. Cinderella's Castle was far more original than Cabin Three, even Roarke had to admit that.

After such shaky beginnings, the morning progressed smoothly. Sherry dressed to work out in the exercise room, then ate lunch with the girls, who chatted easily. Sherry took a couple of minutes to joke about the signs, hoping to reassure them that everything was fine. But she didn't mention Longfellow, although the name of the make-believe ghost could be heard now and again from various tables around the mess hall.

Throughout the meal, Sherry had only a fleeting look at Roarke. He came in, made his announcements and joined the teachers at their table for the noontime meal. He spoke to several counselors, but went out of his way to avoid Sherry, she noted. She hadn't expected him to seek her out for conversation, but she didn't appreciate being ignored, either.

Following lunch, Sherry slipped into the exercise room. Ginny was already there working out with the weights.

"Hi," the young assistant greeted, revealing her pleasure at seeing Sherry.

"Hi," Sherry returned, climbing onto the stationary bicycle and inserting her feet into the stirrups. Pedaling helped minimize the effects of all the fattening food she was consuming at camp.

Ginny, strapping a five-pound belt around her own waist, studied Sherry. "You should wear weights if you expect the biking to do any good."

"No thanks," Sherry said with a grin. "I double-knot my shoelaces; that's good enough."

The teenager laughed. "I heard you had a run-in with Mr. Roarke this morning. How'd you make out?"

"All right, I suppose." Sherry would rather let the subject drop with that. The events of the morning were best forgotten.

"From what I heard, he's been on the warpath all day."

"Oh?" She didn't want to encourage the teenager to gossip, but on the other hand, she was curious to discover what had been happening.

"Apparently one of the kids got caught doing something and was sent into Mr. Roarke's office. When Mr. Roarke questioned him, the boy said Longfellow made him do it. Isn't that the ghost you told the girls about not so long ago?"

Sherry's feet went lax while the wheel continued spinning. Oh dear, this just wasn't going to be her day.

"Something else must have happened, too, because he looked as mad as a hornet right before lunch."

Sherry had barely had time to assimilate that when Lynn appeared in the doorway, her young face streaked with tears.

"Lynn, what happened?"

Sherry's friend glanced at Ginny and wiped the tears from her pale cheek. "Can we talk alone?"

"Sure." Sherry immediately stopped pedaling and climbed off the bike. She placed her arm around the younger girl's shoulders. "Tell me what's upset you so much."

"I-it's Mr. Roarke."

"Yes," she coaxed.

"He found some of the notes I'd written to Peter. He wants to talk to us first thing in the morning . . . the morning—we both know what that means. I . . . I think we're both going to be fired."

Chapter Seven

Sherry woke at the sound of the alarm and lay with her eyes open, savoring the dream. She'd been in a rowboat with Roarke in the middle of the lake. The oars had skimmed the water as he lazily paddled over the silver water. Everything was different between them. Everything was right. All their disagreements had long since been settled. The pros and cons of a friendly ghost named Longfellow were immaterial. All that mattered was the two of them together.

The looks they'd shared as the water lapped gently against the side of the small boat reminded Sherry of the evening they'd sat on the porch and gazed into the brilliant night sky. Stars were in Sherry's eyes in her dream, too, but Jeff Roarke had put them there.

With a melancholy sigh, she tossed aside the covers and sat on the edge of the mattress. It was silly to be so affected by a mere dream, but it had been so real and so wonderful. However, morning brought with it the chill of reality, and Sherry was concerned for Lynn and Peter. She had to think of some way to help them.

After dressing, she held in a yawn and walked across the thick lawn to the staff room. Her arms were criss-crossed over her ribs, but Sherry couldn't decide if it was to ward off a morning chill or the truth that awaited her outside her dreamworld. Birds chirped playfully in the background and the sun glimmered through the tall timbers, casting a pathway of shimmering light across the dewy grass, giving Sherry hope.

At the staff room, Sherry discovered that only a couple of the other counselors had arrived. Roarke was there, standing at the podium in the front, flipping through his notes.

With the warm sensations of the dream lingering in her mind, Sherry approached him, noted his frown and waited for him to acknowledge her before she spoke. Uncomfortable seconds passed and still Roarke didn't raise his head. When he did happen to look up, his gaze met hers, revealing little. Sherry realized that he hadn't forgotten their heated discussion. He'd been the one to suggest that they delay talking because things were getting out of hand. But from the narrowed, sharp appraisal he gave her it was all too apparent that his feelings ran as hot today as they had the day before.

"Miss White." He said her name stiffly.

Sherry grimaced at the chill in his voice. "Good morning."

He returned her greeting with an abrupt nod and waited. There had never been a woman who angered

Roarke more than Sherry White. This thing with the ghost she'd invented infuriated him to the boiling point, and he'd been forced to ask her to leave his office yesterday for fear of what more he'd say or do. His anger had been so intense that he'd wanted to shake her. *Wrong,* his mind tossed back—it had taken every ounce of determination he possessed, which was considerable, not to pull her into his arms and kiss some common sense into her.

The power she had to jostle his secure, impenetrable existence baffled him. He'd never wanted a woman with the intensity that he wanted Sherry, and the realization was frightening. A full day had passed since their last encounter, and he still wasn't in complete control of his emotions. Even with all this time to cool his temper, she caused his blood to boil in his veins.

No other counselor had been granted the latitude he'd given her. He'd turned a blind eye to her other schemes, accepting lesson plans that stated she would be teaching a study on centrifugal force when he knew she was planning on cooking popcorn. The evening sessions weren't the only rule he'd stretched on her behalf. The other counselors would question the integrity of his leadership if they knew about Ralph. But the ghost—now that was going too far. The truth about Longfellow had driven him over the edge. She'd abused his willingness to adapt to her creativity and in the process infuriated him.

Although his emotions were muddled, no woman had intrigued him the way Sherry did, either. He couldn't seem to get her out of his mind. He had enough problems organizing this camp without entertaining romantic thoughts about one impertinent counselor.

"You wanted something?" he asked, forcing his voice to remain cool and unemotional.

"Yes...you said yesterday that you thought it'd be best if we continued our discussion later."

Roarke glanced at his watch. "There's hardly time now."

"I didn't mean this minute exactly," Sherry answered. He was making this more difficult than necessary.

"Is there something you'd like to say?"

"Yes."

"Then this afternoon would be convenient," Roarke said coldly. He might be agreeing to another meeting, he told himself, but he couldn't see what they had left to say. He'd been angry, true, but not completely unreasonable. Nothing she could say would further her cause.

Sherry tried to smile, but the effort was too much for her. "I'll be there about one o'clock."

"That would be fine."

By now the small room was filled to capacity, and she walked to the back, looking for a chair. Lynn had saved her a seat, and Sherry sank down beside her friend, disappointed and uncomfortable. Twenty minutes into the day and already her dream was shattered. So much for lingering looks and meaningful gazes. She might as well be made of mud for all the interest Jeff Roarke showed her.

The announcements were dealt with quickly, but before Roarke could continue, Fred Spencer, the counselor for the older boys, raised his hand.

"Fred, you had a question?"

"Yes." Fred stood and loudly cleared his throat. "There's been talk all over camp about Longfellow. Who or what is he?"

Sherry scooted so far down in her chair that she was in danger of slipping right onto the floor. Fred Spencer was a royal pain in the rear end as far as Sherry was concerned.

"Longfellow is a friendly ghost," Roarke explained wryly. "As I understand it, he derived his name from Henry Wadsworth Longfellow, the poet."

Still Fred remained standing. "A ghost?" he shouted. "And just whose idea was this nonsense?" A hum of raised voices followed, some offended, others amused. "Why I've heard of nothing else for the past twenty-four hours. It's Longfellow this, Longfellow that. The least bit of confusion with kids can become a major catastrophe. These children come to this camp to learn responsibility. They're not gaining a darn thing by placing the blame on an imaginary spirit."

Unable to endure any more, Sherry sprang to her feet. "I believe you're putting too much emphasis on a trivial matter. The camp is visited by a friendly ghost. It doesn't need to be made into a big deal. Longfellow is for fun. The children aren't frightened by him, and he adds a sense of adventure to the few weeks they're here."

"Trivial," Fred countered, turning to face Sherry with his hands placed defiantly on his hips. "I've had nothing but problems from the moment this...this Longfellow was mentioned."

"Sit down, Fred," Roarke said, taking control.

Fred ignored the request. "I suppose you're responsible for this phantom ghost, Miss White? Just like you were with those ridiculous signs?"

Sherry opened and closed her mouth. "Yes, I invented Longfellow."

"I thought as much," Fred announced with profound righteousness.

Again the conversational hum rose from the other staff members, the group quickly taking sides. From bits and pieces of conversations that Sherry heard, the room appeared equally divided. Some saw no problem with Longfellow while others were uncertain. Several made comments about liking Sherry's style, but others agreed with Fred.

Roarke slammed his fist against the podium. "Mr. Spencer, Miss White, I would greatly appreciate it if you would take your seats."

Fred sat, but he didn't remain silent. "I demand that we put an end to this ghost nonsense."

A muscle in Roarke's jaw twitched convulsively and his gaze lifted to meet and hold Sherry's. "I'm afraid it's too late for that. Word of Longfellow is out now, and any effort to do away with him would only encourage the children."

Grumbling followed, mostly from Fred Spencer and his cronies.

"My advice is to ignore him and hope that everyone will forget the whole thing," Roarke spoke above the chatter.

"What about Miss White?" Fred demanded. "She's been nothing but a worry from the moment she arrived. First those ridiculous signs and now this. Where will it end?"

"That's not true," Lynn shouted, and soared to her feet in an effort to defend her friend. She gripped the back of the chair in front of her and glared at the older man. "Sherry's been great with the kids!"

"Miss Duffy, kindly sit down," Roarke barked, raising his hands to quiet the room. The noise level went down appreciably, although the controversy appeared far from settled. He spoke to Fred Spencer with enough authority to quickly silence the other man. "This is neither the time nor the place to air our differences of opinion regarding another counselor's teaching methods."

Sherry wasn't fooled. Roarke wasn't defending her so much as protecting the others from criticism should Fred take exception to another's techniques. Fred Spencer's reputation as a complainer was as well-known as Gretchen's.

"If the staff can't speak out, then exactly whose job is it?" Fred shouted.

"Mine!" Roarke declared, and the challenge in his voice was loud and infinitely clear.

"Good, then I'll leave the situation in your hands."

From her position, Sherry could see that Fred wasn't appeased. Nor did she believe he would quietly drop the subject. From the beginning, she'd known he disagreed with her efforts with the children. Whenever he had the chance, he put down her ideas and found reason to criticize her.

The remainder of the meeting passed quickly, but not fast enough as far as Sherry was concerned. She and Lynn walked out of the staff room together.

"I can't believe that man," Lynn grumbled. "His idea of having fun is watching paint dry."

"Miss Duffy."

Roarke's cold voice stopped both women. The teenager cast a pleading glance at Sherry before turning around to face her employer.

"I believe we have an appointment."

"Oh, yes," Lynn said with a wan smile. "I forgot."

"I'm afraid that's part of the problem," Roarke returned with little humor. "You seem to be forgetting several things lately."

Sherry opened her mouth to dilute his sarcasm, but one piercing glare from Roarke silenced her. This wasn't her business. She didn't want to say or do anything to irritate him any more. Her greatest fear was that after the events of the morning, Roarke wasn't in any mood to deal kindly with Lynn and Peter. With a heavy heart, Sherry returned to her cabin.

Ginny had roused the girls and there was the typical mad confusion of morning. As usual there was fighting over the bathroom and how long Jan and Jill hogged the mirror to braid each other's hair.

"My mattress has got more lumps than the Cream of Wheat we had the other day," Gretchen muttered, sitting on the side of the bed and rubbing the small of her back.

Pamela was stroking Ralph's head with one finger inserted between the bars of the cage; both girl and rodent appeared content.

Sally and Wendy were already dressed, eager to start another day, while Diane slumbered, resisting all wake-up notices.

Sherry walked over to the sleeping youngster's bunk and pulled out the Hardy Boys novel and flashlight from beneath her pillow. Once she'd turned the ten-year-old on to Judy Blume, Beverly Cleary and other preteen series books, there had been no stopping her. Diane's favorite had turned out to be John D. Fitz-gerald's Great Brain books. The dry textbook material had been replaced by fiction, and a whole new world had opened up to the little girl. Now Sherry had to teach Diane about moderation. "Sleeping Beauty," she coaxed softly, "rise and shine."

"Go away," Diane moaned. "I'm too tired."

"Ken-Richie hasn't shown up yet," Wendy muttered disparagingly. "I wonder if Longfellow's ever going to bring him back." She might have mentioned the ghost, but her narrowed gaze surveyed the room, accusing each one who was unlucky enough to fall prey to her eagle eye.

"Hey, don't look at me," Sally shouted. "I wouldn't take your stupid Ken-Richie if someone paid me. *Batrachoseps attenuatus* are my thing."

"What?" Gretchen demanded.

"The California Slender Salamander," Wendy informed her primly. "If you were really so smart you'd know that."

"I'm not into creepy crawly things the way you are."

"I noticed."

"If my American Express card can't buy it, I don't want it," Gretchen informed her primly.

"It's nearly breakfast time," Sally encouraged Diane, roughly shaking the other girl's shoulder. "And Wednesday's French toast day."

"I don't want to eat," Diane murmured on the tail end of a yawn. "I'd rather sleep."

"Listen, kiddo," Sherry said, bending low and whispering in the reluctant girl's ear, "either you're up and dressed in ten minutes flat, or I won't loan you the other books in the Hardy Boys series."

Diane's dark brown eyes flew open. "Okay, okay, I'm awake."

"Here." Sally handed her a pair of shorts and matching top and Sherry looked on approvingly. The girls were developing rich friendships this summer. Even Gretchen, with her constant complaining and her outrageous bragging, had mellowed enough to find a friend or two. She still found lots of things that needed to be brought to Sherry's attention, like lumpy mattresses and the dangers of sleeping too close to the window. Her credit card was flashed for show when her self-worth needed a boost, but all in all, Gretchen had turned into a decent kid.

Feeling sentimental, Sherry looked around at the group of girls she'd been assigned and felt her heart compress with affection. These seven little wizards had securely tucked themselves into the pocket of her heart. She would long remember them. The girls weren't all she'd recall about this summer, though. Memories of Roarke would always be with her. Her stay at the camp was nearly half over and already she dreaded leaving, knowing it was doubtful that she'd see Roarke again. The thought brought with it a brooding sense of melancholy. For all their differences, she'd come to appreciate him and his efforts at the camp.

Much to Sherry's surprise, and probably Fred Spencer's too, the occupants of Cabin Two arrived in the dining hall precisely on time without stragglers. French toast was a popular breakfast, and when the girls had finished, Pam slipped Sherry an extra piece of the battered bread and asked if she would feed it to Ralph.

"Sure," Sherry assured the child. "But I'll tell him it's from you."

The blue eyes brightened. "He likes you, too, Miss White."

"And I think he's a great mascot for our cabin," she admitted in a whisper.

Once the mess hall had emptied, Sherry poured herself a steaming cup of coffee and paused to savor the first sip. She had just raised the cup to her lips when Lynn entered the room, paused to look around and, seeing Sherry, hurried across the floor.

"How'd it go?"

Lynn bit her lower lip and dejectedly shook her head. "Not good, but then I didn't expect it would with Mr. Roarke in such a lousy mood."

"He didn't fire you, did he?"

"I'm afraid so."

"But..." Sherry was so outraged she could barely speak. She hadn't believed he'd do something so unfair. True, the two had broken camp rules, but so had she, so had everyone. It wasn't as though Lynn and Peter were overtly carrying on a torrid romance. No one was aware that they cared for each other. If Roarke hadn't found their notes, he wouldn't even have known they were interested in each other.

"I have to pack my bags," Lynn said calmly, but her voice cracked, relaying her unhappiness. "But before I go I just wanted to tell you how much I enjoyed working with you." Tears briefly glistened in the other girl's eyes.

Flustered and angry, Sherry ran her fingers through her hair and sadly shook her head. "I don't believe this."

"He was upset, partly because of what happened this morning, I think, and other problems. There's a lot more to being camp director than meets the eye."

Sherry wasn't convinced she would have been so gracious with Roarke had their circumstances been reversed.

"Listen," Sherry said and braced her hands against her friend's shoulders. "Let me talk to him. I might be able to help."

"It won't do any good," Lynn argued. "I've never known Mr. Roarke to change his mind."

While chewing on her lower lip, a plan of action began to form in Sherry's befuddled mind. Sure, she could storm into Roarke's office and demand an explanation, but they'd just end up in another shouting match. As the camp director, he would no doubt remind her that whom he chose to fire or hire was none of her concern. The risk was too great, since he could just as easily dismiss her. Following the events of the past few days, she would be cooking her own goose to openly challenge him.

Her plan was better. Much better.

"Don't pack yet," Sherry said slowly, thoughtfully.

"What do you mean?"

"Just that. Go to your quarters and wait for me there."

"Sherry—" Lynn's brow creased with a troubled frown "—what do you have in mind? You don't look right. Listen, Mr. Roarke isn't having a good day—I don't think this would be the time to talk to him." Lynn paused, set her teeth to chewing at the corner of her mouth and sighed. "At least tell me what you have in mind."

Sherry shook her head, not wanting to answer in case her scheme flopped. "Don't worry. I'll get back to you as soon as possible."

"Okay," Lynn agreed reluctantly.

Sherry headed directly to Roarke's office, knocking politely.

"Yes."

Sherry let herself inside. "Hello."

He hesitated, then raised his pen from the paper. This morning was quickly going from bad to worse. He'd been angry when he'd talked to Lynn and Peter. Angry and unreasonable. He'd dismissed them both unfairly and had since changed his mind. Already, he'd sent a message to the two to return to his office. He never used to doubt his decisions. Everything had been cut-and-dried. Black or white. Simple, uncomplicated. And then Sherry had tumbled into his peaceful existence with all the agility of a circus clown, and nothing had been the same since. He wanted to blame her for his dark mood. She occupied his mind night and day. Fiona was insipid tea compared to Sherry's sparkling champagne.

Sherry tempted him to the limit of his control. A simple smile left him weak with the longing to hold her in his arms. The energy it required for him to keep his hands off her was driving him crazy and weakening him. The situation between them was impossible, and his anger with Lynn and Peter had been magnified by his own level of frustration. And here she was again.

"Is there something I can do for you, Miss White?"

Her steady gaze held his. "I came to apologize."

"What have you done this time?"

His attitude stung her ego, but Sherry swallowed down her indignation and continued calmly. "Nothing new, let me assure you."

"That's a relief."

Her hand touched the chair. "Would you mind if I sat down?"

Pointedly, he glanced at his watch. "If you insist."

Sherry did, claiming the chair. "Things haven't gone very smoothly between us lately, have they?" she began in an even, controlled voice. "I decided that perhaps it would be best if we cleared the air."

"If it's about Longfellow—"

"No," she interrupted, then sadly shook her head. "It's more than that."

For several moments, he was silent, giving Sherry time to compose her thoughts. She'd come on Lynn and Peter's behalf, yearning to turn circumstances so he would rehire the two teenagers. That had been her original intention, but now that she was in his office, she couldn't go through with it. What she felt for this man was real, and their minor differences were quickly forming a chasm between them that might never be spanned unless she took the first leap. She turned her palms up and noted that his hard-sculpted features had relaxed. "I'm not even sure where to start."

"Miss White—"

"Sherry," she cried in frustration. "My name is Sherry and you damn well know it." Abruptly, she made a move to stand, her hands braced on the chair arms. "And this is exactly what I'm talking about. I don't call you Mr. Roarke, yet you insist upon addressing me formally, as if I were...I don't know, some stiff, starched counselor so unbending that I refuse anyone the privilege of using my name."

Roarke's gaze widened with her outburst. "You came to apologize?" He made the statement a question, confused by her irrational behavior. Sherry was too gutsy to be ambivalent. Whatever it was she had to say was real enough to sincerely trouble her.

"That was my original thought," she said, standing now and facing him. "But I'm not sure anymore. All I know is that I want things to be different between us."

"Different?"

"Yes," she cried, "every day, it seems, there's something that I've done to displease you. You can't even look at me anymore without frowning. I don't want to be a thorn in your side or a constant source of irritation."

"Sherry—"

"Thank you," she murmured, interrupting him with a soft smile. "I feel a thousand times better just having you say my name."

The frown worrying Roarke's brow relaxed, and a slow, sensuous smile transformed his harsh features. "Although I may not have said it, I've always thought of you as Sherry."

"But you called me Miss White."

"The others..."

Briefly, she dropped her eyes, remembering Fred Spencer's dislike of her. "I know."

"I haven't been angry with you; it's just that circumstances have been working against us."

"I realize I haven't exactly made things easier."

Sherry didn't know the half of it, Roarke thought. At least once a day he'd been placed in the uncomfortable position of having to defend her from the jealousy and resentment of some of the others. But she was by far the most popular counselor in camp, and neither he nor anyone else was in any position to argue her success.

"I know, too," she continued, "that you've turned your head on more than one occasion while I've bent the rules and disrupted this camp."

"Bent the rules," he repeated with a soft laugh. "You've out-and-out pulverized them."

Sherry sighed with relief; she felt a hundred times better to be here with him, talking as they once had in the moonlight. How fragile that truce had been. Now, if possible, she wanted to strengthen that.

"It's important to me, Roarke—no matter what happens at camp—that we always remain friends."

Looking at her now, with the sunlight streaming through her chestnut hair, her dark eyes imploring his, searing their way through the thickest of resolves, it wasn't in Roarke to refuse her anything.

"You can be angry with me," she said. "God knows I give you plenty of reasons, but I have to feel deep down that as long as we share a foundation of mutual respect it won't matter. You could call me Miss White until the year 2000 and it wouldn't bother me, because inside I'd know."

Roarke was convinced she had no idea how lovely she was. Beautiful. Intelligent. Witty. Fun. He felt like a boy trapped inside on a rainy day. She was laughter and sunshine, and he'd never wanted a woman as badly as he did her at this moment.

He stood and moved to her side. Her gaze narrowed with doubt when he placed his hands on her shoulders and turned her to face him. "Just friends?" he asked softly, wanting so much more. After the first week he'd thought to send her straight back to Seattle, because in a matter of only a few days, she'd managed to disturb his orderly life and that of the entire camp. He hadn't. Her candor and wit had thrown him off balance. But staring at her now, he realized her eyes disturbed him far more. She had beautiful, soulful eyes that could search his face as though she were doing a study of his very heart.

Sherry's palms were flattened against Roarke's hard chest; her head tilted back to question the look in his eyes. Surely she was reading more than was there—yet what she saw caused her heartbeat to soar. "Roarke?" she questioned softly, uncertain.

"I want to be more than friends," he answered her, lowering his mouth to hers. "Much more than friends."

Her lips parted under his, warm and moist, eager and curious. For weeks, she'd hungered to feel Roarke's arms around her and experience the taste of his kiss. Now that she was cradled securely in his embrace, the sensation of supreme rightness burned through her. It was as though she'd waited all her life for exactly this moment, for exactly this man.

His arms tightened around her slender frame as he deepened the kiss, his mouth moving hungrily over hers, insistently shaping her lips with his own. Roarke's spirit soared and his heart sang. She'd challenged him, argued with him, angered him. And he loved her, truly loved her. For the first time in his life, he was head over heels in love. He'd thought himself exempt from the emotion, but meeting Sherry had convinced him otherwise.

"Sherry," he groaned. His hands pushing the hair back from her face, he spread eager kisses over her face.

Sherry's world was spinning and she slid her hands up his chest to circle his neck, clinging to the very thing that caused her world to career out of control. She was irrevocably lost in a haze of longing.

Roarke groaned as she fit her body snugly to his. His mouth crushed hers, sliding insistently back and forth, seducing her with his moist lips until hers parted, inviting the plunder of his tongue into the soft recesses of her mouth.

Sherry thought she'd die with wanting Roarke. He tore his lips from hers and held her as though he planned never to let her go. His arms crushed her, but she experienced no pain. Physical limitation prevented her from being any closer, and still she wasn't content, seeking more. His arms were wrapped around her waist, locked at the small of her back. She rotated her hips once, seeking a way to satisfy this incredible longing.

"Sherry, love," he groaned, "don't."

"Roarke, oh, Roarke, is this real?"

"More real than anything I've ever known," he answered, after a long moment.

She moved once more and he moaned, drew in a deep, audible breath and held it so long that she wondered if he planned ever to breathe again.

Raising her hands, she lovingly stroked his handsome face. "I feel like I could cry." She pressed her forehead to his chest. "I'm probably not making the least bit of sense."

Gently, he kissed the crown of her head. "I've wanted to hold you forever."

"Roarke," she said solemnly, raising her eyes to meet his. Her heart was shining through her gaze. "You can't fire Lynn and Peter. Please reconsider."

The words were like a knife ripping into his soul. Roarke released Sherry and stepped back with such abruptness that she staggered a step. "Is that what this is all about?"

Her eyes mirrored her bewilderment. "No, of course not," she murmured, but she couldn't meet the accusing doubt in his eyes. "Originally I came because Lynn told me you'd dismissed both her and Peter, but..."

"So you thought that if you could get me to kiss you, I'd change my mind."

That was so close to the truth that Sherry yearned to find a hole, curl up in it and magically disappear. The words to explain how everything had changed once she'd arrived at his office died on her lips. It would do no good to deny the truth; Roarke read her far too easily for her to try to convince him otherwise.

She didn't need to say a word for him to read the truth revealed in her eyes. "I see," he said, his voice heavy with rancor.

Sherry flinched. She had to try to explain or completely lose him. "Roarke, please listen. I may have thought that at first, but..."

The loud knock against the door stopped her.

His face had become as hard as stone and just as implacable. "If you'll excuse me, I have business to attend to."

"No," she cried, "at least give me a chance to explain."

"There's nothing more to say." He walked across the room and opened the door.

Lynn and Peter stood on the other side. Instantly Lynn's gaze flew to Sherry, wide and questioning.

"Come in," Roarke instructed, holding open the door. "Miss White was just leaving."

Arching her back, Sherry moved past Peter. As Sherry neared Lynn, the other girl whispered, "Your plan must have worked."

"It worked all right—even better than she dared hope," Roarke answered for her with a look of such contempt that Sherry longed to weep.

Chapter Eight

"Sherry, I'm sorry," Lynn said for the tenth time that day. "I didn't think Mr. Roarke could hear me."

Sherry's feet pedaled the stationary bike all the more vigorously. She'd hoped that taking her frustration out on the exercise bike would lessen the ache in her heart. She should have known better. "Don't worry about it. What's done is done."

"But Mr. Roarke hasn't spoken to you in a week."

"I'll survive." But just barely, she mused. When he was through being angry, they'd talk, but from the look of things it could be some time before he'd cooled down enough to reason matters through. There was less than a month left of camp as it was. For seven, long, tedious days, Roarke had gone out of his way to avoid her. If she were in the same room, he found something important to distract him. At the staff meetings, he didn't call upon her unless absolutely necessary and said "Miss White" with such cool disdain that he might as well have stabbed a hot needle straight through her heart.

By the sheer force of her pride, Sherry had managed to hold her head high, but there wasn't a staff member at Camp Gitche Gumee who wasn't aware that Sherry White had fallen from grace. Fred Spencer was ecstatic and thrived on letting smug remarks drop when he suspected there was no one else around to hear. Without Roarke to support her ideas, Fred was given free rein to ridicule her suggestions. Not a single thing she'd campaigned for all week had made it past the fiery tongue of her most ardent opponent.

When Sherry proposed a sing-along at dusk, Fred argued that such nonsense would cut into the cabin's evening lessons. Roarke neither agreed nor disagreed, and the suggestion was quickly dropped. When she'd proposed organized hikes for the study of wildflowers, there had been some enthusiasm, until Fred and a few others countered that crowding too many activities into the already heavy academic schedule could possibly overextend the counselors and the children. A couple debated the issue on Sherry's behalf, but in the long run the idea was abandoned for lack of interest. Again Roarke remained stoically silent.

"Maybe you'll survive," Lynn said, breathing heavily as she continued her sit-ups, "but I don't know about the rest of us."

"Roarke hasn't been angry or unreasonable." Sherry was quick to defend him, although he probably wouldn't have appreciated it.

"No, it's much worse than that," Lynn said with a tired sigh.

"How do you mean?"

"If you'd been here last year, you'd notice the difference. It's like he's built a wall around himself and is closing everybody off. He used to talk to the kids a lot, spend time with them. I think he's hiding."

"Hiding?" Sherry prompted.

"Right." Lynn sat upright and folded her arms around her bent knees, resting her chin there. "If you want the truth, I think Mr. Roarke has fallen for you, only he's too proud to admit it."

Sherry's feet pumped harder, causing the wheel to whirl and hiss. A lump thickened in her throat. "I wish that were true."

"Look at the way he's making himself miserable and, consequently, everyone else. He's responsible for the morale of this camp, and for the past week or so there's been a thundercloud hanging over us all."

To disagree would be to lie. Lynn was right; the happy atmosphere of the camp had cooled decidedly. As for Roarke caring, it was more than Sherry dared hope. She wanted to believe it, but she sincerely doubted that he'd allow a misunderstanding to grow to such outrageous proportions if he did.

"Have you tried talking to him?" Lynn said next. "It couldn't hurt, you know."

Maybe not, but Jeff Roarke wasn't the only one with a surplus of pride. Sherry possessed a generous portion of the emotion herself.

"Well?" Lynn demanded when Sherry didn't respond. "Have you even tried to tell him your side of it?"

The door to the exercise room opened, and both women turned their attention to the tall, muscular man who stepped inside the room.

"Roarke," Sherry murmured. Her feet stopped pumping, but the rear wheel continued to spin.

He was dressed in faded gray sweatpants and a T-shirt, a towel draped around his neck. Just inside the door, he paused, looked around and frowned.

"Here's your chance," Lynn whispered, struggling to her feet. "Go for it, girl." She gave Sherry the thumbs-up sign and casually sauntered from the room, whistling a cheery tune as she went.

Sherry groaned inwardly; Lynn couldn't have been any more obvious had she openly announced that she was leaving to give the two time to sort out their myriad differences. Sherry nearly shouted for her to come back. Talking to Roarke in his present frame of mind would do no good.

While continuing to pedal, Sherry cast an anxious look in Roarke's direction. He ignored her almost as completely as she strove to ignore him. Lifting the towel from his neck he tossed it over the abdominal board of the weight gym and turned his back to her. The T-shirt followed the towel and he proceeded to go about bench-pressing a series of weights.

Without meaning to watch him, Sherry unwillingly found her gaze wandering over to him until it was all she could do to keep from staring outright. The muscles across his wide shoulders rippled with each movement, displaying the lean, hard build.

The inside of Sherry's mouth went dry; just watching him was enough to intoxicate her senses. His biceps bulged with each push.

The bike wheel continued to spin, but Sherry had long since given up pedaling. She freed her feet from the stirrups and climbed off. Her legs felt shaky, but whether it was from the hard exercise or from being alone with Roarke, Sherry couldn't tell.

"Hello," she said, in a voice that sounded strange even to her own ears. Nonchalantly, she removed the helmet with the tiny side mirror from her head. "I suppose you're wondering why I'd wear a helmet when I'm pedaling a stationary bike," she said, hoping to make light conversation.

Sweat broke out across Roarke's brow, but it wasn't from the exertion of lifting the weights. It demanded all his concentration to keep his eyes off Sherry. Ignoring her was the only thing that seemed to work. "What you wear is none of my concern," he returned blandly.

"I—I don't feel like I'm really exercising unless I wear the helmet," she said next, looking for a smile to crack his tight concentration. She rubbed her hand dry against her shorts. The helmet hadn't been her only idea. She'd strapped a horn and side mirror onto the handlebars of the bike and had later added the sheepskin cover to pad the seat.

Roarke didn't comment.

He looked and sounded so infuriatingly disinterested that Sherry had to clear the tears from her throat before she went on.

"Roarke," she pleaded, "I hate this. I know you have good reason to believe I plotted...what happened in your office." She hesitated long enough for him to consider her words. "I'll be honest with you—that had been exactly my intention in the beginning. But once I got there I realized I couldn't do it."

"For someone who found herself incapable of such a devious action, you succeeded extremely well." He paused and studied her impassively.

"I w-want things to be different. I don't think we'll ever be able to settle anything here at camp, so I'm proposing that we meet in town to talk. I'll be in Ellen's Café tomorrow at six...it's my day off. I hope you'll meet me there."

Roarke wanted things settled, too, but not at the expense of his pride and self-respect.

"Answer me, Roarke. At least have the common courtesy to speak to me." His manner was so distant, so unconcerned that Sherry discovered she had to look away from him or lose her composure entirely.

"There's nothing to say," he returned stiffly.

The prolonged silence in the room was as irritating as fingernails on a blackboard. Sherry couldn't stand it any more than she could tolerate his indifference.

"If that's the way you wish to leave matters, then so be it. I tried; I honestly tried," she said, with such dejection that her voice was hardly audible.

Pointedly, Roarke looked in another direction.

With the dignity of visiting royalty, Sherry tucked her helmet under her arm, lifted her chin an extra notch and left the room. A hot tear slipped down the corner of her cheek. She let it fall, then gave in to the others that came in quick succession. Jeff Roarke was a fool!

"Miss White, Miss White!" Diane ran across the campus to her side and stopped abruptly, cocking her head as she studied her counselor. "You're crying."

Sherry nodded and wiped the moisture from her face with the back of her hand.

"Are you hurt?"

"In a manner of speaking." Diane was much too perceptive to fool. "Someone hurt my feelings, but I'll be all right in a minute."

"Who?" Diane demanded, straightening her shoulders. From the little girl's stance, it looked as though she was prepared to single-handedly take on anyone who had hurt her friend and counselor.

"It doesn't matter who. It's over now, and I'll be fine in a minute." Several afternoons a week, Sherry sat on the lawn and the children from the camp gathered at her feet. As a natural born storyteller, she filled the time with make-believe tales from the classics and history. The children loved it, and Sherry enjoyed spending time with them. "Now what was it you needed?"

Shyly Diane looked away.

Sherry laughed. "No, let me guess. I bet you're after another book. Am I right?"

The youngster nodded. "Can I borrow the last book in the Great Brain series?"

"One great brain to another," Sherry said, forcing the joke.

"Right. Can I?"

Sherry looped her arm around the child's small shoulders. "Sure. This story is really a good one. Tom contacts the Pope... well, never mind, you'll read about it yourself."

They'd gone about halfway across the thick carpet of grass when a piercing scream rent the air. Startled, Sherry turned around and discovered Sally running toward her, blood streaming down her forehead and into her eyes, nearly blinding her.

"Miss White, Miss White," she cried in terror. "I fell! I fell!"

Sherry's stomach curdled at the sight of oozing blood. "Diane," she instructed quickly, "run to the cabin and get me a towel. Hurry, sweetheart."

With her arms flying, Diane took off like a jet from a crowded runway.

"I saw it happen," Gretchen cried, following close on Sally's heels and looking sickly pale. "Sally slipped and hit her head on the side of a desk."

"It's fine, sweetheart," Sherry reassured the injured youngster. She placed her hand on the side of Sally's head and found the gash. Pressing on it gently in an effort to stop the ready flow of blood, she guided the girl toward the infirmary.

"Gretchen, run ahead and let Nurse Butler know we're coming."

"It hurts so bad," Sally wailed.

"I'm sure it does, but you're being exceptionally brave."

Breathless, Diane returned with the towel. Sherry took it and replaced her hand with the absorbent material.

The buzzer rang in the background, indicating that the next class was about to start.

Gretchen and Diane exchanged glances. "I don't want to leave my friend," Gretchen murmured, her voice cracking.

Both Gretchen and Diane were frightened, and sending them away would only increase their dismay and play upon their imaginations, Sherry reasoned.

"You can stay until we're all sure Sally's going to be fine. Now, go do what I said."

Gretchen took off at a full run toward the nurse's office, with Diane in hot pursuit. By the time Sherry reached the infirmary, Kelly Butler, the wife of the younger boys' counselor, had been alerted and was waiting.

"Miss White, I'm scared," Sally said, and sniffled loudly.

"Everything's going to be fine," Sherry assured her miniscientist, standing close to her side.

"Will you stay with me?"

"Of course." Sally was her responsibility, and Sherry wouldn't leave the child when she needed her most—no matter how much blood there was.

"This way." Kelly Butler motioned toward the small examination room.

While maintaining the pressure to the gash, Sherry helped Sally climb onto the table. Gretchen and Diane stood in the doorway, looking on.

"You two will have to stay outside until I'm finished," the nurse informed the two.

Both girls sent pleading glances in Sherry's direction. "Do as she says," Sherry told them. "I'll be out to tell you how Sally is in a few minutes."

Halfway through the examination Sherry started to feel light-headed. Her knees went rubbery, and she reached for a chair and sat down.

"Are you all right?" Kelly asked her.

"I'm fine," she lied.

"Well, it isn't as bad as it looks," the nurse said. She paused to smile at the youngster. "We aren't going to need to take you into Arrow Flats for stitches, but I'll have to cut away your bangs to put on a bandage."

"Can I look at it in a mirror?" The shock and pain had lessened enough for Sally's natural curiosity to take over. "If I don't become a biochemist, then I might decide to be a doctor," Sally explained haughtily.

Sherry's nauseated feeling continued, and forcing a smile, she stood. "I'll go tell Diane and Gretchen that Sally's going to recover before they start planning her funeral."

"Thanks for staying with me, Miss White," Sally said, gripping the hand mirror.

"No problem, kiddo."

"You're going to make a great mom someday."

The way she was feeling caused Sherry to sincerely doubt that. The sight of blood had always bothered her, but never more than now. Taking deep breaths to dispel the sickly sensation, she stood and let herself out of the examination room.

Her two charges were missing. Sherry blinked, but Jeff Roarke, who sat in their place didn't vanish. The light-headed feeling persisted, and she wasn't sure if he was real or a figment of her stressed-out senses.

"How is she?" he asked, coming to his feet.

"Fine." At the moment, Sally was doing better than Sherry. "Head wounds apparently bleed a lot, but it doesn't look like she's going to need stitches."

Roarke nodded somberly. "That's good."

"Where are Diane and Gretchen?"

"I sent them back to class," he told her. "I heard how you took control of the situation."

Sherry bristled. "I suppose you'd prefer to believe that I'd panic when confronted with a bleeding child."

"Of course not," he flared.

Trying desperately to control the attack of dizziness, Sherry reached out and gripped the edge of a table.

"You've got blood on your sweatshirt," Roarke said.

Sherry glanced down and gasped softly as the walls started spinning. She wanted to comment, but before she could the room unexpectedly went black.

Roarke watched in astonishment as Sherry crumpled to the floor. At first he thought she was playing another of her silly games. It would be just like her to pull a crazy stunt like that. Then he noted that her coloring was sickly, almost ashen, and immediately he grew alarmed. This wasn't any trick, she'd actually fainted! He fell to his knees at her side and tossed a desperate look over his shoulder, thinking he should call the nurse. But Kelly was already busy with one patient.

He reached for Sherry's hand and lightly slapped her wrist. He'd seen someone do this in a movie once, but how it was supposed to help, he didn't know. His own heart was hammering out of control. Seeing her helpless this way had the most unusual effect upon him. All week he'd been furious with her, so outraged at her underhandedness that he'd barely been able to look at her and not feel the fire of his anger rekindled. He wasn't particularly proud of his behavior, and he'd chosen to blame Sherry for his ill-temper and ugly moods all week. He'd wanted to forget she was around, and completely cast her from his mind once the summer was over.

Seeing her now, he felt as helpless as a wind-tossed leaf, caught in a swirling updraft of emotion. He loved this woman, and pretending otherwise simply wasn't going to work. She was a schemer, a manipulator...and a joy. She was fresh and alive and unspoiled. The whole camp had been brought to life with her smile. Even though this was her first year as a counselor, she took to it as naturally as someone who had been coming back for several summers. Her mind was active, her wit sharp and she possessed a genuine love for the children. They sensed it and gravitated toward her like bees to a blossoming flower.

She moaned, or he thought she did; the sound was barely audible. Roarke's brows drew together in a heavy frown, and he gently smoothed the hair from her face. He'd never seen anyone faint before and he wasn't sure what to do. He elevated her head slightly and noted evidence of fresh tears. Dealing with Sally's injury hadn't been the source of these. From everything Gretchen and Diane had told him, Sherry had handled the situation without revealing her own alarm. No, he had been the one who'd made her cry by treating her callously in the exercise room.

Roarke's eyes closed as hot daggers of remorse stabbed through him. The urge to kiss her and make up for all the pain he had caused her was more than he could resist. Without giving thought to his actions, he secured his arms beneath her shoulders and raised her. Then tenderly, with only the slightest pressure, he bent to fit his lips over hers.

Chapter Nine

Sherry didn't know what was happening, but the most incredible sensation of warmth and love surrounded her. Unless she was dreaming, Roarke was kissing her. If this was some fantasy, then she never wanted to wake up. It was as though the entire week had never happened and she was once again in Roarke's arms, reveling in the gentleness of his kiss. The potent feelings were far too wonderful to ignore, and she parted her lips, wanting this moment to last forever. She sighed with regret when the warmth left her.

"Sherry?"

Her eyes blinked open and she moaned as piercing sunlight momentarily blinded her. She raised her hand to shield her vision and found Roarke bending over her.

"Roarke?" she asked in a hoarse whisper. "What happened?"

"You fainted."

She surged upright, bracing herself on one elbow. "I did what?"

Roarke's smile was smug. "You fainted."

It took a moment for her to clear her head. "I did?"

"That's what I just said."

"Sally..."

"Is fine," he reassured her. "Do you do this type of thing often?"

Sherry rubbed a hand over her face, although she remained slightly disoriented. "No, it feels weird. I've never been fond of the sight of blood, but I certainly didn't pass out because of it."

"When was the last time you had something to eat?"

Sherry had to think about that. Her appetite had been nil for days. She wasn't in the habit of eating breakfast unless it was something like a quick glass of orange juice and a dry piece of toast. This morning, however, she hadn't bothered with either breakfast or lunch.

"Sherry?" he prompted.

"I don't know when I last ate. Yesterday at dinnertime, I guess." She'd been so miserable that food was the last thing she'd wanted.

Roarke's frown deepened, and his arm tightened around her almost painfully. "Of all the stupid—"

"Oh, stop!" She jerked herself free from his grip and awkwardly rose to her feet. "Go ahead and call me stupid... but why stop with that? You've probably got ten other names you're dying to use on me.''

Roarke's mouth thinned, but he didn't rise to the bait. The last thing he'd expected was for her to fight him. This woman astonished him. She was full of surprises and... full of promise. Even when she was semiconscious, she had shyly responded to his kiss. He was embarrassed by the impulse now. Who did he think he was—some kind of legendary lover?

"You're coming with me," he commanded.

"Why? So you can shout at me some more?" she hissed at him like a cat backed into a corner, seeking a means of escape.

"No," he returned softly. "So I can get you something to eat."

"I can take care of myself, thank you very much."

Roarke snickered. "I can tell. Now stop arguing."

Sherry closed her mouth and realized what a fool she was being. For an entire week, she'd wanted to talk to him, spend time alone with him, and now when he'd suggested exactly that, she was making it sound like a capital offense.

Roarke led the way out of the infirmary, and Sherry followed silently behind him. The cooking staff were busy making preparations for the evening meal, and the big kitchen was filled with the hustle and bustle of the day. Roarke approached the cook, who glanced in Sherry's direction and nodded as Roarke said something to him.

Roarke returned to her. "He's going to scramble you some eggs. I suggest you eat them."

"I will," she promised, then watched helplessly as Roarke turned and walked out of the mess hall, leaving her standing alone.

Ellen's Café in Arrow Flats was filled with the weeknight dinner crowd. Sherry sat at a table by the window and studied the menu, although she'd read it so many times over the past twenty minutes that she could have recounted it from memory.

"Do you want to order, miss?" the young waitress in the pink uniform asked. "It looks like your friend isn't going to make it."

"No, I think I'll hold off for a few more minutes, if you don't mind."

"No problem. Just give the signal when you're ready."

"I will." Sherry felt terrible. More depressed than she could remember being in months. She'd really hoped tonight with Roarke would make a difference. She'd put such high hopes in the belief that if they could get away from the camp to meet on neutral ground and talk freely, then maybe they could solve the problems between them.

Just then the café door whirled open. Sherry's gaze flew in that direction, her heart rocketing to her throat as Roarke stepped inside. His gaze did a sweeping inspection of the café, and paused when he found Sherry. He sighed and smiled.

To Sherry it seemed that everyone and everything else in the restaurant faded from view.

"Hi," he said, a bit breathlessly, when he joined her. He pulled out the chair across the table from her and sat. "I apologize for being late. Something came up at the last minute, and I couldn't get away."

"Problems at the camp?"

Forcefully, he expelled his breath and nodded. "I don't want to talk about camp tonight. I'm just a lonely college professor looking for a quiet evening."

"I'm just a sweet young thing looking for a college professor seeking a quiet evening."

"I think we've found each other." Roarke's grin relaxed the tight muscles in his face. He'd convinced himself that Sherry had probably left when he didn't show. They both needed this time away from camp. He'd been miserable and so had she.

He was here at last, Sherry mused silently. Roarke was with her, and the dread of the past pain-filled minutes were wiped out with one Jeff Roarke smile.

"Have you ordered?"

Sherry shook her head and lowered her gaze to the memorized menu. "Not yet."

Roarke's eyes dropped, too, as he studied his own. Choosing quickly, he set it beside his plate. "I highly recommend the special."

"Liver and onions? Oh, Roarke, honestly." She laughed because she was so pleased he was there, and because liver and onions sounded exactly like a meal he'd enjoy.

"Doubt me if you will, but when liver hasn't been fried to a crisp, it's good."

Sherry closed her menu and set it aside. "Don't be disappointed, but I think I'll go with the French dip."

Roarke grinned and shook his head. "I never would have believed Miss Sherry White could be so boring."

"Boring!" She nearly choked on a sip of water.

"All right, all right, I'll revise that." Laugh lines formed deep grooves at the corners of his eyes. "I doubt that you'll ever be that. I can see you at a hundred and ten in the middle of a floor learning the latest dance step."

Sherry's hand circled her water glass. "I'll accept that as a compliment." But she didn't want to be on any dance floor if her partner wasn't Jeff Roarke, she added silently.

The amusement drained from his eyes. "What you said yesterday hit home."

Sherry looked up and blinked, uncertain. "About what?"

"That you wanted things to be different between us. I do too, Sherry. If we'd met any place but at camp things would be a hell of a lot easier. I have responsibilities—for that matter, so do you. Camp isn't the place for a relationship—now isn't the time."

Nervously, her fingers toyed with the fork stem. She didn't know what to say. Roarke seemed to be telling her that the best thing for them to do was ignore the attraction between them, pretend it wasn't there and go on about their lives as though what they felt toward each other made no difference.

"I see," she said slowly, her high spirits sinking to the depths of despair.

"But obviously, that bit of logic isn't going to work," Roarke added thoughtfully. "I've tried all week, and look what happened. I can't ignore you, Sherry, it's too hard on both of us."

The smile lit up her face. "I can't ignore you, either. As it turns out, I'm here and you're here."

His eyes held hers. "And there's no place else I'd rather be. For tonight, at least, we're two people with different tastes and life-styles who happened to meet in an obscure café in Arrow Flats, California."

Sherry smiled and nodded eagerly.

The waitress came and took their order, and Sherry and Roarke talked throughout the meal and long after they'd finished. They lingered over coffee, neither wanting the evening to end.

They left the café when *the* Ellen herself appeared from the kitchen and flipped the sign in the window to Closed. She paused to stare pointedly at them.

"I have the feeling she wants us to leave," Roarke muttered, looking around and noting for the first time that they were the only two customers left in the café.

Sherry took one last sip of her coffee and placed her paper napkin on the tabletop.

Roarke grinned and scooted back his chair to stand, and Sherry rose and followed him out of the restaurant.

"Where are you parked?" he asked.

"Around the corner."

He reached for her hand, lacing her fingers with his own. The action produced a soft smile in Sherry. Something as simple as holding her hand would be out of the question at camp. But tonight it was the most natural thing in the world.

"It's nearly ten," Roarke stated, surprise lifting his husky voice.

It astonished Sherry to realize that they'd sat and talked for more than four hours. Although they hadn't touched until just now, she'd never felt closer to Roarke. When they were at camp it seemed that their differences were magnified a thousandfold by circumstances and duty. Tonight they could be themselves. He'd astonished her. Amused her. Being with Roarke felt amazingly right.

He hesitated in front of the Ford station wagon. The camp logo was printed on the side panel.

Roarke opened the driver's side for her, and Sherry tossed her purse inside. They stood with the car door between them.

"Roarke?" she whispered, curious. "This may sound like a crazy question, but yesterday when I fainted... did you kiss me?"

His grin was slightly off center as he answered her with a quick nod of his head. He'd felt like a fool afterward, chagrined by his own actions. He wasn't exactly the model for Prince Charming, waking Sleeping Beauty with a secret kiss.

"I thought you must have," Sherry said softly. She'd felt so warm and secure that she hadn't wanted to wake up. "I was wondering is all," she added, a little flustered when he didn't speak.

Roarke caressed her cheek with his right hand. "Are you worried you'll have to pass out a second time before I do it again?"

She smiled at that. "The thought had crossed my mind."

"No," he said softly, sliding his hand down her face to the gentle slope of her shoulder. "Just move out from behind the car door."

Smiling, she did, deliberately closing it before walking into his arms. Roarke brought her close, breathed in the heady female scent of her and sighed his appreciation. His lips brushed against her temple, savoring the marvelous silken feel of her in his arms and the supreme rightness of holding her close. He kissed her forehead and her cheek, her chin, then closed her eyes with his lips.

His gentleness made Sherry go weak. She slipped her arms up his chest and around his neck, letting his strength absorb her weakness.

Roarke paused to glance with irritation at the streetlight, and suddenly decided he didn't care who saw him with Sherry or any consequences he might suffer as a result. He had to taste her. He kissed her then, deeply, yearning to reveal all the things he couldn't say with words. Urgently, his lips moved over hers with a fierce tenderness, until she moaned and responded, opening her mouth to him with passion and need.

Sherry's husky groan of pleasure throbbed in Roarke's ears and raced through his blood like quicksilver. He kissed her so many times he lost count, and she was weak and clinging to his arms. His own self-restraint was tested to the limit. With every vestige of control he possessed, he broke off the kiss and buried his face in her shoulder. He drew in a long breath and slowly expelled it in an effort to regain his wits and composure. He couldn't believe he was kissing her like this, in the middle of the street, with half the town looking on. Holding her, touching her, had been the only matters of importance.

"I'll follow you back to camp," he said, after a long moment.

Still too befuddled to speak, Sherry nodded.

Roarke dropped his arms and watched reluctantly as she stepped away. It was all he could do not to haul her back into his arms and kiss her senseless. From the first moment that he'd watched her interact with the children, Roarke had known that she was a natural. What he hadn't guessed was that this marvelous woman would hold his heart in the palm of her hand. He couldn't tell Sherry what he felt for her now; to do so would create the very problem he strove to avoid between staff members. Romance and camp were like oil and water, not meant to mix. To leave her doubting was regrettable, but necessary until the time was right. Never, in all the years that he'd been camp director, had Roarke more looked forward to August.

Roarke was busy all the following day. Even if he'd wanted, he wouldn't have been able to talk to Sherry. They passed each other a couple of times but weren't able to exchange anything more than a casual greeting. Now, at the end of another exhausting day, he felt the need to sit with her for a time and talk. For as long as he could, he resisted the temptation. At nine-thirty, Roarke decided no one would question it, if they saw him sitting on her porch talking.

As he neared her cabin, he heard the girls clamoring inside.

"I saw Buttercup," one of the girls cried, the alarm in her voice obvious.

Roarke glanced around, and sure enough, there was his calico, snooping around the cabin, peeking through the window. Naturally, Sherry's girls would be concerned over the feline, since they continued to house the rodent mascot. Every other cabin had welcomed Buttercup, but the cat had made his choice obvious and lingered around Sherry's, spending far more time there than at all the others combined. Roarke wasn't completely convinced it was solely the allure of Ralph, the hamster, either. Like almost everyone else in camp, the feline wanted to be around Sherry. Roarke watched with interest whenever Fred Spencer voiced his objections. It was obvious to Roarke that the man was jealous of Sherry's popularity, and his resentment shone through at each staff meeting.

"I saw him, too!" The commotion inside the cabin continued.

Roarke climbed the three steps that led to the front door and crouched down to pick up his cat.

"Now," Sherry's excited voice came at him from inside the cabin.

Just as he'd squatted down the front door flew open, and he looked up to find Sherry standing directly in front of him, pointing a Thompson submachine gun directly at his chest.

Before he could shout a warning, a piercing blast of water hit him square in the chest.

Chapter Ten

The blast of water was powerful enough to knock Roarke off balance. Crouched as he was, the force, coupled with the shock of Sherry aiming a submachine gun at him, hurled him backward.

"Roarke," Sherry screamed and slapped her hand over her mouth, smothering her horror, which soon developed into an out-and-out laugh.

Buttercup meowed loudly and scrambled from Roarke's grip, darting off into the night.

"Who the hell do you think you are?" Roarke yelled. "Rambo?" With as much dignity as he could muster, he stood and brushed the grit from his buttocks and hands.

"Mr. Roarke said the H-word." Righteously, Gretchen turned and whispered to the others.

Six small heads bobbed up and down in unison. Unlike Sherry, they recognized that this wasn't the time to show their amusement. Mr. Roarke didn't seem to find the incident the least bit humorous.

"I'm going to say a whole lot more than the H-word if you don't put that gun away," he shouted, his features tight and impatient.

Doing her utmost to keep from smiling, Sherry lowered her weapon, pointing the extended barrel toward the hardwood floor. "I apologize, Roarke, I wasn't aiming for you. I thought Buttercup was alone."

"That cat happens to be the camp pet," he yelled. He paused and inhaled a steadying breath before continuing. "Perhaps it would be best if we spoke privately, Miss White. Girls, if you'd kindly excuse us a moment."

"Oh, sure, go ahead," Gretchen answered for the group, and the others nodded in agreement.

"Sure," Jill and Jan added.

"Feel free," Sally inserted.

"Why not?" Diane wanted to know.

The amusement drained from Sherry's eyes. So much for the new wonderful understanding between them and the evening they'd spent together in town. Roarke knew how much she hated it when he sarcastically called her Miss White. No one did it quite the way he did, saying her name with all the coldness of arctic snow. Snow White. That's what the girls liked to call her when she wasn't around, although they didn't think she knew it.

Sherry stepped onto the porch and Roarke closed the door. "I do apologize, Roarke." Maybe if she said it enough times he'd believe her.

"I sincerely doubt that," he grumbled, swatting the moisture from his shirt. "Good grief, woman, don't you ever do anything like anyone else?"

"I was protecting Ralph," she cried, growing agitated. "What was I supposed to do? Invite Buttercup in for lunch and break seven little girls' hearts?"

"I certainly don't expect you to drown him."

"Fiddlesticks!" she returned heatedly, staring him down. "You're just mad because I got you wet. Believe me, it was unintentional. If I'd known you were going to be on the other side of the door, do you honestly think I would have pulled the trigger?"

"You'll do anything for a laugh," he countered.

Sherry was so furious, she could barely speak. "I might as well have, you're a wet blanket anyway." Following that announcement, she marched into the cabin and slammed the door.

Regret came instantly. What was she doing? Sherry wailed inwardly. She'd behaved like a child when she so much wanted to be a woman. But Roarke always assumed the worst of her, and his lack of trust was what hurt most.

Roarke had half a mind to follow her. He opened his mouth to demand that she come back out or he'd have her job, but the anger drained from him, leaving him flustered and impatient. For a full minute he didn't move. Finally he wiped his hand across his face, shrugged and headed back to his quarters, defeated and discouraged.

That night, Roarke lay in bed thinking. Sherry possessed more spirit than any woman he'd ever known. He would have loved to get a picture of the expression on her face once she realized she'd blasted him with that crazy weapon. But instead of laughing as they should have, the episode had ended in a shouting match. It seemed he did everything wrong with this woman. Maybe if he hadn't kept his nose buried in a book most of his life he'd know more about dealing with the opposite sex. Fiona was so much like him that they'd drifted together for no other reason than that they shared several interests. As he lay in bed, Roarke wasn't sure he could even remember what Fiona looked like.

He'd never been a ladies' man, although he wasn't so naive as to not realize that the opposite sex found him attractive. The scars of his youth went deep. The bookworm, four-eyes and all the other names he'd been taunted with echoed in the farthest corners of his mind. As an adult he'd avoided women, certain that they would find his intelligence and his dedication to the child genius a dead bore. He was thirty, but when it came to this unknown, unsettling realm of romance, he seemed to have all the social grace of a sixteen-year-old.

"Miss White," Pamela called into the dark silence.

"Yes?" Sherry sat upright and glanced at the bedside clock. Although it was well past midnight, she hadn't been able to sleep. "Is something wrong, honey?"

"No."

The direction of the small voice told Sherry that Pamela's head hung low. "Come here, and we can talk without waking the others." Sherry patted the flat space beside her and pulled back the covers so Pam could join her in bed.

The little girl found her way in the dark and climbed onto the bed. Sherry sat upright and leaned against the thick pillows, wrapping her arm around the nine-year-old's shoulders.

"It's Ralph's fault, isn't it?" Pamela said in a tiny, indistinct voice.

"What is?"

"That Mr. Roarke yelled at you."

"Honey," Sherry said with a sigh, "how can you possibly think that? I squirted Mr. Roarke with a submachine gun. He had every right to be upset."

"But you wouldn't have shot him if it hadn't been for Ralph. And then he got mad, and it's all my fault because I smuggled Ralph on the airplane without anyone knowing."

"Mr. Roarke had his feathers ruffled is all. There isn't anything to worry about."

Pamela raised her head and blinked. "Will he send you away?"

Knowing that Roarke could still find out that she'd deceived him on the application form didn't lend her confidence. "I don't think so, and if he does it'd be for something a lot more serious than getting him wet."

Pamela shook her head. "My mom and dad shout at each other the way you and Mr. Roarke do."

"We don't mean to raise our voices," Sherry said, feeling depressed. "It just comes out that way. Things will be better tomorrow." Although she tried to give them confidence, Sherry's words fell decidedly flat.

Throughout the staff meeting the following morning Sherry remained withdrawn and quiet. When Roarke didn't seek her out when the session was dismissed, she returned to her cabin. The girls, too, were quiet, regarding her with anxious stares.

"Well?" Gretchen finally demanded.

"Well, what?" Sherry asked, pulling a sweatshirt over her head, then freeing her hair from the constricting collar. When she finished, she turned to find all seven of the girls studying her.

"How did things go with Mr. Roarke?"

"Is he still angry?"

"Did he yell at you again?"

Sherry raised her hands to stop them. "Everything went fine."

"Fine?" Seven thin voices echoed hers.

"All right, it went great," Sherry sputtered. "Okay, let's move it—it's breakfast time."

A chorus of anxious cries followed her announcement as the girls scrambled for their sweaters, books and assorted necessities.

For most of the day Sherry stayed to herself, wanting to avoid another confrontation with Roarke. However, by late afternoon, she felt as if she was suffering from claustrophobia, avoiding contact with the outside world, ignoring the friends she'd made this summer. There had to be a better way!

Most of the classes had been dismissed, and Sherry sat on the porch steps of her cabin, watching the children chasing one another about, laughing and joking. The sound of their amusement was sweet music to her ears. It hadn't been so long ago that she'd wondered about these minigeniuses, and she was pleased to discover they were learning to be children and have fun. Several of the youngsters were playing games she'd taught them.

A breathless Gretchen soon joined Sherry, sitting on the step below hers. As was often the case when Sherry was within view of the children, she was soon joined by a handful of others.

"Will you tell me the story about how the star got inside the apple again?" Gretchen asked. "I tried to tell Gloria, but I forgot part of it."

"Sure," Sherry said with a grin and proceeded to do just that. Someone supplied her with an apple and a knife, and she took the fruit and cut it crosswise at the end of the story, holding it up to prove to the growing crowd of children that there was indeed a star in every apple.

Fred Spencer approached as she was speaking, pursing his lips in open disapproval. Sherry did her best to ignore him. She didn't understand what Fred had against her, but she was weary of the undercurrents of animosity she felt whenever he was near.

"Shouldn't these children be elsewhere?" he asked, his voice tight and sightly demanding.

Sherry stood and met the glaring dislike in the other man's eyes. "Okay, children, it's time to return to your cabins."

The small group let out a chorus of groans, loudly voicing their protest. Reluctantly, they left Sherry's side, dragging their feet.

"Oh, Miss White," Gretchen murmured. "I forgot to give you this." She withdrew an envelope from her

pocket. The camp logo was stamped on the outside.
"Mr. Roarke asked me to give this to you. I'm sorry I
forgot."

"No problem, sweetheart." Sherry reached for the
letter, her heart clamoring. Although she was dying to
read what Roarke had written, Sherry held off, staring at her name, neatly centered on the outside of the
business-size envelope. Fleetingly, she wondered if
Roarke had decided to fire her. Then she realized that
he wouldn't have asked Gretchen to deliver the notice; he had more honor than that.

With trembling fingers and a pounding heart, she
tore off the end of the envelope, blew inside to open
it and withdrew a single sheet. Carefully unfolding it,
she read the neatly typed sentence in the middle of the
page: Midnight at Clear Lake. Jeff Roarke.

Sherry read the four-word message over and over
again. Midnight at the lake? It didn't make sense. Was
he proposing that she meet him there? The two of
them, alone? Surely there was some other hidden
meaning that she was missing. After the incident with
Buttercup, he had her so flustered she couldn't think
straight.

During the evening, Sherry flirted with the idea of
ignoring the note entirely, but as the sun set and dusk
crept across the campgrounds, bathing the lush property in golden hues, she knew in her heart that no
matter what happened she'd be at the lake as Jeff
Roarke had requested.

At five minutes to midnight, she checked her seven
charges to be sure they were sleeping and woke Ginny
long enough to tell her she was leaving. As silently as

possible, Sherry slipped from the cabin. The moon was three-quarters full and cast a silken glow of light on the pathway that led to the lake's edge.

Hugging her arms, Sherry made her way along the well-defined walkway. Roarke's message hadn't been specific about where she was to meet him, although she'd read the note a hundred times. She pulled the letter from the hip pocket of her jeans and read the four words again.

"Sherry."

Roarke's voice startled her. Alarmed, Sherry slapped a hand over her heart.

"Sorry, I didn't mean to frighten you."

"That's all right," she said, quick to reassure him. "I should have been listening for you." He looked so tall and handsome in the moonlight, and her heart quickened at the sight of him. Loving him felt so right. A thousand times over the past few days she'd had doubts about caring so much for Roarke, but not now. Not tonight.

"Shall we sit down?"

"It's a beautiful night, isn't it?" Sherry asked as she lowered herself onto the sandy beach. They used an old log to lean against and paused to gaze into the heavens. The lake lapped lazily a few yards from their feet, and a fresh cool breeze carried with it the sweet, distinctive scent of summer. The moment was serene, unchallenged by the churning problems that existed between them.

"It's a lovely evening," he answered after a moment. He drew his knees up, crossed his legs and sighed expressively. "I'm pleased you did this, Sherry. I felt badly about the episode with the squirt gun."

"You're pleased I did this?" she returned. "What do you mean?"

"The note."

"What note? I didn't send you any note, but I did receive yours."

"Mine!" He turned then to study her, his gaze wide and challenging.

"I have it right here." Agilely, she raised her hips and slipped the paper from her pocket. It had been folded several times over, and her fingers fumbled with impatience as she opened it to hand to him.

Roarke's gaze quickly scanned the few words. "I didn't write this."

"Of course you did." He couldn't deny it now. The stationery and envelope were both stamped with the Camp Gitche Gumee logo.

"Sherry, I'm telling you I didn't write that note, but I did receive yours."

"And I'm telling you I didn't send you one."

"Then who did?"

She shrugged and gestured with her hand. She had a fair idea who was responsible. Her wizards! All seven of them! They'd plotted this romantic rendezvous down to the last detail, and both Roarke and Sherry had been gullible enough to fall for it. It would have angered Sherry, but for the realization that Roarke had wanted these few stolen moments badly enough to believe even the most improbable circumstances.

Roarke cleared his throat. He could feel Sherry's mounting agitation and sought a way to reassure her. He wasn't so naive as not to recognize that her girls must be responsible for this arrangement. Hell, he didn't care. She was sitting at his side in the moonlight, and it felt so good to have her with him that he didn't want anything to ruin it.

"It seems to me," he said slowly, measuring his words, "that this is Longfellow's doing."

"Longfellow?" Sherry repeated. Then she relaxed, a smile growing until she felt the relief and amusement surge up within her. "Yes, it must be him."

"Camp Gitche Gumee's own personal ghost—Longfellow," Roarke repeated softly. He paused, lifted his arm and cupped her shoulder, bringing her closer into his embrace.

Sherry let her head rest against the solid strength of his shoulder. Briefly she closed her eyes to the swelling tide of emotion that enveloped her. Roarke beside her, so close she could smell his after-shave and the manly scent that was his alone. He was even closer in spirit, so that it was almost as if the words to communicate were completely unnecessary.

Silence reigned for the moment, a refreshing reprieve to the anger that had so often unexpectedly erupted between them. This was a rare time, and Sherry doubted that either would have allowed anyone or anything to destroy it.

"We do seem to find ways to clash, don't we?" Sherry said, after a long moment. They'd made a point of not talking about life at camp when they'd had dinner, but tonight it was necessary. "Roarke, I want you to know I've never intentionally gone out of my way to irritate you."

"I had to believe that," he said softly, gently rifling his fingers through her soft dark hair. "Otherwise I would have gone a little crazy. But maybe I did anyway," he added as an afterthought.

"It just seems that everything I do—is wrong."

"Not wrong," he corrected, his voice raised slightly. "Just different. Some of your ideas have been excellent, but a few of the other counselors . . ."

"Fred Spencer." Roarke didn't need to mention names for her to recognize her most outspoken opponent. Almost from the day of her arrival, Fred had criticized her efforts with the children and challenged her ideas.

"Yes, Fred," Roarke admitted.

"Why?"

"He's been with the camp for as long as we've been operating, dedicating his summers to the children. It's been difficult for him to accept your popularity. The kids love you."

"But I don't want to compete with him."

"He'll learn that soon enough. You've shown admirable restraint, Sherry. The others admire you for the way you've dealt with Fred." He turned his head just enough so that his lips grazed her temple as he spoke. "The others nothing; *I've* admired you."

"Oh, Roarke."

His arm around her tightened, and Sherry held her breath. The magic was potent, so very potent. His breath fanned her cheek, searing her flushed skin.

Without being aware that she was rotating her head toward him, Sherry turned, silently seeking his kiss.

Roarke's hand touched her chin and tipped her face toward him. Sherry stared up at him, hardly able to believe what she saw in his eyes and felt in her heart. His gaze was full of warmth and tenderness and he was smiling with such sweet understanding. It seemed that Roarke was telling her with his eyes how important she was to him, how much he enjoyed her wit, her creativity. Her.

Slowly he bent his head to her. Sherry slid her hands up his shoulders and tilted her head to meet him halfway. He groaned her name, and his lips came down to caress hers in a long, undemanding, tender kiss that robbed her lungs of breath.

The kiss deepened as Roarke sensually shaped and molded her lips to his. Sherry gave herself over to him, holding back nothing. He kissed her again and again, unable to get enough of the delicious taste of her. She was honey and wine. Unbelievably sweet. Sunshine and love. He kissed her again, then lifted his head to tenderly cup her face between his large hands and gaze into her melting brown eyes.

"Roarke?" she said his name, not knowing herself what she would ask. It was in her to beg him not to stop for fear that something would pull them apart as it had so often in the past.

"You're so sweet," he whispered, unable to look away. His mouth unerringly found hers, the kiss lingering, slow and compelling so that by the time he raised his head Sherry was swimming in a sea of sensual awareness.

"Roarke, why do we argue?" Her hands roamed through his hair, luxuriating in the thick feel of it between her fingers. "I hate it when we do."

"Me, too, love. Me, too." His tongue flickered over the seam of her lips, teasing them at first, then urging them apart. And when she did open her mouth, his tongue plunged inside to intimately explore the silken hollow with such thoroughness that Sherry was left weak with desire, clinging to him as the only secure thing in a world that had unexpectedly gone spinning off course.

"Sherry, love," he whispered, and inhaled deeply. "We have to stop."

"I know," she answered and nodded.

But neither loosened the embrace. Neither was willing to forsake the moment or relinquish this special closeness growing between them.

Roarke rubbed his moist mouth sensuously against hers. Back and forth, until Sherry thought she would faint with wanting him. When she could tolerate it no longer, she parted her lips and once again they were tossed into the roiling sea of passion.

Without warning, Roarke stopped.

Kissed into senselessness, Sherry could do nothing to protest. Breathing had taken on an extraordinary effort, and she pressed her forehead to his chest while she gathered her composure.

"Roarke," she whispered.

"In a minute."

She raised her gaze enough to view the naked turmoil that played so vividly across his contorted features.

"I'm sorry," she told him. "So sorry for what happened with Lynn and Peter that day. Sorry for so many things. I can't have you believing that I'd use you like that. I couldn't... I just couldn't."

His smile was so gentle that Sherry felt stinging tears gather in her eyes.

"I know," he said softly. "That's in the past and best forgotten."

"But, Roarke, I..."

He placed his index finger across her lips, stopping her. "Whatever it is doesn't matter."

Sherry's wide-eyed gaze studied him. She dreaded the moment he learned the whole truth about her. "But I want to be honest."

"You can't lie," he said as his hands lovingly caressed the sides of her face. "I've noticed that about you."

"But I have—"

"It doesn't matter now, Sherry. Not now." Unable to resist her a moment longer, he bent low and thoroughly kissed her again.

Any argument, any desire for Sherry to tell him about the falsified references was tossed aside as unimportant and inconsequential. Within a few weeks the camp session would be over, and if he hadn't discovered the truth by then, she would simply trust that he never would. Later, much later, she'd tell him, and they could laugh about it, her deception a source of amusement.

Roarke stood, offering Sherry his hand to help her to her feet. She took it and pulled herself up, then paused momentarily to brush the sand from her backside and look out over the calm lake. This summer with Roarke would always be remembered as special, but she didn't want it to end. The weeks had flown past, and she couldn't imagine ever being without him now.

With a sigh of regret to be leaving the tranquil scene, Roarke draped his arm over her shoulder and guided her back to the main campgrounds.

"My appreciation to Longfellow," he whispered outside her cabin door.

They shared a secret smile, and with unspoken agreement resisted the urge to kiss good-night.

"I'll tell the girls—Longfellow—you said so," she murmured.

Roarke continued to hold her hand. "Good night, Sherry."

"Good night, Roarke." Reluctantly he released her fingers, moved back and turned away.

"Roarke?" she called, anxiously rising onto her tiptoes.

He turned around. "Yes?"

She stared at him, uncertain; her feet returned to the porch. It was in her mind to ask his forgiveness for everything she'd done that had been so zany and caused him such grief. She yearned to confess everything, clean the slate, but anxiety stopped her. She was afraid that a confession now would ruin everything. She could think of only one thing to say. "Friends?"

"Yes," he answered and nodded for emphasis. Much more than friends, he added silently. Much more.

* * *

Things changed after that night. Roarke changed.
Sherry changed. Camp Gitche Gumee changed.

It seemed to Sherry that Roarke had relaxed and
lowered his guard. Gone was the stiff, unbending
camp director. Gone was the tension that stretched
between them so taut that Sherry had sometimes felt
ill with it. Gone were the days when she'd felt on edge
every time they met. Now she eagerly anticipated each
meeting.

Roarke spent less time in his office and was often
seen talking to the children. The sound of his amusement could frequently be heard drifting across the
campgrounds. He joked and smiled, and every once
in a while, he shared secret glances with Sherry. These
rare moments had the most curious effect upon her.
Where she'd always been strong, now she felt weak,
yet her weakness was her strength. She'd argued with
Roarke, battled for changes, and now she was utterly
content. The ideas she'd fought so long and hard to
instill at the camp came naturally with her hardly saying a word.

The late afternoons became a special time for
Roarke and Sherry with the camp kids. All ages would
gather around the couple, and Sherry would lead an
impromptu songfest, teaching them songs she'd
learned as a youngster at camp. Some were silly songs,
while others were more serious, but all were fun, and
more than anything, Sherry wanted the children of
Camp Gitche Gumee to have fun.

Soon the other counselors and staff members joined
Sherry and Roarke on the front lawn, and music be-

came a scheduled event of the day, with two other musically inclined counselors taking turns leading the songs. Within a week, as if by magic, two guitars appeared, and Sherry played one and Lynn the other, accompanying the singers.

Someone suggested a bonfire by the lake, and the entire camp roasted marshmallows as the sky filled with twinkling stars.

When they'd finished the first such event in the history of the camp, Gretchen requested that Sherry tell everyone about Longfellow, and after a tense moment, Sherry stepped forward and kept the group spellbound with her make-believe tales.

To her surprise, Roarke added his own comical version of a trick the friendly spook had once played on him when he'd first arrived at the camp. Even Fred Spencer had been amused, and Sherry had caught him chuckling.

The night was such a success that Sherry was too excited to sleep. Her charges were worn-out from the long week and slept peacefully, curled up in their cots. Sherry sat on top of her bed and tried to read, but her thoughts kept wandering to Roarke and how much had changed between them and how much better it was to be with him than any man she'd ever known.

The pebble against her window caught her attention.

"Sherry?" Her name came on a husky whisper.

Stumbling to her feet, she pushed up the window and leaned out. "Who's there?"

"How many other men do you have pounding on your window?"

"Roarke?" Her eyes searched the night for him, but saw nothing. "I know you're out there."

"Right again," he said, and stepped forward, his hands hidden behind his back.

Sherry sighed her pleasure, propped her elbows against the windowsill and cupped her face with her hands. "What are you doing here?"

He ignored the question. "Did you enjoy tonight?"

Sherry nodded eagerly. "It was wonderful." *He* was wonderful!

"Couldn't you sleep?" he asked, then added, "I saw your light on."

"No, I guess I'm too keyed up. What about you?"

"Too happy."

Sherry studied the curious way he stood, with his hands behind him. "What have you got?"

"What makes you think I have anything?"

"Roarke, honestly."

"All right, all right." He swept his arm around and presented her with a small bouquet of wildflowers.

The gift was so unexpected and so special that Sherry was speechless. For the first time in years she struggled to find the words. She yearned to let him know how pleased she was with his gift.

"Oh, Roarke, thank you," she said after a lengthy moment. "I'm stunned." She cupped the flowers in her hand and brought them to her face to savor the sweet scent.

"I couldn't find any better way to let you know I think you're marvelous."

Their eyes held each other's. "I think you're marvelous, too," she told him.

He wanted to kiss her so much it frightened him—more than the night they'd sat by the lake. More than the first time in his office. But he couldn't. She knew it. He knew it. Yet that didn't make refusing her easy.

"Well, I guess I'd better get back."

Sherry's gaze dropped to the bouquet. "Thank you, Roarke," she said again, with tears in her throat. "For everything."

"No." His eyes grew dark and serious. "It's me who should be thanking you."

He'd been gone a full five minutes before Sherry closed the window. She slumped onto the end of her bed and released a sigh. In her most farfetched dreams, she hadn't believed Jeff Roarke could be so wonderfully romantic. Now she prayed nothing would happen to ruin this bliss.

Chapter Eleven

"Sleepy and Grumpy are at it again," Wendy told Sherry early the next morning. "Diane doesn't want to wake up and Gretchen's complaining that she didn't sleep a wink on that lumpy mattress."

With only a week left of camp, the girls seemed all the more prone to complaints and minor disagreements. Sherry and the other counselors had endured more confusion these past seven days than at any other time in the two-month-long session of Camp Gitche Gumee.

"Say, where'd you get the flowers?" Jan and Jill blocked the doorway into Sherry's room. Jill had long since lost her tooth, making it almost impossible to tell one twin from the other.

Sherry's gaze moved from Jan and Jill to the bouquet of wildflowers Roarke had given her. They had withered long before, but she couldn't bear to part with them. Every time she looked at his gift she went all weak inside with the memory of the night he'd stood outside her window. The warm, caressing look in his eyes had remained with her all week. She'd never dreamed Jeff Roarke could be so romantic. Pulling herself up straight, Sherry diverted her attention from the wilted wildflowers and thoughts of Roarke. If she lingered any longer, they'd all be late to the mess hall.

Taking charge, Sherry stepped out of her room and soundly clapped her hands twice. "All right, Sleeping Beauty, out of bed."

"She must mean me," Gretchen announced with a wide yawn and tossed aside her covers.

"I believe Miss White was referring to Diane," Wendy said, wrinkling up her nose in a mocking gesture of superiority.

"I was speaking to whoever was still in bed," Sherry said hurriedly, hoping to forestall an argument before it escalated into a shouting match.

"See," Gretchen muttered and stuck out her tongue at Wendy, who immediately responded in kind.

"Girls, please, you're acting like a bunch of ten-year-olds!" It wasn't until after the words had slipped from her mouth that Sherry realized her wizards *were* ten-year-olds! Like Roarke, she'd fallen into the trap of thinking of them as pint-size adults. When she first arrived at camp, she'd been critical of Roarke and the others for their attitudes toward the children. She realized now that she'd been wrong to be so judgmental. The participants of Camp Gitche Gumee weren't normal children. Nor were they little adults, of course, but something special in between.

Moving at a snail's pace that drove Sherry near the brink of losing her control, the girls dressed, collected their books and headed in an orderly fashion for the dining hall. Sherry sat at the head of the table, and the girls followed obediently into their assigned seats.

"I hate mush," Gretchen said, glaring down at the serving bowl that steamed with a large portion of the cooked cereal.

"It's good for you," Sally, the young scientist, inserted.

Diane nodded knowingly. "I read this book about how healthy fiber is in the diet."

Gretchen looked around at the faces staring at her and sighed. "All right, all right. Don't make a big deal over it—I'll eat the mush. But it'll taste like glue, and I'll probably end up at Ms. Butler's office having my stomach pumped."

When Roarke approached the front of the mess hall and the podium, the excited chatter quickly fizzled to a low murmur and then to a hush.

Sherry's gaze rested on the tall director, and even now, after all these weeks, her heart fluttered at the virile sight he made. She honestly loved this man. If anyone had told her the first week after her arrival at camp how she'd feel about Jeff Roarke by the end of the summer, she would have laughed in his face. She recalled the way Roarke had irritated her and his dictatorial ways—but she hadn't known him then, hadn't come to appreciate his quiet strength and subtle wit. She hadn't sat under the stars with him or experienced the thrill of his kisses.

Now, in less than a week, camp would be dismissed and she'd be forced to return to Seattle. Already her mind had devised ways to stay close to Roarke in the next months. A deep inner voice urged her to let him speak first. Most of the times they'd clashed had been when Sherry had proceeded with some brilliant scheme without discussing it with Roarke first. No— as difficult as it would be, she'd wait for him to make the first move. But by heaven that was going to be hard.

When Roarke's announcements for the day were completed, the children were dismissed. With an eager cry, they crowded out of the mess hall door to their first classes.

Sherry remained behind to linger over coffee. Soon Roarke and Lynn joined her.

"Morning," Sherry greeted them both, but her gaze lingered on Roarke. Their eyes met in age-old communication, and all her doubts flew out the window and evaporated into the warm morning air. No man could look at her the way he did and not care. Her tongue felt as if it was stuck to the roof of her mouth and her insides twisted with the potency of his charm.

"The natives are restless," Lynn groaned, cupping her coffee mug with both hands.

"Yes, I noticed that," Roarke commented, but his gaze continued to hold Sherry's. With some effort he pulled his eyes away. Disguising his love for her had become nearly impossible. Another week and he would have the freedom to tell her how much he loved her and to speak of the future, but for now he must bide his time. However, now that camp was drawing to a close, he found that his pulse raced like a locomotive speeding out of control whenever he was around her. His hands felt sweaty, his mouth dry. He'd discovered the woman with whom he could spend the rest of his life and he felt as callow as a boy on his first date.

"The kids need something to keep their minds off the last days of camp," Sherry offered.

"I agree," Lynn added. "I thought your suggestion about a hike to study wildflowers was a good one, Sherry. Whatever became of that?"

Fred Spencer had nixed that plan at a time when Roarke might have approved the idea, had he not been so upset with Sherry. She couldn't remember what had been the problem: Longfellow or their first kiss. Probably both. It seemed she'd continually been in hot water with Roarke in the beginning. How things had changed!

"Now that I think about an organized hike, it sounds like something we might want to investigate," Roarke commented, after mulling over the idea for a couple of minutes.

Sherry paused, uncertain, remembering Fred. "What about . . . you know who?"

"After a couple more days like this one, Fred Spencer will be more than happy to have you take his group for an afternoon."

"We could scout out the area this morning," Lynn suggested, looking to Sherry for confirmation.

"Sure," Sherry returned enthusiastically. She'd had a passion for wildflowers from the time she was ten and camped at Paradise on Washington state's Mount

Rainier with her father; hiking together, they'd stumbled upon a field of blazing yellow and white flowers.

"Then you have my blessing," Roarke told the two women, grinning. "Let me know what you find and we'll go from there."

When Sherry and Lynn returned to camp after their successful exploratory hike of the area surrounding the camp and the lake, there was barely time to wash before lunch. Although Sherry was eager to discuss what she'd found with Roarke, she was forced into joining her girls in the mess hall first.

The wizards chattered incessantly, arguing over a paper napkin and a broken shoelace. Wendy reminded everyone that Ken-Richie was still in the hands of a no-good, lily-livered thief and she wasn't leaving camp until he was returned.

The meal couldn't be over soon enough to suit Sherry. The minute the campers were excused, she eagerly crossed the yard to Roarke's office. He hadn't made an appearance at the meal, which was unusual, but it happened often enough not to alarm Sherry.

When she reached his office, she noted that he was alone and knocked politely.

"Come in." His voice was crisp and businesslike.

He looked up from his desk when Sherry walked into the room, but revealed no emotion.

"Is this a bad time?" she asked, hesitant. She could hardly remember the last time he'd spoken to her in that wry tone. Nor had he smiled, and that puzzled her. Her instincts told her something was wrong. His eyes narrowed when he looked at her, and Sherry swallowed her concern. "Do you want me to come back later?"

"No." He shook his head for emphasis. "What did you find?"

"We discovered the most beautiful flowers," she said, warming to the subject closest to her heart. "Oh, Roarke, the trail is perfect. It shouldn't take any more than an hour for the round trip, and I can show the kids several different types of wildflowers. There are probably hundreds more, but those few were the ones I could identify readily. The kids are going to love this."

Her eyes were fairly sparkling with enthusiasm, Roarke noted. Seeing her as she was at this moment made it almost impossible to be angry. His stomach churned, and he looked away, hardly able to bear the sight of her. The phone call had caught him off guard. He'd had most of the morning to come to grips with himself and had failed. Something had to be done, but he wasn't sure what.

"When do you think we could start the first hikes? I mean if you think we should, that is." He was so distant—so strange. Sherry didn't know how she should react. When she first entered the office she'd thought he was irritated with her for something, but now she realized it was more than anger. He seemed distressed, and Sherry hadn't a clue if the matter concerned her or some camp issue. Several times over the past couple of months, she'd been an eyewitness to the heavy pressures placed upon Roarke. He did a marvelous job of managing Camp Gitche Gumee and had gained her unfailing loyalty and admiration.

"Roarke?"

"Hmm?" His gaze left the scene outside his window and reluctantly returned to her.

"Is something wrong?"

"Nothing," he lied smoothly, straightening his shoulders. "Nothing at all. Now regarding the hike, let's give it a trial run. Take your girls out this afternoon and we'll see how things go. Then tomorrow morning you can give a report to the other counselors."

Sherry clasped her hands together, too excited to question him further. "Thank you, Roarke, you won't regret this."

His stoic look was all the response he gave her.

As Sherry knew they would, the girls, carrying backpacks, grumbled all the way from the camp to the other side of the small lake. The pathway was well-defined, and they walked single file along the narrow dirt passage.

"Just how long is this going to take?"

"My feet hurt."

"No one said the Presidential Commission on Physical Fitness applied at Camp Gitche Gumee."

Listening to their complaints brought a smile to Sherry's features. "Honestly," she said with a short laugh, "you guys make it sound like we're going to climb Mount Everest."

"This is more like K-2."

"K-what?" Jan and Jill wanted to know.

"That's the highest peak in the Himalayas," Sally announced with a prim look. In response to a blank stare from a couple of the others, she added, "You know? The mountain system of south-central Asia that extends fifteen hundred miles through Kashmir, northern India, southern Tibet, Nepal, Sikkim and Bhutan."

"I remember reading about those," Diane added.

Gretchen paused and wiped her hot, perspiring face with the back of her hand. "You read about everything," she told her friend.

"Well, that's better than complaining about everything."

"Girls, please," Sherry said, hoping to keep the peace. "This is supposed to be fun."

"Do we get to eat anything?" Jan muttered.

"We're starved," Jill added.

The others agreed in a loud plea until Sherry reminded them that they'd left the mess hall only half an hour before.

"But don't worry," she said, "it's against camp policy to leave the grounds without chocolate chips." Sherry did her best to hide a smile.

Pamela laughed, and the others quickly joined in.

For all their bickering, Sherry's wizards were doing well—and even enjoying themselves. With so much time spent in the classroom in academic ventures, there had been little planned exercise for the girls.

"We'll take a break in a little bit," Sherry promised.

"It's a good thing," Gretchen muttered despairingly.

"Really," Sally added.

"Don't listen to them, Miss White," Pamela piped in, then lowered her voice to a thin whisper. "They're wimps."

"Hey! Look who's calling a wimp a wimp!"

In mute consternation, Sherry raised her arms and silenced her young charges. Before matters got out of hand, she found a fallen log and instructed them to sit.

Grumbling, the girls complied.

"Snack time," Sherry told them, gathering her composure. She slipped the bulky backpack from her tired shoulders. "This is a special treat, developed after twenty years of serious research."

"What is it?" Sally wanted to know, immediately interested in anything that had to do with research.

Already Gretchen was frowning with practiced disapproval.

Sherry ignored their questions and pulled a full jar of peanut butter from inside her pack. She screwed off the lid and reached for a plastic knife. "Does everyone have clean hands?"

Seven pairs of eyes scanned seven pairs of hands. This was followed by eager nods.

"Okay," Sherry told them next, "stick out an index finger."

Silently, they complied and shared curious glances as Sherry proceeded down the neat row of girls, spreading peanut butter on seven extended index fingers. A loud chorus of questions followed.

"Yuk. What's it for?"

"Hey, what are we suppose to do with this?"

"Can I lick it off yet?"

Replacing the peanut butter in her knapsack, Sherry took out a large bag of semisweet chocolate chips.

"What are you going to do with that?"

"Is it true what you said about not leaving camp without chocolate chips?"

"Scout's honor!" Dramatically, Sherry crossed her heart with her right hand, then tore open the bag of chocolate pieces, holding it open for the girls. "Okay, dip your finger inside, coat it with chips and enjoy."

Gretchen was the first to stick her finger in her mouth. "Hey, this isn't bad."

"It's delicious, I promise," Sherry told her wizards as she proceeded from one girl to the next.

"It didn't really take twenty years of research for this, did it?" Sally asked, cocking her head at an angle to study her counselor.

Sherry grinned. "Well, I was about twenty when I perfected the technique." She swirled her finger in the air, then claimed it was all in the wrist movement.

The girls giggled, and the sound of their amusement drifted through the tall redwoods that dominated the forest. Sherry found a rock and sat down in front of her wizards, bringing her knees up and crossing her ankles.

"When I was about your age," she began, "my dad and I went for a hike much like we're doing today. And like you, I complained and wanted to know how much farther I was going to have to walk and how long it would be before I could have something to eat and where the closest rest room was."

The girls continued licking the chocolate and peanut butter off their fingers, but their gazes centered on Sherry.

"When we'd been gone about an hour, I was convinced my dad was never going back to the car. He kept telling me there was something he wanted me to see."

"Can you tell us what it was?"

"Did you ever find it?"

"Yes, to both questions," Sherry said, coming to her feet. "In fact, I want to show you girls what my father showed me." She led them away from the water's edge. The girls trooped after her in single file, marching farther into the woods to the lush meadow Sherry had discovered with Lynn earlier in the day.

A sprinkling of flowers tucked their heads between the thick grass, hidden from an untrained eye.

"This is a blue monkshood," Sherry said, crouching down close to a foot-tall flower with lobed, toothed leaves and a thin stalk. Eagerly the girls gathered around the stringy plant that bloomed in blue and violet hues.

"The blue monkshood can grow as tall as seven feet," Sherry added.

"That's even bigger than Mr. Roarke," Diane said in awe.

At the sound of Jeff Roarke's name, Sherry's heart went still. She wished now that she'd taken time to talk to him and learn what he'd found so troubling. His eyes had seemed to avoid hers, and he'd been so...so distant. The minute they returned to camp, Sherry decided, she was going directly to his office. If she wasn't part of the problem, then she wanted to be part of the solution.

"Miss White?"

"Yes?" Shaking her head to clear her thoughts, Sherry smiled lamely.

"What's this?" Wendy pointed to a dwarf shrub with white blossoms and scalelike leaves that was close by.

"These are known as cassiopes." Sherry pronounced the name slowly and had the girls repeat it after her. "This is a hearty little flower. Some grow as far north as the arctic."

"How'd you learn so much about wildflowers?" Gretchen asked, her eyes wide and curious.

"Books, I bet," Diane shouted.

"Thank you, Miss White," Gretchen came back sarcastically.

"I did study books, but I learned far more by combining reading with taking hikes just like the one we're on today."

"Are there any other flowers here?"

"Look around you," Sherry answered, sweeping her arm in a wide arch. "They're everywhere."

"I wish Ralph were here," Pamela said with a loud sigh. "He likes the woods."

"What's this?" Sally asked, crouched down beside a yellow blossom.

"The western wallflower."

Gretchen giggled and called out, "Sally found a wallflower."

"It's better than being one," came the other girl's fiery retort.

"Girls, please!" Again Sherry found herself serving as referee to her young charges.

"I don't want camp to end," Wendy said suddenly, slumping to the ground. She shrugged out of her backpack and took out her Barbie and Ken dolls, holding them close. "But I want to go home, too."

"I feel the same way," Sherry admitted.

"You do?" Seven faces turned to study her.

"You bet. I love each one of you, and it's going to be hard to tell you all goodbye, but Camp Gitche Gumee isn't my home, and I miss my friends and my family." As much as she'd yearned to escape Phyliss, Sherry knew what she was saying was in fact, true. She did miss her father and her individualistic stepmother. And although California was beautiful, it wasn't Seattle.

"Are you planning to come back next year, Miss White?" Pam asked timidly.

Sherry nodded. "But only if you and Ralph will be here."

"I come back every summer," Gretchen said. "Next year I'm going to have my mother request you as my counselor."

Sherry tucked her arm around the little girl's shoulders and gently squeezed. "What about the lumpy mattress?"

"I said I was going to request you as my counselor, but I definitely don't want the same bed."

Sherry laughed at that, and so did the others.

The afternoon sped past, and by the time they returned to camp, Pam had gotten stung by a bee, Jan and Jill had suffered twin blisters on their right feet and Sally had happened upon two varieties of skipper moths. With a little help from her friends, she'd captured both and brought them back to camp to examine under her microscope.

The tired group of girls marched back into camp as heroes, as the other kids came running toward them, full of questions.

"Where did you guys go?"

"Will our counselor take us on a search for wildflowers, too?"

"How come you guys get to do all the fun stuff?"

"Miss White."

Jeff Roarke's voice reached Sherry, and with a wide, triumphant grin she turned to face him. The smile quickly faded at the cool reception in his gaze, and his dark, brooding look cut through her like a hot needle.

"You wanted to see me?" Sherry asked.

"That's correct." He motioned with his hand toward his office. "Lynn has agreed to take care of your girls until you return."

Lynn's smile was decidedly weak when Sherry's gaze sought out her friend's. Sherry paused, heaved in a deep breath and wiped the grime off the back of her neck with her hand. Her face felt hot and flushed. So much for her triumphant entry into Camp Gitche Gumee.

"Would you mind if I washed up first?" she asked.

Roarke hesitated.

"All right. A drink of water should do me."

They paused beside the water fountain, and Sherry took a long, slow drink, killing time. She straightened and wiped the clear water from her mouth. Again, Roarke's gaze didn't meet hers.

"I-it's about the references, isn't it?" she asked, trying her best to keep her voice from trembling. "I know I shouldn't have falsified them—I knew it was wrong—but I wanted this job so badly and—"

It didn't seem possible that Roarke's harsh features could tighten any more without hardening into granite. Yet, they did, right before her eyes.

"Roarke," she whispered.

"So you lied on the application, too."

Sherry's mind refused to cooperate. "Too? What do you mean, too? That's the only time I ever have, and I didn't consider it a real lie—I misled you is all."

His look seared her. "I suppose you 'misled' me in more than one area."

"Roarke, no...never." Sherry could see two months of a promising relationship evaporating into thin, stale air, and she was helpless to change it. She opened her mouth to defend herself and saw how useless it would be.

"Are you finished?" Roarke asked.

Feeling sick to her stomach, Sherry nodded.

"This way. There are people waiting to see you."

"People?"

At precisely that moment the door to Roarke's office opened and Phyliss came down the first step. With a wild, excited cry, she threw her arms in the air and cried, "Sherry, baby, I've found you at last."

Before Sherry had time to blink, she found herself clenched in her stepmother's arms in a grip that would have crushed anyone else. "Oh, darling, let me look at you." Gripping Sherry's shoulders, the older woman stepped back and sighed. "I've had every detective agency from here to San Francisco looking for you." She paused and laughed, the sound high and shrill. "I've got so much to tell you. Do you like my new hairstyle?" She paused and patted the side of her head. "Purple highlights—it drives your father wild."

Despite everything, Sherry laughed and hugged her. Loony, magnificent Phyliss. She'd never change.

"Your father is waiting to talk to you, darling. Do you have any idea what a wild-goose chase you've led us on? Never mind that now...we've had a marvelous time searching for you. This is something you may want to consider doing every summer. Your father and I have had a second honeymoon traveling all over the country trying to find you." She paused and laughed. "Sherry, sweetheart," she whispered, "before we leave, you and I must have a girl-to-girl talk about the camp director, Mr. Roarke. Why, he's handsome enough to stir up the blood of any woman. Now don't try to tell me you haven't noticed. I know better."

Flustered, Sherry looked up to find Roarke watching them both, obviously displeased.

Chapter Twelve

"Roarke, please try to understand," Sherry pleaded.

A triumphant Phyliss and Virgil White had left Camp Gitche Gumee only minutes before. Her stepmother had evidently decided to look upon Sherry's disappearance as a fun game and had spent weeks tracking her down. It was as if Phyliss had won this comical version of hide-and-seek and could now return home giddy with jubilation for having outsmarted her stepdaughter.

As if that wasn't enough, Phyliss stayed long enough to inspect the camp kitchen and insist that Sherry tint her dark hair purple the minute she returned to Seattle—it was absolutely the in thing. She also enumerated in embarrassing detail Sherry's "many fine qualities" in front of Roarke, then paused demurely to flutter her lashes and announce that she'd die for a stepson-in-law as handsome as he was.

Sherry was convinced the entire camp sighed with relief the minute Phyliss and her father headed toward the exit in their powder-pink Cadillac. As they drove through the campgrounds, Phyliss leaned over her husband and blasted the horn in sharp toots, waving and generously blowing kisses as they went.

During the uncomfortable two hours that her parents were visiting, Sherry noted that Roarke didn't so much as utter a word to her. He carried on a polite conversation with her father, but Sherry had been too busy keeping Phyliss out of mischief to worry about what her father was telling Roarke.

Now that her parents were on their way back to Seattle, Sherry was free to speak to the somber camp director. She followed him back to his office, holding her tongue until he was seated behind the large desk that dominated his room.

"Now that you've met Phyliss you can understand why I needed to get away. I love her . . . in fact, I think she's wonderful, but all that mothering was giving me claustrophobia."

Roarke's smile was involuntary. "I must admit she's quite an individual."

Without invitation, Sherry pulled a chair close to Roarke's desk and sat down. She crossed her legs and leaned forward. "I-I'm sorry about the references on the application."

"You lied." His voice was a monotone, offering her little hope.

"I—I prefer to think of it as misleading you, and then only because it was necessary."

"Did you or did you not falsify your references?"

"Well, I did have the good references, I just equivocated a little on the addresses...."

"Then you were dishonest. A lie is a lie, so don't try to pretty it up with excuses."

Sherry swallowed uncomfortably. "Then I lied. But you wouldn't have known," she added quickly, before losing her nerve. "I mean, just now, today, when I mentioned it, you looked shocked. You didn't know until I told you."

"I knew." That wasn't completely true, Roarke thought. He'd suspected when the post office returned the first reference and then two of the others; but rather than investigate, Roarke had chosen to ignore the obvious for fear he'd be forced to fire her. Almost from the first week, he'd been so strongly attracted to her that he'd gone against all his instincts. Now he felt like a fool.

Sherry's hands trembled as she draped a thick strand of hair around her ear. She boldly met his gaze. "There are only a few days of camp left. Are...are you going to fire me?"

Roarke mulled over the question. He should. If any of the other counselors were to discover her deception, he would be made to look like a love-crazed fool.

"No," he answered finally.

In grateful relief Sherry momentarily closed her eyes.

"You understand, of course, that you won't be invited back as a counselor next summer."

His words burned through her like a hot poker. In one flat statement he was saying so much more. In effect, he was cutting her out of his life, severing her from his emotions and his heart. The tight knot that formed in her throat made it difficult to speak. "I understand," she said in a voice that was hardly more than a whisper. "I understand perfectly."

Sherry made her way to her cabin trapped in a haze of emotional pain. Lynn's words at the beginning of the camp session about Roarke's placing high regard on honesty returned to taunt her. The night they'd sat by the lake under the stars and kissed brought with it such a flood of memories that Sherry brushed the moisture from her cheek and sucked in huge breaths to keep from weeping.

"Miss White," Gretchen shouted when Sherry entered the cabin. "I liked your stepmother."

"Me, too," Jan added.

"Me, three," Jill said, and the twins giggled.

Sherry's smile was decidedly flat, although she did make the effort.

"She's so much fun!" Wendy held up her index finger to display a five-carat smoky topaz ring.

Costume jewelry, of course, Sherry mused. Phyliss didn't believe in real jewels, except her wedding ring.

"Phyliss told me I could have the ring," Wendy continued, "because anyone who appreciated Barbie and Ken the way I did deserved something special."

"She gave me a silk scarf," Diane said with a sigh. "She suggested I read Stephen King."

"Is her hair really purple?"

"She's funny."

Sherry sat at the foot of the closest bunk. "She's wonderful and fun and I love her."

"Do you think she'll visit next year?"

"I...I can't say." Another fib, Sherry realized. Phyliss wouldn't be coming to Camp Gitche Gumee because Sherry wouldn't be back.

"She sure is neat."

"Yes," Sherry said, and for the first time since she'd spoken to Roarke, the smile reached her eyes. "Phyliss is some kind of special."

"Miss White, Miss White, give me a hug," Sally cried, her suitcase in her hand. Sally was the first girl from Sherry's cabin to leave the camp. Camp Gitche Gumee had been dismissed at breakfast that morning. The bus to transport the youngsters to the airport was parked outside the dining room, waiting for the first group.

"Oh, Sally," Sherry said, wrapping her arms around the little girl and squeezing her tight. "I'm going to miss you so much."

"I had a whole lot of fun," she whispered, tears in her eyes. "More than at any other camp ever."

Tenderly, Sherry brushed the hair from Sally's forehead. "I did, too, sweetheart."

Goodbyes were difficult enough, but knowing that it was unlikely she would ever see her young charges again produced an even tighter pain within Sherry. She'd grown to love her girls, and the end of camp was all part of this bittersweet summer.

"Miss White," Gretchen cried, racing out of the cabin. "Miss White, guess what?"

Wendy followed quickly on Gretchen's heels. "I want to tell her," the other girl cried. "Gretchen, let me tell her."

A triumphant Wendy stormed to Sherry's side like an unexpected summer squall. "Look!" she declared breathlessly and held up the missing Ken-Richie.

"Where was he?" Sherry cried. The entire cabin had been searching for Ken-Richie for weeks.

"Guess," Gretchen said, hands placed on her hips. She couldn't hold her stern look long, and quickly dissolved into happy giggles. "I was sleeping on him."

Sherry's eyes rounded with shock. "You were sleeping on him?"

"I kept telling everyone how lumpy my mattress was, but no one would listen."

"Little wonder," Wendy said. "You complain about everything."

"Ever hear the story of the boy who cried wolf?" Sally asked.

"Of course, I know that story. I read it when I was three years old," Gretchen answered heatedly.

"But how'd Ken-Richie get under Gretchen's mattress?" Sherry wanted to know.

Wendy shuffled her feet back and forth and found the thick grass of utmost interest. "Well, actually," she mumbled, "I may have put him there for safe-keeping."

"You?" Sherry cried.

"I forgot."

A pregnant pause followed Wendy's words before all four burst into helpless peals of laughter. It felt so good to laugh, Sherry decided. The past few days had been a living nightmare. In all that time, she hadn't spoken to Roarke once. He hadn't come to her. Hadn't so much as glanced in her direction. It was as though she were no longer a part of this camp, and he had effectively divorced her from his life.

Past experience in dealing with Roarke had taught Sherry to be patient and let his anger defuse itself before she approached him. However, time was running out; she was scheduled to leave camp the following day.

"The bus is ready," Sally said, and her voice sagged with regret. She hugged Sherry's middle one last time, then climbed into the van, taking a window seat. "Goodbye, Miss White," she cried, pressing her face against the glass. "Can I write you?"

"I'll answer every letter, I promise."

Sherry stood in the driveway until the van was out of sight, feeling more distressed by the moment. When she turned to go back to her cabin, she found Fred Spencer standing behind her. She stopped just short of colliding with his chest.

He frowned at her in the way she found so irritating.

"One down and six to go," she said, making polite conversation.

"Two down," he murmured, and turned to leave.

"Fred?" She stopped him.

"Yes?"

She held out her hand in the age-old gesture of friendship. "I enjoyed working with you this summer."

He looked astonished, but quickly took her hand and shook it enthusiastically. "You certainly added zip to this year's session."

She smiled, unsure how to take his comment.

"I hope you don't think my objections were anything personal," the older man added self-consciously. "I didn't think a lot of what you suggested would work, but you proved me wrong." His gaze shifted, then returned to her. "I hope you come back next summer, Miss White. I mean that."

Fred Spencer was the last person she'd ever expected to hear that from. "Thank you."

He tipped his hand to his hat and saluted her. "Have a good year."

"You, too."

But without Roarke, nothing would be good.

By three that afternoon, Sherry's cabin was empty. All her wizards were safely on their way back to their families. The log cabin that had only hours before been the focal point of laughter, tears and constant chatter seemed hollow without the sound of the seven little girls.

Aimlessly, Sherry wandered from one bunk to another, experiencing all the symptoms of the empty-nest syndrome. With nothing left to do, she went into her room and pulled out her suitcase. Feeling dejected and depressed, she laid it open on top of her mattress and sighed. She opened her drawer, but left it dangling as she slumped onto the end of the bed and reread the book the girls had written for her as a going-away present. Tenderly, her heart throbbing with love, she flipped through each page of the fairy tale created in her honor.

The girls had titled it *Sherry White and the Seven Wizards*. Each girl had developed a part of the story, drawn the pictures and created such a humorous scenario of life at Camp Gitche Gumee that even after she'd read it no less than ten times, the plot continued to make her laugh. And cry. She was going to miss her darling wizards. But no more than she would miss Roarke.

A polite knock at the front of the cabin caught Sherry by surprise. She set the book aside and stood.

"Yes." Her heart shot to her throat and rebounded against her ribs at the sight of Jeff Roarke framed in the open doorway of the cabin.

"Miss White."

He knew how she detested his saying her name in such a cool, distant voice, she thought. He was saying it as a reminder of how far apart they were now, telling her in two words that she'd committed the unforgivable sin and nothing could be the same between them again.

"Mr. Roarke," she returned, echoing his frigid tone.

Roarke's mouth tightened into a thin, impatient line.

"Listen," she said, trying again. "I understand and fully agree with you."

"You do?" His brows came together in a puzzled frown. "Agree with me about what?"

"Not having me back next year. What I did was stupid and foolish and I'll never regret anything more in my life." Her actions had cost her Roarke's love. Because there was nothing else for her to do, Sherry would leave Camp Gitche Gumee and would wonder all her life if she'd love another man with the same intensity that she loved Jeff Roarke.

"Fred told me the two of you had come to terms."

Sherry rubbed her palms together. Fred had smiled at her for the first time all summer. Sherry could afford to be generous with him.

"He isn't so bad," she murmured softly.

"Funny, that's what he said about you."

Sherry attempted a smile, but the effort was feeble and wobbly at best.

With his hands buried deep within his pockets, Roarke walked into the cabin and strolled around the room. The silence hung heavy between them. Abruptly, he turned to face her. "So you feel I made the right decision not to ask you back."

She didn't know why he insisted on putting her through this. "I understand that I didn't give you much of a choice."

"What if I made another request of you?"

Sherry's gaze held his, daring to hope, daring to believe that he would love her enough to overcome her deception. "Another request?"

"Yes." In an uncustomary display of nervousness, Roarke rifled his fingers through his hair, mussing the well-groomed effect. "It might be better if I elaborate a little."

"Please." Sherry continued to hold herself stiff.

"Camp Gitche Gumee is my brainchild."

Sherry already knew that, but she didn't want to interrupt him.

"As a youngster I was like many of these children. I was too intelligent to fit in comfortably with my peers and too immature to be accepted into the adult community."

Sherry just nodded.

"The camp was born with the desire to offer a summer program for such children. I regretted having hired you the first week of camp, but I quickly changed my mind. Maybe because I've never experienced the kind of fun you introduced to your girls, I tended to be skeptical of your methods." He paused and exhaled sharply. So many things were rummaging around in his head. He didn't know if he was saying too much or not enough.

"I'm not sure I understand," Sherry said.

"I'd like you to come back."

"As a counselor?"

"No." He watched the joy drain from her eyes and tasted her disappointment. "Actually I was hoping that you'd consider becoming my partner."

"Your partner?" Sherry didn't understand.

Silently, Roarke was cursing himself with every swear word he knew. He was fumbling this badly. For all his intelligence he should be able to tell a woman he loved her and wanted her to share his life. He rubbed his hand along the back of his neck and exhaled again. None of the things he longed to tell her were coming out right. "I'm doing this all wrong."

"Doing what? Roarke," she said. "You want me to be your partner—then fine. I'd do anything to come back to Camp Gitche Gumee. Work in the kitchen. Be a housekeeper. Even garden. All I want in the world is here."

"I'm asking you to be my partner for more reasons than you know. The children love you. In a few weeks' time, you've managed to show everyone in the camp, including me and Fred Spencer, that learning can be fun. There wasn't a camper here who doesn't want you back next year."

"As your partner what would be my responsibilities?"

"You'd share the management of the camp with me and plan curriculum and the other activities that you've instigated this summer."

Some of the hope that had been building inside her died a silent death. "I see. I'd consider it an honor to return in any capacity."

"There is one problem, however."

"Yes?"

"The director's quarters is only a small cabin."

"I understand." Naturally, he'd want his quarters.

Roarke closed his eyes to the mounting frustration. He couldn't have done a worse job of this had he tried. Finally he just blurted it out. "Sherry, I'm asking you to marry me."

Joy crowded her features. "Yes," she cried, zooming to her feet. Her acceptance was followed by an instantaneous flood of tears.

"Damn it, now I've made you cry."

"Can't you tell when a woman is so overcome with happiness that she can't contain herself?" She wiped the moisture from her cheeks in a furious action. "Why are you standing over there? Why aren't you right here, kissing me and holding me?" She paused and challenged him, almost afraid of his answer. "Jeff Roarke, do you love me?"

"Dear God, yes."

They met halfway across the floor. Roarke reached for her and hauled her into his arms, burying his face in the gentle slope of her neck and shoulder while he drew in several calming breaths, feeling physically and mentally exhausted. He'd never messed anything up more in his life. This woman had to love him. She must, to have allowed him to put her through that.

Being crushed against him as she was made speaking impossible. Not that Sherry minded. Her brain was so fuddled and her throat so thick with emotion that she probably wouldn't have made sense anyway.

Roarke tucked his index finger beneath her chin and raised her mouth to meet his. His hungry kiss rocked her to the core of her being. Countless times, his mouth feasted on hers, as though it were impossible to get enough of her. Not touching her all these weeks had been next to impossible, and now, knowing that she felt for him the same things he did for her made the ache of longing all the more intense.

Freely, Sherry's hands roved his back, reveling in the muscular feel of his skin beneath her fingers. All the while, Roarke's mouth made moist forays over her lips, dipping again and again to sample her sweet kiss.

"Oh, love," he whispered, lackadaisically sliding his mouth back and forth over her lips. "I can't believe this is happening." He ground his hips against her softness and sharply sucked in his breath. "Nothing can get more real than this."

"Nothing," she agreed and trapped his head between her two hands in an effort to study him. "Why?"

"Why do I love you?"

Her smile went soft. "No, how can you love me after what I did?"

"I met Phyliss, remember?"

"But..."

"But it took me a few days to remember that you'd tried to tell me about the references."

"I did?"

Resisting her was impossible, and he kissed the tip of her pert nose. "Yes. The night at the lake. Remember? I knew then, or strongly suspected, but I didn't want to hear it, didn't want to face the truth because that would have demanded some response. Yet even when I was forced to look at the truth, I couldn't send you away. Doing that would have been like sentencing my own heart to solitary confinement for life.''

"Oh, Roarke." She leaned against him, linking her hands at the base of his spine. "I do love you."

"I know."

Abruptly, her head came up. "What about school?"

"What about it?"

"I've only got one year left."

"I wouldn't dream of having you drop out," he rushed to assure her. "You can transfer your credits and finish here in California."

Sherry pressed her head against his heart and sighed expressively. "I may give up school for a year or two and go back later."

"But why? There's no reason for you to delay your education because of marriage."

Lifting her head, Sherry pressed her finger over his lips. "I want a baby, Roarke. Your baby."

Roarke met the intensity of her gaze with all the deep desire of his own. He wanted Sherry to share his life. She was marvelous with the youngsters, and having her work with him at Camp Gitche Gumee would be an advantage to the camp and the children. But with all of his plans, he hadn't paused to think of their having a child of their own. The love he felt for her swelled within him until he felt weak with it. And strong, so strong that he seemed invincible.

"Someday we'll be sending our own wizards to this camp," Sherry told him.

Roarke's hold on her tightened.

"The girls told me you were my prince," she said, her gaze falling on the book her wizards had created.

"We're going to be so happy, Sherry, my love."

"Forever and ever," she agreed, just as the book said.

* * * * *

Bestselling Author

Jasmine Cresswell

May 1995 brings you face-to-face with her latest thrilling adventure

Desires & Deceptions

Will the real Claire Campbell please stand up? Missing for over seven years, Claire's family has only one year left to declare her legally dead and claim her substantial fortune—that is, until a woman appears on the scene alleging to be the missing heiress. Will DNA testing solve the dilemma? Do old family secrets still have the power to decide who lives and dies, suffers or prospers, loves or hates? Only Claire knows for sure.

MIRA The brightest star in women's fiction

MJCDD

Take 4 bestselling love stories FREE

Plus get a FREE surprise gift!

Fifty red-blooded, white-hot, true-blue hunks
from every State in the Union!

Look for MEN MADE IN AMERICA! Written by some
of our most popular authors, these stories feature some
of the strongest, sexiest men, each from a different state
in the union!

Two titles available every month at your favorite
retail outlet.

In May, look for:

A TIME AND A SEASON
by Curtiss Ann Matlock (Oklahoma)
SPECIAL TOUCHES
by Sharon Brondos (Wyoming)

In June, look for:

THE WAITING GAME
by Jayne Ann Krentz (Washington)
ALL IN THE FAMILY
by Heather Graham Pozzessere (Virginia)

You won't be able to resist MEN MADE IN AMERICA!

In June, get ready for thrilling romances and FREE BOOKS—Western-style—with...

WESTERN *Lovers*

You can receive the first 2 Western Lovers titles FREE!

June 1995 brings Harlequin and Silhouette's WESTERN LOVERS series, which combines larger-than-life love stories set in the American West! And WESTERN LOVERS brings you stories with your favorite themes... "Ranch Rogues," "Hitched In Haste," "Ranchin' Dads," "Reunited Hearts" the packaging on each book highlights the popular theme found in each WESTERN LOVERS story!

And in June, when you buy either of the Men Made In America titles, you will receive a WESTERN LOVERS title absolutely FREE! Look for these fabulous combinations:

◆ Buy ALL IN THE FAMILY
by Heather Graham Pozzessere (Men Made In America) and receive a FREE copy of BETRAYED BY LOVE by Diana Palmer (Western Lovers)

◆ Buy THE WAITING GAME
by Jayne Ann Krentz (Men Made In America) and receive a FREE copy of IN A CLASS BY HIMSELF by JoAnn Ross (Western Lovers)

Look for the special, extra-value shrink-wrapped packages at your favorite retail outlet!

HARLEQUIN® ♥ *Silhouette*®

WL-T

Silhouette celebrates motherhood in May with...

**Debbie Macomber
Jill Marie Landis
Gina Ferris Wilkins**

in

*Three
Mothers
& a Cradle*

Join three award-winning authors in this
beautiful collection you'll treasure forever.
The same antique, hand-crafted cradle
connects these three heartwarming romances,
which celebrate the joys and excitement of
motherhood. Makes the perfect gift for yourself
or a loved one!

A special celebration of love,

Only from

Silhouette®

—where passion lives.

Announcing
the New Pages & Privileges™ Program
from Harlequin® and Silhouette®

Get All This FREE
With Just One Proof-of-Purchase!

- **FREE Travel Service** with the guaranteed lowest available airfares plus 5% cash back on every ticket

- **FREE Hotel Discounts** of up to 60% off at leading hotels in the U.S., Canada and Europe

- **FREE Petite Parfumerie** collection (a $50 Retail value)

- **FREE $25 Travel Voucher** to use on any ticket on any airline booked through our Travel Service

- **FREE Insider Tips Letter** full of fascinating information and hot sneak previews of upcoming books

- **FREE Mystery Gift** (if you enroll before May 31/95)

And there are more great gifts and benefits to come!
Enroll today and become Privileged!

(see insert for details)

 PROOF-OF-PURCHASE

Offer expires October 31, 1996

BR-PP1

If you are looking for more titles by

DEBBIE MACOMBER,

don't miss these heartwarming stories by one of
Silhouette's most popular authors:

Silhouette Special Edition®

#09756	BRIDE ON THE LOOSE+	$3.39	☐
#09798	HASTY WEDDING	$3.39	☐
#09831	GROOM WANTED*	$3.50	☐
#09836	BRIDE WANTED*	$3.50	☐
#09842	MARRIAGE WANTED*	$3.50	☐
#09937	SAME TIME, NEXT YEAR	$3.75 U.S.	☐
		$4.25 CAN.	☐

+Those Manning Men
*From This Day Forward

Men Made in America

#45152	BORROWED DREAMS	$3.59	☐

TOTAL AMOUNT	$
POSTAGE & HANDLING ($1.00 for one book, 50¢ for each additional)	$
APPLICABLE TAXES*	$_____
TOTAL PAYABLE	$_____
(check or money order—please do not send cash)	

To order, complete this form and send it, along with a check or money order
for the total above, payable to Silhouette Books, to: **In the U.S.:** 3010 Walden
Avenue, P.O. Box 9047, Buffalo, NY 14269-9047; **In Canada:** P.O. Box 636,
Fort Erie, Ontario, L2A 5X3.

Name:_____

Address:_____ City:_____

State/Prov.:_____ Zip/Postal Code:_____

*New York residents remit applicable sales taxes.
Canadian residents remit applicable GST and provincial taxes.   SDMBACK6

V *Silhouette* ®